DEC   2002

Fic DOOLING
Dooling, Richard
Bet your life :
novel /

D0098946

BET YOUR LIFE

ALSO BY RICHARD DOOLING

CRITICAL CARE

WHITE MAN'S GRAVE

BLUE STREAK: SWEARING, FREE SPEECH,
AND SEXUAL HARASSMENT

BRAIN STORM

BET YOUR LIFE

<< A NOVEL >>

RICHARD DOOLING

HarperCollinsPublishers

ALAMEDA FREE LIBRARY
2200-A CENTRAL AVENUE
ALAMEDA, CA 94501

BET YOUR LIFE. Copyright © 2002 by Richard Dooling. All rights reserved. Printed in the United States of America. No part of this book may be used or reproduced in any manner whatsoever without written permission except in the case of brief quotations embodied in critical articles and reviews. For information, address HarperCollins Publishers Inc., 10 East 53rd Street, New York, NY 10022.

HarperCollins books may be purchased for educational, business, or sales promotional use. For information, please write: Special Markets Department, HarperCollins Publishers Inc., 10 East 53rd Street, New York, NY 10022.

FIRST EDITION

Designed by Joseph Rutt

Printed on acid-free paper

Library of Congress Cataloging-in-Publication Data

Dooling, Richard.
Bet your life: a novel / Richard Dooling.—1st ed.
p. cm.
ISBN 0-06-050539-7 (alk. paper)
1. Insurance investigators—Fiction. 2. Insurance crimes—Fiction.
3. Omaha (Neb.)—Fiction. I. Title.

PS3554.O583 B47 2002
813'.54—dc21
2002024952

02 03 04 05 06 WB/RRD 10 9 8 7 6 5 4 3 2 1

A. M. D. G.

FOR MIKE BECKER AND CHARLIE PARKER

"*There's one way to find out if a man is honest—ask him. If he says yes, he's a crook.*"

—GROUCHO MARX

BET YOUR LIFE

1

THE SMELL TEST

IN MY LINE OF WORK, we call it the f-word. Not the too familiar obscenity but a close cousin and mercenary variant called fraud. I work in the Special Investigations Unit of Reliable Allied Trust, where I investigate insurance fraud. Truth be told, we don't do all that much investigating; it's more about odor management. Fraud runs through the insurance business like waste through a treatment plant, and the vice presidents in marketing and sales and product development don't care. If they pay out on too many rotten claims, they charge it back to their honest customers by raising premiums. Our marching orders in Special Investigations are to "process" the fraud just enough to keep the stench away from the corner offices and off the front page. Meanwhile, out in the cube village where I work, the aroma seeps into our clothes.

Every day the network routes me three or four claims that failed the smell test over in General Processing. The subject line says, "Attn: Carver Hartnett, Special Investigations Unit," and when I click on the folder icon, the virtual file opens containing all of the supporting medical records, accident reports, claim forms, and death certificates that were scanned in and uploaded by the document-management and knowledge-index jockeys downstairs.

I like computers as much as the next gaming geek, and I appreciate the efficiencies of scanning in the documents instead of carting them around in manila folders. But the veteran investigators all say that the computers and the scanning are just more proof that management is barely interested in actually doing anything about insurance fraud. Those of us trained by real investigators, like Old Man Norton, know that if you really want to smell out a fake claim, you need a file with real papers in it—the accident reports, medical records, claim forms, obituaries, and newspaper clippings—the ones that the fraudster actually held and doctored with Wite-Out or computer imaging or by cutting and pasting photocopies. If you can get your hands on those, you can almost detect fraud by divination, same way a dowser finds water with his rod—some say it's a real smell. Something's not right, so we study the handwriting, the layout, stray marks, margin alignments, the obituary date, the slightly different fonts in one blank on a form that otherwise appears to be an original—all become runes with elusive meanings, and soon the papers give off the unmistakable scent of human deception.

The old-school investigators also yearn for the days when it mattered if you busted a scammer and saved a bogus claim getting paid. Nowadays, the computers don't even flag the tricky ones. Instead they send me three or four laughable virtual "special claim" files, and within five minutes I determine that they don't just smell special, they stink so high in heaven they make the angels weep. No investigation necessary.

I don't really smoke, except during certain periods of my life. These certain periods tend to pop up at work, where, if I need a cigarette, I can find one and avoid buying a whole pack. The company provides a smoking break room with separate ventilation, and also a canopied veranda out front with huge sand pit ashtrays, but all the smokers in the building prefer the fire escape. It overlooks a satellite pediatric clinic operated by one of the big hospitals in town. All day long, nervous mothers drive up in minivans, unpack toddlers from their car seats, and haul them in to see pediatricians. We look on, charmed by the cherubic faces blooming with ruddy innocence, while we squint and suck death into our lungs.

The day my friend Lenny got fired, I'd been out on the fire escape enjoying one of those periods of my life by smoking a Marlboro I'd bummed off a woman from Procurement. When I got back to my workstation, I found a "While You Were Out" electronic sticky blinking on my monitor from my fellow investigator, and daily obsession, Miranda Pryor, advising me that Old Man Norton's assistant had come by in my absence:

Carver,

Dagmar was here looking for you and Lenny—Mr. Norton has some questions about the life insurance claims on the twenty dead Nigerians.

She said she'd call you later.

Miranda

Lenny, who works out of the cube to my right, wasn't at his desk. The latest issue of *PC Gamer* was still open on his keyboard, which meant that he'd left in a hurry—maybe he was already in Old Man Norton's office discussing dead Nigerians. I stalled, skimmed an article in the *John Cooke Fraud Report* about infant life insurance policies and "baby farming" in the Soviet Union, and hoped I'd be able to check stories with Lenny before Norton called me in.

Miranda probably knew more about what was up with the dead Nigerians, but she was on the phone denying a bogus auto claim. I leaned closer to the cellulose prefab wall between us, closed my eyes, and felt her voice resonate within, as if a tuning fork or a frequency transponder were embedded in my limbic system, stimulating my pleasure circuits, secreting dopamine, serotonin, and erotic neurotransmitters until my entire scalp tingled in sync with the inflections of her voice.

When Miranda denies an insurance claim by phone, she first consoles the would-be claimant with a free vocal massage (for male callers it's closer to a vocal frottage) because her voice is a delicate inveigling rasp textured by fifty-dollar bottles of wine, designer chocolates, and, I imagined, other mysterious and intriguing bad habits. The party on the other end gets an earful of gregarious patter sparkling with authentic concern, and soon Miranda sounds as if she's ready to propose a dinner-date. Until she gets the information she needs to deny the claim, whereupon the telephone romance ends.

The male scam artists always call her back, just so they can listen to her deny their claim again. They're lucky and don't know it, because they've never been alone with her, never touched her, kissed her, or drunk a glass of Napa Valley syrah with her. If they had, they'd be damned to an eternal recurrence of the same longing, twenty, thirty times a day, as I am.

As usual, just as I entered the deepest trance, Miranda said, "Okay, then. Bye-bye," and my eyes jittered open to the fluorescent disappointment of the real world.

Her adjustable chair squeaked, and her beatific smile—framed in lustrous black tresses—popped up over my cube wall. Two years ago, when she showed up in the cube to my left, I can't say that I swooned, but I didn't look past her either. If you superimposed the scientist's X-Y axis on her exquisite features, she lacked the perfect bilateral symmetry of those nubile babes you see in magazine articles belaboring the evolutionary psychology of beauty. Her face is wide, almost round, her lips overdone, swollen and carnal, as if hornets or scorpions had stung them. A pale scar blemishes the hollow of her throat where at the age of eight she'd needed a tracheotomy tube after being hospitalized with pneumonia. Photos of her would not launch ships or send alpha males on a quest for their next trophy wife, but if those guys ever saw the real thing, orbited and entered her gravitational pull, felt her breathless vitality, saw her rosy glow, they'd end up just like me.

She snickered behind her hand, made big blue eyes at me, and whispered, "Old Man Norton is asking about the Nigerian life claims."

I stood up, just in time to watch her yawn and swell herself against the seams of my favorite blouse—a peach-colored, microfiber affair that clung and shimmered like satin every time she breathed. She reached back between her shoulder blades and adjusted the strap of her bra. Her breasts stirred. The neck of her blouse opened (two buttons undone). A little crucifix of white gold tumbled out and dangled below her throat on its fragile chain.

I leaned into her cubicle for a whiff of perfumes and lotions and the little scented holy cards she hung from her bulletin board. My shelf was stacked with DVDs, CD-ROMs, and computer manuals; hers was an artful shrine of knickknacks, mementoes, and religious icons. She had a little brass twin photo frame that opened like a small Bible and had First Communion snapshots of herself and her big sister, Annette, who had been born with some weird giant mole and had to have surgeries her whole life for it.

Annette was a cutie, too, but for me Miranda came from another world.

She drinks too much and she's unstable, I thought, taking another look at the little prayer cards and statuettes spread all over her workstation. *Life with her would be a living hell.* Truths I told myself that failed to console me, because I wanted to spend eternity with her if she'd let me—no matter how badly it might turn out.

"I have an idea," said Miranda.

Early that morning I had watched her pucker in her compact mirror and smear Black Honey lipstick around her mouth, and now I didn't want to think about what she was saying, I just wanted to watch her lips move and feel her voice reverberate in my brain stem. She had an Iowa, family-farm work ethic bred into her, which made me wonder whether if I paid her by the hour, she would agree to read ancient, guttural Arabic poetry aloud to me, so I could just watch her mouth move without being distracted by the meaning of words.

She turned pensive, careful, intense, and examined a piece of paper. Then she said, "Why don't you come into my cubicle and violate me. Cup my large breasts in your hands. Whisper filth in my ear. Force yourself on me, you big brute. Make me want you. Leave me handwritten notes describing the trashy lingerie you'd like to buy for me."

She tossed aside a swath of lustrous black hair, tucking it behind her right ear. She picked up another piece of paper and appeared to be reading from it. Respirations ceased as I watched her lips part for a berry-shaped breath mint.

"Then I'll sue the company for sexual harassment and punitive damages," she said. "After I win big, we move in together and split the proceeds. Game?"

I couldn't breathe or speak. Her lips puckered when her tongue moved the mint from one cheek to the other, and just as I concluded it was time for action, not words, she blew right by me to the rabbit punch line.

"I got a claim just like it right here," she said, waving the form at me. "Howler Manufacturing buys employment-litigation insurance from us, which means we promise to cover claims if they get sued for harassment or discrimination. A secretary sues Howler Manufacturing for sexual harassment, because her boss, the Howler CEO, lost control of himself, came into her cubicle and violated her by cupping her large breasts in his hands, whispered filth in her ear, forced himself on her, the big brute, made her want him against her will, and left her notes about buying her trashy lingerie."

She paused for another taste of the mint, then continued.

"The jury awards the secretary four hundred thousand plus attorneys' fees for sexual harassment under Title Seven. Howler sends in the claim asking us to cover. I do a little checking. He said, she said; his address, her address. They live together! They moved in with each other after the verdict came down. She quit the company, because she wants to be a full-time mom to the kid she had with the CEO whom she sued for sexual harassment. Now they want us to cover the four hundred thousand in damages he paid to his girlfriend?"

"Don't pay it," I said. Always safe advice in this department.

"Duh," she said, "but they'll get a lawyer and sue us, and Old Man Norton will settle. And then?"

Our eyes met, and we shared the sullen dread that haunts any good fraud investigator.

"That's right," she said. "They'll get away with it."

2

OLD MAN NORTON

Before I could tear myself away from Miranda's tales of sexual harassment and insurance fraud, Dagmar called with instructions for me to join Lenny in Old Man Norton's office. I'd never get to check stories with Lenny about the twenty dead Nigerians, because I'd arrive just in time to miss his version of events, and then I'd have to go live with my own. The timing was no accident: Old Man Norton's instincts kept him at least two moves ahead of everybody else in the insurance business.

Dagmar Helveg had been with Norton for nineteen years, fifteen years longer than the next senior person in Special Investigations, who is Lenny. As Norton's assistant, she interviewed prospective investigators and terminated the unwanted by giving them the business end of a Danish accent that slid along a scale from northern Minnesota to East Berlin. When she interviewed Lenny for the first time she must have worn a uniform or a brown shirt, with her hair in a severe bun. For whatever reason, from day one, Dagmar reminded Lenny of Colonel Klink from *Hogan's Heroes*, maybe because Lenny had taped every episode and sometimes said, "Ho-GAN!" without even realizing it. Then Lenny began insisting that Dagmar had cooperated with the Nazis when they invaded Denmark during World War II. When we laughed at him, Lenny hacked into the Dag's personnel file and found scanned documents showing her date of birth as 1938, meaning that she was a toddler when the Nazis invaded Denmark in 1940 and seven years old when the Third Reich collapsed in 1945 and Hitler committed suicide. Lenny claimed the docs were forgeries—worse: forgeries of forgeries. He said that if we hired an outside firm to investigate Dagmar the way we go after some of these scam kings, we'd find a trail of intrigue, espionage, and body bags leading all the way back to Bergen-Belsen.

Even though I'd been summoned, I couldn't just waltz into Norton's office unannounced; I had to check in with Comrade Helveg at her chief-of-staff sentry booth. She called up my appointment on her computer screen, selecting "Arrived" from the drop-down list of options in the dialogue box. Rumor in the Information Technology group is that this automatically calls up my performance profiles, personal, and personnel information and displays them on a fifteen-inch LCD monitor disguised as a book rest on Norton's desk.

Once I was entered in the system, she assured me that the meeting was no big deal, disarmed me with a smile, grand-mothered my fears away, then waved me on in to watch Old Man Norton wreak mayhem, havoc, and cold-blooded slayage on my partner, Lenny Stillmach.

Inside, Norton's office feels like a small, carefully lit theater equipped with the latest presentation technologies. High-definition digital flat panels take up most of two upholstered walls on either side of the entrance, and the back walls (flanking Norton at center stage) are glass and chrome opening on a vista of Omaha, Nebraska—the insurance capital of the Midwest— nestled in a bend of the Missouri River, and across the water in the middle distance Harveys and Harrah's casinos, the dog tracks and porn emporiums of Council Bluffs, Iowa.

Norton looked seventy-five at least, but career employees said that he was barely sixty, and that his age had been accelerated by a genetic disorder or metabolic syndrome that prematurely and preternaturally turned him into one of the Three Wise Men before he'd qualified for Social Security. Marinating his liver in scotch every night for forty years probably didn't help either. As he told it, he'd started with Dewar's, had moved to single malts, then coastal Highland Single Malts, on to an Islay-only liquid diet, until his palate became so refined and life too short to drink any but "the best" from some obscure Islay distillery that bottled its wares out of numbered single casks. Yes, Norton was prematurely aged and pickled, but he was still a handsome guy with a complexion burnished and cured by seasonal ski trips and sailing expeditions. He had blown-dry silver hair to go with his dark, business-casual shirts and Italian slacks—all conspiring to produce the aura of a maestro at a soirée, or a mysterious Person in Black at a film festival, anything but an old insurance executive.

I made my way over to where Lenny Stillmach was sitting and jittering his skinny legs, alone front row center before the stage formed by Norton's Herman Miller executive workstation. Lenny is one of those guys who turn dangerously good-looking at age nineteen and then spend the rest of their lives ravaging their classical good looks with romantic substance abuse. In the flower of his decadent youth, Lenny's features were still attractively ripe, spoiled only by missing body art. Piercings are tolerated at Reliable but not the jewelry that goes in them. As Dagmar put it in one of her e-mail fiats defining the outer limits of the dress code and the meaning of *business casual*: "Employees will remove all body jewelry and fishing lures from their self-inflicted puncture wounds before coming to work." And nothing looked worse than Lenny's fine flesh with his studs and earrings out, leaving big empty holes around his ears, nose, and mouth, looking like he'd perforated himself with a nail gun. At work Lenny wore long-sleeved, button-down oxfords to hide his barbed-wire biceps tattoos, and in two-ply double-pinpoint Egyptian cotton he looked almost respectable, depending on the pants and whether he had slept in them.

Norton swiveled on an executive Aeron throne bristling with lumbar tension and tilt controls, greeted me with a nod, and motioned for me to take a seat somewhere in the half circle of captain's chairs. Each chair had its own halogen track light (with motion detectors), so when I took a seat a cone of light shone in my face and made it hard to see what Norton, the Bland Inquisitor, was up to behind his desk. All I could see were the software manuals and database guides stacked sideways on the workstation's shelves, so the box that said ORACLE in big red letters looked like a label he'd made for himself.

Lenny couldn't quite look him in the eyes either, as he wound up his version of how we denied the life insurance claims of the twenty dead Nigerians named Mohammed Bilko. Lenny was never any good in meat-to-meat confrontations. Ideas erupted in his brain as Visio diagrams or structured queries, MPEG files, dynamic web pages with Macromedia Flash add-ins, or at the very least HTML e-mails, and he resented it when people forced him to express himself in a sequence of slow, imprecise English words spoken in plodding real time. With no keyboard, pointing device, and screen in front of him, he often seemed surly and taciturn, like an accomplished scholar obliged to use his third or fourth language over a 28K connection.

"Recapping," Norton said, "you denied twenty different Nigerian life insurance claims during one telephone conversation with a single Nigerian lawyer?"

Norton glanced down and made a note with an elegant pen. They say the "pen" is a stylus, mouse, and pointing device for the screen embedded in the LCD-equipped polycarbonate "book rest."

"Fire up a search engine, type in *Nigeria* and *fraud*, and see what you get," Lenny said, making a misguided appeal to common sense. "Twenty guys named Mohammed Bilko? All from Nigeria? All represented by the same lawyer? Yep, I denied them."

"Let's hope so," Norton said. "I'd fire you if you didn't deny them. My question is: Did you deny them because the claimants were Nigerian? In other words, did you discriminate against the twenty dead Mohammed Bilkos because of their national origin?"

By most estimates, bank fraud and insurance fraud are the leading industries in Nigeria, second and third only to the country's corrupt international oil business, the envy of all West Africa, topped only by the trading of arms and cash for blood diamonds in Liberia and Sierra Leone. But Title VII of the Civil Rights Act of 1964 prohibits discrimination based on national origin, which means it is against the law for us to publicly admit that all day every day we deny any claim filed by a Nigerian national. I held my breath and hoped that Lenny had the good sense to obey the law and lie outright.

"No," Lenny muttered, "I didn't discriminate against any of the Nigerian claims. I denied them all equally."

Worse than I thought. He was poisoning himself on toadstools from the dark side of his bipolar personality. He'd probably just had his lithium levels adjusted, which sometimes provoked self-destructive behaviors, like being flip about the EEOC using "testers" to probe our claims-processing practices for national origin discrimination. Still, Lenny was a diagnosed manic-depressive and therefore certifiably "disabled" within the meaning of the Americans with Disabilities Act, so maybe his job was safe.

"Did you deny the claims because the insureds or the claimants were Nigerian?"

Old Man Norton was lobbing them slow over the plate, but Lenny just glowered at him and refused to swing, so Norton shifted his gaze over to me instead, as if I were on first and ready to steal second.

"We denied the claims of the twenty dead Nigerians named Mohammed Bilko because they were fraudulent," I said, "not because they were Nigerian."

"Hartnett, did *you* talk to the alleged Nigerian attorney?"

"No," I said. "I reviewed the files, called the lawyer to deny the claims, and left a message for him. Then I went out for a smoke and told Lenny to deny the claims if the guy called back."

Old Man Norton glanced down at the book rest once, then his eyes found Lenny's.

"Did you tell the lawyer that you were denying the claims because they were Nigerian claims?"

Lenny flushed in his cone of light, the vasculature of his face providing measurable somatic manifestations of the mental state called guilt, easily detected by the heat-sensitive, infrared mini-camera on Norton's desk, which (according to the boys down in Information Technology) makes a digital video record of every meeting and saves it to a remote server.

"I don't remember," said Lenny.

I suspect that Old Man Norton had version 5.0 of the Israeli voice-analysis software called Truster booted up, which meant that Lenny was a dying man, expiring from vocal stress patterns, recorded as proof positive that he was telling one big porky pie after another. That's why I had told the truth, even about going out for a smoke, because a white lie can touch off enough stress patterns in a session to make your whole story look bogus.

Norton looked up at Lenny with a friendly smile and nodded. "That should do it, Lenny. Carver and I can finish up without you."

Lenny traipsed out, and without looking up, Old Man Norton told me with the index finger of his left hand to wait, while his right hand made a few "notes" on the book rest.

The flat panel on the wall over my right shoulder was displaying the new multimedia history of Reliable Allied Trust (the standard screen saver on all the company's wall-mounted monitors), which included archive photos of Old Man Norton's dad (sometimes known as Dead Man Norton), hired as a Special Investigation man in 1932, sitting at his rolltop desk with files stacked all over it, its pigeonholes stuffed with claim forms. Soft audio kicked in, probably because a sensor had detected the attention of my eyes, and the narrator described how Cecil Norton cut his teeth working for the railroads, examining claimants who could feign apoplexy, paralysis, petit mal seizures, internal hemorrhage, joint dislocations, hysteria, everything from the well-defined "nervous breakdown" to coma. A newspaper headline spun onto the screen like a newswire at a Sunday matinee: RELIABLE ALLIED WINS INSURANCE FRAUD VERDICT.

The streaming video presentation is shown to all new claims agents during the first day of orientation to put them in the proper "Special Investigations" mind-set. I could feel Old Man Norton's eyes on me, so I beamed with pride and tried to look like a professional, deeply touched by Reliable Allied Trust's proud heritage of busting fraud rings. Norton saw right through that to what I was really thinking about.

"When my father was busting fraud rings back in the forties and fifties, he had a staff of thirty men," said Norton. "In those days, this company did about a fourth of the business we do today. His budget for the Special Claims Unit was five times what mine is now. And that's not adjusting for inflation."

Despite careful editing by the company's Media Department, the presentation unavoidably highlighted the declining manpower in the Special Investigations Unit. In the forties, fifties, even the sixties, insurance investigators were the heroes and truth seekers of countless TV programs and feature films. Most of Dead Man Norton's small army were ex-cops or ex-FBI men and bloodhounds for phony signatures or tampered dates and figures on carbon-copied or photocopied checks or forms. Those were the salad days of fraud busting, and most of those guys had travel budgets bigger than what Old Man Norton could offer his entire department these days.

"We worked with the best detectives in town, worked with Hoover's G-men, helped homicide dicks solve murders. When I started, we still chased down witnesses and reviewed documents, receipts, forms, claim checks, any piece of paper we could get our hands on. We didn't just interview claimants and witnesses. We found friends and neighbors, classmates, lovers, enemies of witnesses. We found any piece of paper or person who could help us find the truth."

"Those were the good old days," I said.

"And the cynics," hissed Norton, "the cynics say it was all because we'd do anything to deny a claim, and that's a lie. My father told management to pay many an accidental death claim that the authorities had called a suicide out of laziness or to protect their local businesses from wrongful death suits."

Much as we disliked Norton, you had to feel for him when the subject of the glory days came up. It was damn sad, because these days the entire department consisted of me, Lenny, and Miranda. If Norton griped about staffing, the official line from the senior VPs was that we didn't need more investigators in Special Claims because our productivity had been enhanced by the company's considerable capital expenditures for state-of-the-art information technologies. Instead of thirty investigators burning shoe leather, using street smarts, and pawing through files in document repositories and government buildings, the senior VP of Policyholder Services imagined us using computers and search engines to achieve the same results. The truth was that we sat in our cubes and had to take shit from management for denying twenty patently bogus Nigerian life insurance claims. That's how far the fraud defense business had fallen.

"I have to ask you about the Nigerian life claims," said Old Man Norton, glancing down where he probably had a summary of them in a spreadsheet.

I drove right up the middle and told him about the twenty different life insurance claims for twenty different guys named Mohammed Bilko, all represented by a Nigerian attorney named Mohammed Bilko. I told him how I renamed each special claim folder: Mohammed1, Mohammed2, Mohammed3 . . . and how by the time I got to Mohammed4, I noticed that someone had taken the trouble to provide each Mohammed Bilko with a different well-documented cause, mechanism, and manner of death. Mohammed5, for instance, was crushed under his motorcar while repairing an oil leak, whereas Mohammed4 had been trapped in an elevator during a hotel fire, his charred remains identifiable from dental records, and Mohammed3 had drowned when his fishing boat capsized off the coast of Liberia. The unexpected attention to detail was endearing, and the twenty tales of untimely, gruesome death were compelling narratives on the order of Scheherazade's *1001 Arabian Nights*, accompanied by customized medical records and accident reports and photos of twenty different mutilated Nigerian corpses. Even Miranda (the Dr. No of Special Claims, the Bride of Frankenstein Denies Again, Cruella De Vil when it came to spotting claims that were real dogs), even she momentarily suspended disbelief and was moved to sudden pity for the twenty fictitious widows, all named Fatima Bilko.

The cardinal trait of a bogus claim is excessive documentation, and the Bilko claims came with novellas attached. Instead of filing a simple claim form, scammers try to inspire confidence in investigators by attaching every record or report that might help the investigator approve payment on the spot. But in Special Investigations, every superfluous piece of paper screams red flag, thee attests too much, and my exact words to Lenny were: "These

Mohammed Bilko claims are fat frauds. If that Nigerian lawyer calls back, tell him all twenty claims are denied." That's when I went out and had a cigarette with the woman from Procurement.

Old Man Norton made another notation, and a tinny fanfare erupted from the flat panel where a digitally enhanced sepia photo appeared featuring Cecil "Dead Man" Norton and a doctor examining a "banana peeler" back in the 1940s, when a scammer could earn five grand a week slipping on banana peels in railroad cars. If the dining cars ever served banana splits or fruit salad or Bananas Foster, they stopped, and management banned bananas from coming anywhere near passenger trains. This didn't stop the banana gangs who always carried their own peels on board, concealed in handbags and suit-coat pockets.

Dead Man Norton's nose for a stinky claim was legendary, but he also worked overtime with the postal authorities and the FBI sending scam artists to prison. Nowadays, management loathes the expense and publicity of criminal investigations. It's easier to just deny the claims and let the crooks go file with some other company. And they do. The Dead Man Nortons of the insurance business are all dead, which for scammers means that jail is more a distant possibility than an immediate deterrent, a calculable risk well worth taking.

Old Man Norton set his stylus aside and folded his hands.

"You're young," he said. "You don't really understand the Fall of Man until you've fallen once or twice yourself."

I nodded and grinned, as if I knew just how this questionable adage fit in with my version of the twenty dead Mohammed Bilkos.

"It's ironic," said Old Man Norton. "All day long we deal with fraud and deception"—and then he paused.

I thought: *Is he done? Or is he waiting for me to finish for him? Maybe it's a corporate motivational slogan I'm supposed to know? Or maybe Norton was just spouting random wisdom in his perceived role as the oracle of the Omaha insurance business?*

"—and Lenny can't even tell us a decent lie."

I heard the soft click of a mouse button somewhere on Norton's console, and an audio clip of Lenny's recorded conversation with the Nigerian lawyer began to play.

"We don't pay on bullshit life claims," said Lenny's voice. "Are these the same Mohammed Bilko claims you tried to file with Northeastern Benefit last year? Did you change anything except the company names and the policy numbers?"

The Nigerian lawyer, EEOC tester—whatever he was—launched a thickly accented diatribe against Lenny, our company, the rapacity and insular greed of Western insurance corporations. He demanded payment in the name of the Geneva Circumvention, the World Trade Orientation, the Nuremberger Tribes, and the International Monastery Fund.

The Nigerian lawyer was dead serious, which made Lenny lose it. "Are these Mohammed Bilkos the same Nigerian exchange students who moved to the U.S. in 1997, changed their names to Mohammed Bilko, bought term life insurance from Northeastern Benefit, moved back to Nigeria, waited until they were outside the two-year contestability periods for life insurance claims, then faked their deaths, collected, and moved to the Bahamas?"

The audio clip kept playing, and it captured Lenny at his finest: "I think somebody told me about a retirement community for dead Mohammed Bilkos down there in the Bahamas. Isn't there a resort on Nassau Beach named after them? Villa de

Mohammed Bilko, or something? Where they enjoy a fake afterlife to go with their fake deaths?"

(I've said worse, and it's a veritable pastime in Special Investigations to allow your cube neighbors to listen in while you lay
waste to an unsavory speculator with an especially odiferous
claim. Lenny made two mistakes: He failed to sniff the line first
for recording devices, and he didn't check the caller-ID software
and make sure that the call wasn't coming from Washington,
D.C., where the EEOC lives.)

"This is not fraudulent claims," the Nigerian lawyer/tester/
whatever protested, and his voice rose to an imperial Afro-
Oxford-Cambridge accent that I could easily imagine being
declaimed from the witness stand when Lenny is arraigned before
a Hague tribunal investigating insurance war crimes. "This is
invidious discrimination against deceased Nigerians!"

"Make a sign and hang it on your refrigerator door with mag-
nets," said Lenny. "Make a tape of this conversation and play it back
to yourself whenever you feel the need to call: We don't pay on Nigerian death claims. Understand? You sabby, Mr. Wunga Bunga?"

Old Man Norton gave me one of those grave, patriarchal
looks brimming with clichés—everything from *It's lonely at the
top* to *I'm counting on you, son.*

"This could be big for you," he said. "I need somebody to
take over as the main IT man in the Special Investigations Unit."

So much for Lenny's manic depression protecting him from
termination. But wait, something was missing. Crucify a certified
fraud examiner and computer-use professional who's worth twice
what you're paying him? Because he lost his temper while denying twenty Nigerian fraud claims? Norton knew as well as the
next middle manager that the Equal Employment Opportunity

Commission was about as dangerous as a giant bureaucratic hive of human gerbils. An EEOC investigator's job is to run a paper treadmill attached to toothless gears designed to power the agency's main goal: lifetime employment. At most, Lenny's national-origin discrimination against twenty dead Nigerians might cause the EEOC to issue a steady stream of regulatory forms for us to complete and return according to instructions.

Norton tapped on his book rest. "You've had two years in Special Investigations?"

I nodded. "I started two years after Lenny."

"Seen the new annual report?"

Norton handed me a glossy one, fresh off the press.

"Turn to page twenty-nine."

I did and found a nice black-and-white of me, the same one they had run in the company newsletter when Lenny and I had been recognized for record low claims-loss ratios. If Lenny didn't have holes all over his face, he'd have been in the photo, too.

"First time management has paid attention to Special Investigations in five years. Two years and three million in bogus claims that were dropped after we sicced you on them. You need your own budget and a bigger expense account."

Lenny's numbers were at least as good as mine, and look what happened to him.

Lenny and I had gotten sore butts pulling all-nighters getting Reliable connected to the special claims databases, ChoicePoint, Equifax, the Fraud Defense Network, and the state and federal insurance-fraud databases. Lenny was the first guy to go in and index all fields in the company's life insurance databases. Then we wrote a program that isolated all of those claims coming out of the viatical-fraud outfits in Florida, Texas, and Philadelphia. It wasn't hard or particularly noble work, but we were both good at outwitting fraudsters.

I wanted to walk around Norton's desk, assume control of his desktop, and pull up that PowerPoint presentation that Lenny and I put together on viaticals. Seven and a half million dollars in claims that Reliable didn't have to pay because Lenny's program flagged dozens of viatical policies before they came due. *What's a viatical?* That's exactly what the rest of the industry was asking when Lenny and a few other computer-use wizards at other life insurance companies uncovered mass fraud in the secondary market, where terminally ill patients bought and sold life insurance policies on themselves called viaticals.

The industry was born at the height of the AIDS epidemic, before the disease could be treated with any success. Back then viaticals were called "life benefits"; they were and still are legal, and they work this way: Suppose you are dying from AIDS, too sick to work, and desperate for money to pay your medical bills. All you have left is your life insurance policy, which will be worth, say, one hundred thousand dollars when you die in two years. So you sell the policy to a viatical company for sixty thousand and get money you can spend right now, *before* you die, on medicine or on taking your lover to Tahiti while you're still alive. The viatical company resells your policy to its investors, and together they will earn forty thousand dollars—a 40 percent return—on their investment in your life insurance policy when it "matures," meaning when you die.

"Man," I said, "Lenny is the main viatical-fraud guy. If you let him go—"

"Nothing wrong with viaticals, per se," said Norton, "only the fraudulent ones. You can find those as well as Lenny."

A two-man job, at least. Look at the setup: an unregulated industry where investors bet on how fast AIDS victims will die. It's an engraved invitation to start a fraud farm. For instance, suppose you have AIDS, but you don't have a life insurance policy to sell. No problem. If you don't look too sick yet, just go in and apply for a life insurance policy. Don't call attention to yourself by asking for too much money. Just make it for forty thousand or so, what the companies call a "jet-issue" policy, meaning the salesperson, whose commission is at stake, does an eyeball medical assessment of you, because the death benefit is so low it's hardly worth the cost of a medical work-up. On the application where it asks, "Have you tested positive, been diagnosed, or treated for acquired immune deficiency syndrome (AIDS), AIDS-related complex (ARC), human immunodeficiency virus (HIV) or any other immune system disorder?" check the box that says "NO" and hope they don't make you take a blood test. If the insurance company issues the policy, you get a piece of paper in the mail that will be worth forty thousand dollars when you die. All you have to do is pay the premiums. Forty grand isn't much money, but don't worry, you can do it to ten or twelve different insurance companies, then sell all of those policies for fifty cents on the dollar to your local viatical company. That's not perfectly legal; that's insurance fraud.

"We found hundreds of AIDS victims—some of whom owned ten or twenty life insurance policies apiece, at twenty or thirty different life insurance companies—who had applied for so-called jet-issue low-dollar life insurance policies, lied from top to bottom on the applications, then sold the policies and irrevocably assigned their death benefits to Miami Viatical or Philadelphia Partners."

Norton had heard enough of my stealth defense of Lenny Stillmach and cut me off.

"Two salary bumps last year and a bonus," said Norton. "That's how we show our appreciation for him saving us money. Lenny's great with machines, but you heard what happens on the phone with a human being. This Nigerian nonsense was just the straw that broke his back. He has plenty of other problems."

I could feel Norton taking a read on how much Lenny had told me about any other problems. Then he smiled at me, his eyes twinkling with conspiratorial greed.

"My only concern is that if we don't pay you more, somebody will steal you."

I was still carrying my screaming new Dell home machine on a credit card, so I let that one hang there, in case it turned into something more valuable than a compliment.

"Found yourself a gal yet?" he asked.

Not again! I shook my head. "Gals find me, sir."

"I'll bet they do," said Norton. "I mean a wife. Family. I don't like single investigators on a steady diet of special claims for too long. It changes the way you look at the human race."

As if that would bother anybody in Special Investigations?

"Pretty soon," he said, "you don't trust anybody except your family, if you're lucky enough to get one before—"

Before I get fired for discriminating against dead Nigerians?

"You know what I'm talking about," he continued, oblivious to my internal repartee. "Before you think that every human being on the planet is a liar and a con and a cheat who will tie his own children in bed and burn down the house just to collect the insurance money."

Or before I think that my boss would stomp a harmless idiot savant and genius from Mars like Lenny for telling the truth?

"A young man unmarried is a menace to society," said Norton, wagging his finger at me and nodding at the flat panel video. "That's what my dad always said. He believed in family, too. God. Family. Cornhusker football."

Go Big Red. And we all grew up with shrines to coach Bob Devaney or Tom Osborne in our partially finished basements. Amen. Hallelujah.

Speaking of not being able to tell a decent lie! Norton can't admit that he doesn't like his male Special Investigations men to be single for the same reason that J. Edgar Hoover didn't like homosexual FBI agents: because they supposedly were security risks, susceptible to being bought off with sexual favors. It was a hangover from the old days, when insurance investigators actually had travel budgets and conducted field investigations in Swindleville, Louisiana, or Scab Hill, Pennsylvania, Deadfish, Idaho, or Nub City, Arkansas, where whole towns ran fraud rings. When the adjusters and investigators came to town trying to find out how a community of 350 souls could file 275 slip-and-fall claims a year, they were usually met by a chamber of commerce representative, a blonde in a tight black dress who wanted to discuss the problem claims over dinner and drinks. After highballs and pork steaks and a couple of shots of Wild Turkey or Rebel Yell whiskey, she would start thinking out loud about losing control of herself and doing something impulsive to get the claims paid.

To old-schoolers like Norton, a married man had a powerful incentive not to get caught in a badger game or blackmailed over a statutory rape charge in Mingo County, West Virginia, where the sheriff, the town doctor, the coroner, and the local insurance agent all had a nice Appalachian health-and-accident fraud racket in place.

Norton opened a folder. A real, paper one, which told me it was more than just any old Special Claims file.

"This was one of Lenny's files," he said, passing it across the graphite expanse of the workstation and into my cone of light. "Why don't you look it over and then close it out for me. Heartland Viatical. Heard of it?"

"Sure," I said. "Operated by a South Omaha lawyer—Hector Something?—who ran a lot of ads looking for investors to buy term life policies owned by terminally ill patients who needed their death-benefits paid here, instead of hereafter. Hector's outfit promised viatical investors twenty-five-percent returns on 'insurance-grade' investments, and the state attorney general began an investigation to see if old Hector was keeping his promises."

Norton looked a little chilly and annoyed. "Did Lenny tell you all of that?"

My theory is that old lushers like Norton just stop reading at some point, or more likely they instantly forget whatever they've read; text passes before their eyes without leaving a trace anywhere in the shrinking ventricles of their pickled brains.

"I didn't know Lenny had a file on it," I said. "I read about Heartland Viatical in the paper."

"The *Omaha World-Herald*?" asked Norton.

To an insurance executive with a one-acre spread and a Dan Witt home out in Linden Estates, "the paper" means the *Omaha World-Herald*. To a working Special Claims man, "the paper" means the *John Cooke Fraud Report*, the scandal sheet of everybody in the fraud defense industry.

"John Cooke," I said. "Front page, on the money the viatical companies are making."

"Legitimate companies, then?" asked Norton, looking curiously relieved. "I'm sure Heartland Viatical paid at least one investor twenty-five percent returns. It's a plain nothingburger with a side of fried goose eggs to me unless they're running viatical fraud on us."

The folder contained some docs and a few printouts from Lenny's machine detailing the web research he'd done on Heartland Viatical.

"The CEO is a lawyer named Hector Crogan," said Norton. "His brother-in-law is Heartland's president, a doctor—Raymond Guttman, M.D.—from one of those med schools down in the Caribbean."

I spotted a yellow sticky containing Lenny's tiny, left-handed, backward-slanted printing, probably written weeks ago, before he could imagine that one day soon I would be in Norton's office casting lots for the garments and the files he'd left behind.

Norton kept yammering.

"Lenny did his web thing and found out that Hector Crogan, J.D., was disciplined by the state bar of California in 1995 for getting a little too intimately involved in his client's auto accident fraud enterprise in Orange County."

Right, I remembered Lenny saying how Crogan had defended a capper, the middle manager on swoop-and-squats. The capper rounds up the rusty old sedans, fills them with personnel, then heads out on the freeway to box in a Lexus or a Mercedes and make sure the well-insured target rear-ends the Pinto in front of it filled with hired Mexicans and Indians. The capper fills out the claim forms for back, neck, soft tissue—four to six grand apiece, easy—and the money goes to the lawyer, the capper, the runners, and forty bucks a head for the meat riding in the car.

"But Crogan wasn't running the ring," said Norton. "He just defended the capper, who was in the usual tight crack between the crime boss and the FBI."

Norton stabbed a prematurely wrinkled and age-spotted finger at the Heartland folder.

"Run Heartland's policies in your spreadsheets, and you'll see there are no viatical-fraud flags. Heartland buys life policies, but most of them aren't low-dollar, jet issue. They're legitimate, big-dollar policies with routine medical, blood, urine, and the rest, and nobody lied about their health to get them, so it's not viatical fraud, and I doubt they'd bother with swoop-and-squats in Omaha, Nebraska."

Whatever. Norton knew a lot about the file already, so why did he need me to close it out for him?

"Hector and his brother-in-law both kept their licenses," added Norton, "professionals in good standing, et cetera. Could be nothing more than two guys who went astray in L.A., then came to the insurance capital of Mid-America to make a fresh start with Heartland Viatical."

I get it. It's a TV-movie pitch.

"Finish up where Lenny left off," said Norton. "If you smell something, let me know. Otherwise, just close it for me."

He got up and beamed me one of his grandest smiles, followed by a reliable handshake.

"You want me to set you up with a nice girl from a good family?"

3

RAVE

Miranda was right—Lenny needed commiseration. It was Friday, less than ten shopping days till Christmas. A flatland winter grinding down to the shortest day of the year, but it would be nothing but a long cold one for poor Lenny.

Miranda and I left Reliable at five sharp and shoe-skated on salt-and-gravel-dusted snowpack down to Lenny's favorite haunt, the Upstream, a brew pub and restaurant installed in a renovated, old-time fire station. Lenny was at the bar chasing Bushmills with microbrews that smelled like fermented bran muffins. He looked like he'd just been toaded from his favorite multiuser dungeon. Nothing excessive, just the usual too much of everything. The lithium was medication for his manic depression, and I knew about that because I'd seen him toxic before. Doctors drew his blood once a month to monitor him. But I'd also seen him chop up Ritalin with a razor blade and snort it, pop amyls, do meth—anything to leaven his daily bread of smoking pot. Even the better classes in town can't escape crank out here in the Midwest, where the fields along the highways are dotted with trailer labs manned by brain-dead meth merchants cooking vats of white-cross paste for fuel and profit. One look into their eyes and you believe the time-honored maxim that addicts treat themselves. But Lenny was no speed freak; his tastes ran to pharmaceuticals and designer pot strains, sometimes Ecstasy or mushrooms. In a dark room after too much wine, he'd admit to experimenting with a sterile needle or two in his college days. Moderation was a distant memory, an adolescent phase Lenny had crashed through like the sound barrier over fifteen years ago, and he had no intention of regressing.

Miranda bought a round, and Lenny gave us the blow-by-blow on how the Dag had posted security outside Norton's door. Fake cops had escorted him back to his cube, where they powered down his machine, gave him two cardboard boxes, and told him to clean out his space. He'd gone straight home, where he tried to log on to the network and found all of his user and admin profiles had been deleted. In two hours he'd gone from a guy with root privileges on the servers to a stranded J. Random Hacker with revoked network privileges, the cyber equivalent of the detective in a bad movie surrendering his gold badge to the chief.

Finding another job wouldn't be too tough. Omaha has trouble holding on to young talent, and the brains tend to drain to the coasts or to Denver, Chicago, Minneapolis, or St. Louis. In the nineties, shortly after Level 3 Communications chose Denver for its headquarters instead of Omaha, Reliable Allied Trust and a lot of other local businesses hired headhunters to conduct nationwide dragnets searching for technology workers. People like Lenny and Miranda were prime targets because they had grown up in or around Omaha and so had at least one reason to come back and live in the middle of a moonscape the local paper called "the Midlands," the TV stations called "the Heartland," and Lenny called "the Mid-Heartland."

In Lenny's case, the headhunters had found him working at a San Jose electronic-gaming company called City of Dis Entertainment, where he had once made good money as a senior software engineer. His depressive phases had interrupted a few key projects, and soon the talented Lenny wasn't quite cutting it when it came to competing for stock options and cash bonuses. He drifted downward at Dis until he was assigned to corporate investigations, better known around Silicon Valley as "Dumpster diving"—he was the guy paid to grab documents from the trash bins of his company's competitors and paw through them in search of carelessly discarded proprietary information. His bosses kept telling him commercial espionage was perfectly legal, right up to the night Lenny had off and the cops arrested the guy working his shift.

Lenny had been a good find for Reliable. He was already an investigator of sorts, he had lots of technology experience, and his many personality defects rendered him "not quite right" on the West Coast, which meant his talents could be had for half price here in the Mid-Heartland.

Lenny drained his glass of microbrew and was ready to brain dump on the subject of Norton's sphincterish behavior, but it was hard to concentrate when every stray male in the place was watching Miranda and sensing that she didn't belong to me or Lenny. Lenny knew about a rave supposedly taking place in a barn on the Omaha Indian Reservation up north, reportedly safe and bustproof because it was not on state or federal land, or some other insane excuse to believe in a frontier hell's half acre where the government couldn't arrest you for rampant polydrug use.

Miranda got up to use the little girls' room, while all the little boys watched.

Lenny waited till she was out of earshot.

"Did you bring my vitamins?" he asked.

I had a friend of a friend who carried Lenny's favorite brand of Ecstasy, and sometimes I picked some up for him. I didn't like doing it, but he gave me unremitting shit about it if he asked for some and didn't get any. He also laughed at me when I wouldn't take money from him for the pills. He didn't want to hear my careful, rabbinical distinctions between using (sharing drugs with somebody) and dealing (selling drugs to somebody), even though the laws made the same distinctions.

So every now and again, I'd pick him up some. I had five of them in an envelope and pressed them into his hand.

"Don't tell our hall monitor," he said, nodding where Miranda had been. He fished one out and popped it in his mouth like a breath mint. "I plan on raving whether we make it to the reservation or not."

I shook my head when he offered one because I favor a fuel mix of sinsemilla and the best scotch I can afford, and I wasn't in the mood for uncharted waters. Miranda could be talked into smoking pot on special occasions, but unlike Lenny, who was an expert in all forms of alcohol, Miranda was mainly a wine snob.

She slithered back onto her stool and sipped a pinot noir.

"I'll buy you a glass of this Saintsbury," she said. "That'll cheer you up."

I didn't worry about Lenny mixing Bushmills and beer and wine with Ecstasy because alcohol and drugs never affected him in the normal way. His loft condo in the Old Market was six blocks from Reliable's offices. I'd gone home for lunch with him before and seen him swat shots of tequila, do bong blasts of hydro-grown, blue Indica, then go back to the office, where I watched him configure a secure network server, thinking in Free BSD and speaking in VI. I was more worried about the mindless stunt he'd pulled in Norton's office, because it meant Lenny's manic cycle could be kicking in. If so and if the past was any guide, Lenny would soon become Napoleonic (except he'd get more done than Napoleon ever did, because Napoleon slept once in a while).

Lenny swallowed the rest of his wheat beer and said, "I feel like harvesting an army of zombie machines and executing a tribal flood into Norton's network. Send him a Godzillagram thank-you note."

If Lenny was on his way to manic, he could manage a tribal flood in the space of an evening. During his manic phases, Lenny booked flights to Moscow, Rio, Stockholm, and Hong Kong; he wrote presidents, kings, and dictators via FedEx First Overnight, stamping "PRIVILEGED" and "CONFIDENTIAL" all over the envelopes; he cabled investment brokers who had never heard of him and told them to sell the blue chips in his IRA and buy all the titanium futures they could get their hands on; he'd order a hundred engraved invitations to a wine-tasting party at his place, tomorrow night at six, regrets only, then he'd mix and burn five custom CDs for the occasion. After that, he'd drain off a tumbler of single malt, then wind down with a Whitehall Lane merlot or Stags' Leap reserve from his Vinotemp, stand-free wine cellar, maybe recite this year's Darwin Awards while swirling his glass and swigging, tell a few code warrior lies. Later he'd stop by Sushi

Ichiban for a dragon roll and saki, then head on across the river to the casinos for a drink. He'd empty his wallet at the blackjack table, make it home by about three A.M., and go on-line, where he'd try to win it all back playing Delta-Strike at a hundred bucks a head shot in real money.

Later, he'd celebrate by hooking up on-line with Tanya, his ex-girlfriend, in California. They'd both been heavy users and geeks at Dis Entertainment, where they would meet in the supply room after hours and go down on each other. Lenny moved to Omaha, and they'd lost touch, so to speak, and Tanya had married a dentist and had two kids. Then the dentist had been paralyzed with a C3 fracture in a freak combination Firestone-tire blowout, cell-phone accident, and SUV rollover. The jury awarded twenty-four million dollars for loss of consortium among many other things, because Tanya's husband couldn't move anything south of his lower molars, had some possible brain damage and lots of pneumonia thrown in, so Tanya was getting nothing in the prime of her sex life. She couldn't leave the poor guy, and the thought of adultery was too much for her. Instead, she and Lenny used to hook up late at night with web cams and stereo headphones and experiment with various new technologies for simulating sex on-line. Him watching her, her watching him. She called it psychological adultery. She wasn't saying it was right, but it wasn't as wrong as actual sex with another man while her husband was still alive.

After about a week of being the whirling dervish of on- and off-line Omaha, Lenny would suddenly not show up for work. His sister and his mom would open his condo with their key and take him in for crisis stabilization and partial hospitalization at the Methodist Richard Young Center, where, after a lithium adjustment and some IV Valium, Lenny would take a seventy-two-hour nap. Three or four days later he'd be back at work and worth every penny Reliable paid him. Norton knew Lenny's bipolar drills, and knew he was getting Lenny at a bargain rate because of it.

Miranda moved away from someone who was smoking, and she seemed distracted and ticked off, probably at Norton. I could tell she thought Lenny was being shot at dawn for not using his napkin, and maybe she and I would be next if we picked up the wrong fork.

We tossed back what was left of round two, and the bartender put a six-pack of Coronas and a lime in a brown bag for us. Lenny and I raced for shotgun in Miranda's Audi and the proximity it would provide to her in the driver's seat. Of course we'd be taking her car; she didn't like riding in other people's cars or staying in other people's houses. She never said a word about it, she just always ended up driving, and if we went anywhere for late-night drinks and small talk, it was her place. Every now and again, after three or four drinks, she'd let me touch her; when that happened I had to move fast, because an hour later she'd be in bed. Alone.

I got shotgun, then Miranda missed a turn and went looking for an entrance ramp to 480 East, so she could get over to Iowa and I-29 for the trip north to the reservation. It must have been Indian Night, because when she crested the hill on Dodge Street, there it was: Mutual of Omaha, the biggest insurance company in town, with the biggest skyscraper west of downtown to prove it. And emblazoned on top, a five-story rendition of Mutual's corporate logo—a stylized profile of a stoic Indian chief wearing a headdress. All we needed now was for "Cherokee Boogie" to come on the radio. Mutual has kept the Indian-head logo for over fifty years despite the recent outrage of the Correctness Crowd against the Washington Redskins, the Atlanta Braves, the Kansas City Chiefs, the St. John's Redmen, and the San Diego State Aztecs. According to the company's website, the headdress image honors the "qualities and characteristics of the Plains Indians." Lenny, who was something of an Indian buff, and, like Norton, an ardent fraud historian, told a different story.

The name Omaha may sound like a calf bawling for its mother, but it's not a cattle or corn derivative. The city takes its name from a tribe of Indians, the Omahas, who once ruled the Plains, until they were scammed clean by the Washington White-skins. In the padded cell of Lenny's imagination, Mutual of Omaha's logo was a portrait of Blackbird, the most powerful chief the Omaha Indians ever had, and revered, by Lenny at least, as the founding father of the life insurance industry. I'd checked Lenny's historical facts and found them mostly accurate—namely, there was a great chief of the Omahas named Blackbird, and the stories Lenny told about him could be found in history books. But I never heard from anybody else that the Mutual of Omaha insurance logo was a portrait of the great Omaha chief.

Miranda laughed whenever Lenny got to riffing on some left-field theory, like how Dagmar was in Hitler's inner circle, or how Old Man Norton didn't really exist because he was made out of microscopic nanobots and computer-generated holographic images propagated by management, or how Blackbird founded the life insurance industry, so we were in for a reprise of the whole story on our way to an alleged rave at the Omaha reservation.

Chief Blackbird had reigned during the golden age of the Omahas at the end of the eighteenth century. According to

Lenny and the history books, Blackbird was a mighty, ruthless warrior and a shrewd businessman, who also had a weakness for the ladies. Early on, he made handsome profits fleecing the white French fur traders whenever possible. Somewhere along the line one of the traders told Blackbird about the powers of arsenic, then sold the chief pounds of the stuff on demand. Blackbird ingeniously employed the toxin to work "magic"—meaning, he poisoned any rivals to his power, prophesying their death and graciously accepting the adulation of his tribe when his uncanny predictions came true.

According to the explorers and fur traders, when Blackbird ruled the tribe at its peak, the Omahas considered themselves superior to all other tribes and nations of men, and thought all of nature, including the human race, was created especially for their comfort and aggrandizement. This patrician sensibility meant they saw eye-to-eye with white people, who also thought the rest of the human race was created for their comfort and aggrandizement, the difference being that white people not only considered themselves superior, they acted like it, with a vengeance.

Before long, Blackbird and four fifths of his tribe were wiped out by smallpox, brought west by the white man, who also chased all the buffalo away and made a killing selling firewater. What was left of the Omaha tribe were toothless dupes gullible enough to engage in "treaties" with the white man.

Finally, on March 16, 1854, the U.S. government made the Omahas a lucrative offer for their lands and brought the Indian chiefs to Washington for a powwow. Security was foremost in the minds of the Omahas, because their numbers were dwindling and they were now forced to organize longer hunting expeditions, taking them deeper into the territories of their sworn enemies, the Sioux. The new treaty promised the Omahas cash and fringe benefits designed to entice them to move to their new homeland, including the "protection" promised in the now famous Article Seven of the treaty, which Lenny had once printed and read aloud to us:

> *Article Seven:* Should the Omahas determine to make their permanent home north of the due west line named in the first article, the United States agree to protect them from the Sioux and all other hostile tribes, as long as the President may deem such protection necessary; and if other lands be assigned them, the same protection is guaranteed.

Blackbird was long dead and would never have fallen for such an obvious scam from a bunch of transparent fraudsters who were the color of corn silk. Instead, the first chief signing the treaty was Logan Fontenelle, the only chief who could read, write, and speak English. Indians and white men alike admired him, because he was well educated and half French. Once Fontenelle signed, all the other chiefs did, too.

Maybe Logan Fontenelle knew some English and had done some reading, but he should have had his lawyer look the thing over and play with the wording before he signed it. Yes, the agreement promised "protection," but only for "as long as the President may deem such protection necessary." The day after signing the treaty, President Franklin D. Pierce must have deemed the promised protection unnecessary, because when it came time for the big move to the reservation, no protection had been provided.

The Omahas were ordered out of town anyway, and the well-spoken Logan Fontenelle gave what can only be called an "I Have a Nightmare" speech at Bellevue (just south of Omaha) before the Omahas set out; the Nebraska State Historical Society has preserved portions of this famous address. Logan said that it was cold-blooded murder to place the unarmed and defenseless Omahas in the path of their ancient foes, the Sioux. He drew his revolver and said, "This is good for six Sioux. We will go and meet our fate."

Shortly afterward, a mob of Sioux attacked an Omaha hunting party and killed Logan Fontenelle. Three dead Sioux were found near the great chief's body. Nobody in Omaha ever heard of Blackbird; instead we have Fontenelle Boulevard, Fontenelle Forest Nature Association, the old Fontenelle Hotel, even Fontenelle Hair & Tanning, probably out of gratitude for Logan being good enough to sign his death warrant and get out of town.

They were tales any student of fraud, including me and Miranda, would love, but this was the second time I'd heard them, and it was still like nailing down a drop of mercury getting Lenny to explain just how they proved that the Mutual of Omaha Indian was Chief Blackbird. Right about when Miranda and I could have congratulated ourselves on keeping Lenny's mind off of his sudden joblessness, he came back around to it and spent a good twenty minutes in the backseat performing verbal rampage on Colonel Klink and Old Man Norton.

"Last Monday a credit card company sent a registered letter to Human Resources and garnished my Reliable wages," he said.

"Norton freaked. I guess he can discriminate against me for being broke, but I can't discriminate against Nigerians for being scam artists. There's a garnishment statute says he can't harass me over bad debts, but so what?"

That gave me the willies, because I had several credit cards near the max myself, even though I always found money for the interest payments before they showed up in my credit rating. That might be hard to do if, like Lenny, I was suddenly missing a salary.

Lenny cursed Norton, Norton's mother, Norton's religion, even took Dead Man Norton's name in vain; then he cussed us because we'd forgotten a bottle opener for the Coronas.

I told Lenny that Norton had given me the Heartland file and asked him about Hector and his brother-in-law.

"Why don't you ask Miranda," he said. "She had the Heartland file before me."

Miranda was busy dialing the Omaha Indian Reservation into the dashboard GPS destination finder. I kept my eyes on her and waited for an explanation, but she just shrugged.

"So," I said, "this Heartland file is a Black Death ship looking for a port? Norton thinks there's something there, and he'll go through two certified fraud examiners and a computer use professional to find it?"

Lenny was unimpressed with my instincts. "Miranda already told Norton that she thought Crogan's old company had recruited sick people in San Francisco, New York, and Miami to apply for fifty-K jet-issue policies—no blood, urine, or EKG. Paying them to lie like Judas and 'clean-sheet' their life applications by answering 'no' to the entire list of 'have you ever had' questions, specifically the one that says, 'Have you tested positive, been diagnosed, or treated for acquired immune deficiency syndrome, AIDS-related complex, human immunodeficiency virus, or any other immune system disorder?' Then, the insurance companies issued the policies, unwittingly insuring the life of AIDS victims, who, in those days, used to die like clockwork within two or three years.

"Hector's old California company was buying the policies from them before the ink could dry (thus the name 'wet-ink' viaticals), and maybe even coaching HIV-positive, proposed insureds about how to fill out the applications to their advantage. Only problem was that once the new protease inhibitors arrived on the scene, the AIDS victims stopped dying on time."

"We're partying too far out of bounds," Miranda said. "The fun is too much. I think we should go back downtown and work for a few more hours."

She popped open the glove and tried to change the subject by handing Lenny a Swiss Army knife, but he stayed on topic while prying the caps off Coronas and slicing up the lime.

"Norton gave me the Heartland file," said Lenny, "and I found some evil shit on Hector Crogan in a California *Daily Reporter,* ethics and disciplinary proceedings. He works cheek by jowl with a doctor, Ray Guttman, and Ray has a history of writing a few too many prescriptions for friends, God love him.

"I gave my machines a good whiff and turned them loose on Hector and Dr. Guttman. I treed Hector's former law partner at an IP address in L.A., but the guy had well-maintained firewalls, so I had to go other places for the info."

"Where?" I asked. "Fraud86? ChoicePoint?"

"Some there," said Lenny, "but mostly from deep inside."

"Deep inside what?" I asked. "Deep inside Heartland?"

"Deep inside the Tomb of the Unknown I-Told-Ya-But-I-Didn't-Tell-Ya," said Lenny, "which means I can't tell ya. Dead man's talk. Hector's new company, Heartland Viatical, doesn't show up on our programs because he's using straw owners with different names and addresses to hold the policies for him for two years, until they become incontestable. I told Norton I thought Crogan and his partner were running swoop-and-squats out in Orange County, *and* representing the capper. Guttman has a history of being disciplined by the Medical Board of California because he helped a terminal cancer patient do the Kevorkian with a big injection of potassium chloride in a California mercy-killing case.

"That was then, and this is now, and maybe things changed. Besides, I can't prove what went on in California, and apparently neither could the prosecutors, if all Hector and Ray ever got was disciplined by the bar and medical board."

Without proof, we both knew it was not the kind of thing Lenny could take to Old Man Norton. Norton dealt with senior VPs who wanted beyond-a-reasonable-doubt-type evidence before they'd go public with fraud charges. In the meantime, as I've said, if too many bogus claims got paid, the actuaries could adjust the equations to produce a premium increase. And according to the latest e-mail from FDN, fraud caused an estimated $96.2 billion in increased premiums for 1999 alone, stolen by clever vermin who feed on the rest of us. To stop them, somebody like me or Lenny or Miranda not only had to catch the scammers, we then had to sweet-talk management into letting us go to the authorities.

"Hector probably used to be dirty," said Lenny. "Now he and his brother-in-law, Dr. Ray Guttman, have a new angle, maybe even a semilegitimate angle. If you party with Ray, ask him to bring his black bag." Lenny sniffled and rubbed his nose suggestively. "They may be scamming somebody, but not us insurance companies. They may try to work a side deal with you. If they do, let us know, and we'll tell you how to handle them."

Us? We'll? As in him and Miranda? But before I could ask him, Lenny's cell phone rang. It was somebody named Planet, in Sioux City, Iowa, calling to tell us that the tribal police had busted the rave and were searching cars and arresting ravers. We turned around and headed back south, while Lenny pulled out a glass pipe and a bud. Miranda didn't like that, but I think she cut him slack because of his reduced circumstances. She opened the windows and drove five miles under the speed limit, even though Lenny said that would put her right in the Iowa State Patrol's profile for somebody with drugs. By the time we'd smoked that, he'd talked Miranda into taking him to the casino for a few hands.

It was Friday night, and the parking lot, which takes up 10 percent of Council Bluffs proper, was jammed with cars and a forced march of gamers, their breath hanging around their heads like fog balloons.

After the long haul over frozen blacktop to the casino, I took Miranda to the bar, where we drank more pinot noirs by the glass. Lenny wandered off to find his fortune.

I didn't get much more on Heartland, but I could tell she was pissed that Norton had gone behind her and lateraled the file to Lenny, and now to me. Instead, we talked about her dad's failing organic produce farm back in Ottumwa, Iowa. How her dad had artificial ankles and knees because rheumatoid arthritis had turned his joints to wormwood. How her mom had to take panic-attack and antianxiety drugs because she had agoraphobia and had to live on a farm nine miles outside of Ottumwa and was terrified of the huge blue sky soaring to infinity in all four directions. How her only sister, Annette, needed skin grafts to patch the holes where the giant mole had been. How the insurance company paid for the original lesion removal but—surprise!—wouldn't pay for the skin graft repairs because they were "cosmetic surgery."

I knew Miranda sent money home to them, knew she had investments, didn't know what kind. She usually had a *Wall Street Journal* under her arm in the morning, whereas Lenny and I would be swapping *Gamer* and *PC Magazine*s.

After a bit, she asked the bartender for two glasses of the twenty-year-old Graham's. She had money. So did Lenny—he used to, anyway. Not me. I was still paying car loans and low-limit credit cards. I even had a consumer bank lien on my car and one of my student loans was in default, so I was a long way from ordering vintage port. When we went to Jams for high-end food and wine, Miranda usually grabbed the check and insisted.

Once the port was gone, she didn't last long. It was probably ten o'clock at the latest when she said she'd had enough, and we went looking for Lenny.

We found him playing two hands at a table with a twenty-five-dollar minimum, a five-thousand-dollar maximum, and a dealer who looked like Charlize Theron. I worried about the manic thing again, because Lenny was revved, Action Jackson with deep pockets on Fat Street. He was in no mood to leave, with a thousand or so stacked in front of him, and hanging on his left arm studying his technique, a striking, raven-haired beauty, whom Lenny introduced by saying, "This is Rosa," as he colored up on his chips.

Miranda and Rosa gave each other quick smiles and nods, as if they'd met before and had nothing to say about it. Instead Miranda yawned behind her hand and said, "We're ready to head out, Lenny."

Lenny leaned over and listened to Rosa whisper something in his ear. He nodded and said, "I'm coming with you guys, but I'm playing one last hand."

Then he pulled a Lenny and decided to go home double rich or nothing broke. He colored up to one big black-and-gold thousand-dollar chip and slid it out to the winner's circle.

Maybe Charlize was new, or maybe she just took a certain pleasure in her calling. She cooed and made goo-goo eyes at his big chip, then started sliding cards out of the shoe.

Lenny got two eights and gave out with a war whoop when Charlize showed a six up. Any mutt would split the eights; it was practically required, no matter what the bet, so the hand went on hold while Lenny consulted the ATM machine up front and a small fan club formed at his table.

He came back with a shot of Glensomething and cash on the barrel for another black-and-gold chip. He slid the chip out to cover the second eight, just in time for Charlize to turn—gasps all around—a third eight.

Lenny pondered the layout for all of ten seconds before leaving for the ATM again, and the spectators began arranging themselves for better views of the high-stakes contest.

"Shouldn't you stop him?" Miranda asked me. "What if he loses?"

"He knows what he's doing," I said. "She's got a six up. I can't say I wouldn't do the same."

"No doubt!" said Rosa. "He has to do it."

"Where's he bank?" whispered Miranda. "I can't get more than three hundred at a time out of Commercial Federal."

"Cash advances on credit cards," I said, "not bank withdrawals, and he's got enough plastic on him to fill out that card shoe."

Lenny returned with financing and a shot of Grand Marnier for Miranda. He remained standing, the better to survey his portfolio of three $1,000 eights.

Charlize turned over eight number four like it was destiny itself. She looked at Lenny like he was a wizard in the Voodoo Zone, and again he had no real choice—he had to split the eights, and now he needed four grand on the table. Actually he needed more, because what if he had to double down on a ten or an eleven? How many times do mere mortals get to play four live blackjack hands against a dealer with a six up?

"Okay, then," Lenny said to Charlize and Rosa, "if I split the eights again and win it, you're both coming with me to Saint Kitts to help me spend it." Rosa giggled, and Charlize shimmied under her dealer's smock and purred to him about a four-day weekend ahead of her with nobody and no place to go, acting like she'd let him jump her bones right there in the pit if he was man enough to put another thousand on the table.

Lenny made his way through thronging admirers and kibbitzers and out to the ATM, again, where from the looks of it he maxed out four different cards. The fans cheered his arrival back at the table like Romans hailing Caesar's return from Gaul. Lenny squared up across from Charlize and bought a fourth black-and-gold chip.

Charlize licked her lips and gave Lenny a dangerous smile for good luck. The next card out of the shoe was a three on his first eight, for eleven, which—of course!—he'd be crazy not to double down on, and this time he had the extra cash on hand for chip number five. Next card, a nine for twenty. Applause. Then she turned an ace on the second eight (more applause on the nineteen), a king on the third eight, and a queen on the fourth eight. Lenny had two hands at eighteen, one at nineteen, one at twenty. Great hands, especially against a six, but not twenty-ones.

Her bottom card was a queen, and Lenny loved all three of them: Charlize, the queen, and the six, for a hard sixteen. Time for her to bust. Nobody was breathing when she slipped the last card out of the shoe. A five of spades. She let it fall out of her hand like a used dagger. Then she snapped her gum and shrugged, like it was the ninth or tenth time that shift she'd hit a hard sixteen for twenty-one and sucked five dime bets out of a soft fish named Lenny.

Lenny was white as a turnip and motionless—like he was buried in wet sand from the neck down. A collective groan from the crowd, and then everybody, including Rosa, moved away from him without saying a word.

4

DELTA-STRIKE

The Audi was mostly quiet during the hop across the river back to Omaha. I felt sorry for Lenny, but I also knew that nothing short of cash could repair the fiscal carnage wrought by Lady Luck and her nymphet daughter Charlize. Lenny was already into me for fifteen hundred dollars, money I'd see in six months if he found a job right away, and I had interest running on my own debts. We took him back to his place in the Old Market, and I managed to console him along the way without once mentioning money.

We dropped him at his front door—a good thing, too, because he'd shot another single malt on his way out of the casino and was in no shape to drive. He even lit a cigarette in the back of the car without asking Miranda's permission, but she just clenched her jaw and held her tongue. He asked me if I wanted one and smirked when I said no, because he knew why—so

Miranda wouldn't find out about those certain periods of my life when I smoke.

He seemed steady when he climbed out of the car, but there was a hint of muzzy in his voice.

"I'd offer you a ride," he said, "but I figure you'd rather have Miranda drive you back to your place, even if I were sober."

He was drunk enough to say what we all knew. Lately she'd been letting me chase her more than she let him. Not that it ever led to anything more than occasionally smashing mouths and breathing heavy. My used Explorer was in the shop, and I was looking forward to some quality time alone with Miranda on the way back to my place—I could ask her in for a drink, and she could say no.

"I'll give you the lowdown on Heartland before you get too far into it," said Lenny over his shoulder, "unless you want to tell him, Miranda?"

Lenny looked more deranged than usual, and Miranda worried me with one of her looks, like I was supposed to crawl out of the car and carry Lenny on my back out to Father Flanagan's Boystown. *He ain't heavy, Father. He ain't crazy, either. He's my brother!*

"Lenny, you're okay, right?" she called after him.

"I scorn pain," Lenny said. "I laugh at debts. Either they'll go away, or I will."

He opened the door to his building and staggered over the threshold, while we tried to decipher that one.

Miranda said good-bye with a tap on her horn and wheeled the Audi out onto Dodge Street. She opened the windows and the sunroof, even though it was December, and headed west, trying to shoo the cigarette smoke out of her car with her gloved hand.

"What's with Heartland?" I asked.

I watched the moon glow on her skin, the frigid night wind strewing her hair against the headrest, her reindeer eyes lambent with the reflected glow of minimalls, billboards, Christmas lights, and fast food restaurants, her upper lip flexing like Cupid's Bow as she worked over the chewing the gum I'd given her.

"You know Lenny," she said. "He's got more angles than a rhombohedron. I'll let him explain it to you."

She turned up the volume on the CD player, and I watched her moving with the bass of the Beta Band. She knew what I was thinking about, and she didn't mind talking about it. To her, it was our problem and nobody's fault, a result of mismatched neurochemical disorders, incompatible lusts and phobias, even though I hoped that we might someday blend them carefully to produce some intriguing hybrid fetishes.

By the time she pulled up in front of my place I was transitioning from drunk to sleepy, until she put it in park and looked at me like she might share those lips.

"You wanna come up?"

"I shouldn't," she said, but she leaned closer to me, and let me kiss her.

I went easy, hoping I could make it last, but this time her lips opened first, and I could feel heat coming off of her in perfumed waves. Pretty soon we were going at it. I went after her with both hands, feeling her up through her goose down vest, and looking for a way in.

I had to watch my hands. I even had a dream about it once. We were on her leather couch, and she had all of her clothes off. I was armless, and she let me devour every part of her with my lips and tongue. The dream ended when she said, "See? Now you can do whatever you want because you don't have any hands."

I even meant to try it next time in the real world. See what would happen if I never touched her with my hands and instead just licked her ear, her neck, the scar in the hollow of her throat, her sternum, keep probing lower. You never know what dreams mean.

The wine made me forget that plan. I got my hands inside the vest and got a hold of her breasts. For a second, I thought this was the night, because she didn't pull back right away. I was jazzed and ready to start my whole life over with her, right there on the leather seats. But when I went around back to undo her bra, the fever broke. She disengaged and rearranged her clothes.

She looked on the verge of tears, so I apologized, but she shook her head and said it wasn't my fault. No shit, it was her fault, otherwise we'd be doing it right now on the center console. No sense arguing with her. Like any common scammer who tried to sneak a bogus claim past her, I was well aware that Miranda knew twenty different seductive and compelling ways to say no.

"I'm worried about what Lenny said," she mumbled.

"He's fine," I said. "No, he's not fine. He's fucked up."

"Let's both check on him," she said. "Make sure he's okay. You should stop him before he gets himself so messed up like that."

"Stop him? He's a force majeure straight out of our coverage exceptions. Hurricane Lenny. He's okay, but I'll call him to make sure."

She kissed her fingertip and touched it to my lips.

"Thanks. I'll call him, too," she said.

I climbed out. She wiped her finger off on the custom leather seat and drove away.

I got the mail out of my box and trudged up to 202B, the enigma of Miranda playing over and over in my head.

Some of the biggest lies get told with nobody saying a word.

She wasn't that way. She seemed genuinely conflicted about sex, or sex with me—I had to find out which. If she was involved with someone else, she didn't talk about him. Or was it a her? That might mean that she couldn't talk about it, for whatever reason. I once chased a woman all over town for months only to find out she was in love with a married man and sworn to vows of absolute secrecy. Worse, she intended to be faithful to the faithless rat.

Lenny's theory was that Miranda's apparent chastity was a Catholic thing, even though he and I had both been raised that way, and we'd dated lots of good Catholic girls for whom sex and piety coexisted in harmony. If religion was her problem it was an affliction she didn't discuss much. Unlike Lenny and me, she still went to church every Sunday, and every morning during Lent and Advent. Lenny for one claimed that she was one of those controlled nymphomaniacs we used to hear about in college: A woman who was saving a thousand and one nights of raging lust for one man, her husband.

Maybe, but I suspected that she had other bugs in her ant farm. Somebody might have abused her or hurt her. She told me that her mom was one of those sexually liberated types who belabored the specifics in graphic detail before Miranda and her sister Annette had even had their first periods; gave them both night terrors with anatomically correct images and drawings from *Our Bodies, Ourselves*. Miranda and Annette had stayed up late giggling and grossing each other out by whispering, "Then the man puts his erect penis inside the woman's vagina." "Ewwwww! Stop it!" Miranda said it had been disgusting enough to put two prepubescent girls off their feed for a day or two, but she was laughing when she told me about it.

She'd worked in Minneapolis for a few years and still visited there off and on, so maybe she was involved with somebody up there?

I threw my shit in a chair and went to get four aspirin and a quart of bottled water to ward off the effects of mixing liquor. Before I got the aspirin down, the NetPhone beeped and my big IBM flat panel came out of sleep mode.

It was Lenny. Had to be full manic by now if he wanted to play Delta-Strike after losing five grand. He had a new map loaded called Storm Alley, and he was taking the terrorist role. His name was SnowKiller, and he was packing a Colt M4 A1 carbine with silencer and C4 explosives. He was inside an abandoned warehouse complex with hostages and a VIP.

"Dirk, are you there?" asked Lenny's tinny, NetPhone voice. "If you are, I got a VIP peeing in her leopard-skin panties because she knows you're a pussy and can't save her."

I grabbed the mouse and said, "SnowKiller, everybody knows you got substance abuse problems. You're too fucked up to take on a Navy Seal."

I grabbed the mouse and pulled up my favorite skin, Dirk Stone, Seal Team 6. I had exactly twenty thousand dollars and 6.5 minutes to plan and execute a siege, kill Lenny, and rescue the VIP. Delta-Strike is money-driven: A thousand-dollar fine for each wound incurred or hostage accidentally killed. Head shots are fatal, game over, unless you're part of a clan, in which case a head shot turns you into a spectator.

I didn't scrimp on firepower, because I've been caught far from home too many times with nothing but melee weapons. I bought a Kevlar vest, two concussion grenades (flash bangs), and a Benelli M3 Super 90 shotgun. I moved out into the alley where rescue and police vehicles had secured the perimeter. I got direct sound-board audio on the helicopter blades whomping overhead, and my screen pulsated with red strobes coming off the emergency vehicles.

"I've got women and children tied up in a meat locker in here, Dirk," said Lenny. "I've got a VIP, too. Say hello to the voluptuous international fashion model and actress, Renata Vixen."

Renata screamed, begging me to save her, and Lenny laughed. I heard fabric ripping and missy gasps of terror from Renata, as she fought off Lenny's brutish advances somewhere inside the warehouse.

"I'm tearing Renata's flimsy clothes off, Dirk," said Lenny. "First I'm gonna splatter your giblets all over the wall, then I'm gonna despoil Renata on a butcher's block out on the slaughterhouse floor. Come and save her if you can, you pussy."

Lenny was always gabby, and he loved using human shields. But he was also wasted on X and booze. I grabbed the Benelli because it's great in close quarters, and the shape Lenny was in, he wouldn't know I was in the environment until I was pointing it at the back of his head.

He said he was in the warehouse meat locker with Renata and the two kids, so I figured he was really down at the loading dock. I busted in the overhead door on one of the bays, tossed a flash bang in to blind him, then killed him with a head shot before he even saw me.

Renata swooned and told me I was her hero. She was wearing a leopard-skin halter, a black leather miniskirt, sheer black nylons, and black stilettos. As usual, the close brush with violent death had a paradoxical effect on her libido. She told me to meet her upstairs in the tankage loft, so she could express her profound gratitude to me in a special, intimate way.

"Hey, Lenny!" I hollered. "Not bad for a pussy, huh?"

I clicked on Renata's halter and she peeled it off for me. I wouldn't mind spending some time with those, but I planned to waste Lenny one more time first. I reloaded the environment and put myself back out in alley, where I spent my winnings on an M249 Para light machine gun for the next round.

The NetPhone hissed. Nothing but silence.

"Lenny?"

I figured he'd gone to stealth and white noise, probably planning to pop the bolts on the fire exit and waste me with the Colt before I knew he was playing again. So I charged the warehouse and came in through a window off the fire escape, figuring I'd cap Lenny before he could look up.

But faster than Lenny, drunk or sober, SnowKiller met me on the catwalk with a Mac-10. I couldn't get a clear shot at him, because he had two kids and Renata tied to him as human shields.

SnowKiller was a pure low-ping bastard, twice as fast as Lenny on a good day. He wheeled on me and took me out with four head shots before I could move my finger on the trigger.

I went to the chat window and typed:

CarvedMeat: Dirk, here, who's your low-ping buddy? We both know you ain't that good.

SnowKiller answered with six more head shots, then a flash bang whited-out my screen. Only the chat box was open, where words appeared, letter by letter:

GothicRage86: I win.

5

HYDE69.EXE

I GRABBED A REAL phone and speed-dialed Lenny. Nobody answered, then voice messaging clicked in: "This is Lenny. Leave a message, or send an e-mail to Attila-at-Home-dot-com."

"Lenny," I said, "call me. We got switched on the server or something. Somebody broke in on us with a fat pipe for a connection. Way, way fast! I'm a high-ping whiner. Who the fuck is GothicRage86? Just call me back, Lenny! And if you're doing this yourself, it ain't funny."

Lenny ran a website called WeirdHarold.com, which was a spoof of the *Omaha World-Herald,* and one feature of the site was a web cam of Lenny's computer desk called Attila-at-Home cam, where users could click in and see him playing on his home machine, whenever he was in a sociable e-mood.

I clicked on Zone Alarm for an IP address and identity of the intruder, if there was one. Nothing but twelve-hour-old zombie scans. But maybe they had cut in on Lenny's machine? Highly unlikely, because if anybody could make his machine invisible to Internet predators, it was Lenny. Which meant somebody was there *with* him?

Lenny was probably messing with my head. Maybe he'd spliced in one of his high-speed, low-ping tournament-level pals as a ringer?

I pinged Lenny's machine, and the packets came back trace route normal. Then I probed the usual ports with some screwy packets trying to see what services he had running. He was invisible, firewalls up and running. Nothing amiss. If there had been an intruder, they had permissions that I didn't have. I figured I'd wait ten minutes, then try and raise him with an instant message or a NetPhone call. I tried to get on the Attila-at-Home cam, but it gave me a "404 page not found," which meant he'd turned the thing off.

In the meantime, I thought about going back into the warehouse to find Renata and have my way with her in the meat locker.

Truth is, sex with pleasure partners and game personalities depresses me, because it's not sex with Miranda. Lenny had told me all about his on-line adventures with Tanya, while her husband was gorked out in the next room, and I knew all about the new singles sex sites offering anonymous, two-way encounters with streaming audio and video, but I wasn't interested. Sex with real women in meat space was even more depressing, because it ate up a lot more time than cybersex, and for what? Either way I got the same thing: sex with someone who is not Miranda.

I backed out of Delta-Strike, opened a DOS Window command line, pinged Miranda's machine (something I did a lot), and found she was up and running, also. Any decent instant messaging program would tell me whether she was up, but it would also tell her that I was on-line. I had the usual desire to "watch" her for a few minutes first before letting her know that I was on-line. Then she could type to me if she was in the messaging mood, even though it made almost no sense in a local area code—unless you preferred text to human contact, which she often unapologetically did.

Reliable gives all of its Special Claims investigators free, always-on, high-speed connections from home, on the theory that we geeks will do at least some work at home and, maybe more important, we geeks will purge ourselves of whatever else we do on-line at home, instead of at work.

Maybe I should call Miranda. Hadn't she told me to check on Lenny? I could call and tell her that I'd played Delta-Strike with him, and he seemed okay, but then space aliens and gremlins broke in and flamed me and then he didn't answer the phone.

I pinged her again and probed her ports for an opening. Why was she up and on her machine? Miranda wasn't a heavy user. Not like Lenny, who was almost always on; he called his work machine Jekyll and his home machine Hyde, and he frequently connected Hyde to zero-knowledge, anonymous privacy portals, which in essence rent you a "nym"—an untraceable pseudonymous digital identity—and then erase any trace of you when you're done using it.

I'd been here before: probing her machine for the heck of it to see if she was on-line, then wondering what she was doing if she was.

The difference this time was that I now had the means to see what she was doing on-line, if I was vile enough to use them. See,

Miranda is an ace when it comes to finding people or information using browsers or search engines, but she doesn't know much about security, or the real world. She relies on keywords, Boolean logic, and metasearch on the job, and she relies on Lenny and me to protect her from the outside world by keeping her ports reserved and her system interiors uncorrupted. Her mistake was trusting us.

A few months back, Lenny and I had gone over to her place to eat La Casa's pizzas, slosh high-end wines, and get her new machine up and running. We set it up on a fiber-optic connection, installed her firewalls, partitioned her hard drive—the nouveau-geek equivalent of a barn raising. I tested her shields myself at the Gibson Research Shields Up! site. She scanned clean and was invulnerable to corruption behind a virtual private network firewall.

Then, a few weeks ago, she'd called late and said she was getting IP stack errors on the machine we'd set up for her, which I jumped on as an invitation to go over and reconfigure her stack. While I was in there checking her kernel and her system registry, I found a little spoor left by Lenny, the Internet freebooter and predator of cyberintimacies. It was a Back Orifice program appropriately named hyde69.exe, and he'd preflagged it as "quarantined," so her antivirus software wouldn't detect it running at boot time. It was a tiny, well-concealed code back door for Lenny, which would allow him to visit Miranda's machine whenever he wanted, with full privileges, "watch" her while she was on-line, even record all of her keystrokes in a copycat file to be perused at his leisure.

Hyde69.exe was the mark and spoor of BeastMaster Lenny—another one of his obsessions out on a leash. My first thought was to serve him right then and there and tell her what he'd done. But she was in the midst of pouring me a Leonardini reserve cabernet (my reward for fixing her machine), and I could feel her warming up to another sordid tale of insurance fraud. If her voice was all I could have, I wanted as much of it as possible. So I let her go on, while I terminated the hyde69 task, removed the launch instructions from the boot sequence, deleted hyde69.exe from her hard drive, and silently cursed Lenny's self-indulgent depredations.

Miranda approached, carrying two Riedel lead crystal goblets (thirty-ounce), three fingers of ruby-red in each—the kind of glass that says: Tonight's activity is wine. She nuzzled the mouth of the bowl for a long, slow whiff of cab fumes, the way she and Lenny always did before rhapsodizing about "the nose" half the night. They were the wine nuts, and we were all of us old-movie buffs (the only kind of movie you can rent deep in the Mid-Heartland on a Friday night). Miranda handed me the wine, and I could see her slip into my favorite character sketch in her repertoire: a dead-on rendition of the savvy dame in another film noir about murder for insurance money. She set my wineglass at my elbow and smiled at me, as if I were playing the piano in a gin joint in *Key Largo* and she was my chanteuse, sashaying over to sing a number while I accompanied her on the computer keyboard.

She gave me a hard look and wrapped her elegant wrist around the monster goblet.

"Suppose you and I fall in love and get married," she said.

"I would love that," I said.

She dropped a beat but picked right up. "I'd think about it," she said, "but you'd want marriage to be like a life insurance policy. You'd want a two-year contestability provision, so you could rescind the deal at any time during the first two years."

"No," I said. "I'll do it any way you want it. What's good for you? Next week?"

"How about never," she said. "Is never good for you?"

She wrinkled her nose at me, then slipped back into her role. "Anyway, we're married, and we start our own dot-com e-business together," she continued, running her fingers once through my hair. "We sell sex toys and erotic paraphernalia on a site called HarmlessLust dot-com." She snagged a tissue and wiped the fingers she'd run through my hair. "We both work real hard and get rich. By sheer willpower we transform ourselves into valuable assets, and to protect our investment in ourselves we take out five-million-dollar life policies on each other."

She draped herself over the minibar and gave me the limp wrist, the painted eyelids, the decadent, hooded gaze, the dulcet, low-throated croon of Lauren Bacall in *The Big Sleep* or Barbara Stanwyck in *Double Indemnity*.

"I need more background," I said. I was not about to miss her performance, but I was also staring at the empty, blinking cursor where Lenny's hyde69.exe program had been. I knew why the conniving pervert had done it, because I was right behind him in line at the peep show: imagining what it would be like to access Miranda's system, anytime. Day. Night. Just check in on her whenever I wanted, and see what she was up to.

She was on the other side of the screen, and too far into her acting binge to notice anything I was doing.

"But I got a thing going with your best friend, Al," she continued, "who just happens to be a cardiologist and an Ironman triathlete. Al and I can't keep our hands off each other. You start getting suspicious that I'm seeing someone, but who? Not your best friend, Al. Never! After a while, I don't come home once or twice, and you go medieval possessive on me and threaten to dissolve the marriage, the business, the insurance, unless I come clean and tell you whose ceiling I've been moaning at lately."

"How old am I?" I asked her.

"You're almost fifty," she said, "with a family history of heart disease but no symptoms. I'm thirty-five and looking twenty-eight. On top of all that, our dot com stock plummets ninety-five percent, and I could use five million. Oh, I forgot, my boyfriend, Al, and I recently determined that you are emotionally abusive, and I'm a psychologically battered woman forced to take action because my situation is intolerable. Your buddy, Al the cardiologist (my boyfriend), tells you it's time for a routine physical, blood and urine, and a twelve-lead EKG."

"Uh-oh," I said. "I feel chest pains coming on." I looked up across the top of the monitor to let her know how much I admired her routine. Then I was back at that blinking cursor on her screen and thinking how easy it would be to leave my own little remote-access program behind. I'd only use it once, I told myself, to check back in a week or two and make sure that Lenny hadn't sent her another Trojan horse by e-mail. I wouldn't leave anything as vulgar as Back Orifice. How about that Trojan horse written in C named Girlfriend? Or a Sub-Seven variant?

By then Miranda's eyes had the key-cold gleam of Lady Macbeth contemplating murder to collect insurance money, and she said, "Maybe you think it's unusual when I say I want to tag along with you when you go in for the EKG. 'We'll go to lunch after?' I say. Maybe it seems peculiar when, instead of the usual

EKG tech, you wind up alone in the room with your best buddy, Al the doctor and me, your wife."

"I like you as my wife," I said, "but please don't hurt me."

Then it was almost automatic, like somebody else was doing it, not me. I downloaded a SubSeven remote-access program called Rubicon.exe from the web and then looked for an inconspicuous folder in C:\Programs where I could hide it. Her WindowsUpdate folder had two-hundred-plus objects in it, plenty crowded and out of the way, so I pasted Rubicon.exe in and went back to her desktop.

It was just a bit of code, I told myself, but it wasn't. It was a covert act of intimacy, a breach of trust, a violation of her machine's integrity. Exactly. I almost erased it then and there, but then I realized it gave me the power to access her machine and erase it any old time, so I left it there and listened to her story instead.

"Maybe you don't want to know what's happening," she said, "when Al the doctor grabs the paddle electrodes of the defibrillator? Maybe you think, *Hey, those aren't part of the EKG equipment, are they?* He doesn't bother to synchronize with your cardiac rhythm before he zaps you with a thousand joules."

"Go on," I said. "It really happened?"

"Two years ago. Sacramento, California," she said. "It was on the *Fraud Info Newsletter* today."

The ingenuity of the scheme enchanted her. Dying in a doctor's office could be negligent or unusual, but doctors kill patients every day, and the body count almost never inspires a homicide investigation. No marks on the body, no trace poisons, no blunt trauma, only paddle-electrode burns, the high voltage dispersed by gel pads. Why? Because the poor husband had suffered a heart attack, of course, whereupon his good friend the doctor repeatedly attempted cardio version and defibrillation but could not resuscitate the patient.

I exited back out to her desktop, just as she came around the monitor stand and slid onto a stool next to me.

"Wicked," I said.

She sniffed the cabernet again, took a sip, held it in her mouth, swallowed. At such times her lips, her throat, her slender hands were too much for me, but I couldn't look away. She's the definition of "fetching" when she's role-playing the latest insurance crime.

She was a farm girl from Ottumwa, Iowa, an apparent virgin when it came to personal experiences of fraud or depravity. After just two years in Special Claims, she still hadn't had sex with anybody, as far as we knew, but she was jaded when it came to insurance fraud. She knew a thousand different scams a speculator could use to, uh, shuck her out of ten grand. She had nothing but contempt for low-level operators and saved all of her admiration for murderers who had the sheer face and steady hands needed to pull off million-dollar stings involving cloak-and-dagger intrigue, offshore money laundering, industrial-strength shredders, and bodies buried under poured concrete. The sordid, high-octane frauds made her eyes light up with horror and fascination, as if she stood in awe of villains who could accomplish such gargantuan feats of evil without the slightest compunctions of conscience.

"You'd have to be oozing evil right out of your pores to kill your husband with paddle electrodes," she said, looking as if she wanted to be Catwoman and was constrained only by habits of conscience configured into her neural networks by the Sisters of the Sacred Heart of Duchesne Academy, in Omaha.

"Turbo evil," I said. "Stephen King could make a whole novel out of it, and a screenplay, to boot. How'd they get caught?"

"The usual," she said. "They turned on each other."

I'D LEFT THE SubSeven program running on her machine, and now here I was for the third or fourth time, on the verge of slipping in the back door. I wasn't worried about getting caught, because I knew that if Lenny came looking for hyde69.exe processes and got squat, he'd be so afraid that we'd figure out it was him he wouldn't say boo about a missing Back Orifice file.

I decided to sleep on it. I didn't want to enter her machine as the lovesick puppy with a head full of booze; I wanted my wits about me when I took that step. Why do something I might regret in the morning?

I left my machine up and running, slid onto the couch, and looked for the TV remote. When I saw it across the room, my eyes fell shut; even TV was just not worth the effort, and I slipped below the waves in the sea of sleep.

6

THE FINAL CARTOON

B y definition the supernatural is elusive and almost intangible. Sometimes the only symptom is a stirring in the roots of the hair accompanied by a premonition, some preconscious awareness operating outside the bandwidth of the five senses. Cops call it the "blue sense," the primal and uncanny ability to smell danger like ozone in a dark alley, where a professional killer waits with a gun, an 0-and-2 felony count, fire in the belly, and a suicide's resolve to stay out of prison.

I woke up with it. Instead of being hung over on wine, port, brandy, and Lenny's superpotent bud, I sat up and gasped, breathless, hyperaware. I'd been dreaming, maybe was still dreaming and seeing 3:37 A.M. glowing in green on an LCD readout below the surveillance camera in the darkness of my maximum security prison cell. I heard another prisoner being tortured somewhere off in another cell block, his screams of horror resounding in the cement-and-steel gangways. He was pleading

with his sadistic keepers, begging them to spare him. And just as
his words took shape—reverberating in the afterechoes of his
agony—I recognized his voice. It was Lenny.

Maybe the coming catastrophe infected even my memory of
waking. Whether I was imprisoned in a dreamscape penitentiary
or just passed out in a cheap West Omaha apartment with fiber-
board walls trimmed in vinyl—either way, I knew that Lenny
was in mortal peril and beyond my help.

I got off the couch and went for my machine, thinking I'd try
to raise him on instant messaging, or ping him and see if he was
up and running his machine or playing another game in the full
manic phase. And just as I reached out to touch the keyboard, up
popped the message window. I was sure it was Lenny, as sure as I
knew he was in trouble, but it wasn't him.

WantonMP: You theere?

It was Miranda! I was afraid she'd caught me sniffing her ports,
or knew I'd been lurking earlier. Had she found the back door?

CarvedMeat: Hi, M. I thought you were going to sleep?

WantonMP: I'm worrieda bout Llenny, somethings' worng
with him.

The apprehensions I'd had about GothicRage86 and his
cryptic message became flesh—cold, certain, and dreadful. I
typed:

CarvedMeat: Did you talk to him?

Miranda, normally an impeccable typist, even when
e-mailing or instant-messaging, typed:

WantonMP: We were instant-mESsaging aand he starteDd typing slloppy nonsense lal over the screen. I started thinking it wsa somebody else, or he'd had one of those breaks. I think we should gover there now!! I'm calling on the phone.

And it rang at my elbow.

She was more than worried; she was afraid, and the way her voice was breaking up, it wasn't just for Lenny.

"I don't want to go over there by myself," she said.

"Pick me up," I said. "No car. Remember?"

"I'm leaving right now," she said.

I wrote "3:45 A.M." on a pad next to the computer. I printed the instant-messaging exchange I'd had with GothicRage86, which was still on my screen, folded it, stuffed it in my jeans, and went down to meet her.

WE BUZZED LENNY from his entryway, but he wasn't answering. Miranda stabbed the touch pad with her thumb and pleaded with him under her breath, "C'mon, Lenny." I wanted to think that Lenny had a bankroll stashed somewhere and had gone back across the river to wager it all on a comeback, but I knew he didn't have a crying dime to his name, and we both knew something was wrong.

"Maybe I should call his sister?" I said. "She has a key."

Miranda opened her purse and yanked out a chain of keys and smart cards. She grabbed a key rimmed in red plastic, stabbed it in the lock, and cranked the dead bolt open with a fluency plainly acquired by practice. Before I could ask her about it, she was banging her clogs on the metal stairs, running up to

Lenny's place, cursing him through her clenched teeth, leaving me behind to wonder why she had a key and, more important, why she didn't want me to know she had a key.

I took the stairs two at a time and caught up with her at the door to Lenny's loft, where she used a second key, this one rimmed in green, to unlock another dead bolt. The steel door groaned when it swung open, sounding just like those squawky doors in a game of Delta-Strike.

Sometimes, you enter a room, and life starts over in an alien place where all the old rules, habits, and assumptions are useless— a place that makes you agree with the philosophers who say that the pleasures of this world are nothing more than the torments of hell seen backward in a mirror. Or worse, that this world is just another planet's hell. You step off a plane in a Third World country run by an authoritarian junta, or you ride a transit beam to another galaxy, where the hatch of the excursion module opens and you are disgorged onto the blasted heath of hell, a place so evil the temperatures approach absolute zero and superconductivity kicks in: your dead best friend's condo, where you find him in his boxers, frozen in a half crouch over the keyboard, his head tilted against the computer monitor, chin settled on the back of his crumpled right fist, a travesty of Rodin's *The Thinker* (with Monitor and Keyboard), a tableau done in cooling white meat.

Miranda stifled a gag reflex and sketched a sign of the cross, then dry-heaved and coughed into Lenny's wastebasket. Movies condition us to expect that evil is usually accompanied by a maelstrom of clamor and bloodshed, but Lenny's place was a cone of silence, with evil inscaped an inch thick until it deadened the acoustics like tapestries, and all we could hear was the blood thrumming in our ears like cryogenic locusts.

The only dead bodies I'd seen were in institutions where the liberal use of narcotics and sedatives had gentled my grandparents into perpetual night. Lenny's was the first corpse I'd encountered in the wild, as it were, but when I saw the bloodless, marmoreal pallor of his profile, I knew just what to do. Nothing.

His lips were colorless, eyes flat and lusterless, fingernails white as bones. His complexion was almost translucent, like mother-of-pearl, where I could peer inside his purpling interiors and almost see myself lying next to him on the bier, derogate, stone deaf to all elegies, blind to bosoms heaving with grief and tendresse for us, the dead guys.

Miranda covered her face with her hands, but her eyes were transfixed, staring through the webwork of her fingers, unable to look away.

"Lenny!" I yelled, and moved toward him, as if maybe I'd think of something to do on the way.

He'd been dead long enough for his blood to settle, and somewhere midway down his torso, the waxy whiteness of his head and neck shaded to blue and purple, like the bleeding edge of a bruise darkening all the way down below his knees where the gravity of oxygen-poor blood had turned his naked feet the color of hell's violets.

It was past horrible, but I tried not to be too concerned. He couldn't be dead. Six hours ago he was doubling down with thousand-dollar chips, leering at beautiful women, and puckering up to a single malt. If anybody could take you to school, give you a facial, pull a sick gimmick, like making you think he was dead, it was Lenny. He was clever enough to pull off just about any-thing, but not dead. He couldn't be. I was expecting a big giggle, a sound clip, or a note on his chair asking us how we liked his new wax dummy. Some explanation other than death would appear any second. It was just a matter of being patient and not panicking. While I waited, I admired Lenny's new high-end gaming mouse: a Razer Boomslang 3000, looking like a small sleek Batmobile idling, ready to roar away on the fiber-optic freeway.

When there's nothing to be done, people often do something anyway, because nature and human nature alike abhor vacuums, and nothing sucks the air right out of a room like death. I had the useless idea that Lenny's body should be lowered to the floor, and Miranda decided this was an emergency, so she called 911. I lifted Lenny by the shoulders and saw that his nose had bled on his hands and the keyboard—not a lot of blood, just the kind of thing you might get after—

Then I saw the hand mirror on his computer desk piled with tiny snowbanks of purple powder, a razor blade, a rolled-up diskette label (he'd left all of his dollar bills at the casino), pill vials, some with pills and labels, some with neither. They reminded me of the one time I said to him, "I hope somebody besides you is keeping track of all those pills." And Lenny had blown me off. "I was born with scrambled neurochemistry," he said. "A hundred years ago I would have been Lizzie Borden or Jack the Ripper, but thanks to lithium and selective serotonin reuptake inhibitors, I'm just a slack-master named Lenny Stillmach. Guys like me need a friendly doctor, somebody who keeps up with neuropharmacology and better living through chemistry."

Miranda was behind me giving the 911 operator the address and answering questions I couldn't hear. "What do you mean, how do we know?" she said. "He's not breathing, he's not moving—he's dead."

I put one of my hands under the nape of his neck and the other under his right thigh, lifted him out of the office chair, and lowered him to the floor. I arranged him in the supine position, aligned his tattooed arms and his plum-colored legs.

"Fuck, Lenny," I said. So far, it was indeed a sick joke, and it just kept going, with no punch line. My face burned and tears drabbled onto his naked chest.

When I moved to center his head and close the eyelids over his unnerving stare, I heard Miranda gasp and stop talking on the phone. I looked up at her; she had covered the phone with her hand.

"Don't touch his blood," she said, horror and grief raveling her face. She held her hand out to stop me. "Don't touch his blood. He—" And then she talked again into the phone to the 911 operator. "We don't know how long. He was dead when we got here."

The word *blood* was like she had yanked the chain on a bare lightbulb in a dark cellar and the luciform glare of revelation fell on Lenny's carcass. His remains looked like something left by Satan the predator, who had ambushed Lenny, had fallen upon him in the dead of night and stripped him of the magic pelt of life. Nothing left but a body bag of skin and bones forlorn in fallen flesh. He'd always been skinny—not sickly, just too thin— and six months ago he went through a phase where he looked certifiably anorexic, but we both attributed his weight loss to his cravings for what he called "S&M," substances and medications, which he was more fond of than nutrition.

"Lenny has AIDS," said Miranda; she was looking at me but talking into the phone. "Yes. HIV positive."

Now Miranda was off the phone, shuddering next to me, the two of us looking down at dead Lenny.

"He didn't tell anybody," she said, "unless he had to. He wasn't sick with it yet, but he was HIV-positive."

"How'd he—" I began.

She pulled strands of her hair away from her chin where they'd stuck in flecks of saliva; she wiped her mouth on the sleeve of her leather jacket.

She shook her head. "It wasn't that long ago that he found out he was positive," she said. "I don't think he knew for sure how he got it."

I scanned the pill vials again: lithium, Celexa, Ritalin, Percocet, OxyContin, blah blah, on down the line, no names I didn't recognize, no Crixivan or Viracept, nothing that looked like the stuff you'd take if you had AIDS. I'd seen stray pill vials aplenty around his place over the years, but I'd never seen so many together in one place, never noticed the doctor's name before, either—the same on every vial: Raymond Guttman, M.D.

My ears rang with silence and burned with shame as I took a moment to consider whether I might have accidentally swapped blood with him on the basketball court, passing a joint, sharing a razor. What about the time he sliced open his hand when we were splitting firewood at his mom's? He was a mess of blood, and I'd helped him clean the wound with peroxide.

We heard sirens, and Miranda shook harder, on her way to a full-blown grand mal of grief and terror.

I heard a beep and looked up at Lenny's monitor, which must have come out of sleep mode when I moved his hands on the keyboard. His screen slowly brightened like dawn breaking on the frozen plains of a new world naked, where Lenny's browser had several sessions open: The window on top was an XXX site churning out animated GIFs and JPGs of porn stars in daisy chains of blow jobs and cluster fucks being dished up by a server off in some infernal cyberspace basement. And behind it, the map still loaded from the Delta-Strike game we played. Only half of the man-machine hybrid named Lenny Stillmach was dead; the other half was still up and running.

AIDS? Lenny? He'd never acted gay, and the porn on the screen was plainly hetero. So maybe he was bi, or gay—a double agent and master of deception. Or maybe those needles he'd played with in college weren't really sterile. Or his number came up, like the time he'd won twelve grand at the tables over at Harrah's and had celebrated by saying yes to a hooker. She'd been flirting with him forever, or at least since she'd seen those black-and-gold thousand-dollar chips stacked in front of him. He couldn't say no, and next morning he swore it was all safe sex, and that he'd paid her double for superior skillful service. And then he tested positive, and now he's dead. But HIV positive doesn't jump up and kill you at the keyboard. Something else happened.

Window number three was a chat session open on his desktop, with the Attila-at-Home Web Cam Commander running for a Net meeting. The incoming video window was dark and blank. If someone had had a camera going on the other side, that someone was gone now. Then I glanced up and saw Lenny's Intel Pro PC camera mounted on the top rim of his monitor, it's glass eye staring right back at me, a tiny red light under the lens on the base blinking red. The Attila-at-Home Web cam was on and transmitting.

"Turn it off!" Miranda cried.

I wasn't sure if she meant turn off the porn, or if she was tracking with me: namely, maybe somebody was on the other side of the Attila-at-Home camera . . . watching. Maybe they'd been watching when Lenny had—

"Turn it off!" she yelled. She reached under his computer desk, grabbed the power strip, and started yanking out the plugs to the backup power supply, the web cam, the monitor, the machine.

"Miranda," I said. "Don't—"

"You want somebody seeing him like this? You want that human garbage on the screen when the ambulance gets here?"

I looked up again at the dark monitor and listened to the hard disk and the cooling fans spin down, realizing that if somebody had been there watching when Lenny died, any trace of the onlooker was probably evaporating from volatile memory, unless one of Lenny's programs had kept a visitor's log.

I heard Miranda sobbing and calling Lenny's name, but the stillness of his body seemed to soak up words before I could hear them.

"Carver, the ambulance is coming. The cops, the EMTs. What do we tell them?"

I looked at Lenny and the pill vials and the tidy little rows of powder on the mirror. It didn't occur to me there was much to tell. It was just a beautiful idea named Lenny being desecrated and mutilated by gangs of ugly facts.

"Are we just going to let them find all of this that he was taking? Tell them what he was doing?" She glanced in horror again at the monitor. "What about his mom? The newspaper?"

"It's over," I said. "We can't make it look any different than it is."

I heard voices and footfalls on the metal stairs.

7

THE REGIONAL
INVESTIGATOR

The specter of Lenny's corpse temporarily obliterated our considerable theoretical knowledge about dead bodies and the medical and legal procedures for determining the cause, mechanism, and manner of death. For years Miranda and I had seen folder after virtual folder of court files, autopsy reports, medical-examiner and coroner affidavits, emergency-room records, police reports, and death certificates, all containing the statements of witnesses—expert, official, unofficial. But we didn't think of ourselves as witnesses about to give statements; we were just two fashionably dissolute slackers who'd found one of our own slumped against the terminal, dead. Official statements never occurred to us, even after the first Omaha police officer arrived.

She was thirtyish and slight in two-tone blues and a black leather utility belt festooned with the tools of her trade. She took our names and addresses, asking for identification and our relationship to the deceased, but she pointedly did not ask us for any details about Lenny or how we'd found him dead in his condo.

When Miranda started telling her how we'd found him slumped over the keyboard, the officer asked her to please wait until the regional investigator arrived to tell her story. Then she took Miranda by the hand and helped her over to Lenny's couch on the far side of the room.

Two EMTs arrived wearing double plastic gowns, hairnets, double surgical gloves and masks, as if Lenny's place were the hot zone of an Ebola virus outbreak. They had a high-tech gurney and life-support equipment in tow, but one look at the body and the hurry left them.

I made a move to join Miranda and console her, but the officer met me halfway and motioned me onto a stool at the breakfast bar of Lenny's trendy loft kitchen.

"Mr. Hartnett, sir, it would be better if you sat here and waited for the regional investigator."

Miranda covered her face and sobbed. I started to get up again.

"It would be better if you stayed there until the regional investigator gets here. He's on his way and should be here any minute."

Her tone of voice and the glint in her eye came with a subtext: *Just obey,* she seemed to be saying, *then I won't have to give you any painful lessons.*

If I didn't obey, I sensed I'd be the latest proof that she never missed a chance to be as ruthless as the next male prick.

She went back to confer with the EMTs, who were calling in on radios about needing an autopsy, notifying the Douglas County coroner; it looked to be a drug overdose, accidental or otherwise, but no one had examined the body.

How many times had I seen in print the words "witnesses were sequestered and interviewed separately," but the sectors of my brain containing occupational data were inaccessible; system resources were being consumed by a painful urge to hold Miranda and commingle our sorrows.

The regional investigator was a burly, late-middle-aged plain-clothesman named Charlie Becker with eyes as black and lustery as obsidian. His face seemed to have settled long ago into a single, impassive expression that gave no clue to his feelings or thoughts. He looked like he'd gone to bed drunk watching late-night TV, until his phone woke him up an hour ago. But here he was, showered, shaved, and dressed like a middle manager, in a sport coat and tie. He had to be sixty at least, with thin hair past gray and on the way to white, but he looked like he could still knock me down if he had to. He seemed agreeable enough, accustomed to the routine: the cause of death appeared self-evident, and he'd soon be back home in bed.

He went first to the body, listening to the EMTs and the policewoman, who handed him a clipboard and briefed him on details. He fished his reading glasses out, grunted, and stooped to squint at the pill vials and the rows of powder on the mirror. Again, I heard them on the radio describing Lenny's death as an "apparent drug overdose" and "no apparent indication of foul play." Afterward, Becker came over and introduced himself.

While we spoke, the uniformed officer was taking more name, rank, and serial-number information from Miranda at the door, and Becker saw me noticing.

"Officer McAllister will take Ms. Pryor to the station—it's just down the street—and you can ride over with me. We'll take your statements there, and then I'll have an officer bring you back here to collect your vehicle."

By now a photographer had arrived, and Becker went over to discuss some of the shots he wanted of Lenny and of the pill vials and paraphernalia scattered on the computer table.

I saw him stop and look at the web cam, first from the front, then from each side.

"Is that a camera?" he asked, fishing out his glasses again and squinting at it.

I nodded. "It feeds video into his computer, and out to the Internet if he wants to connect with somebody else. It's called Attila-at-Home cam."

Becker made a face but then said, "I like cameras. So it's like a video camera, but that small?"

"Yes," I said. "They used to be herky-jerky, but they're better quality now."

"So he was slumped over the keyboard. Was the computer on?"

"No," Miranda blurted. "No, it wasn't on."

Becker looked from Miranda to me, and then to Officer McAllister, who steered Miranda toward the door.

"Was the computer on?" he asked me.

"I—I didn't really notice," I said.

"Who moved the body?" asked Becker.

For the first time since he walked in the door, Becker looked at me hard, like I might matter.

I opened my mouth to answer and locked up. Becker was already making a note on his clipboard about how I'd moved the body. He looked at his watch, then walked toward the door and motioned for me to come along. I decided now was the time to show him the instant message I'd printed on my machine, tell him about the Delta-Strike game and GothicRage86. When the coroner did the autopsy and found drugs in Lenny's system, this would be written up as a suicide or an accidental overdose. Maybe it was, but I was almost sure that I'd played somebody else in the second game of Delta-Strike, and maybe that somebody else had been here and used Lenny's souped-up machine to kick my ass and then sign off as GothicRage86. The Razer Boomslang gaming mouse would explain some of the agile, deadly maneuvers by GothicRage86, assuming whoever was at the controls was sober and played at the Cyberathlete Professional League level.

I handed Becker the instant-messaging screen printout I'd done from my home machine. He squinted, jerked his head, and grimaced every time I described the game or how I had received the message. I called his attention to the last line:

GothicRage86: I win.

"He was slumped over the keyboard when you found him?"
"He was."
"Now you're saying that earlier tonight you played a game on his computer?"
"No," I said. "I was in my apartment on my computer playing Lenny in a game called Delta-Strike."
"Lenny was at your place earlier playing computer games?" asked Becker.

I am not a tech snob who lords it over nonusers, and I was prepared to explain the Internet and how two or more players could "meet" there and play games together. But Becker was not in the mood for an introduction to peer-to-peer networking.

"Look," he said. "I don't mess with computers—"

He left the second half of his sentence unsaid, the *or with peo-ple who use them* part.

"I don't touch 'em. And if there's a dead body in the room and the computer is still on, or we see something else . . . not right, then I have a Dilbert come and look at the computer."

Becker's tone was dismissive, as if he'd be surprised to find anything but pornography on the Internet, most of it child pornography, from what he'd heard. He probably once expected computers to go the way of CB radios and was still incredulous that huge segments of the population chose to spend their waking hours clattering on keyboards and peering into screens, but he was not about to join them in their folly. He had all the RAM he needed in his number-2 Dixon Ticonderoga pencil.

"Two people in two different places can use two different computers to log on to the Internet and play each other in a game," I began.

His eyes skipped away from mine.

"See?" I said, and showed him the text of the instant messaging again, where it said:

CarvedMeat: Dirk, here, who's your low-ping buddy? We both know you ain't that good.

"Who's Dirk?" asked Becker.

"That's me," I said.

Becker looked down at his clipboard and said, "Carver Hartnett? Seventy-eight-oh-two Pacific Meadows?"

"Dirk is the nickname I use when I play the game," I explained. "Lenny uses the nickname SnowKiller."

Becker grunted and suppressed a chuckle at the macabre aptness of Lenny's game moniker.

"So maybe he changed his name to Gotham68 or whatever?" asked Becker, losing what little interest he'd had in the message and turning his scrutiny on me, wondering if maybe I had served myself at the smorgasbord of Lenny's minipharmacopoeia.

"I'm what you might call a gamer, sir," I said. "I've played Delta-Strike since it hit the Net years ago."

My plan was to tell him the naked truth, unless he displayed an aversion to it, in which case I'd adapt the truth to his liking, or else go back to the standard, preposterous lies we tell each other to make it through the average day.

Becker shrugged and moved for the door again. Maybe Sherlock Holmes and Kojak and Columbo and every other movie or TV homicide detective walked around *noticing* things at the scene of a death, but Becker acted as if he wanted to get out of there noticing as little as possible.

"I've also played Delta-Strike a lot with Lenny, and I don't think it was him playing in the second game. For instance, Lenny's never used a Mac-10, and he's nowhere near as fast as GothicRage was."

I could see pink serous fluid flush from the veins in the whites of his eyes as they fastened on me. "Mac-10?"

"Players choose a profile. You can be a counterterrorist named Dirk, let's say, or you can be a terrorist named SnowKiller, and then you can buy weapons. Lenny always used the SnowKiller profile and the Colt M4 A1 carbine with silencer."

Becker looked at the screen again.

"Shooter games, right?" he asked. "Like, blowing people's heads off on the screen?"

"Well, yeah," I said, and I sensed that he had me pegged as a refugee of the Littleton, Colorado, Trenchcoat Mafia. "It's like going to the firing range," I added. "Even the government uses first-person shooter games to train police and military personnel."

I was all set to convince him that it was my patriotic duty to be a heavy gamer because I might be called upon to serve in the next tactical air war against Iraq, where I would use my computer-gaming skills to guide air-launched cruise missiles into the ventilation shafts of Saddam Hussein's fortified bunkers, but Becker interrupted me.

"Look," he said, "I'll have a Dilbert look at the machine and tear it apart if he needs to. In the meantime, we're going to do an autopsy on Mr. Lenny and see how much there is of whatever he had inside of him and whether it was enough to kill him. If we find something not right, then we'll have them check the computer to see if somebody besides him was in here using it. Would that suit you?"

"Yes," I said.

"Good," he said. "Now let's go down the street to the station, and you can help me make my report."

8

DEATH UNKNOWN

THE FLOOR MATS OF Becker's Taurus wagon were strewn with fast food refuse and Cornhusker paraphernalia. The interior reeked of stale smoke, and the armrest on my side had a scabby black cigarette burn that looked like a cancer lesion on a vinyl lung. The dashboard featured none of the usual cop hardware or barking radios. Becker had a radio, but it was off; he presumably didn't need it because he kept his cell phone mashed against his ear at all times, while the police operators patched callers in and out to create one seamless, never-ending phone call. "Was she dead when they got there?" he said into phone, presumably talking to another officer dealing with another body somewhere else in Omaha. "And what time was that? Did they just stop by for a visit at two A.M.? Okay, then, put him on."

He lit an Old Gold filter (a brand I hadn't seen since they killed my granddad), and I took one when he offered it. I am descended from Irish Catholic railroad and road-construction workers, most of whom have a cigarette after alcohol or sex, or when somebody dies. The Hartnett clan marks the passing of their own with plenty of eating, drinking, and smoking, even if the deceased died of cirrhosis of the liver and lung cancer, in which case having a drink and smoking a cigarette are expressions of solidarity with the dearly departed.

So I smoked one in Lenny's memory, while Becker drove the five blocks from the Old Market loft to the police station, steering with the meaty palm of his cigarette hand and muttering routine questions into the cell phone he held in the other.

"How did they get in? What were they doing there? And what time was that?"

He wheeled the Taurus into a marked space at the station and snapped the phone shut without saying good-bye. I heard him say "Friday night" under his breath, though technically it was Saturday morning, and then the words he'd spoken to whomever during the drive over arrived in central processing, like the rumble of thunder lagging along after a flash of lightning: *What were they doing there?*

What were *we* doing there? Did *we* just stop by for a visit? How did *we* get in? I could imagine how Miranda might plausibly end up with a key, but then why didn't she just whip it out and say, "I've got a key?"

I saw Officer McAllister leading Miranda through the plate-glass front door of the station as we drove up, and realized I wasn't going to hear Miranda answer any of these questions.

Once Becker and I were inside, Miranda was nowhere in sight. Becker showed me into a conference room with a steel table, a coffeemaker, and a tray of coffee filters, powdered creamers, and sugar packets. He poured coffee into Styrofoam cups for us and slid some forms under the clamp of his clipboard.

"Okay," he said, and nodded for me to go ahead.

"We called him because we were worried about him," I said.

"We being you and Ms. Pryor?" he asked. "Were you two together when you called?"

I detected a tiny smile beneath his immobile cheeks. Becker was a regular guy with a healthy curiosity about who serviced Miranda's affections. Lenny? Me? Some other lucky guy? I had a feeling that the subject would come up, and Becker would have the usual trouble believing Miranda was a single, unattached drone working in a cube farm at an insurance company.

"No," I said. "I called Lenny first, then Miranda called him later, and then she called me and said she was worried about him."

I sketched him a five-panel cartoon of Friday night, beginning with Terminator Norton ending Lenny's career at Reliable, on to the Upstream, skipping over the drive to the Indian rave that wasn't, on to the casino where Lenny didn't do so well at blackjack, and ending with the freaky Delta-Strike game, and Miranda calling me.

"What time was it when you tried to call Lenny?" Becker asked.

"Right after we played Delta-Strike. I called from my apartment. I'd say eleven, eleven-thirty. Right before I went to bed."

"Was Lenny doing drugs when you were out with him? Was he taking pills? Was he drinking heavy?"

Becker had probably been here a thousand times before. He didn't want to know if *we* were doing drugs. Just Lenny. Was Lenny doing drugs?

"Yeah," I said. "He took medications for depression, and—he may have smoked some marijuana—"

I barely paused, but he was all over it.

"I work in homicide," said Becker. "I'm covering this weekend for the regional investigator, because his wife is dying of brain cancer out at Methodist Hospital. The point is, I work in homicide, not vice and narcotics. If you and your friends do drugs, we don't care. In homicide, we *like* drugs. If your friend took too many drugs, and drugs killed him, then it's not a homicide. I write 'cause of death unknown' in this report because that's what we call a mess like this. Then I wait for my autopsy protocol. Meantime, we all go home to bed."

His contempt for duplicity was palpable, and just like us, he'd probably seen plenty of it in his line of work. We found it in tampered dates on medical records and forged physicians' signatures on disability claims; Becker saw it on the faces of suspects, or in the sheepish reticence of an industry rookie like me trying to hide pot smoking from a homicide detective.

"We drank a lot," I said, "and Lenny probably smoked some pot."

I was prepared to do the easy thing and level with him about the Ecstasy and the purple lines on Lenny's mirror, probably chopped-up tablets of OxyContin, the latest designer opiate. When he needed some, Lenny called it Vitamin O; when he came in late because he'd taken too much of it, he called it the Great Satan. Or maybe it was a purple stimulant chopped up and snorted to enhance gaming prowess. I was worried about what Miranda would say. She was more than a little paranoid about recreational drug abuse. She didn't want Lenny in her car if he had pot on him, so he routinely lied to her about whether he was carrying any. She smoked his fancy strains and hydroponic hybrids of pot only on special occasions and only after putting damp towels under all the doors and burning scented candles first, like she was back in a college dorm room. If Becker asked her about drugs, the Miranda I knew would say, "Drugs? What drugs? We just said no to drugs a long time ago," and then our stories wouldn't exactly match. But she had to know that under the circumstances there was no use hiding it, because they'd test Lenny's blood for everything.

"Pills?" asked Becker.

"Probably," I said. "I don't know what kind, though. Probably from the bottles on his computer table?"

He shook his head and grinned at me, like I was a kid going on too long with a game of make-believe and he was the dad who'd graduated head of the class from the Academy of Hard Knocks and he was getting ready to send me there if I didn't quit messing around.

"Needles? Anything by needle?"

I shook my head no, and meant it, mostly.

"Did he ever say he took needle drugs, or did you ever see him do them?"

"Uhm. No."

His cell phone trilled, and he flicked it open like a slasher whipping out a switchblade.

"Becker," he said into the mouthpiece.

His eyes were aimed at me, but they blanked, like he was on hold or adrift in a patch of dead cellular air, so I filled it.

"Busy night, huh?"

"It's Friday, and the holidays are coming," said Becker. "This time of year people get together with their families, they get drunk, and they fight. Sometimes fighting ain't enough and only killing will do."

He arranged for another dead body to be processed—an old lady who slipped, fell through a glass shower door, and bled to death on floor, from the sound of it—while I looked out the plate-glass window and into the lobby of the station, searching for any sign of Miranda.

After a few more terse instructions, Becker snapped his phone shut and poured us both more coffee.

"You say Lenny took medicines for depression? Did he see any psychiatrists or counselors for a diagnosed type of mental illness? If you know? Was he mentally ill?"

I shrugged. "Mentally ill" seemed excessive to me for someone of Lenny's capabilities, but if Becker needed a few half truths to occupy the blanks on his forms, I wouldn't object. Doctors treated Lenny for mental illness, so I guess that made him mentally ill. I thought of him more as a telecosmic visionary on the fiber-optic frontier, a man at ease in the age of spiritual machines, and he could make them do amazing things. Sure, he had mental illnesses and substance-abuse problems to manage like the rest of us, and maybe he was more willing than most to risk excess, but suicidal? Not. Reckless? Never fatally so, until now. Wacky? Yes. Dangerous to himself or others? Never.

Becker checked his facts by going back over the forms and making blunt statements barbed with inflected question marks. I was expected to nod after each one, so we could get the paperwork over with and go home.

"He liked pills, he liked dope?" said Becker.

I shrugged and nodded.

"He told you that the credit card companies had garnished his wages? He got fired?"

Nod.

"According to your . . . your girlfriend, Ms. Pryor . . . you say she told you that Lenny had AIDS?"

He took an extra eyeful of me on the word *girlfriend,* waited for me to correct him, then kept going when I just nodded.

Miranda was a private person who respected the privacy of others. She'd be wanting to hide the AIDS from them about now, too, just like she'd be wanting to pretend we were model citizens who never went near drugs. But it was too late to hide AIDS—she'd said that right into the phone. That's why the EMTs showed up looking like astronauts in a semiconductor-clean room, so of course Becker would be thinking dirty needles, or gay, or both.

"So, Lenny lost his job," said Becker. "Then he lost five thousand dollars in one blackjack hand over at Harrah's?" He made another note. "And then maybe he took too much of something?"

"He didn't commit suicide," I said.

Becker snorted, almost smirked. "I'm glad we agree on that," he said.

He had a certain pitch-perfect facetiousness, barely detectable and therefore eminently deniable, in case anybody noticed and took offense.

"Families hate that word. That's why if there's no foul play we leave it a death unknown, even if it's a suicide. Used to be the insurance companies didn't like a suicide, either; they wouldn't pay on them. But for accidents they'd pay double indemnity, just like in the movies."

He waited for me to catch up again. Knowledge, especially insurance knowledge, seemed to be stored in a separate partition of my brain that I couldn't access from the desolate desktops of the Grief 4.0 operating system.

"Reliable Allied Trust Insurance Company," he said, reading from his report. "That's where you and Ms. Pryor and Mr. Stillmach all worked?"

I nodded and recovered enough memory to see where he was going. Back in Dead Man Norton's day, insurance companies refused to pay for a suicide. That led to ugly trial coverage on the front page of the newspaper, with the likes of Dead Man Norton on the stand telling a jury that he wasn't going to pay death benefits to a sobbing widow and kids, because the deceased was a crook who killed himself to defraud the insurance company. Or it was even worse if the cops found the guy hanging from a ceiling hook with a belt around his neck, porno and lubricants everywhere, and a printout from a website extolling the carnal delights of autoeroticasphyxiation to enhance orgasm during masturbation. Suicide or accident? You decide.

"It's different nowadays," I said. "If a guy commits suicide in the first two years he owns the policy, then it's true, we don't pay the death benefit; we just refund the premiums paid, with interest. 'A push is a push,' as Lenny used to say in blackjack lingo. It goes along with the two-year contestability period. The same is true if we find out the guy lied on his life insurance application by saying he didn't smoke when really he was a two-pack-a-day man, or by writing 'no' in the answer box for the question 'Have you seen a doctor or received medical treatment for cancer in the last five years?' when actually he'd gone AWOL from the ICU with a pancreatic tumor the size of a summer squash inside him. If we want to call him on it, we've got two years to claim fraud and rescind the policy. After two years, we have to pay, even if we know we're paying scam money to a fraudster."

"So, maybe somebody should make sure about the suicide coverage," he said. "Just in case his blood comes back a river of toxic waste, and somebody like, oh, his insurance company, let's say, might have a financial interest in calling him a suicide."

Not even Norton would go that low, or maybe he would if enough money was involved.

"Lenny probably had simple group term life insurance from Reliable," I said. "That would pay the same whether it's accident, suicide, or murder, as long as he had the policy for at least two years. He started at Reliable four or five years ago, and the policy came with his job benefits. Chances are it started running then. But Lenny didn't kill himself."

"Oh," said Becker, "because he would have told you if he was thinking about doing that?" Another deniable insinuation resonating with the same creeping facetiousness. "When you dropped him off at his place, did he say anything? What were his last words?"

I felt sicker when I remembered them, and Becker waited, knowing he had something on the line.

"He said," I began, and my tongue got stuck in my dry mouth. "He said, 'I laugh at debts. Either they'll go away, or I will.'"

Becker's face barely moved, but he pursed his lips as he wrote down Lenny's last words.

"Damn," I said.

"Did Lenny tell you that he had AIDS?"

The AIDS again, and Becker was using it to suggest that maybe I didn't know Lenny as well as I thought I did. If he was a true friend, why would he keep such a devastating secret from me? I almost resented him, as if Becker had handed me an insulting note that Lenny had written to me just before he died.

"He never looked that sick," I said. I was resorting memories, trying to figure out how Lenny could pull all-nighters and drink me and Barnacle Bill and everybody else in the bar dead drunk before going home to bed if he was dying from AIDS? "You don't just up and die from AIDS, you get sick first, right?"

Becker shrugged. To him it was all academic, unless it was murder. I didn't think anybody had killed Lenny, but I wanted to know what had happened, and Becker wouldn't bother to find out, unless something was "not right," as he liked to put it.

"Maybe Lenny got too far gone and lost track of what he was taking," I said, "but I think somebody was there with him. Somebody else played that Delta-Strike game. It wasn't Lenny."

Becker looked off me again and went into his windup.

"So, we have to wait for the autopsy results and medical-examiner reports to come in," he said. "It depends what kind of drugs they want to test for—probably a lot from the looks of things. Might take a week before we get complete toxicology. Sometimes they have to mail specimens around the country from Omaha and wait for the lab results. In the meantime, it's a death unknown. We like to get the apartment turned back over to the family within a few days, so they can get in there and tell us if anything is missing. If you think Lenny was murdered by a character from a computer game, well, I'll tell that to the Dilbert I send out to look at the machine. And I'll have the Evidence Unit dust the keyboards.

Where they will find my fingerprint on the space bar I touched to bring the machine out of sleep mode.

"And the Razer Boomslang," I said. "The gaming mouse."

"What?" he asked.

We made a point of looking each other in the eye, even though we were aliens from different galaxies who by some cosmic coincidence happened to share a common language—English— that did nothing to bring us any closer to an understanding.

"We'll dust the razor hootenanny," he said.

Becker finished up his forms and poured me a fresh cup of coffee.

"You sit tight, and I'll be right back."

He took his clipboard with him, and during the twenty minutes he was gone I considered the suicide angle. Yes, Lenny took drugs, lots of them, all the time, meaning he was an experienced user well acquainted with his substances, mixes, and limits, and unlikely to accidentally take too much of something. But Becker was not the guy to test my sophisticated-user theory on. Better to wait for the blood tests. In the meantime, I needed to figure a way to go back and boot up Lenny's machine and find out if GothicRage86 was Lenny or somebody else, and, if it was somebody else, whether they'd been there with him in his condo or just hiding somewhere in the game map before it started. Even if Becker told a police IT geek to look at Lenny's machine, he wouldn't know enough to tell his Dilbert what to look for.

Becker was gone long enough to make me wonder if he'd forgotten about me and gone home. Then I saw him walking back down the hall with his cell phone mashed to his ear.

He finished the call on the other side of the glass, then came in and sat down across from me.

"After the Upstream," he asked, "did you go anywhere else before the casino?"

Miranda must have told him we were going to the rave that had been busted? No way, how would that look in the *Omaha World-Herald*? The headline would be something restrained, like RAVING ECSTASY BINGE ENDS IN TRAGEDY, with a caption: *Drugs Snuff Out Another Young Heartland Life*. Before the first paragraph ended, we'd be mentioned as insurance investigators for Reliable Allied Trust.

"We went for a drive on I-twenty-nine," I said.

"Where were you going?"

"A party somewhere."

"What kind of party? Where?"

"It was a rock concert, I think. Lenny said it was on an Indian reservation. We barely got out of town when he got a phone call from somebody and changed his mind. Then he wanted to go to the casino."

I was thinking about the Ecstasy I'd given Lenny, and staying as far away from it as possible. Becker seemed satisfied, but he quizzed me again about what drugs Lenny had taken.

After that, he showed me out to a chair in the lobby, where I nursed another cup of bitter coffee and waited for Miranda. I watched the hands of the station clock creep toward 6 A.M., thinking about how, after a finite number of clock ticks, I would join Lenny out at Calvary Cemetery, where the Catholics in town keep their dead. Meanwhile, I was in a police station thinking about new and hateful ways to kill time before time finished its subtle and insidious business of killing me.

At ten after six, Becker and Officer McAllister came out of a conference room with Miranda and offered us a lift back to the car. Miranda still looked like a shock victim, pale and sick to death of police procedures, so I told McAllister we'd walk the five blocks back to Miranda's car.

All the way back to her place, Miranda obsessed about what might have been if he'd taken one less pill, snorted one less row of purple powder, drunk one less single malt scotch or glass of wine, or if God had only let him win that blackjack game.

"You didn't tell them anything about us smoking pot or about Lenny's drugs, did you?" she asked.

She read it all over my face. "Carver!"

"They're going to run every fluid in his body through a spectrograph and find every single drug he took last night. Why lie about pot?"

"Because," she said, "it makes us look negligent. Like we should have taken better care of him."

What if I'd called her right after the Delta-Strike game and told her about GothicRage86? And what if we'd gone over to see what was up with Lenny? Before he'd stopped breathing. What then?

I wasn't the what-if type. Were we supposed to take care of him because he'd lost five thousand at blackjack? If he'd won the blackjack game, he probably would have fucked himself up even worse to celebrate.

Outside it was still dark under a low December fog. The buildings along Fifteenth Street looked like vacant mausoleums or temples abandoned by a civilization lost, at least for the weekend. Most of the snow had melted and refrozen, leaving a skin of dirty ice tufted here and there with blobs of black snow. Miranda teetered in her clogs on the slick cement and grabbed my upper arm for balance. We could pass for a normal couple out for a walk at an abnormal hour, except that death had complexioned our faces with the unmistakable pallors of woe.

The fog hung over us like limestone formations on the ceiling of an underground cave, and we were lost, wandering somewhere far below the earth's surface, searching the underworld for the soul of Lenny Stillmach.

9

NORTON SCRUBS
HIS HANDS

I STOOD BY LENNY," said Norton. "I cut him slack from here to Doomsday."

He was ensconced in the throne of his graphite workstation, trying to get on with Monday-morning business, and peeved at Lenny Stillmach for disrupting the entire department by killing himself. The wake was tonight, the funeral tomorrow morning. In Norton's mind, Lenny had overdosed himself into a soft afterlife. He left the rest of us behind to do all the work, and if Lenny were still alive Norton would kill him for it. Now two days of useless grieving would tear holes in the week's productivity numbers, and year-end meant it was impossible to catch up.

Worse were the volatile rumors in Special Claims that Lenny had committed suicide only because Norton had fired him and left him without so much as severance pay to service the interest on his gambling debts. Norton moved to contain gossip and control spin before it undermined department morale. We were all underpaid, and it was important to keep the Special Claims work group energized and on a common mission against the evil scam artists who prey on our customers by submitting fraudulent insurance claims. If the people in Special Claims started thinking their leader was an evil manager with a hollow heart, it might divide or dilute their unmitigated hatred for mere scammers. If it came to that, Norton wouldn't hesitate to point at the true villains—the powers that took over after his dad, Dead Man Norton, died. Some MBA with a spreadsheet upstairs was probably to blame, because he'd decided that Norton only needed two investigators under him, not three, so somebody had to go overboard.

He called me in first because he needed my considered opinion that Lenny killing himself had nothing to do with Norton firing him. My job was to listen while Norton convinced himself out loud that Lenny's suicide was a random tragedy—no more Norton's fault than if daredevil Lenny had died in a one-car accident on a dirt road out past the back side of beyond.

"How's your mom doing out there in Sun City?" Norton asked.

"Oh." I looked up, and he was smiling, affectionate, benevolent. "She's fine. She likes the golf."

"Good," he said. "And your dad up in Minneapolis?"

This time I caught him glancing at his book rest. Christ, it was him and his contact manager. What's next? *Didn't you tell me that he's a Vikings fan and a scratch golfer and that he took a trip to Easter Island last spring?*

"He's fine," I said. "You wanted to see me about Lenny?"

"We were *there* for Lenny through sickness and health, of *all* kinds," said Norton. "We let him be his own person, but he was in slow-motion self-destruct. This was bound to happen. Now.

Next week. Next year. Bound to. That kind of hard living catches up to you. It's like going to the casinos every weekend: You don't need an actuary to tell you that eventually math will get the better of luck."

If Lenny did kill himself, he was probably driven to it by homespun platitudes like these, so full of cloying Midwestern wisdom we choked on them when Norton pushed them down our throats. I was in my designated chair, under my own personal cone of light, and I must have made a face, or given off a reading, because Norton instantly shifted gears.

"Lenny was talented," Norton said. "One of those self-destructive geniuses. He'll be missed, but I can't have my investigators invidiously discriminating against dead Nigerians and abusing them, live! On tape! Then lying to my face about it. Lenny gave me no choice. Him killing himself last night—that was bound to happen."

"I don't think he committed suicide," I said.

Norton looked like he hadn't thought about that until just now. "Meaning he *accidentally* killed himself? Does it matter? Either way he killed himself."

Norton's obsessive hand washing was verging on perseveration, and why was he doing it in front of me? If this kept up, we'd be talking about our feelings soon. He could have called in Colonel Dagmar for a Nazi Secret Service confab and worked off his obsessive denial on her. He could have called his second wife, Docia (even though technically he and Docia were separated); he frequently talked her into spending a special weekend with him—then he could have displaced and transferred some anxiety her way. Instead, he chose me as his guilt therapist, probably because, like his first wife, his second wife was sick to death of

ALAMEDA FREE LIBRARY

playing Freud to Norton's Wolf Man. He didn't want another divorce on his curriculum vitae—it would make people wonder about his emotional stability—so he called in me instead of Docia to minister to his needs. My job was to sit in the audience and vouch for the stories he told himself from the high-tech stage of his office minitheater.

"I had to let him go," said Norton. "You know how the EEOC can be once they come after you."

When people are stressed and conflicted in this way, they often say the exact opposite of what they mean—the way Norton was saying that he'd fired Lenny over the EEOC and the dead Nigerians, but really he'd fired him because of what? The garnishment? For hard living in the first degree? Cost cutting come down from upstairs? Certainly not because Lenny discriminated against the twenty dead Nigerians named Mohammed Bilko.

"It's not even correct to say that Lenny was terminated," said Norton. "It was a mutual understanding. That's what we were doing before you joined us on Friday. We mutually agreed that things were not working out and that something had to change. It was Lenny who suggested that we go our separate ways. He thanked me for giving him the idea of moving on. It was a mutual solution to our ongoing mutual problems."

If he said "mutual" again I was going to resign and go get a job over at Mutual of Omaha's *Wild Kingdom* working with Marlin Perkins and his sidekick, Jim; I could get away from the likes of Norton and spend some time with spotted hyenas in the African bush. I didn't nod, I didn't wink, but Norton still felt entitled to assume I would politely abide his ritual lying. His skull was like one of those transparent shells on the new multi-colored computers: I could see inside and watch while his operating system purged his conscience of all open files on Lenny Still-mach. Then he could get back to the business of making his year-end numbers.

Dangerous thoughts, because Norton is sensitive to even trace amounts of contempt, which he usually repays with a frontal assault, the way he'd gone after poor Lenny last Friday. But I was ready for him this time, or so I thought.

"Did you talk to Lenny about the Heartland Viatical file?" he asked.

He glanced down at his screen. The bastard! He probably kept a laptop on his nightstand and ran voice-analysis software whenever he pillow-talked with his wives. Maybe that's why they moved out!

"Lenny didn't say much about Heartland," I said. "He summarized the web research he'd done on them and Hector Crogan. Was there something he was supposed to tell me?"

Questions are good, I'm told, because they confuse the software, which is designed primarily to detect vocal stresses in true or false statements, not open-ended questions.

Norton tapped the screen and glared.

"I moved that file over to you because two years ago I asked Lenny to investigate Heartland Viatical for fraud. He came back two weeks later and told me they were clean. After that, I found out that Lenny *dated*, more than *dated*, had been *involved with* a Heartland Viatical sales agent while he was supposed to be investigating them. Apparently it went on for months, probably still was going on right up to the end. He never told me anything about this *relationship*."

Relationship?

I held off asking if it was a man or a woman that Lenny was

"involved with" in Norton's feverish imagination. I could find that out for myself. Either way, Norton clearly didn't know about the AIDS. A Special Investigations man with AIDS "dating" a viatical-settlement broker? AIDS victims were the bread and butter of the viatical companies. Norton wouldn't dither a minute away pondering that one, he would have fired Lenny when he found out about it. Maybe that's what happened?

"See what I meant about him having *other problems?*"

I weighed the likelihood that Lenny would have a fling with a crooked viatical broker against Norton's unremitting paranoia about single investigators having sex with fraudsters. Norton's version came up the likely suspect, and Norton promptly confirmed.

"Found yourself a gal yet?"

Not again! I shook my head, ignored the question, and defended the honor of the dead.

"If Lenny was chasing a viatical rep around in public, then he was probably at least half on the job and trying to investigate any way he could, which wouldn't preclude having a little fun along the way."

Unless, of course, he had AIDS. Something I didn't want to think about just then. He probably had chatted up a babe in the target organization and used standard, hacker social engineering on her, hoping for the off chance that she'd be gullible or careless enough to divulge clues to her username and password along the way—names of her cats, her address, nicknames, best of all, chat-room IDs or instant-messaging usernames. Then he could access Heartland's servers at 2 A.M. and roam their networks at will plundering any files he needed.

I'd done it before, with his help. Borderline illegal—okay,

actually it's outright illegal, but criminals running scam outfits don't complain to the FBI when they get hacked, and their network security usually has plenty of well-known holes. Nine times out of ten, they never even know they were hacked, and if they catch you the tenth time, they can't prove it was you or your machine.

"Did he say anything about dating a Heartland Viatical sales rep?"

"No way," I said.

"How about Miranda?" he asked, his eyes steady on me. "Did she say anything about the Heartland file?"

"No," I said. Nothing but the easy truth. Maybe I was safe after all.

Norton clasped his hands together and leaned into his cone of light so I'd be sure to see gravity tugging his slack features into overdone solemnity. "I don't think Lenny gave me everything he had on Heartland Viatical."

That went without saying, but I spied an opening.

"You want me to go through his machine and search it for files containing references to Heartland Viatical?"

Norton would have this done anyway; I volunteered for the job because I wouldn't mind getting into Lenny's work machine and searching his files for any reference to GothicRage86, too, or maybe a suicide e-mail note? Some explanation for what happened? Or what if Lenny had expropriated a username and password for the chance to get inside Heartland? If that stuff existed, it would be on at least one of his machines. On the way to the Indian rave, when I'd asked him where he'd gotten his information on Hector Crogan and Heartland Viatical, he said it was from deep inside. "Some on the Fraud Eighty-six site, some on

ChoicePoint," he'd said, "and some from deep inside the Tomb of the Unknown I-Told-Ya-But-I-Didn't-Tell-Ya." Real dead man's talk, as it had turned out.

Norton looked away, and I didn't need software to detect stress in his voice.

"I had Lenny's machine taken down to the IT Department on Saturday. I asked Eric to retrieve all of the company files and proprietary information. I'll send you copies of any Heartland files they find."

Always two steps ahead.

"Just so I'm sure—I am investigating Heartland Viatical for what?"

"I want you to find out if Lenny sandbagged me and held back evidence of viatical fraud at Heartland, because he was mattress wrestling one of Hector Crogan's sales reps."

"Okay," I said. I almost asked him again for access to Lenny's machine, but if I went that route, I'd have better luck going down to IT myself.

"I asked Miranda to look into the Heartland file, too," said Norton and watched me to see if I seemed surprised. "I don't think she gave me everything, either."

He could take that up with her, and I said as much with the look on my face.

"Lenny and Miranda," he said, and shook his head. "They sat five feet apart in the same row of cubes, right?"

"Just me in between," I said.

"That's why it's so strange," said Norton, his tone a masterful blend of innocence and suggestiveness. "Why would two people sitting five feet apart with just you in between send each other e-mails, sometimes dozens of e-mails a day, back and forth, for weeks?"

I flashed on Miranda having Lenny's loft key in her purse. My face got hot, and I found myself looking into one of Norton's minicams, its infernal infrared eye staring right back at me. It was sampling my face, torso, hands for thermal fluctuations. I was emitting dermatome thermographs consistent with an intense emotional state, which meant I needed a good excuse for having one.

"Lenny isn't even in the ground yet," I said. "And people are pawing through his e-mails?"

"You offered to do the same sixty seconds ago," Norton said. "Check your employee handbook and your personnel file. It's in bold type with a signature box under it. Every employee initials it when they sign on here and before they get their first paycheck: 'I acknowledge that the Reliable Allied Trust insurance company owns my work computer and all of the software, data, and information contained in it, including my e-mails.'"

He stood up to shoo me out.

"I'm trying to meet privately with each person in the department about this terrible business. I'll have to get back to you on the Heartland matters. But just so I'm clear." He peered at me through the titanium frames of his reading glasses, then took them off and squinted at me. "Lenny told you nothing about his dealings with Heartland?"

"No," I said. "Only that he'd researched them and Hector Crogan on-line."

"And Miranda?"

"She didn't say anything," I said.

"All right, then I see no need to tell her about this particular assignment," said Norton.

I didn't say, "Okay," thereby preserving my right to complain later about being assigned to investigate my friends.

Norton reached over and shook my hand.

"We're lucky to have you, young man," he said. "I'll send you any Heartland files we find on his system."

Outside his office, at Helveg's sentry booth, the Dag studied me for signs of conspiracy to spread hateful rumors about her boss causing Lenny's suicide.

When I got back to my cube, I found a note on my keyboard.

> *Where are you?*
> *Norton wants to see me.*
> *Lunch after?*
>   *M.*

Norton had me going and Miranda coming.

10

LENNY'S COVERAGE

I WENT BACK TO my cube and tried not to think about whether Miranda and Lenny had something going. Norton wouldn't make up stuff like e-mail traffic, and he never gave away information for free, so he had a purpose in telling me. Because he wanted me to look into it? With him being the only one with access to Lenny's e-mail? Ah! Knowing Lenny, the e-mails were encrypted, so Norton knew about how many times they'd written but nothing about content. I suppose Miranda and Lenny could have been forwarding Internet jokes back and forth. *Robert Parker Wine Advocate* bulletins and Wine Spectator Selections and Best Buys? Not to their home machines, but to the next cube? I withheld judgment, pending submission of a valid claim with supporting documents. That seemed the proper mind-set for a Special Claims investigator.

Maybe Norton was right. Maybe a steady diet of fraud rewires your brain, makes you bitter and suspicious of people you're supposed to love. Makes you paranoid and irritable, just the way I felt when I saw the pink "While You Were Out" icon blinking on my screen and found a message—taken by the Dag—for me to call Addie Frenzer over at Omaha Beneficial. Thanks, Addie! Now the Dag would report to Norton that I'd been contacted by forces behind enemy lines, that I was fielding overtures from our biggest competitor, second only to Mutual of Omaha.

Addie was a thirtyish single mom in the Special Investigations Unit, and she had a girlfriend Lenny liked (had liked) named Natalie Fleming, also in the same department at Beneficial. Lenny and I had double-dated Natalie and Addie now and again, and they liked to get a little wild, which in Omaha, Nebraska, left little in the way of public venues. So by the end of the night, we'd wind up in Lenny's loft, where Addie usually came after me, or else she let me come after her. She was smart and funny, but she was already north of thirty and had a kid with hearing aids, goggle glasses, and enough special needs to feed an army of specialists. Only saints and millionaires need apply for the prospective husband vacancy, and in between she passed the time with guys like me.

Her face was nothing special, but she had a shape that made you want to grab on, and she was better than average in bed—something I say about less than half the women I go with. She was usually game for a night or a weekend together. She never cared if I didn't call till the next time I called, and she never hissed or pouted about it if she called and I had something else. I collected my fair share of rain checks from her, especially if I called too late after cocktails at the Kennel Club, where all the women more interesting than her were already spoken for.

Addie was also one of the few special claims professionals around town with more and better information than anybody except Lenny, and maybe Old Man Norton. She was well connected in the industry, on both the new, wired IT side and the old-boy, Knights Of Aksarben network on the other. She worked herself up the food chain because she needed money to pay the specialists and therapists who took care of her kid.

We didn't usually call and leave each other messages at our offices. We used our home phones and e-mails or, in her case, a transient Yahoo account, where I wrote her at Fraud-Maven19@yahoo.com. She'd probably read Mike Kelly's column in the *World-Herald,* where Lenny's death had been described as a "tragedy, cause unknown, but an autopsy has been ordered," and then she'd called to commiserate.

Her message got me vexing again over the damn AIDS thing—how it forced me to rethink every angle of Lenny's social life. For instance, what were Lenny and Natalie doing back at his place after they dropped Addie and me off at mine? Was he crazy? Sometimes. Would he sleep with a woman and not tell her he had AIDS? Never.

I eased into my chair and logged on, figuring I'd go after at least one question I could answer—the one Inspector Becker had posed during our interview: What kind of life insurance did Lenny have? Did it matter under the terms of his policy whether it happened accidentally? He had to be outside the two-year contestability period of any policy he got here, and then it wouldn't matter if he'd done himself on purpose. Once his mom got past the shock of it and started getting the bills, she'd be asking me the same questions.

All I remembered about the policy Reliable gave me was signing a sheaf of papers during orientation week related to "job benefits," one of which was a life insurance policy; probably the same kind of policy Lenny had. I remembered getting stuck at the blank box labeled "beneficiary," where I was supposed to write the name of the lucky person who would collect the benefit if I died. I was twenty-six years old with no kids and still holding an immortal hand in life's poker game. I was more concerned about free parking in the building than free life insurance. If I ever knew the death benefit of my own life insurance policy, I'd forgotten it, because I had no intention of collecting it. I put my mom down as the beneficiary and forgot the rest.

I found Leonard Stillmach's record file in the policy database. Twenty-nine years old, nonsmoker (hah!) with a straight term group policy for one hundred thousand dollars. Been in effect since thirty days after his hire date, or four years, the duration of his tour in Special Investigations at Reliable. Just what I had expected. I checked the beneficiary, figuring I'd find his mom's or his sister's name there, but instead listed under "primary beneficiary" was a Rosa Prescott, 17321 Orchard Circle, and a zip code out West where the housing developments turn into treeless prairies dotted with luxury homes, Starbucks minimalls, and office parks. Was Rosa an old girlfriend? Some gal he fell for one night at the casino—and that *was* the gal's name on his arm at the casino. She was a fine-looking woman, but a hundred thousand dollars? To *her* instead of his mom, or his retarded sister? And sure enough, I could see where, six months ago, Lenny had changed the beneficiary from his mom to Rosa. Rosa must have done something special for him one night, and then he must have come in next morning in full manic mode and put her name into a change-of-beneficiary request.

Whoever she was, Rosa was in for a hundred grand because Lenny was dead. Case closed. Becker and nobody else would care if it was a suicide because his policy was outside the two-year contestability period. Maybe I should personally deliver the check to her so I could find out what all the fuss was about.

I called Addie Frenzer, and she picked up right away.

"I'm running out to lunch," she said. "Why don't you call me right back on my cell. It's digital."

She meant 'it's secure,' and she didn't want to talk on a business line when the business was run by the likes of Old Man Norton, so I took the elevator downstairs and called her cell phone from a booth in the lobby.

"We got a problem over at our place with your friend who passed away," said Addie.

She was all business and cold as an antique cash register, so I held off reminding her that Lenny had been her friend, too; that as I remembered it she'd once let him drink Chandon sparkling wine out of her navel.

"We have a policy that our company issued to Leonard Stillmach, two years and three weeks ago, a life insurance policy. Term."

"Face amount?" I asked.

"Five hundred thousand."

What's a single guy, late twenties, doing with a half-million-dollar life policy? At another company? He was still young, so the premiums wouldn't be too bad, maybe three or four hundred a year, maybe more for risk factors like mental illness. Real money to a guy in debt, and wasted money unless he was a dad with unfed mouths to think about.

"Is it contestable?"

"Incontestable," said Addie. "He bought it two years and ten days ago."

Maybe Lenny *was* worried about his mom, or his little sister, who had Down syndrome and a job wheeling carts at a local grocery-store chain. So he bought a half-million-dollar policy on himself? For them? So he could give away his hundred-thousand-dollar policy to Rosa? It didn't make sense.

"Beneficiary?" I asked.

"Until last Monday, it was a Raymond Guttman," she said.

"Address?"

"Heartland Internal Medicine Associates," she said, "over off Center Street in that defunct shopping mall."

"We got a policy on Lenny here, too, for a hundred K, that lists a Rosa Prescott as the primary beneficiary."

"That's gotta be an older policy," she said.

"Four years," I said. "Why would it be old?"

"Rosa Prescott works with Heartland Viatical. She's a finder—I mean, she's a viatical-settlement broker. I think she used to be a hospice nurse. Now she goes to all of those AIDS and cancer support groups, hospices, and assisted-living communities with a minivan and a megaphone saying, 'Bring out your almost dead! If you're dying, we're buying!' Then she hauls them over to Heartland and helps them sell their life insurance policies for a cut of the face amount. They stopped using her as the interim beneficiary on viaticated policies years ago, because her name was popping up all over the country in the life insurance databases."

She scoffed, and her voice got sharp around the edges. "Database wizards like you and your friend Lenny caught people like her with all of your fancy search algorithms, remember?"

"Addie—"

"That's why I'm wondering, 'Gee! How did this one get by them over there at Reliable Allied Trust, where my friend Carver Hartnett works?'"

"You said until last Monday it was Raymond Guttman, then what happened?"

"Oh, come on, Carver! Last Monday they transferred ownership of the policy to—brace yourself—Heartland Viatical and listed it as the irrevocable beneficiary, future premiums to be paid by Heartland Viatical."

We both had a good idea what Lenny had done. He'd bought a policy on his own life for five hundred thousand, held it for almost two years, and then sold it to Heartland Viatical, but the transfer and change of beneficiaries didn't raise any viatical flags because, until a week ago, it was owned by an individual, Raymond Guttman, not a viatical company. But Guttman was just a straw man for Heartland.

All of it was perfectly legal as long as Lenny didn't already have AIDS when he'd bought the Omaha Beneficial policy. If he did, I didn't want to own up to knowing him. It's one thing to die personally disgraced, and I fully expect to do so someday myself, but if Lenny had "clean-sheeted" life insurance applications (that is, lied on them about having AIDS) and then sold the policies to Heartland for fifty cents on the dollar, his legacy would be total professional disgrace. The scandal would contaminate the whole department, all the way to the corner office, where Old Man Norton sat basking in the heritage of that paragon of fraud busters, Dead Man Norton. *"Reliable Allied?"* they'd say at the next Fraud Defense Convention. *"Isn't that the place where they had that viatical fraudster working right in their own department for four years before they caught on?"*

When she had heavy artillery at hand, Addie didn't hesitate to use it.

"We both got good smellers, Carver. And this one smells like Grandpa's breath when he came home drunk from Anna Wilson's cathouse. Maybe you know things you can't tell me? Like was Lenny almost dead with something? Is this something I should talk to *Natalie* about?"

"I don't know for sure, Addie. Maybe. Maybe Lenny told Natalie, and you can tell me." I wondered if Addie had a cellphone edition of Truster 6.0 running, a newer version than Norton's because she had a bigger technology budget. "All we know for sure is he's dead. Let me see what I can find out about him and Heartland," I offered, "and you ask Natalie."

"Or we could just swap," she said. "I'll find out about everything, and I'll let you guys pay this one for half a million. I can't waste time waiting for you to call back, Carver. I gotta find out about this any way I can."

I knew she had no choice but to go to the Network and send fiber-optic feelers out to the industry information sites looking for anybody else with policies owned by Leonard Stillmach, and within a few days it would all come back around to Old Man Norton.

"Give me one week," I said.

"Two days," she said. "Then I go to the fraud-defense sites. In the meantime, it's hard to get me by phone at work. I'm moving around a lot, so use my cell and make sure you use the Yahoo e-mail address, and send it with some of those fancy formats and fonts that Lenny used. He was always so good with graphics."

All code: We weren't going to talk about Lenny or Heartland Viatical on the phones at work. Any e-mail was going to anonymous Yahoo accounts, and everything was going to be encrypted using a program Lenny had told us about called Pretty Good Privacy. Standard procedure for investigators at different companies swapping black-market information, and please delete everything after you read it. Or at least copy it into a new file and make sure you don't bring any software watermarks or hidden source document information with it.

"I've got the same fonts and graphics program that Lenny used," I said.

"I hope that's all you have in common with him," Addie said. "He lied on the application, too, Carver. He said he didn't have any other life insurance policies with other companies. Tell me right now that I am not gonna find out that you knew what this maniac was doing to us?"

"Addie, Lenny's dead."

"That's right," she said. "He's dead, and now we're supposed to write a check for a half a million dollars to Hector Crogan and Heartland Viatical. I don't want to pay it, Carver, but it looks incontestable. At least find a way to make the money go to Lenny's family. I don't want to fund these viatical buzzards. I'll ask Legal if we can pay it to the court and let a judge award the proceeds."

"Two days," I said. "Let me find out for sure what he did."

11

THE FRAUDULENT
AND THE MALICIOUS

WHEN MIRANDA EMERGED FROM what Lenny used to call "Norton's environment" a half hour later, her muscles were tensile tight under a longish, belted, black cashmere sweater dress. She had a magic shawl around her shoulders that looked like an Expressionist painting, a dark mural in bold strokes—burgundy, blood, chocolate—all flickering with a light that seemed wholly their own, like phosphorescence. Normally, I'd have looked forward to hearing all about the shawl's pedigree over wine somewhere: how it was made from nanoengineered fabrics, the latest offspring of Mother Nature and Father Fiber Technology, or how the ethereally soft yarn was pashmina—spun from the underbelly hair of Himalayan ibex found above fourteen thousand feet and handwoven by blind, crippled, Nepalese tapestry-craft eunuchs. How each shawl has at least one tiny unique flaw for two reasons: no other shawl in the whole world could be exactly like it, and because only God can make a thing of perfect beauty.

"We need to talk," she said.

And more. Old Man Norton had scanned our nerves to frazzles with his biometric surveillance, so instead of sitting around the office and profaning the memory of Lenny by pretending to work, we left. We went to lunch at a walk-down hideaway joint with dark wooden booths called the Rendezvous Bar & Grill, where we skipped the grill part and went straight for liquid anesthesia and truth serum in a solitary booth at the back.

I let her savor a few mouthfuls of petite syrah first, while I sipped a house scotch on cracked ice. We didn't normally indulge at lunch, but it was already two in the afternoon; we'd decided not to go back to Reliable before the wake, and we had plenty to drink about. I asked her straight out if Lenny had something going with Heartland Viatical.

Behind the condiment set and the stoppered cruets of vinegar and olive oil was a single Christmas-tree light glowing inside a medieval-looking sconce with a red scrim, festooned with dusty plastic shoots of artificial mistletoe. Miranda twirled the stem of her wineglass, and her shawl glimmered in the fake candlelight, looking like one of those iridescent capes you see in the sword-and-sorcery games, and she had the fantasy shape underneath to go with it.

"He was thinking about selling his life policy," she said. "He needed money, and not just for gambling. He was spending two thousand dollars a month on AIDS medicines."

So she'd known, and hadn't told me.

"I should have stopped him from messing himself up, and I should have stopped him from gambling, while you were letting him run around selling viaticals on himself to a company he's supposed to be investigating?"

"It was *his* policy. Same group term policy we all got when we started. He owned it. He could sell it. Nothing wrong with viaticals per se."

Did she get that from her session with Norton?

Her cheeks flushed all the way down to the scar in the hollow at the base of her neck. I could hold off on telling her till after the funeral, but it couldn't wait.

"I'm not talking about his Reliable policy, Miranda. Two years and ten days ago Lenny bought a five-hundred-thousand-dollar policy on himself from Omaha Beneficial. A few weeks ago he sold it to Raymond Guttman and Heartland Viatical."

That stopped her good—either the policy, or that I knew about it.

"Omaha Beneficial called me this morning," I said. "I've got two days to find out what Lenny did, or they'll post Leonard Stillmach inquiries all over the Fraud Defense Network, run his name right up the flagpole. You know what this will look like. We're the viatical experts, remember?"

She was sorting events along the same timeline I was. "If he'd bought the policy two years ago—"

"When did he say he got AIDS?"

"Not very long ago," she said. "It wasn't two years ago. That's for sure."

"When he lost all the weight?" I asked. "That was just a few months ago."

"I don't remember," she said. "Maybe."

In Inspector Becker parlance, something was "not right." For half a million in coverage, Omaha Beneficial would have hired a private lab to test Lenny's blood for HIV and done a lot more—a urine test, an EKG, maybe even a chest x-ray. And two years ago Lenny must have passed it, because he had the five-hundred-thousand-dollar life insurance policy to prove it. For a half million, Omaha Beneficial probably also kept Lenny's specimens frozen in storage somewhere, and if they had to they would gene-test them against his remains, to see if he'd used a stand-in to qualify his lab work—and why would he do that? Because he *knew* he had AIDS, lied on the application about it, and then had somebody else show up to give blood and urine for him. But wait. What did it matter now? He didn't *die* of AIDS, he overdosed, supposedly, and it didn't matter if he'd done it on purpose, because he was outside the contestability period for suicide.

"This keeps getting worse," she said. Tears glistened in her eyes and seeped into her mascara. "I knew he had AIDS. I knew about his debts. I knew he was thinking about selling his Reliable policy. But I didn't know he had a policy at Omaha Beneficial. I don't want to think about what that means."

She thought about it anyway, and her face turned whiter than Lenny's did when he lost the five grand at Harrah's. I figured she was thinking about the scandal it would cause in the company and in the industry, but she had bigger ideas.

"Do you believe in hell, Carver?"

Maybe Lenny had been right about the Catholic thing. Maybe the stress of his death had touched off fulminating religious phobias. If faith were her problem, it might be more endearing than irritating, same as if she were afraid of black cats or getting off elevators on the thirteenth floor. If she was Christ-bitten, then maybe she wouldn't give it up to me unless I was a good, kind, devout suitor who swore on the family Bible that he intended to marry her. I'd been raised Catholic and could take Communion, put my hand on a Bible, and sing with the choir, but I had trouble carrying a tune in the key of devoutness.

"Maybe," I said. "It depends. You mean flames and devils?"

"That's how you end up there," she said. "You go through your whole life thinking maybe there's a hell, but if there is, you're not the type of person who would go there. Same way you think you won't get cancer or die, at least not for a good long while. Even when you're old, you still think: *Probably won't happen for a good long while, if I just stay healthy.* Then one day you get sick and you never get well. You get so sick you pass out for good and wake up at hell's mouth, where you abandon all hope. That's probably just how it happens. Nobody plans on dying, and nobody plans on going to hell, and then, hello, you're there, and it's too late to do a damn thing about it."

Whew. So this was lunch.

Unlike her I was just the sort of person who'd end up in hell if there is such a place, so I avoided thinking about it. But I liked to talk to Miranda, and if she wanted to talk about hell, I'd let her.

"Is it that you're afraid of going there?" I asked her. "Or are you afraid that's where Lenny is?"

"If he was a scam king who conned Omaha Beneficial out of half a million?" she asked. "Then wouldn't he be down there with all of the other liars for hire?"

Her eyes clouded up with dread, so I tried to keep things in perspective for her.

"C'mon, Miranda, you know the numbers. Insurance fraud's running at about ninety-six billion dollars a year in this country alone. If all of those fraudsters formed a corporation they'd be in the Fortune One Hundred. Do you think God sends all of those people to hell?"

A merciful God would send Lenny the scammer to some

afterlife minimum security facility out east of Eden, Nebraska—
a federal halfway house with liberal furlough and visitation policies, where Lenny's punishment would be to keep the hedges
trimmed and the pool and sand traps raked.

She stared into the burgundy shadows and crimson gloom of
her wineglass, as if she'd found a peephole to the netherworld and
was looking for him down there among the thronging hordes of
anguished souls bereft.

"No," she said, her voice softening to a sepulchral moan. "It's
the road to Life that's steep and narrow, and few there are who
find it. Scammers don't find it, right? They lie to gullible people
and steal their money."

I could read her mind and share some of the same childhood
memories of the Gospels read aloud every Sunday at mass. For the
wicked, Damnation's Gate is wide, and the road's clear, four lanes
downhill. In the *Inferno*, Dante put the Fraudulent and the Mali-
cious in a special ditch in the Eighth Circle of Hell, just one rung
up from the Ninth, where Satan himself is upside down in the ice.
The fraudsters bob in moats of boiling pitch, and every time they
come up for air, demons rake their flesh with sharp hooks.

I hated insurance cheats as much as she did, but boiling
pitch and meat hooks seemed cruel and unusual even for the
likes of them.

"You think God would send a manic-depressive creature of
addictions like poor Lenny to hell?"

She nodded. "Especially if—" and she stopped.

Oh, no. Not the old-fashioned, Baltimore-catechism stuff!
Was she worried about the suicide angle? And if I called it ridiculous, she'd probably quote me chapter and verse on the taboo and
how the Almighty hath fixed his canon against self-slaughter.

Come to think of it, even Dante went along with it. The Wood of the Suicides was Eighth Circle, too—two troughs down the bloody slope to the Ninth.

"But God doesn't send people to hell," she explained. "People go there because they are ashamed of themselves, because their sins have been written in stone, and everything they whispered in dark locked rooms has been proclaimed from the rooftops at high noon. When that happens, they are so ashamed that all they want to do is be alone. Forever."

I hadn't gone to Sunday mass in a good ten years, but I'd read all about these fancy new hell theories, where the modern theologians try to tell you that hell is just an eternal mental state—the pain of loss or the remorse of conscience—a kind of Hell Lite for liberal weenies. Deep down I knew that if hell existed, it was a real place full of ruthless, venal people, like the commodity pits at the Chicago Board of Trade, Disney World, or oral arguments before the United States Supreme Court.

"But instead of being alone, they end up in hell," she said, and her eyes flashed like falling stars. "They get thrown into a pit with all of the other horrid, hateful people who ever lived."

Another persistent misconception, I thought. Hell could be a real place, and it could last forever, but who said it had to be crowded? It's probably spored and honeycombed with special, made-to-order chambers. It could be no more crowded than a pretrial conference in divorce court with your second ex-wife's extended family of lawyers, or the waiting room of your hair-transplant surgeon where you're reading a glossy pamphlet on the pros and cons of minimicrografting versus follicular-unit transplantation.

Or maybe at first it's just you, all by yourself at a table of dead soldiers in a Council Bluffs strip joint at 3 A.M. It's normally clean, but tonight it smells like stick perfume and vomited beer, which must have been left by the early crowd, because by sheer good luck you're the only one in the audience. Out comes the hot new dancer, "Amsterdam," pronounced like the city, and as far as you know neither you nor Amsterdam has thrown up yet. Amsterdam is an attractive, fortyish show matron with tobacco-stained teeth and breast implants that look like the plastic surgeon used inverted Tupperware bowls. She's really grinding to Def Leppard's "Pour Some Sugar on Me," and then she strips down to stretchmarks, veiny cellulite, pasties, and a G-string—right when Nine Inch Nails's "Closer" comes over the sound system. Did she plan it that way? Fucking great service if so. She's a pretty good dancer, and at the break she comes over and lets you buy her an eight-dollar drink and takes you up on a cigarette, too. You can just tell that even if you weren't the only one in the audience, she'd have come over and sat with you anyway. Her son's in Douglas County Jail, she says by way of introduction, otherwise she'd be back in Vegas by now. She makes a joke about no greenery no scenery. Blow jobs are twenty bucks if you wear a condom and fifty if you don't.

Miranda caught the waiter's eye and ordered another round by looping her finger over our glasses.

"My sister, Annette, did something bad once to get money," Miranda said. "I told you she was born with a huge mole, and she had to have cosmetic surgeries, really expensive ones. She cheated on her—"

My cell phone vibrated, and the caller-ID said "Reliable Ins. 2357," the Dag's extension.

I showed it to Miranda, and she said I should get it.

Worse than Dag, it was Norton using her extension. Grumpier than I left him, and he wanted one of us to come in "first thing after the funeral tomorrow" and handle "the mess that Mr. Stillmach has left for us."

I let him grouse long enough to assure myself that Addie hadn't jumped the gun and told him about the policy at Omaha Beneficial. No. Norton wanted to report that he'd had a call from the Sauer & Ferryman Funeral Home, and they were seeking disclosure of the beneficiary on Lenny's life insurance policy, so they could propose the usual deal for an assignment of the benefits. Any reputable funeral director or mortuary services provider would do the same, especially if Lenny wasn't the only one in the Stillmach family with an iffy credit rating.

According to Norton, the funeral home stood ready to extend credit for a bare bones—make that bare-basics—package of bereavement services, but Lenny's mom was said to be deeply distressed by the sudden loss of her son and was ordering premium services—two-stage arterial embalming, preparation and presentation of the body for viewing at a wake the night before, denominationally appropriate grief therapies—in this case, administered by a Catholic priest and attendant altar boys, transportation from the wake chapel to the cathedral for the funeral, motorcade and escort to Calvary Cemetery after, graveside services and interment ceremonies, burial plot to include a lined and reinforced concrete vault—all followed by brunch and beverages at St. Dymphna's parish center.

Fifteen thousand dollars, at least, according to Norton. Ferryman was inquiring after the right to protect itself by attaching a portion of any life insurance policy owned by Mr. Stillmach, probably only a small percentage of the total policy payout.

Almost painless after the tax-free windfall from a good insurance policy. According to the insurance consumer surveys, most policy owners intend for their policy benefits to go first and foremost to pay funeral and burial expenses, and to spare loved ones the anguish and expense of arrangements for a proper ceremony. I'd heard the spiel a hundred times, and Ferryman had Mrs. Stillmach's consent, if she was indeed the policy beneficiary.

All of which brought Norton to the real reason he had called: He had pulled up Lenny's policy in the database to provide Sauer & Ferryman with the name of the legal beneficiary.

I took a big swig off the scotch without making a sound.

"Heartland Viatical is listed as the beneficiary," said Norton. "Did you know about this?"

It seemed like a week ago, but at nine that very morning, today, Monday, the day of the wake, I'd looked up the record of Lenny's life policy in Reliable's database and found Rosa Prescott listed as the beneficiary. My watch said four now, and somewhere in between somebody had changed the beneficiary. Maybe some customer-service keypuncher had entered a change-of-beneficiary request and it was just a coincidence that it happened today. Or maybe somebody else changed it? I'd check the file for the change-of-beneficiary form tomorrow. In the meantime, questions are good, I'm told.

"It doesn't have a person's name there?" I asked, looking over at Miranda, who was listening right along.

"Just Heartland Viatical, Incorporated," said Norton, "four-one-five-one Center Street. Listed as the irrevocable beneficiary, future premiums to be paid by Heartland Viatical, Incorporated."

12

THE EXQUISITE CORPSE

THE VISITATION AND WAKE were held out off of Eighty-fourth Street, where Interstate 80 bends south looking for a way around Omaha to Lincoln, where it's zoned "light industrial" with truck plazas and outlet malls clustered around the exit ramps. The big one-story, white-brick Sauer & Ferryman Funeral Home would have fit right in, except it had the façade of a Victorian mansion cemented on the front end and a canopied archway out the back in case of inclement weather.

On the way there Miranda told me that Lenny's mom had called her with life insurance questions, and Miranda had told her to call Norton, or else have the funeral directors call him. Lenny's mom said that Aron Ferryman was also dickering with the infamous Father Fogarty, the pastor of the grand old St. Dymphna's Cathedral, for a Catholic wake, funeral, and burial. As a former altar boy who'd served mass in St. Dymphna's Cathedral—the flagship of the diocese—I remembered some of how that would work.

Lenny's mom was technically a parishioner because she still lived north of Bemis Park in the same sagging wreck of a house Lenny had grown up in—a late-nineteenth-century grand manse in terminal decline, a period home at the end of its sentence, with a crumbling carriage house out back propped up by exterior four-by-four beams, and cars on blocks up and down the busted brick alleys. But Lenny wasn't a member of St. Dymphna's, didn't even live in the parish, and old Father Fogarty probably saw Lenny's mom at mass on Christmas or Easter, but not both.

The cathedral was still the nominal heart of the archdiocese, but the money had all moved west to the suburbs and gated communities. Fogarty was left with aging parishioners living in declining neighborhoods and a beloved landmark of a white-elephant cathedral to maintain. It wasn't uncommon to have eight or nine funerals a week for eight or nine faithful senior citizens, old-timers whose families had been tithing to St. Dymphna's Cathedral since the Great Depression. Fogarty wouldn't be happy about providing funeral services for a faithless slacker cyborg like Lenny who worshipped computers instead of the Eucharist and never came to church.

I knew, because I'd been an altar boy for Fogarty at the funeral of the notorious city councilman Michael Muldoon. To most, it was only a parish legend, dismissed by reputable old-timers as apocryphal rumor, but I'd been there, had seen and heard it firsthand.

Muldoon was a personal-injury lawyer and public drunk who'd married wealth and then won a city-council seat by running on his Irish Catholic heritage, even though he hadn't been to church since his first wedding. He drank himself to death at the age of fifty—got away early from life's party without once being called an alcoholic, because in those days it was still an insult. As my grandma used to put it, "Mr. Muldoon had the failing." The family wanted services held at the cathedral, even though Muldoon had fallen so far away from Mother Church that they could just as well have hauled his body over for services at Mount Sinai Synagogue.

Father Fogarty did his duty, gave the Muldoon clan their funeral, and even showed up to say the mass himself. But just before the procession started down the center aisle of the nave, Fogarty paused in the narthex at the back of the cathedral, where only us altar boys, the pallbearers, and the funeral director could hear him. The old priest turned around, knocked on the casket like it was an outhouse door, and said, "Are you in there, Michael Muldoon? I just want to be sure it's you in there, Muldoon, because the only times I saw you were when your mother carried you in here to get baptized, your first wife dragged you in here to get married, and your kids brought you back to get buried."

Lenny's family would be lucky to get a no-frills funeral mass said by a newly ordained seminary grad, who would stammer through a plain-vanilla homily prominently featuring the parable of the Prodigal Son. On the other hand, if somebody showed up with a generous donation, or even if Mrs. Stillmach had been a poor parish widow who'd given her mite to help put the new slate roof on back in 1972, then Fogarty would pull out the stops and make Lenny's funeral something special.

Somebody must have brokered a deal with Ferryman before we got there, because Lenny's wake was decidedly upscale, held in the main parlor, and he had a huge two-tone metal casket with silver trimmings. The casket was backed up by banked and tiered floral arrangements, even though the obituary in the *World-*

Herald had said, "In lieu of flowers, the family requests donations to the Methodist Richard Young Center" (where Lenny had taken those three-day naps after his manic attacks).

When we went from the greeting room to the viewing room, we passed by a woman in a black gown playing a violin. And instead of a junior priest presiding over the questionable death of a former parishioner, Pastor Fogarty was there to handle it himself, with an altar boy and a thurifer swinging a silver censer of smoldering incense. Miranda exchanged pleasantries with Father Fogarty, while he gave me the evil eyeball as somebody he used to know who stopped going to church.

After that, we filed in the rows of chairs and kneelers and took our places facing Lenny. I could feel Miranda building to the occasion, shuddering every now again and snuffling into one of her silk hankies. She unpacked a rosary that had the heft and medieval odor of a sainted relic, with huge weathered wooden beads worn smooth by generations of fingers, real hand-wired silver links, and a silver-and-ebony crucifix. She'd shown it to me and Lenny once before at her place, had drawn it out of the carved cedar box where she kept it on the mantel and had told us its story. Her great-great-grandmother had died of consumption back in Antwerp clutching this very rosary to her bosom. Then Miranda's great-grandmother, Zoe, had brought it over on the boat from Belgium after World War I and had given it to Miranda's grandmother, who'd wisely skipped over Miranda's irreligious, hippie mom and passed it to Miranda, instead. When Lenny first saw it, he wanted to take it over to Harveys Casino and see if it would bring him some sorely needed luck, but she'd told him no, because she was afraid he'd take it to Sol's Jewelry & Loan and pawn it.

Whenever I saw a rosary it reminded me of my grandpa—the

one who died from Old Gold Filters—because near the end there, when he had only a week or so left in him, the nurses found him on the floor of his room at Archbishop Bergan Mercy Hospital at two in the morning clutching a plastic rosary. He was far gone with ICU psychosis, and his brain was already seeded with blossoming metastases. He was waving the rosary and yelling at the charge nurse, "Hey! Send somebody in here that knows how to work one of these things! Say, you there, miss! Do you know how to operate one of these things?"

Father Fogarty blessed Lenny's body in the open casket, then looked to heaven.

"Eternal rest grant unto him, O Lord."

"And let perpetual light shine upon him," said Miranda with the rest of the group.

The thurifer lifted the sooty silver cap of the censer by the chain, and Father Fogarty spooned in more incense. Then they walked around Lenny's body wagging the censer at him and sending plumes of smoke drifting across his open casket.

"Glory be to the Father, to the Son, and to the Holy Spirit. As it was in the beginning, is now, and ever shall be, world without end. Amen."

Back in ancient Rome, Christians were captured and fed to the lions in the Colosseum. To escape persecution they hid out in subterranean cemeteries called catacombs, where they huddled together in tombs, stared at dead people, and talked about how the world was going to end in sheets of flaming hellfire by Sunday. Back then, the incense helped take the edge off the necrotic stench. Catholics still like to huddle together and stare at their dead, and they still stand on ceremony and burn incense at the finer funerals, even though these days the body is mostly formaldehyde and emulsifiers by the time it's displayed at a wake, and smells no worse than car wax. And no one really believes in the end of the world anymore, except me.

Miranda pressed the silver-and-ebony crucifix to her lips and fingered the rosary. As if on cue, the mourners broke forth in murmuration, bowing their heads and telling the beads and gauds of their rosaries.

"Hail, Holy Queen, Mother of Mercy, hail, our life, our sweetness, and our hope! To thee do we cry, poor banished children of Eve! To thee do we send up our sighs, mourning, and weeping in this vale of tears! Turn then, most gracious advocate, thine eyes of mercy towards us, and after this, our exile, show unto us the blessed fruit of thy womb, Jesus! O clement, O loving, O sweet Virgin Mary!"

It made my hair roots tingle. It was like hearing someone read Rimbaud or Baudelaire aloud ten years after your last high school French class. Clement? Womb fruit? It was grand and moving, and I used to know what it meant, but now I seemed to be stuck on the verge of understanding without ever getting there, like the night Lenny died and I couldn't access certain parts of my brain.

Miranda knew every word. For her it was all Catholic Burial 3.2. And I noticed that when I came in just right on an "Amen" or a "And let perpetual light shine upon him," she set her hand on top of mine, as if we were an engaged couple grieving together at the funeral of a dear friend. She even discreetly slipped her finger between two of mine and applied pressure in ways mysterious and wonderful—ways she'd never done before.

I'd forgotten what a grim ordeal it is to say five decades of a rosary: fifty Hail Marys in all, with five Our Fathers, the Five Sorrowful Mysteries, and a lot of Ave Marias weeping in vales of tears in between. After the first few, the mob synchronized its murmurings and frantic fingerings, as if they were trying to raise Lenny from the dead or summon the Fates back from antiquity to measure off the lives of every one of us in rosary beads, then cut the threads. Every time I heard the beads clacking, saw the censer swinging, watched Father Fogarty's special gesticulations and blessings, I felt like going Gilgamesh and grabbing a rattle and a drum and flying Lenny's body back to Olduvai Gorge or Shanidar, Iraq, or some other cradle of civilization for an old-fashioned hominid burial, without the incense and the two-tone metal casket and the frantic ritualizing and verbigerations. And if it cost too much to ship a body out of civilization and back to nature, then under the circumstances Lenny would have preferred something more complex, sordid, and interesting, like the Dumpster behind Burger King.

"Eternal rest grant unto him, O Lord."

"And let perpetual light shine upon him."

I had trouble imagining Lenny eternally resting and bathing in perpetual light. I'd read enough autopsy reports and seen enough body photos from the medical examiner's office to know that Lenny had been gutted like a dressed deer, his organs scooped out, weighed, sectioned; his scalp peeled back and forward and the top of his skull sawed off, his brain removed, weighed, sectioned, sliced, and strained. When you got a Catholic corpse, the medical examiners and the funeral directors all work from the same page: Save that face and something to hang it on; you can fake the rest of it.

"Glory be to the Father, the Son, and the Holy Spirit. As it was in the beginning, is now and ever shall be, world without end. Amen."

It would take days before the coroner would release an initial report, and maybe weeks—depending on where they sent the blood and tissue samples—before he would issue a final report containing the definitive cause, mechanism, and manner of Lenny's death. And every time I looked at Lenny in the casket I thought about what would happen if claims on five or ten more life insurance policies at five or ten other life insurance companies came rolling in on Leonard Stillmach, with Rosa Prescott or Heartland Viatical or Hector Crogan or Raymond Guttman as the beneficiary. What if the companies went to court and moved to exhume the body so they could genetically test their blood and urine samples against his remains? See if Lenny, the Mad Hatter of Special Claims, had been HIV positive two years ago and had used a stand-in for blood and urine samples so he'd qualify for their life insurance policies?

Remember thou art dust and to dust thou shall return. Yes, but please don't stink with fraud in between, Lenny!

When the rosary ended, everybody formed a grieving line and took turns going up to a kneeler that overlooked the open casket to spend a few remaining moments with Lenny's remains. I held back and made as if to go out to the lobby, but Miranda looked at me like I was a coward or a deserter, so I fell in behind her.

When I got up there alone with him, I saw it was nothing but a foam-filled Halloween mask made of Lenny's skin still attached to his original neck in a sport coat he'd never worn before. His ears, lips, and nose were missing their body jewelry, and some thoughtful mortician's apprentice had caulked all of the skin holes with cosmetic plaster and spackled over them with flesh-colored rouge. It didn't help, though; Lenny looked like a Ghoul from Galaxy 9 who'd been hit by a death ray that had fried his chips and processors, melted his components and circuit boards, leaving only the putty-colored computer casing of his skin.

I could see the AIDS in him, now that he was dead.

Then I had to go over with Miranda and pay our respects to his mom, who looked even worse than Lenny.

Vera Stillmach was from Guide Rock, Nebraska, where she'd sold the Wigwam Bar & Grill, which had passed to her from her folks. She'd moved to the big city for LPN school at the College of St. Mary's. After that she'd spent thirty years tending the tracheostomies of ex-smokers in the Head and Neck Unit at the VA hospital. Lenny's dad, Wally "Sneaks" Stillmach, had trouble holding jobs and mostly worked on the backside of Aksarben Racetrack as a hot-walker for horse trainers. He'd left Omaha twenty-some years ago, before Lenny got out of grade school.

As Lenny told it, when he was only twelve years old, one of his letters to his dad had come back stamped "deceased." Lenny had soaked his pillow with hot tears, until his mom told him not to worry—it was just Sir Sneaky Stillmach trying to wangle his way out of paying child support by pretending to be dead.

Vera had watched her two boys and their sister run wild with no dad around to whup sense and training into them. Lenny's brother was on work release, and over the years Vera had fetched her kids from emergency rooms, county jails, after-hours clubs, and the dayroom at the Methodist Richard Young Center, but a funeral was too much for her. Dr. Goody must have called in a prescription for her at Wal-Mart, because instead of her usual hard-bitten resolve, Vera had the vacant, lobotomized look of a parent called upon to bury her own child on short notice, present and accounted for only by the grace of Xanax or Ativan. I could almost hear the long, private, wordless conversation she was having with herself, deep inside: *This ain't clockwise clockwork with me going first, the way my ma went before me, and her ma before*

her; this is backassward widdershins wickedness, because there's my
baby boy, dead and gone before me. Why?

She was in no danger of smiling and putting cracks in the mask
of foundation and waterproof makeup she'd patted onto her face.
She must have given up by the time she got to the fine-motor work
of eye pencils and eyeliners, because it looked as if she'd smeared
Rawlings Athletic Eye-Black in the bags and hollows around her
eyes, antiglare war paint for the big game against the heavily
favored Grim Reapers. She couldn't even see me and Miranda,
because it was just her and her kids now, out there naked and trem-
bling under the stadium arc lights on their own twenty-yard line,
while the hooded Reapers lined up opposite—all mounted on
black stallions, their polished scythes shimmering with the white
radiance of eternity. She couldn't hear Miranda and me making
noises about how we didn't know what had happened to Lenny,
and how sorry we were even though it wasn't really our fault. She
couldn't hear us, because the steeds were snorting and whinnying
and pawing the turf at the other end of the field, and then the lead
horseman in the black hood raised his scythe like a royal standard
and shouted: "Take her children, but leave her alive!"

Miranda brought Vera around long enough to recognize us.
Vera thanked Miranda for her prayers and for telling her to call
Norton. Her voice droned in a hollow, robotic monotone about
how the arrangements had all been taken care of by the life insurance man. That nice lawyer who'd been managing Lenny's affairs
and helping him get advance money against his insurance policies
had called her.

"Mr. Crogan took care of everything," said Vera. "He said
not to worry, and it would all be paid out of Lenny's insurance."

13

TO THE MACHINES

No sense talking about what had to be done now, and no sense waiting till after the funeral. If Hector Crogan was paying the bills for premium services, it was because he wanted old Vera on his side before she found out that Lenny had sold life insurance policies to Heartland—policies that could have had her name in the beneficiary slot, if only Lenny hadn't sold them. It meant that Old Man Norton was probably right—again!—and Lenny had something going with Hector or somebody else at Heartland. Only question was: Doing what exactly? So far he'd sold two life policies to them.

In the fraud-defense business it's sometimes a matter of restraining your overly suspicious nature. Maybe Heartland Viatical was a legitimate viatical company, and maybe Lenny was a legitimate AIDS patient with the uncanny foresight to buy a big extra term life policy just before testing HIV-positive. I had ways to find out if Lenny owned other life insurance policies, and I could do it without alerting every special investigator in the country on the Fraud Defense Network. But unless I called Addie soon with a true and accurate account of the life insurance of Leonard Stillmach, that's exactly what she would do.

We needed a computer with a broadband connection. My place was closer to the funeral home, but Miranda's was a lot nicer and came with plenty of good wine. She lived on Jones Street in the Old Market, not two blocks from Lenny's, so close that I could see it gave her the creeps to go home alone these days. Good for me, because I could offer to go home with her, and sometimes she'd even let me stay—on the couch.

She had a condo in an old furniture warehouse that had been converted several times, the first time as a haven for fine arts graduates dressed in basic black Gap activewear. A fire emptied the place in 1997, right about the same time technology fever swept through the town. To lure and accommodate "people of technology" like Lenny and Miranda, the building had been stripped down to the exposed brick walls, supporting beams, and original wood floors, then retrofitted with Sub-Zero and Viking kitchen appliances, granite countertops, slate-and-marble baths with oversized showers, and fiber-optic cable to the main rooms, as well as being prewired for home theater, digital jukeboxes, and five-speaker sound systems—all the connections for every toy in the IT worker's arsenal built right in—and two-foot sound insulation between all shared walls.

Miranda stopped in the frosted glass entryway and unslung a leather handbag embossed in crocodile, pawing through its lined interiors for the smart card on her key chain. The keys jangled on the way out, and no sense pretending I wasn't looking for the ones rimmed in red and green plastic.

She waved the card over the panel detector in the entryway, and the lock clicked open.

"Did Becker ask you about having a key to Lenny's place?"

She pushed the door open, and we walked into the brick atrium, past the fountain, under the skylights.

"Lenny gave it to me a couple months ago. He was going to be tied up in a meeting, so he asked me to go over and let an electrician into his place. Remember when he had those ceiling fans replaced?"

We stopped in front of the tiny elevator with mission-style grilles and real ficus trees on both sides of it. She waved the smart card again.

I remembered the ceiling fans. Sort of. But then why hadn't she just yanked the keys right out? Instead of buzzing him ten times from the entryway?

"I forgot I even had his keys," she said. "All I could think was that something was wrong. I forgot they were on my chain, until you said call his sister, she has a key."

Inside the elevator the top half was all mirrors, and both angles I had on her face said that she didn't want to talk about the key, or about finding Lenny dead.

"And you knew something was wrong because you were instant-messaging him at three in the morning? And he started typing slop, and then you messaged me, and called me on the phone?"

She looked up, and right at me.

"You saw his body," she said. "His blood had settled. Lividity. Rigor. He'd been dead four hours at least. I messaged him around eleven or so, probably right before or right after you guys played."

The night Lenny died was macabre madness for both of us, and memories were not to be trusted. But when I'd woken up that morning in my own nightmare, hearing Lenny being tortured in some afterlife penitentiary, and suddenly Miranda had been right there on my machine, messaging, she'd sounded like she'd just logged off with him. She'd been frantic, said he'd been typing gibberish all over the screen. "I think we should go over there now!" was what she'd typed. And on the phone, the fear in her voice had sounded fresh.

"I checked on him," she said, "and he was acting weird on instant messaging. You checked on him, and he was acting weird in the game. Then we both said, 'Oh, hell,' and went to bed, instead of . . . we should have . . . I don't know how you feel about that."

It was Death's most painful companion—the guilt monster—looming inside, and her soul was Loch Ness. Personally I didn't indulge; I tried feeling guilty a time or two, because it seemed the decent thing to do, but instead of a blushing shamefaced spirit mutinying in my bosom or an avenging angel haunting the halls of conscience, guilt always felt more like I was a dog chewing on concrete. If I regretted not going over to Lenny's place right after the Delta-Strike game, gnawing the gnarly rock of remorse wouldn't undo it. And I was a country mile from the exotic guilt exercises the Catholics used like new personal digital assistants. I hadn't whispered my sins in the dark to old men since my grade school days, and all those sacraments and prayers seemed pointless and habit-forming, like biting your nails or cracking your knuckles. *Bless me, Father, for I have sinned. Everything I said I was sorry for last time, well, I've gone and done them all again. I'm sorry all over again, too.* The dog returns to his vomit, the sow to her mire, the twice-burned fool's bandaged finger wabbles back to the fire, the mailman walks back up the sidewalk, and I confess again to being a congenital liar. *Bless me, Father, for I have sinned, and wrap your purple stole around this one: If I make a perfect Act of Contrition and confess that "I am lying when I say I am sorry for my sins," am I telling the truth?*

She booted her machine for me, then left to fetch wine. I logged on to the Medical Information Bureau database using a borrowed Reliable username and password.

The Medical Information Bureau (MIB) is a private company that acts as a repository of coded information for more than six hundred member insurance companies. Underwriting uses it more than we do, but I had a buddy in underwriting who'd "lent" me his privileges. The MIB was formed in 1902 and for most of the last century was the only pool of insurance data about individuals—the only place member life insurance companies could look up a guy named Leonard Stillmach and try to guess from the coded alerts whether he was an honest customer looking to buy life insurance or an HIV-positive scammer working for a clean-sheeting, wet-inking viatical outfit.

The MIB wouldn't tell me much. The privacy and consumer credit laws keep the gory details confidential, but you can see how many other insurance companies have filed coded reports with the bureau regarding Leonard Stillmach, which usually means that Leonard Stillmach applied for life or medical coverage, and that coverage was issued, denied, or "rated," meaning he was charged extra for risk factors or preexisting conditions. You can't get the particulars, but you can tell if your information matches or doesn't match the information filed by other member companies. I was prepared to see one or two other inquiries, especially if

Lenny had tried for a policy at one place, had been denied, and then had gone to another. What I got instead was a hit list of nine different inquiries on Leonard Stillmach by five different insurance companies: Omaha Beneficial (Addie's company), Metropolitan Life, Pacific Altruistic, Iowa Life & Casualty, and Guaranteed Investment Mutual Trust of Indianapolis.

I printed the list. No way to tell if coverage was granted or declined, but odds were good that Lenny had more life policies. No way to tell the face amounts, dates issued, or beneficiaries without calling contacts at the other companies. If I knew Addie, she'd keep her promise not to broadcast it on the Fraud Defense Network, but she'd have gone to the MIB and the Life Insurance Index by now, and maybe even called her contacts at the companies with policies on him.

I knew a Computer Use geek at Guaranteed Investment Mutual—Pete Westfall—and we'd swapped information on policyholders before. I logged on to my web-based account and sent him an e-mail asking if he had a policy at his company on Leonard Stillmach.

I heard glasses clanking and looked up and over the monitor. I could see Miranda in her kitchen pulling stemware down from the ceiling rack, inspecting it for water spots, and looking for just the right shape of glass to go with the wines she'd selected.

Out of nowhere I remembered Rubicon.exe, the SubSeven Trojan horse I'd left on her machine and had almost used the night Lenny died. I regretted putting it there, but this, unlike mere remorse, I could still do something about. I had no business tampering with her interiors, leaving secret back doors into her home machine. I opened the Programs folder on her directory tree and went in search of the folder where I'd hidden the file. I was going to delete it, then go into the Recycling Bin and permanently delete it. But when the directory of her C: drive popped up, I saw a first-level folder that hadn't been there the last time I'd worked on her machine: "Web Cam Commander"—the same software that Lenny had used to run the web cam he had on his machine.

I searched the top rim of her monitor and the environs of the antique escritoire she used for a computer table. Nothing but a big flat panel monitor and speakers, with a subwoofer stuffed under the table next to the CPU box. No web cam.

I could see her still in the kitchen fondling wineglasses in the ceiling rack like they were hanging clumps of grapes. I felt the usual painful longing watching her shape undulate under the black stretch cashmere. She could make you believe the philosophers who said that the human body is the shadow of spiritual beauty and the best picture of the human soul.

"Miranda, I didn't know you had a web cam on your machine."

I didn't see her drop it, I just heard the sudden hollow plunk followed by glass shattering and skittering across the granite island countertop.

"Darn!" she hollered. "I did it again. It's getting to be like once a month. I didn't even drink any wine yet!"

She stooped and disappeared under the island. I heard a cupboard door bang, and she reappeared with a hand broom and a dustpan and went after the shards of stemware.

"I said I didn't know you had a web cam on this thing."

"I don't," she said. "I mean, I didn't, but Lenny was over one night, and he had a web cam that the IT geeks were testing for AV conferencing. He hooked it up for me and showed me how good the video quality was. He was off on one of his George Gilder telecosmic rants about how our brains will all soon be hooked together by chip implants and fiber optics. Then he showed me some videos of myself. It was like looking into one of those bank monitors for the first time. Very cool. High-quality video, almost like a movie. He said I could keep it for a while, but I told him to take it off because it slowed my system way down."

Huh? If Lenny had removed the Web Cam, why hadn't he uninstalled the software? Or maybe he had, and Web Cam Commander was just one of those empty folders left behind by an imperfect uninstall?

She stooped and swept more glass off the floor. I clicked into the web-cam folder to see if there were still program files inside, and there were, including one named "session.log." I started scrolling over to the "Modified" column, so I could see the date and time of the file, presumably the last time she'd used the web cam.

"Carver, darling," she said, adopting a spot-on Edwardian accent straight out of a Merchant-Ivory adaptation of E. M. Forster or Virginia Woolf. "Be a dear and help me with these."

It was the first playful note to come out of her since Lenny had died. I looked up and saw her holding four crystal glasses out to me through the kitchen pass-through.

I exited to her desktop and went to help her. I could see what she had in mind by the profusion of stemware she handed me. I'd been here before. She wanted me to stay and visit and drink wine with her, so we could help each other through this, so she could work out her morbid neuroses about hell and death and sex and the sacraments, because she could usually count on me not to mock her the way her girlfriends did. After she was done talking and drinking, she wanted me drunk and passed out on the couch, so I wouldn't be crawling into her bed at 2 A.M. and begging for it.

I set the glasses down on a coffee table, cherry inlaid with marble, handmade and old, nothing like the stuff on the showroom floor at Nebraska Furniture Mart.

I thought about risking another peek at the web-cam session log; I hadn't even figured out why I wanted to see it yet. But I knew that if I went back into her machine, she'd come over to see what I was doing, maybe just in time to catch me snooping through her files. Rather than blow my chance at spending the night, I left the Trojan horse in place, so I could come back later and see for myself what was in the session log file, then delete all traces of my minor treachery.

I moved over to the vamp black-red sofa and settled against plump, butter-slick, aniline leather. I shifted the *Wine Spectators* off the top of the magazine pile and flipped through some glossies I'd never heard of, like *Nest* and *Fast Company*. I was trying to decide whether to shove Lenny's life insurance hit list in front of her and wreck what little chance we had of a somber, romantic little interlude in the funeral train of events following Lenny's death.

She came out of the kitchen with a bottle in each hand—a red and a white—both uncorked and ready to pour. The white was in a sleeve of rapid ice decorated with wine motifs from Renoir paintings. She set the bottles on marble coasters, then stepped out of her slingback pumps and dribbled the magic shawl into a silky puddle on a matching leather club chair.

She touched a button on the DVD and filled the place with Pat Metheny, and I watched her shape—outlined in tight black wool—glide through sections and levels of the loft, her hair flowing like liquid midnight behind her in the penumbrae of the track lights.

"Darling," she said in the same mannered British accent, "please fill our glasses and let's soothe ourselves with wine and music."

I poured away, and she came back with spring water and French bread for palate cleansing.

She sat next to me and tried to smile, her face bathed in the rose-colored nimbus of a hanging Tiffany lamp. Her fingernails almost matched the cabernet when she wrapped them around her glass and lifted it my way for a somber toast, backlit by shadowy rose reds from the exposed brick walls.

"To Lenny," she said.

Times like these it was obvious that she matched, coordinated, and accessorized her entire living room until everything—her wardrobe, her framed prints, her furniture, her wall and floor coverings—all went with and belonged together in this single, well-wrought place.

She wasn't vain or fussy or ostentatious about it and preferred, like most accomplished interior designers, that her work be appreciated mainly at the subliminal level. On the wall over the sofa she'd hung an outsized print of Gustav Klimt's *The Kiss* (with applied gold leaf), lit by one dim, gauze-covered track light, so that the jewel-and-russet tones in the painting seemed to bleed right out into the frameless shadows of the room, oozing gold browns and copper blues and madder rose onto her Persian rug, spangling ruby reds and emerald greens all over the knot-work patterns of the paisley chenille throw and the beaded silk shantung pillows.

She completed the tableau by hoisting a small pond of black-cherry-colored wine that went with the leather, the bricks, *The Kiss,* and her lipstick.

A single stargazer lily looked to be made in heaven for the claret bud vase on the butler's table; the raisin-colored flecks of its petals were accented by a folded dark cranberry serviette embroidered with holiday themes—snowflakes and miniature cavorting reindeer—and forming a kind of skirt for the vase, but folded so that all four points of its corners were visible and spread in a perfect fan at the hem. Everywhere I looked, a still life an artist could paint but wouldn't because it was too perfect.

Her face was bone white, the customary glow of the runner at rest chilled by the prospect of death. Her first drink of wine was not the sip of a connoisseur but the gulp of a user. Grief was draining the vital fluids right out of her, making her eyes sink into dark sockets. She killed the big track lights, and in the amber glow of the lamp she looked like an anorexic fashion model who'd smoked too much heroin, except Miranda was being consumed by the real thing, not the pale imitation of substance abuse.

In the car, on the way back to her place, she'd obsessed about how she'd already harrowed hell and satisfied herself that Lenny wasn't there. Now she was worried that he was suffering in purgatory. That meant more work for us back here on planet Earth; mere mortals cannot allay the eternal suffering of the damned, but if Lenny's soul was in purgatory, then he needed prayer to the tenth power to get him out. The prayers of the living are the *only* way out of purgatory, because archangels jam the signals of sinners being held there, and they lose the power to pray for themselves.

She didn't want to be alone any more than I did. After all of the hell talk at lunch and her mastery of all things Catholic at the wake, I could see that she'd been praying with her eyes closed for four days—ever since we'd found Lenny—and for her, "praying" meant watching mental movies of Lenny's soul blistering in sulfurous flames and stewing in the juices of his own unnatural desires.

Part of me liked seeing her this way—haunted, almost desperate—so she'd have a taste for how I felt when she wouldn't let me slip my hands under her blouse.

I moved over next to her and kissed her, even though I knew I wouldn't get anything like tongue until she was halfway into a bottle of wine. I kept after it, and she went semilimp and let her head loll to one side with that familiar, disappointed look in her eye. She was probably thinking that a good and kind man of character and of faith would minister to her in her bereavement. The family heirloom rosary was right there next to her sauvignon blanc. Maybe if I took it up and threw myself mind, heart, body, and soul into another reprise of Eve's banished children mourning and weeping in a vale of tears, maybe then she'd work herself into a fervor and lose control long enough for me to—

No shame? None! Instead of sharing a prayer with her after my buddy's wake, all I could think about was fornication and defiling the sacrament of marriage.

"I want you to stay," she said, "but . . ."

The rules never changed. I could stay. If I brushed my teeth and scrubbed my hands with antibacterial soap, we could cuddle as much as I wanted. She also appreciated it if you sprayed Formula 409 in the bowl after you peed in it. With Lenny dead and all, she'd be more emotional and affectionate than usual. I could hold her, maybe even kiss her. I could slide my hands up and down her black cashmere dress, even rest my hand on her leg, maybe. But I was responsible for keeping myself under control. If I started "gathering momentum," as she called it, which usually meant I was grabbing at her faster than she could push my hands away, then I had to leave.

She handed me a glass and tilted hers in the light for a look at the color.

"But?"

"But we can't do what you're thinking about doing."

"Why not?" It was as if she'd tapped my patella and, instead of my knee jerking, out came what was really on my mind.

Lenny was dead, and I was sick about it. I wanted to fuck like it was our last night on earth, wrap myself around her like a barnacle, and go to sleep forever.

I'd never directly and sincerely asked her to marry me. I was ready to if it came to that. But her answer might obliterate hope and strangle my heart in its cage. If she said no, I'd never see her again, and I'd probably leave town to make sure of it. I wouldn't pretend I could just be friends. What I wouldn't do to be friends with her was just be friends. So instead I waited and probed for hints that she might say something besides no to joining forces.

She didn't answer. Instead, she fingered the beads of the rosary and stared at them as if they were a string of linked mementos commemorating every tragedy in her family's history. Maybe acting the pious Catholic was a convenient excuse, when really it was something else. Because I didn't make enough money? Because I wasn't her type?

"Is it a Catholic thing between us, Miranda? Is that why? Because your catechism says that God put you on the earth to know love and serve Him, same way the African Masai believe God put them on the earth to care for the world's cattle, same way the flagellants think God put them here to beat themselves on the back with chains, same way I think God put me here to make love to you. I don't want to argue about which of us is right. I just want equal time."

She shook her head, as if to say that she wasn't thinking about God at the moment.

Maybe her contempt for small-time fraud operators carried over to the spiritual realm. Maybe only kingpin mortal sinning would grab her interest the same way million-dollar insurance murders inflamed her with fascination most horrible. Maybe I'd have to play the Marquis de Sade and come up with some new intoxicating concoction of sex and blasphemy. In which case, if she suggested that sex before marriage was a sin, my role was to hiss like a snake, dress up in the cunning livery of hell, and whisper to her that sinning was the best part of it, and why didn't she just wear that rosary to bed like a belly chain, while I taught her about the Gnostics, who believed that the only way to avoid a sin was to commit it and be rid of it. The raven can be no blacker than its wings, my darling, so revel in your native night-colored plumage.

Instead, I said, "Lenny dying and all has really got me thinking about my faith."

It was the truth! After staring at Lenny's dead body and saying my first decade of the rosary in over a decade, and reliving the terrors of serving funeral masses for the likes of Father Fogarty, how could I help but think about the faith I'd been raised in? I was ready to return to her womb and be reborn if that's what it took to get my hands inside that black cashmere sweater dress.

"I want to know everything about you."

"You want to be with me," said Miranda. "You want to see me, you want to know everything about me? So far, I feel like an on-line content provider, and you? You're like two eyeballs led around by an erect browser. If I give you what you want—click! You'll move on."

"I won't move on," I said, and as I remember it, I meant it.

"Harder to do than it is to say."

"How would you know?"

"Ringside watching my parents' divorces. Elvis Costello said it best: 'Forever doesn't mean forever anymore.' For people like my parents, 'forever' means 'until it seems like forever.' After that, all vows and bets are off."

I stayed away from the topic of her mom and dad. I once made the mistake of suggesting that she'd acquired her Catholic superstitions from her parents. I knew, for instance, that when her sister, Annette, had been born with the giant birthmark, it confirmed family suspicions that Miranda's mom had committed adultery. Miranda's grandpa on her father's side had said the disfiguration was a sign from God. So I'd imagined her parents as Ma and Pa American Gothic from Grant Wood's Iowa, strict farm-bred Catholics who must have overdone the descriptions of eternal hellfire. But Miranda described her mom as a "failed musician" and a "free-love Woodstock pothead" and her dad as a "nature-cult, back-to-the-land weirdo" who'd graduated from a transcendental-meditation program in central Iowa. They'd literally bet the family farm on the organic food craze and lost. Then her dad got bad arthritis. They got divorced and sent Miranda to a Catholic, all-girl boarding school in Omaha, where along with a good education, she reclaimed the lost family religion as her own.

I'd told her I'd loved her before, and one time after she'd had half a magnum of merlot she said it back to me. Even when she didn't respond in kind I could tell she liked me saying it.

She sipped her wine and put her head on my shoulder. I touched her hair, inhaled it, the way she would sample the nose from one of Lenny's fifty-dollar cabernets.

"If you think it's a sin or something, then blame the sin on me. Draw up the papers; I'll sign them and go to hell for it. Let any curse against you fall on me. Wait. That's Genesis, isn't it?"

I didn't want to overdo it and tip my hand that I'd gone to BibleQuote.com just for her, even though that's exactly what I'd done.

"Rebekah to her son Jacob, who was worried his old man, Isaac, would curse him for his treachery," I said. "Instead Rebekah said, 'Let any curse against you, son, fall on me! Just do as I say.'"

I think she knew I'd been to BibleQuote.com, but she was still touched, as if I'd stopped at the florist and bought her a single long-stemmed rose.

"So, Miranda, let any curse against you fall on me. You stay up here and gorge on Grace and the sacraments, and I'll go to hell for making love to you if that's the problem."

She set down her glass, put her arms around me, kissed my neck.

"I'm sorry," she whispered.

"For what?"

"Could we be faithful to each other?" she asked, still embracing me. "Would you turn on me?"

I pulled her around in front of me so I could look at those perfect china cat eyes shining in their painted settings.

"That's the only way I'm going to do it," she said. "Call me old-fashioned. Forever means forever to me. I have to know you'd be faithful and never turn on me."

She reached her glass and let me drink out of it, then she finished it in a long swallow.

"Look what happens when we turn those husband-and-wife scam teams over to the law. The FBI and the federal prosecutors apply a little pressure, and wham! They turn on each other. 'Send *her* down to the pen in Leavenworth, not me, Officer, it was all *her* idea.' Their marriage vows translate as 'I'm yours until I find a better deal.' Betrayal is the norm."

She seemed a little breathless, and she moved closer to me again, closer than usual. I didn't see any germ wipes or tissues handy. I'd missed some connections along the way from being faithful to each other to scammers turning on each other, but I was willing to go wherever she took me.

"If we were trapped in a big ugly scam together," she asked, "would you turn on me? That's how it can turn out, you know. Sometimes marriage is just like one big ugly scam."

She took my right hand in both of hers, like we were still back at the church and about to say another rosary together. In one eye was the playful glimmer of the actress-investigator warming up for another insurance noir tale, but the other shadowed forth the desperation of Miranda the sinner damned.

"I wouldn't turn on you," I said, "unless you turned on me first."

"That's exactly how they get you," she said. "They make you *think* your lover turned on you. To face them down, you have to *know* I wouldn't turn on you. You have to *know* that no matter who else I scammed, I'd never scam you."

"Never scam me, and never sleep with me. Right?"

"You wouldn't turn on me just for scamming somebody else, would you?"

She kept me in her sights until she knew how I'd feel about that.

"Like an insurance company?" I asked. "Miranda, tell me right now if you were in on something with Lenny?"

I still didn't know who'd changed the beneficiary on Lenny's Reliable policy from Rosa Prescott to Heartland Viatical. Normally if the change-of-beneficiary form had the word *viatical* anywhere on it, the customer-service drones would send it straight to us.

"C'mon, Miranda," I said, "you know I'm gonna find out if you were."

But anybody in Special Investigations could have changed it, too: Norton, Dagmar, Miranda . . .

"Find out about yourself, cowboy," she said. "What about you? I know how to find out a few things, too. Did Lenny ever ask you for any help selling his policies?"

"Me?"

"I wouldn't turn on you," she said, and gave me a long, meaningful look, as if she were waiting for me to confess to an insurance murder so she could prove she wouldn't turn on me.

"Were you helping him sell his policies?" I asked.

She shook her head like I had it all wrong, scooped up her glass, and passed it before my eyes. She was drawing back the curtain at our own private theater, where we could go back to happier times and I could settle in for another show. I'd get my answer later; for now she was off to the land of storybook insurance fraud.

"I'm your loving wife," she said. "I'm a little bit wicked, but that's okay because you're a little bit wicked, too. What matters is that we love each other more than anything else in the world, so we know no matter how wicked we get, we'd never turn on each other."

"I'm betting we got different working definitions of *wicked*," I said.

"We're just wicked enough to get nine or ten life insurance policies with nine or ten different companies on . . . well, let's get them on you, with me the beneficiary. We get those policies in the $250,000 to $500,000 range. Not enough to put you on the radar screen at any one company if you suddenly croak, but policies worth three or four million in the aggregate."

"Where's this one come from? The *Fraud Report*?"

She refreshed my glass for the show.

"We've got two years' worth of premiums to pay on those policies, and we make ends meet any way we can, but somewhere along the line I go out and buy you a watch engraved with your initials. On our next anniversary I get your wedding band engraved with our wedding date, assuming it's not there already. Meanwhile we keep paying on those policies. Heck, we go six months past two years and sail right out of the contestability period and half a year into the incontestable safety zone."

"Wait," I said. "Something tells me we should take out the policies on you instead of me, and I'll be the beneficiary. Can we do that?"

"No," she said, and wagged her finger at me. "The policies are on you, Buster, and once we've had them two and a half years, you announce at work that you're going to take Friday off because you want to go hiking for a three-day weekend up north of town. Come Friday, drive your car down to the St. Francis

Mission House and pick out a drunk transient with the shakes, one just about your size and age. Catch him coming or going a block away from the mission, so nobody sees you talking to him. Give him a bottle and show him you got a lot more in the backseat if he'll just go get his teeth x-rayed for a study Creighton University is doing on dental care and the homeless. Tell him they pay a hundred bucks before and another hundred after. Get him in the car and take him to see our dentist, your high school buddy, who also happens to be just a little bit wicked, just enough to x-ray the bum's teeth and put the pictures of those teeth in your dental file."

I showed her my teeth.

"Now take the bum out for a long ride while he finishes another bottle. Keep your new buddy drinking till after midnight if you can, and help him get those bottles open until he passes out. Then drive him out north of town up in the forested bluffs around Hummel Park. Pull over when you get to the top of Weather Station Hill. Get out and put the engraved watch I gave you on the drunk's left wrist. Put your wedding band on his left ring finger. Strap the shoulder belt on him and prop him up over the steering wheel, roll up the floor mat, stuff it on top of the gas pedal, put it in drive, and let her rip.

"After it crashes into the trees, chase it down and soak him good with a gallon of gas. Toss in a match and run hell-for-leather to where I'm waiting for you in car number two."

"You'll be there waiting?"

"The police will find you burned to bony cinders in your car," she said. "There's only one way to identify the body: your dental records, and those will jibe. You jet on down to Petite St. Vincent with a new name, while I attend your funeral and collect on all the life policies. We pay the dentist two hundred grand (cash, unmarked twenties). And for that, he takes our secret to the grave.

"How do I know you wouldn't just off me and take all of the money?" I asked.

She slowly shook her head. "See? You have to know I wouldn't turn on you, even if you had something going with Lenny."

"Me?" I protested. "I'm not the one—"

Her phone trilled, and she glanced down at the handset's caller-ID.

"V. Stillmach," she said, and picked up.

It was Vera calling to ask if Miranda knew where I was, because she wanted me to be a pallbearer tomorrow. Of course I wasn't there, because Miranda had to keep up medieval appearances, and eleven at night was too late for an unmarried Catholic girl to be entertaining a gentleman caller.

She talked along about how she knew how to find me, and said Mrs. Stillmach should just count on me being a pallbearer.

Then she got up and wandered around the loft with the handset, telling Lenny's mom how peaceful Lenny had looked, what a fine wake it had been, how beautiful the flowers were—all the usual inane patter people serve up when they're trying to be nice.

I could see she was going to be a while and was paying no attention to me, because she'd taken the water pitcher into the kitchen for a refill from the cooler.

I moved over to her machine and got back on. I went straight to the Web Cam Commander folder and found the file where I'd left it. I wouldn't have time to open it and get the session details or the IP addresses of whomever she'd hooked up with; I had time to get the date and time on which she'd last used the web cam that Lenny had supposedly removed when she'd told him to "take it off."

I put the cursor bar on the file named "session.log" and crossed over to the entry under the "Modified" column; the file was dated and time-stamped 12/15/2001 3:39 A.M. The morning Lenny had died. The time? Six minutes before I wrote "3:45" on the pad and went down to meet her for the last ride to Lenny's, and presumably the last time she'd run Web Cam Commander. Maybe it had been her on the other side of Lenny's webcam session?

I flashed to the Intel Pro web cam on Lenny's monitor the morning we'd found him dead, and on her ripping the cords out of the backup power supply. *"Turn it off! You want somebody seeing him like this? You want that human garbage on the screen when the ambulance gets here?"* And then she'd flat-out lied when Becker had asked us if Lenny's machine had been on.

She sauntered around the granite island in the kitchen, one arm folded under her breasts and propping the other up at the elbow, the phone nestled against her ear.

I went back to my on-line e-mail account on the off chance that since it was Monday night, Pete Westfall, who was an "always-on"-type guy, might have already e-mailed back. Nothing from him, but there was one from Addie. Encrypted, meaning I had to be on my own machine to read it. I went to sign off, and *ding*! The chime sounded and a new message came in. This one *was* from Pete. The subject line said: "Leonard Stillmach Query." The body of the message read:

Guaranteed Investment Mutual Trust
Policy #09709064
Face Amount: $300,000
Issue date: 01/05/2000
Beneficiary: Miranda Pryor

Her hips swayed as she took the third corner of the granite island and headed back my way.

I felt like eight-year-old Virginia O'Hanlon getting her question about Santa Claus answered, not by some avuncular senior editor on the pages of the *New York Sun* but by Wicked Uncle Ernie after a three-day bender: "You think Santa Claus flies all over the world with a big bag of toys for six-point-two billion people? If he spends sixty seconds in each house, that's one billion minutes, or sixteen million hours, or six hundred ninety-four thousand days, or twenty-nine thousand *years* to deliver all those presents. Yes, there is a Santa fraud, Virginia, an enormous Santa fraud, and your mom and dad are professional scam artists who've been lying to you since you learned to talk!"

What in hell's name was she keeping from me? Maybe if I opened a few more files, I'd find out she was a double agent selling missile technologies to the Chinese, or maybe she's really a lap dancer across the river at the Bluffs Babylon Club? Or just another fraudster in one of her own play-acted scams: Miranda Pryor, the Scheherezade of insurance fraud, consumed by her own ferocious imagination, until she couldn't tell the real world from the make-believe.

I closed everything down faster than if I'd had a virus alert and met her back at the couch, where she'd put the handset back in its cradle and grabbed her wineglass.

"Is my computer okay?" she asked.

"It's fine," I said.

The storyteller had vanished, the ghost gone out of her machine, and she was just another forlorn pupil in Death's crowded classroom. The wine made her cheeks bloom in new fever colors, but her eyes had burned out, gone cold and dark. She didn't look like somebody who'd just won almost a third of a million in life's lottery, and maybe she hadn't, because the policy was still two weeks inside the contestability period. If she wanted the money, she'd have to sue and fight them for it.

I knew she had *Double Indemnity* with Fred MacMurray and Barbara Stanwyck on DVD and maybe it was time to pull it out and make her watch it. I'd be Hamlet using the old play-within-the-play gambit for the excellent purpose of what? Delaying the inevitable?

So far, she had an explanation for calling me after Lenny had died, and one for not telling me about his AIDS, and another for the key, and for the web-cam software, and she probably had explanations for the session.log and the life policy, too. I didn't even want to hear them. The only way I was going to get the truth about her and Lenny and Heartland Viatical was to go through her machine, then go back to his place and go through his machine, put the two together and—shazam!—study them.

I'd have to tell Addie to post it on the Fraud Defense Network; it was the only way to find out just how many policies he had out there.

The unhappy, beautiful woman slumped next to me on the couch swirling her glass and staring into it like it was hell's kaleidoscope didn't look like she'd have the spine to kill Lenny or anybody else. But policy number three had turned up with her name on it. If Becker knew about that, he'd pull an all-nighter asking her questions about it.

After we finished the wine, she gathered up the glasses and took them away. I kissed her good night and curled up in my designated place on the couch and waited. Every time I heard her clear her throat or click off a light switch, I looked at my watch and started counting again. Her machine was still on, but if I started clicking and clacking around on her keyboard, she'd come and find me pawing through her e-mails.

Instead, I had an idea, a bad one, but after lunching on scotch and downing my half of two wine bottles, how was I to know good from bad when it came to wee-hour ideas like wondering if the gal I'm chasing is a fraudster or a murderer?

I waited, and counted.

At 1:16 A.M., she'd been quiet for an hour.

I put my boots on, grabbed the sport coat I'd worn to the wake and my parka. I found her leather handbag on the table in the entryway. I drew her keys out in slow, silent motion, made sure the one rimmed in red and the one rimmed in green were still there, then slipped out into the winter night.

JEHOVAH'S WITNESSES

THE YELLOW POLICE TAPE was still up, but the weight of it had peeled back half the adhesive on one side of the doorjamb. I put on my wool gloves and touched it, then, whoops! It fell, and how was I to know if it was still off limits? Becker's computer man and the evidence people had surely already been there. Hadn't Becker said that he wanted to turn the place over to the family in a few days? Friday, Saturday, Sunday, Monday, early Tuesday morning? That was more than a few, and I was practically family to Lenny.

I cranked the green-rimmed key in the slot, pushed open the raspy door, and went inside. The place was still colder than Satan's frozen butthole, as if Lenny's furniture and belongings were made out of cleverly painted dry ice that would start smoking any minute. The machine was still off, or more likely Becker's computer techs had powered it down after they finished copying the hard drive.

I powered it back up with a gloved fingertip and took a look around while I waited for it to boot. The pill vials, the razor blade, and the mirror were all gone. Everything else appeared undisturbed, not that I remembered much about that night, other than finding Lenny half naked, dead, and as yet uncovered in shame.

I sat down at his machine. Wearing gloves while working his pointing device and keyboard was going to be a chore, and I didn't plan on sitting in a condo roped off with police tape reading a dead man's junk e-mails in the dead of night. All I wanted to do was copy one big file and a few folders and take them with me.

I didn't know Lenny's passwords, so I had to log on as a new user. From the desktop I went straight to Windows Explorer.

Love or hate Microsoft, they make it easy to quickly locate the nexus of the entire electronic personality. The program is called Outlook, and those who use it have their calendar and scheduler, their contacts, their to-do lists, their memos, and above all their e-mail all contained in one personal folder file, a .pst file, usually called "outlook.pst." If I *opened* the Outlook program, it would open Lenny's personal-file folders, and it would change the date and time of his .pst file. Copying the whole file onto a removable disk wouldn't change the date or time or any other file attributes, and then I could just take them all home where I could peruse them at my leisure. Only trouble is, like any file associated with a Microsoft application, it was a fat hog: in Lenny's case a file called "AttilaTheHun.pst" weighing in at 150 megabytes.

Personal-folder files, like any other files, are easily password-protected, but most users don't take the trouble. At most, the typical Outlook user may have a hidden or password-protected folder set aside inside the program, where he keeps e-mail from

the latest object of his affections at the office, but everything else
is wide open. Why? Because nobody likes to be nagged by password dialogue boxes every time he opens his e-mail program.

Go through someone's personal effects after he or she dies;
there's no better proof that people live entire lives convinced of
their own immortality. Otherwise they'd be a lot more careful
about the stuff they leave behind for their loved ones to find.
Lenny had gobs of subscriber e-mails from sites promising Hot
Asian Teenage Girls, Barely Legal Pussy, XXX Top 100 Hot
Web Cam Sex, everything including Kurt Vonnegut's "Wide
Open Beavers Inside!" And, sure enough, e-mail aplenty from the
Center for AIDS Prevention Studies, the CDC, and other AIDS
information sources.

I read somewhere that the human brain contains one hundred billion neurons, about the same number of stars clustered
together in the large spiral galaxy we live in called the Milky Way.
When those hundred billion neurons hook up via synapses to
make a person—like Lenny, or Miranda, or even Norton—what
you get is a galactic-scale persona of neurons and neuroses. But
instead of being a hundred thousand light-years wide, like the
Milky Way, the vast, deranged Lenny Way had all fit inside a single human skull. Saying I "knew" him because I'd worked with
him, talked to him, e-mailed him, had yucked it up over beers
and joints with him, was like saying I knew the Milky Way
because of the time I'd spent in West Omaha.

Now all that was left of the galaxy formerly known as Lenny
was the text he'd typed into his computer. It was as if the Milky
Way and all of its vast majesty had vanished, leaving behind only
a few insect fossils in a limestone cut along Interstate 80.

Lenny had archived his MP3 music files on a collection of

Iomega Zip 250 disks, and I needed one or more blank disks to put his files on. I grabbed one from the little carousel, stuck it in the drive, and erased it by doing a quick format. According to the label on the case, Gomez, *Liquid Skin,* Ryan Adams, *Heart-breaker,* and the Hangdogs, *Beware of Dog,* had all just lost their magnetic lives in the name of copying Lenny's electronic identity. I copied AttilaTheHun.pst onto the Zip disk, and then I copied all of the session.log files from his Web Cam Commander folder, his "My Documents" folder, his "My Pictures" folder.

I did file searches using the various text strings: "Heartland Viatical," "Crogan," or "GothicRage86." While the searches progressed, I had another thought. I'd originally planned to get into Miranda's system from my home machine and copy her Outlook.pst file, as well as the session.log file I'd found in her Web Cam Commander folder. But here I was on Lenny's machine, and I realized that if I accessed her machine right now, from Lenny's place instead of mine, then I could do so without leaving any traces of my home machine or its address. If she checked her firewall logs or had somebody else do it for her, they'd find traces of Lenny's machine, not mine.

I got past her software firewall okay using the Rubicon.exe program I'd left on her machine. I formatted another Zip disk (good-bye to what looked like the complete works of Alison Krauss and the Fountains of Wayne's *Utopia Parkway*). Miranda's .pst file was ninety megabytes, which would take a good ten minutes to transfer. While I waited, I went back to look at the results of my file search and found that most of the text string hits were in the .pst file I'd already copied. The "GothicRage86" hits were all in his Delta-Strike folder; GothicRage had to be a team member or a frequent opponent, from the looks of it. I copied the most recent of those and headed back out to the desktop to monitor the transfer of Miranda's Outlook file.

Then Lenny's instant-messaging window popped open:

GothicRage86: SnowKiller, what happened Friday night, did you morph into a fucking pussy, again? Where you been?

I decided typing was the best policy, or maybe even loading a map for a game, until I figured out how to handle this one. How well had GothicRage known Lenny if he didn't even know he was dead? Not unusual for a gamer—he could have "known" Lenny for years and never met him. Suppose I told him who I was and what had happened to Lenny? It might spook him and he'd vanish. I wouldn't know who he was or where to find him. Instead I played along, at least until I could find out if GothicRage was physically at Lenny's place the night he died, or if he had just cut into our game somehow. Or maybe Lenny had played on a team that night just before hooking up with me, and GothicRage had still been lurking somewhere in the map?

I panicked for a second, because I wasn't sure if I had to log in before using his instant messaging. I didn't know the AttilaTheHun password.

I started typing anyway, and Lenny's Attila profile popped right up. Whew. Now I could just *be* Lenny.

AttilaTheHun: Friday I was impaired by substances beyond my control, but I can empty a few clips into your gizzard tonight if you're ready. I conked out early Friday night, and next day I heard you kicked my buddy's ass, too. Dirk Stone, Seal Team 6?

Thirty seconds is a long lag in instant-messaging land, and I thought maybe GothicRage had taken off, but then there he was.

GothicRage86: Dude, you passed out at the keyboard. After that, I played your buddy Dirk, and he was a fucking pussy, just like you. Who was Senorita Silk Fox who turned me off of the Attila-at-Home web cam?

AttilaTheHun: Friday night? On Attila cam?

GothicRage86: Yeah, 11 or so. You were bobbing and weaving at the keyboard and then Beauty Betty comes over and switches me out.

AttilaTheHun: Keep describing. On the weekends I got hot and cold running babes in this place. Blonde? Brunette?

GothicRage86: Brunette, lipstick, big ones. Dressed for it. She switched me off the cam.

AttilaTheHun: I think I know who you're talking about. If you were on Attila cam Friday night, you probably still got a shot of her in the cache of your temporary files?

GothicRage86: Maybe.

AttilaTheHun: I wanna pimp her. Send me the image and I'll pull it up in my graphics program. I'll make a cartoon out of it and mail it to her and say, "Bitch, what the fuck you doing switching my friends off Attila-at-Home cam?"

Another pause that lasted way too long.

AttilaTheHun: Never mind if it's a pain. It's just a joke I wanna play on her.

GothicRage86: Not a problem. I was just searching the cache for the Attila images. I only got one of her. You must have had it set on a thirty-second refresh rate. Hey, bring her along as the VIP next time you hole up inside a 747 map.

AttilaTheHun: Cool, send it. Hey, wait a sec, send it to my buddy. He's got FreeHand graphics on his machine. Send it to CarvedMeat@home.com and I'll work on it at his place.

GothicRage86: Got it. Shall I splatter thy brains now fuckface? You pick the map, SnowKiller, and I'll come find you and take you out.

I picked Cartel Headquarters, a map that I'd played Lenny in many times, so I could try to remember how he had played it as we went along. Otherwise, I was going to start doing shit Lenny had never done, and maybe if GothicRage had played Lenny a lot, he'd start to notice. Not to mention I might get killed right off trying to work a Razer Boomslang with wool gloves on.

I took the SnowKiller skin and the Mac-10 and went up to guard the entrance through the vent on the roof. I waited for GothicRage to open the vent and give me a clear head shot.

GothicRage86: Hey, why isn't Attila-at-Home cam on now?

I looked up into the dead eye of the Intel camera.

He was just distracting me while he made his move. I heard his boots clanging on the metal fire escape stairs, but I also heard something else.

A doorbell, and it wasn't sound effects coming from inside the map; it was Lenny's real-world doorbell, which meant that somebody was at Lenny's door at 2 A.M. Why? To check and see how he was doing the night before his funeral? Miranda? Had she noticed the keys were gone? Knew that I'd taken them? Lenny's mom? But why would his mom be ringing her dead son's doorbell? Becker's computer guys? In the middle of the night?

I tiptoed over to the door and listened. I heard a male clear his throat outside, then a peculiar series of grunts and unintelligible speech.

The bell chimed again.

The door had a peephole with a little silver cover.

I leaned up close and slid the cover away. I peeked in the lens, where I could see two well-groomed young guys in suits and thirty-dollar ties of the sort not even lawyers wear anymore. They looked like University of Nebraska Omaha students or Eagle Scouts out raising money for a good cause. The one on the left carried a briefcase and was a tall, wiry blond with a long lean head that drooped forward slightly on his knobby frame. The guy on the right was shorter and even slighter than his companion. Both the savoriest of characters. And the short guy had newsletters and pamphlets or papers of some kind in hand.

Copies of the Watchtower, I thought, *that's it!* If I opened the door they'd offer me a free Bible study session, invite themselves in to share their faith with me, and when I said no thanks they'd leave me a pamphlet warning me about the dangers of blood transfusions. Jehovah's Witnesses made perfect sense. Except it was two in the morning, and they were inside a building with a locked front door and frosted lettering on the glass that said NO SOLICITATIONS? I reared back and refocused, and lost my grip on the silver cover, and it slipped back into place with an audible click.

"FBI," a voice said, "We have a search warrant for this address. Open the door."

Shit. I tiptoed back to the machine and popped out the Zip disk, grabbed the other one with Lenny's files on it, and put them both in the crotch of my underwear, right on top of Mr. Shriveled-in-Panic. Then I powered down the machine.

I went back to the door and carefully slid the cover open again and watched them.

"Federal agents," said the short one on the right. "Open the door."

Or what? I thought. *You'll hold up my tax refund?* Lenny had a steel door. Unless they had six more agents with Plexiglas shields and a battering ram waiting in the wings, I could go lie down and pretend I fell asleep drunk.

Then I saw the tall one lift a set of keys, and I opened the door quick.

There were three of them. Instead of a battering ram, they had a technician's cart in the hallway to the right, with hardware shelving and plastic bins scattered with computer parts and tools: external Iomega drives, external media for the most likely super-floppy and external drives, backup tape machines.

Maybe the FBI had gone into the PC repair business?

A third guy with movie-star, blond good looks manned the cart. He had a thin tan cord that came out of his collar and hooked up to a little, oval, flesh-colored disk that appeared to be stuck to the side of his head. At first I thought it was one of those secret agent earphones, but it didn't go into his ear, it was stuck to the side of his head behind and slightly above his ear.

The short guy arranged a stapled clutch of papers on his clipboard.

"I'm case agent Todd McKnight, Federal Bureau of Investigation," he said. "I have a search warrant for the premises: 1325 Jason Street, number 232. This is Agent Michael Mutton, Evidence Response Team."

His taller partner nodded, and McKnight kept talking.

"And this is Nate Langdon," said McKnight, indicating the handsome guy with the cart. "He's a computer forensic examiner—Computer Analysis Response Team."

Langdon made an odd inarticulate sound in the back of his throat. He interrupted McKnight's introduction, as if he hadn't heard him talking.

"Nate Lahng-DUN," he said.

He didn't seem a bit self-conscious about his speech impediment. Instead he was loud and almost pushy, then he said, "Cahm-pew-tuh For-en-zic Zaminah," accenting all the wrong syllables.

"He's deaf," said McKnight, "but he wears a cochlear implant."

"Oh," I said.

McKnight turned the clipboard around, showed me the search warrant, and pointed at the list of items they were entitled to seize: computers of any kind, disks, diskettes, storage peripherals . . . the list went on, but it all seemed to be computer-related.

He flapped open his federal ID, where I could read his name: Todd D. McKnight.

"Okay," I said.

"Are you Mr. Leonard Stillmach?" asked Mutton.

I don't know why I said it, but I did. Maybe it was because I'd just been pretending to be Lenny with GothicRage.

"Just Lenny," I said.

I figured if he asked me for identification, I'd tell him that Lenny was my nickname. Sure. It was unconscious, a brain spasm and desperate ploy to avoid having to explain why I was there and how I'd gotten in. Mainly it was Charlie Becker I was thinking of, and how I didn't want to explain it to him. These guys didn't even know Lenny was dead, which meant they weren't working with Becker, probably didn't even know Becker.

From the average citizen's point of view, the police are a unitary organization working together at the federal, state, and local levels to apprehend lawbreakers, but I'd worked enough with all three levels of cops to know that wasn't so. The few times I'd worked with FBI on a fraud case, if you mentioned the local cops, they looked right past you, like, *Why would we want them involved?* FBI guys have a college grad's contempt for local cops, who maybe went to a community college. Plus they hadn't said anything about an *arrest* warrant, just a *search* warrant. I was betting that if I gave them their search, they wouldn't care if I was Lenny Stillmach or Jimmy Hoffa.

"Have you been drinking, sir?" asked McKnight.

Goddamn! Sober people have such sensitive sniffers.

"Yes," I said, "I drank some wine with my girlfriend."

Mutton looked at the police tape.

"The tape was down when I came back home a while ago," I said. "I was out."

The deaf guy with the cart didn't seem to hear me, cochlear implant or no.

"It's not our tape," said McKnight. "We don't care about the tape."

He looked over my shoulder toward Lenny's computer table.

"We're here for the computers," said McKnight, and handed me the stapled papers. "Here's your copy of the warrant."

Langdon, the deaf guy with the robotic speech, had a persistent stare that was annoying. I noticed that he reached up and pulled off the disk that was stuck to the side of his head and let it dangle on his lapel.

I looked back at McKnight and his warrant.

"He unhooks the implant sometimes, when he doesn't want to be distracted by people yacking," McKnight explained.

"Oh," I said.

Langdon grinned at me and kept staring, then used sign language to say something to McKnight, who nodded.

"Are you alone? Is anyone else on the premises?" asked McKnight.

"No one else is here," I said.

I didn't step back to let them in, but they walked right in, cart and all, as if it didn't matter whether I invited them in or not.

McKnight walked me over to a space in the middle of the room.

"Arms up and turn around," he said.

He patted me here and there in a cursory fashion. Inside both legs below the crotch was the closest he came to where I had the two Zip disks hidden in my underwear.

"Take a seat on the floor, Mr. Stillmach," said McKnight.

I sat cross-legged and waited. While McKnight watched over me, the tall skinny guy, Mutton, locked the door.

Langdon wheeled his cart over to Lenny's machine and made that funny sound in the back of his throat. He signed something to McKnight.

"Is this the only computer on the premises?" McKnight asked.

"That's it," I said, and I felt Langdon watching me again with that unnerving stare.

"You sit there, sir," McKnight said. "We will conduct the search and remove the property and evidence specified in the warrant."

Mutton walked into Lenny's bedroom, and I could hear him rummaging here and there. Langdon used a digital camera to take photos of the port connections, then unplugged the equipment and loaded it onto his cart. He took the Zip carousel and all of the disks, the Razer Boomslang mouse, the keyboard—every peripheral and connecting cord.

Mutton came out of the bedroom and into the kitchen, where he opened all the cupboards and poked around inside.

After Langdon finished loading his cart, Mutton came out of the kitchen and looked in the closets, the drawers of Lenny's desk, his shelves of videotapes and books, and they all ended up back where I was sitting on the floor.

"Is it normal to do this at two o'clock in the morning?" I asked.

I could see Langdon had his little flesh-colored implant thingy stuck back on his head. He looked at McKnight, then reached up and flicked the disk off, so that it dangled down over his lapel again.

He used sign language to tell McKnight something.

"When we got here, the machine was off," said McKnight. "Were you using your computer when we arrived?"

Langdon leaned forward slightly and kept staring, even lifting his eyebrows slightly as if to say, *"And so?"*

"No," I said.

Now they were both looking at me, silent, as if they were waiting for me to elaborate about how I wasn't on the computer.

"I was reading," I said.

Langdon walked a little closer and looked at me from another angle, like I was a potted plant or a piece of furniture he was thinking about buying. Then he used sign language again to McKnight. And McKnight signed back to him.

Langdon was still staring at me, and lifted his eyebrows again: *And so?*

"What?" I said, looking at Langdon but talking to McKnight. "What does he want?"

McKnight almost apologized for Langdon's behavior.

"We do a lot of these routines," he said. "This is probably the tenth computer seizure deal we've done with specialist Langdon here in the last two or three months, because we had all that tele-marketing fraud, and after that a lot of denial-of-service attacks. Anyway, after about the second or third one, Langdon here up and tells us that deaf people can tell when hearing people are lying just by watching their faces."

McKnight made a high-pitched sound, like he didn't believe it either, but—

Langdon raised his eyebrows. *And so?*

McKnight was almost embarrassed to ask, but he did anyway.

"We're tired of buying him steaks at Gorats every time he's right. All we want to do is prove he's wrong this time, and that you really are Leonard Stillmach. Would you mind showing us some ID?"

15

HOME MACHINE

IT WAS LIKE A nightmare that turned back into just another harmless, weird dream. McKnight handed my driver's license to Langdon, who smiled a big one when he read my name. We were in a cartoon together, and I could see a Gorats twelve-ounce New York strip hovering overhead in his thought balloon.

Langdon took my driver's license over to Lenny's multifunction fax-printer-photocopier, powered it up, and made a copy of it. McKnight looked at the license, then handed it back to me. He told me to sit on the floor again while he called in on his cell and ran me through NCIC (National Crime Information Center).

When he came off the call, he said, "Is this your current address, Mr. Hartnett?"

"Yes," I said.

"Do you have a cell phone?" he asked pleasantly, as if we were two young execs just getting into the networking thing.

I fished in the pocket of my sport coat and found him a card.

He read my cell phone number aloud, and then he said, "If we call that number during the next two weeks, you'll answer it, and you'll be in Omaha, right?"

I shrugged and said, "Okay."

Langdon rolled the cart out of the room. Mutton looked at me once deadpan, and they all left.

Just like that! No questions. No accusations. No hot lights and where-were-you-on-the-night-of-the-fifteenth? And best of all, not a word about Lenny's death, local cops, yellow crime tape. Nothing!

I gave them a good five minutes' head start, and then I jogged back over to Miranda's. I waved her smart card, and the door opened with a soft click. I pushed it in a quarter inch, then gently nudged it, inch by careful inch, stopping and barely breathing whenever I heard anything like a creak in its hinges. If it took me five minutes or an hour, I was going to get those keys back in the purse without making a single sound. I was like the guy in the Edgar Allan Poe story opening the door millimeter by millimeter, stealthy step by stealthy step, for a look at the vulture eye, and about now I was thinking she probably had one.

I left her a note about how I couldn't sleep, had gone home to take a warm bath, and I'd see her at the funeral.

I didn't want to see her again or talk to her until I knew exactly what she knew, till I knew what Lenny had been up to and whether she'd been in on it. Then I was going to strap her in a chair like a POW if I had to, lay it all out, and break her down. Maybe GothicRage would even send a JPG image file of her, reaching over Lenny's body the night he'd died.

Would the FBI call Becker? Tell him they'd found me in

there? I'd have more credibility if I went to Becker first and told him . . . everything? Tell him I'd copied files from both of their machines and was about to solve the case? What case? Well, solve the viatical angles first, and see if they pointed to a case? Tell him there's a life insurance policy for three hundred thousand dollars on Lenny's life, with Miranda Pryor the beneficiary? He'd probably arrest us both and take another long hard look at anything that was "not right."

It was 3 A.M. Becker was probably out looking at new dead bodies. I shouldn't bother him. Between now and noon tomorrow, I could say that I was *going* to tell him everything, but that I had decided to wait for normal business hours, the first half of which would be occupied by my best friend's funeral. If I didn't sleep, that gave me four or five hours to go home and plow through the files I'd—okay, I'd stolen them, but it was under duress because my would-be girlfriend and my dead best friend started looking a lot like those lurid color photos of common fraudsters in the *John Cooke Fraud Report.*

If it was Miranda whom GothicRage was calling Senorita Silk Fox with the big ones and the nice lipstick, it could turn out that there wasn't enough to get her on a murder charge, especially if I never got the image from him. It could end up one of those civil trials for murder, same way it happened with O.J. trying to collect on Nicole's life insurance after he'd slashed her. To convict an insurance murderer of homicide, the prosecutors needed to prove the usual "guilt beyond a reasonable doubt," a standard not easy to meet if the accused has a decent lawyer and the perfect right not to take the stand. The county prosecutors could pass on charging her with murder, but then the insurance companies could refuse to pay her and pay the money into court instead. There the fight would be over money, pure and simple, so instead of the formidable burden of proof "beyond a reasonable doubt," the lawyers had only to meet the burden of proof in a civil action, meaning they had to prove only that it was "more likely than not" that Miranda had got him to name her as a beneficiary, and then . . . ? If she killed him, how did she do it?

Instead of calling Becker, I went home and copied Lenny's and Miranda's .pst files onto my hard drive, where they'd run a lot faster than they would off the Zip. I could open them in two separate windows and compare them side by side, if it came to that.

According to the little digital clock on the task bar it was 4 A.M., and in five hours I was going to be a pallbearer for the person whose inbox was open before me on the screen, and manic Lenny had an inbox with two thousand plus e-mails in it, probably hadn't been cleaned out in months. He had a fat archive file, too, which I'd have to open separately.

I had passed the tired mile marker four stops back, but I didn't want to sleep until I knew what had happened. Like it or not, it was becoming just like a case file, a big one. If the FBI was watching Lenny, he was into something bigger than selling a couple of life policies. Tomorrow people like Norton, Addie Frenzer, and yes, Becker would be asking me questions. The only safe plan was to do what I always did with a big fraud case: make sure that I knew more about it than anyone else. If I had time left before the funeral, I'd take my forty winks; if not, I'd have to motor along on caffeine until tonight.

I found an e-mail from Miranda to Lenny. Subject: "Here's a Giggle!" I right-clicked on it, then selected: "Find all messages from Sender." There were plenty, about books, music, movies; a few said, "Re: Norton Sucks." A couple of others on wine tastings at Omaha Wine Company or the Winery.

I clicked around and sorted them in different ways, until I had all e-mail from her to him sorted by subject and found the ones I was looking for: "Subject: Re: Heartland V." I picked the oldest Heartland thread, from almost two years ago.

I opened his preview pane so I could just click and scan them without opening each one:

> **From:** Miranda Pryor
> **To:** Leonard Stillmach
> **Subject:** Heartland V.
> It would be for Annette, my sister. She had a serious
> skin condition. I told you about it. She has a life policy. She's
> at increased risk for melanoma, which can kill you quick. Is
> that the kind of thing that would qualify her?
> mp

The next one had part of Lenny's last e-mail message to her bracketed at the top:

> **From:** Miranda Pryor
> **To:** Leonard Stillmach
> **Subject:** Heartland V.
> >Your sister wouldn't be doing anything illegal. I
> >didn't do anything illegal—well, maybe a little,
> >but not really—all I did was sell them policies.

>I got the policies legit. They bought them from
>me. I told you they need all the policies they
>can get because they're being investigated.

And underneath Miranda had written:

You keep saying it's not illegal, but my sister is not
terminally ill. If Heartland buys her life insurance policy and
sells it to their investors by telling them that she IS
terminally ill, that's fraud, isn't it?
wantonmp

Same deal on the next one—she was replying to Lenny and
had copied his in above.

From: Miranda Pryor
To: Leonard Stillmach
Subject: Heartland
>OK, pretend Annette sells me her car instead of
>her life insurance policy. I pay her more than
>the car is worth, and then I turn around and sell
>it to an investor for even more than I got from
>her. Did I do something wrong? Pretend I did,
>does that mean Annette did anything wrong?

>Why do I care if Heartland is taking advantage of
>vulture investors who like to bet on when sick
>people will die?

And underneath Miranda had written:

I'll e-mail the Heartland stuff to her, and I'll talk to her about it next time I go back to Ottumwa for a weekend visit.

I'm sure she would sell the policy if she could. She needs money because the plastic surgeons say it will take a series of expensive surgeries.

The social worker at the hospital said it would easily reach 6 procedures, and cost more than $100,000, which insurance won't pay because they say it is cosmetic.
wantonmp

That one was dated November 2000, over a year ago. So if her sister was going to sell the policy, she probably would have done it by now.

Two weeks later in the thread, another one, with a new subject heading.

From: Miranda Pryor
To: Leonard Stillmach
Subject: Qualifying Medical
I've attached two medical journal articles and a paragraph or two from Lycos Health WebMD, which should answer any questions your friend Rosa has about Annette's medical condition.
wantonmp

The articles were from plastic surgery journals: "Excision of Congenital Giant Pigmented Nevus in Adult Patients" and "Risk of Melanoma in Patients with Congenital Melanocytic Nevi and Giant Pigmented Nevi."

The articles were attached web pages, so the digital photos and presentation graphics came with them. About 1 percent of infants are born with pigmented moles called congenital nevi. The worst is the so-called "bathing trunk" nevus (named for the surface area it often covers), described as a "disfiguring, darkly pigmented, nodular patch of skin that is present at birth and may cover large areas of the body."

The first full-color slide was of a three-month-old baby boy whose tiny haunch was a massive black mole. Only medical science can explain such a disfigurement, and before medical science, the horrors probably were blamed on elves leaving changelings in the cradles of tormented parents. It's often said that everything can be explained by faith in a loving God—everything except the suffering of children, and the lesion I saw in the photo would make an infidel of Abraham.

Another slide was of a baby, normal in every respect, except for a band of raised pigmented flesh wrapped around its waist, like some dermal monster from the depths of a nightmare.

According to the article, plastic surgeons can't just cut the nevi away from the skin, because the lesion usually extends all the way into the superficial muscle. The procedures called for a half dozen sessions of something called "tissue expansion," with secondary procedures to remove the expanders, advance skin flaps of normal tissue, and allow for excision of the abnormal skin.

Okay, so she helped her sister sell Heartland a policy. Fraud? Probably not. But she had had no qualms about lying to me. At the Rendezvous, before the wake, when I'd told her about the

Omaha Beneficial policy for five hundred thousand that Addie had called about, Miranda had said: *"I knew he was thinking about selling his Reliable policy. But I didn't know he had a policy at Omaha Beneficial."* She'd implied that she knew only about one policy, his Reliable policy. But here he was freely telling her about selling *policies. "All I did was sell them policies. I got the policies legit."*

I scanned more e-mails looking for some explanation of how Miranda ended up the beneficiary on Lenny's three-hundred-thousand-dollar policy at Guaranteed Investment Mutual.

After reading the "Heartland" subject headings, I searched the body text of every message in his inbox for "Heartland" and found a new series from Rosa Prescott under the subject heading "More Policies."

> **From:** Rosa Prescott
> **To:** Leonard Stillmach
> **Subject:** More Policies
> If you have more, they will buy them. You will get more if you hold them for the two years until they are incontestable.
>
> The accusations of fraud you found on the net are old. Mr. Crogan's former California associates pulled a neat trick and sold a single viaticated life insurance policy to four or five different investors, all of whom believed they were the exclusive owners. That's not what Hector's about. But the problems have followed him here to Omaha.
>
> The Postal Authorities and the FBI and insurance commission guys are sniffing around asking about

Heartland's operations and issuing subpoenas. The company took money from investors, and now it needs to convince the authorities that the money went to buy life insurance policies. Let the doctors argue about who is "terminally ill." In the meantime, they need policies—pure and simple—almost any policies, or else the government will shut them down.

If you bring any other viators with policies in, we can share my commission.

P.S. Did you turn video capture on during the session we had last night? I was dripping hot, I hope you could feel it.
Love,
Rosa

Wayward Lenny and his on-line sex. *Dripping hot?*

That's probably how Miss Rosa got him to go along with selling life policies on himself, because she gave him live web-cam action at 3 A.M. Norton's words came rushing into my forebrain: *"I moved that file over to you because two years ago I asked Lenny to investigate Heartland Viatical . . . he came back two weeks later and told me they were clean . . . Lenny dated, more than dated, had been involved with a Heartland Viatical sales agent."*

Norton's information, it would appear, was reliable, just like the company name.

The sun was coming up, and I'd barely scratched the surface, hadn't even opened Miranda's .pst file yet, because so far I could see both ends of their e-mails on Lenny's. But Miranda's e-mail probably had more info about the sale of her sister's policy, and maybe somewhere an e-mail from her telling Lenny to put her name down on that Guaranteed Investment Mutual Trust policy, just for kicks?

My machine chimed to announce the arrival of more e-mail, and one of the ten or twelve that came in was from GothicRage86@aol.com but with no file attached.

>
> **From:** GothicRage86@aol.com
>
> **To:** CarvedMeat@home.com
>
> **Re:** Attila-at-Home cam
>
> Hey, Carved Meat, nice try, but I think it was you on Lenny's machine earlier. Just a funny feeling. Why would Lenny log on to his own machine as a new user?
>
> And why is it you want a picture of Lenny's girlfriend?
>
> Why isn't Lenny on-line anymore?
>
> He's not answering e-mail either. When he does I'm gonna tell him you were on his machine, unless you wanna try to convince me different?
>
> GothicRage86

16

FUNERAL

St. Dymphna's Cathedral is a gargantuan landmark done in early-twentieth-century Spanish Renaissance revival and built on the highest hill in town. Okay, the highest *bluff*. Groundbreaking to christening took fifty-four years (1905–59), and now the twin bell towers are visible for miles on both sides of the Missouri River.

From afar the cathedral looks like an overwrought Baroque tomb jutting up out of a stand of trees on the prairie. Its cornices, cupolas, and quatrefoils are trimmed in swirling marble swags, friezes, and decorative moldings, with massive flying buttresses of scrolled stone supporting the domes. Skim off the wrought-iron crucifixes and stone crosses, and it would look like the summer palace and seraglio of a Turkish emperor vacationing in Spain shortly after conquering it. In a town dominated by square, white-brick buildings and shopping malls, the cathedral is an architectural red zone where the city planners have quarantined all of the ornaments, filigrees, and masonic braveries in the Mid-Heartland on a single monumental anachronism.

Ascending the granite steps to a row of twelve-foot wrought-iron doors, I had the usual sensation that the bell towers and the rose-windowed façade were slowly toppling forward like the walls of Jericho to crush us grieving human insects and end the world. Inside, the marble pillars soared into arches and vaults spangled with the glittery tesserae of murals that covered the domed ceilings. The diocese had raised the money to restore and preserve the grandeur of the architecture, but the supernatural power that had terrorized me in my Catholic youth was almost all gone. I hoped.

I watched SUVs and minivans unloading out front, soccer moms bullying their children like trail bosses getting after stray cattle, herding the little ones into St. Dymphna's Elementary School next door. And double-parking outside of them, carloads of people coming for the funeral.

It took quite a while for Lenny's family and friends to make their way up front. Lenny's retarded sister was clinging to Vera, and his aunts and grandmas were kissing and splashing tears on each other. We menfolk had official duties in the funeral procession, so we waited in the narthex with Lenny and his casket. The other pallbearers were uncles and neighbors, young and old men I'd met once or twice and got high with, some even from the insurance business, but I didn't know them well enough to talk about death in a familiar way. They were all dressed better than I—in real suits. I wore the same black sport coat and khaki slacks I always wore when I had to dress up. We shook hands and stood around the casket listening to the organ and the choir.

After the high-end wake, the choir was no surprise. I was half

expecting that Hector Crogan would fly in the Mormon Taber-
nacle Choir to sing Palestrina's *Stabat Mater* for Mrs. Stillmach.
The music was loud enough to give us pallbearers an excuse not
to attempt conversation.

More of Lenny's family and friends streamed in the doors. I
knew some of them, and I wound up in a receiving line of sorts, a
line I didn't want to be in. I heard the "He was so young" thing,
over and over. "Cause of death unknown" kept appearing in the
paper, which had everybody thinking that Lenny had committed
suicide, which I hated, because I didn't believe it. Have I said that
before? Maybe I thought about it too much.

First up was Addie. She wriggled her eyebrows and shook her
head just enough to say: *I tried, but it's posted on FDN.*

Maybe by now even more policies had turned up.

She shook my hand, then pulled me down close and said, "I
know the name Miranda Pryor because she works with you,
right?"

"Yeah," I said. "Why?"

"Same way she worked with Lenny?"

Her eyes scorched me like twin lasers.

"Addie, I know what it looks like," I said.

"Yeah," she said. "I hope they come after all Three Muske-
teers."

Then she walked away. I owed her for the blunt warning;
until this fiasco sorted itself out, her allegiances were to the insurance industry, the FBI, and the postal authorities. Hell, she'd
help Norton, too, if it came to that, and it would.

Behind her was Miranda, and she had the old rosary out and
wrapped around her hands, her fingernails painted one shade
lighter than the wooden beads. I watched her walk toward me in

an espresso-colored designer suit, matching heels, and sheer hose. Maybe it was the organ blaring, the smell of lilies, or the emotional turbulence, but I realized that if we ever did get married, it would probably be in this cathedral.

Eyes were on us, because everybody knew that Lenny had been out with me and Miranda the night he'd died, and we were the last to see him alive. Nobody was going to badger us here at high-lamentation tide, but soon people would sidle up to us and ask, "What happened?"

We hugged each other, and I whispered, "We're in trouble."

She looked at me like she knew that, but what else did I have for her?

"Will you sit with me," she said, with the same poorly concealed desperation that I'd appreciated so much late last night.

I showed her the pews where us pallbearers would end up. She squeezed my hand and whispered, "Norton's behind you," then she leaned into me suddenly, for another squeeze, kissed me on the cheek, and whispered, "I love you," and moved off, while us pallbearers tried not to watch her hips because it was a funeral.

Norton wore a black wool sport coat and a dove gray shirt with a silver satin tie, altogether the most elegantly dressed man in the church. His finery highlighted the professional distance between his position as the head of the Special Claims Department at one of the biggest companies in town and the shabby circumstances Lenny had managed to surround himself with at the end of his short life. Norton was here out of noblesse oblige for the mentally disabled, overpaid, salaried employees who ran his information-technology engines.

He shook my hand warmly, then put his arm on my shoulder, then his hand on the back of my head and shook it, just like I was a kid and he was the boss I never had.

He leaned forward, uttered a standard-issue condolence, and then said, "The office. Right after the cemetery. We need to talk. And Brent has sent you some e-mails."

Brent Slipper was Reliable's in-house counsel, which meant we had legal problems.

He took my right hand in both of his and said, "Time heals all wounds."

Father Fogarty did the honors without pausing to knock on the casket, while we pallbearers marched it up in front of the Communion rail and turned it sideways, so everybody could get a good look, study it during the service, and think about Lenny's dead body inside.

I sat one row back from the rest of the casket crew so I could be with Miranda, even though the guys looked at me like it was not protocol to sit with a babe when you were on pallbearer duty. The ceremonies included a concelebrated mass and a customized homily featuring four or five remembrances of Lenny loosely themed around the Five Sorrowful Mysteries. Fogarty put mind, body, heart, and soul into it, and stirred everyone with the proper mix of grief and consolation and the promise of redemption.

He sounded like Anubis reading from the Egyptian *Book of the Dead.* The deluxe service was a long one; I had plenty of time to remember my sins and what I used to think about at daily mass.

I felt Miranda getting the heebie-jeebies next to me whenever eternity was mentioned, and she trembled halfway through the Apostles' Creed where it said, "Christ suffered under Pontius Pilate, was crucified, died, and was buried. He descended to the dead . . . rose again . . . He will come again in glory to judge the living and the dead."

That means he'll judge you, too, Miranda.

But I'd save that for tonight.

"Eternal rest grant unto him, O Lord."

"And let perpetual light shine upon him."

It was all about eternity, and in grade school we had no trouble imagining eternity. We knew it better than our own backyard, because we'd had vivid metaphors wired into our heads and soldered in place with white-hot, nun fervor: *If a bird came, once every one thousand years, to sharpen its beak on the highest mountain in the world, when the mountain had been worn away from the bird sharpening its beak upon it, Eternity would have just begun.*

Normally, Miranda's religious fervors weren't catching, and normally I was merely bemused when she asked if I believed in hell. Here it was different. A casket with my best friend in it, a massive congregation of people who believed in everything I didn't. They were good people going to heaven because they all liked being together for some reason those of us in hell cannot comprehend. I wondered whether, since it meant so much to Miranda, I could see myself coming back to church on Sundays with her. I had my doubts. I had escaped the tractor beams of the Empire Church in the starship of a liberal arts education. I was a free spirit in the deep space beyond the twilight of the gods. Maybe.

I sensed Miranda was glad to have me next to her at a time like this, and she moved closer to me when I hit the timing just right on the "Lord have mercy" and the "Christ have mercy" during the Responses of the Faithful. Father Fogarty waved the altar boys over to meet him at the casket, where they held back the

sleeves of his vestments while the thurifer loaded the censer with
more incense. Then Fogarty took a trip around the casket, cere-
monially swinging plumes of smoke at the four corners. He took
another lap, waving his aspergillum like a grand marshal's swag-
ger stick and sprinkling holy water, first on Lenny's casket, then
on the crowds. I remembered to bless myself when I felt the
sprinkles land on my face.

Miranda and I had talked about the Catholic thing many
times, and I'd told her I didn't want to go back to thinking about
hell all day and going to the Godbox every Sunday. I subscribed
to the theology of Peter DeVries, who said, "It is the final proof
of God's omnipotence that He need not exist in order to save us."

Miranda didn't think that was the least bit funny and argued
that the church wasn't about hell anymore. According to her,
instead of high mass and high terror, it was Mass Lite, probably
created by the same people who'd brought her Hell Lite. She said
being a Catholic was easy nowadays, like being a Lutheran or an
Episcopalian. The church makes a real effort to put on a show of
joy these days. Maybe, but it wasn't something I was going to
experience at a funeral. All I had to accompany me here were hor-
monal memories of sin and death flooding my nervous system,
while I thought about Lenny shut up inside a coffin, full of sin,
and dead in life's prime.

"Eternal rest grant unto him, O Lord."

"And let perpetual light shine upon him."

I lost ten minutes of mass in daydreams and nightmares from
my altar-boy days, and the next time I came around, Father Fogarty said, "Let us offer each other a sign of peace."

I shook hands with everybody in arm's length, and Miranda
gave me a long hug and sobbed against me a few times. When I

looked over her shoulder, I saw Norton sitting with Addie, and instead of exchanging the sign of peace, they were exchanging information. They were working, while my brain was locked up running grief processes, error checking, scanning for corrupted files in the life and times of Lenny Stillmach.

When I got back into his e-mail folders later that night, I could probably figure just when he'd gotten the AIDS and just how he'd played it before and after he'd sold the policies to Heartland.

Maybe Miranda had seen Norton, too. She didn't know Addie, but she'd recognize her as an Industry Someone, and maybe that's why she was clutching me. Miranda also had to think about the best time to file her claim for three hundred thousand dollars as a beneficiary on Lenny's life policy. She'd probably wait until the autopsy and medical examiner stuff came in, and they had a cause of death.

And what would Norton advise Addie or Pete at Guaranteed Investment Mutual Trust to do? If somebody filed a claim for three hundred grand on a Reliable policy under similar circumstances, Norton's first thought would be how to deny the claim, because it was in his job description, and it was still in the two-year contestability period. Sometimes outright denial and the right lawyers could make the other side settle for fifty cents on the dollar or less. But Pete and Norton also had to consider that Miranda would have no trouble attracting a first-rate lawyer, and the first-rate lawyer might take Guaranteed Investment Mutual to trial looking for the death benefit and punitive damages for breaching their duty of good faith to pay on claims.

Guaranteed also had to consider Miranda sitting at the plaintiff's table in a good little Catholic-girl skirt and sweater or vest, a

demure ensemble that would remind the jury of the uniforms
she'd worn as a young lady at Duchesne. Perhaps a small, plain
gold crucifix would be twinkling in the crushed wool of her lapel.
Her lawyer would describe her as a young Catholic woman with
a big heart who sacrificed her free time to care for a dying AIDS
victim. "And when this troubled young man tried to repay his
angel of mercy with the only thing he owned in this world—his
life insurance policy with Guaranteed Investment Mutual
Trust—the company broke the promise it made to Leonard Stillmach. Guaranteed Investment Mutual Trust took Mr. Stillmach's premiums every month for TWO YEARS and then
refused to pay a dime to Miranda Pryor, his angel of mercy,
whose name he'd so carefully written on Exhibit A when he'd
chosen her as his beloved beneficiary."

Guaranteed's best hope would be to ask Norton to process
the policy for them, then Norton could assign Miranda to the file
and hope that she would deny her own claim by sheer force of
habit.

And if Lenny had been the dirty insider for a viatical scam
outfit, Norton would probably call the archbishop and make a
ten-thousand-dollar charitable donation to the Catholic church,
contingent on Lenny's body being buried nowhere near conse-
crated ground.

We struggled through the service until it came time for Communion. I begged off on taking the Eucharist, because I remembered that it is a mortal sin to eat a Host unless you really believe
it's the Body of Jesus Christ. Miranda looked at me with the
usual disappointment, then she took my hand in hers and gave
me another, closer look. This one said, "Believe with me, just for
today, please?" So I went with her.

Fogarty said, "The Body of Christ."

I said, "Amen," and ate my first Host in at least ten years.

I went back to the pew with Miranda, knelt next to her, bowed my head, clasped my hands together, closed my eyes, and moved as close to her as I could.

I wasn't praying. I was pondering whether God would send me to hell because I ate a Host to please Miranda. Would God do this, even if I didn't quite believe in him, Hosts, eternal damnation, or Miranda?

17

NOT RIGHT, NOT WRONG

FATHER FOGARTY RODE WITH Vera Stillmach at the head of the motorcade over to Calvary Cemetery for a graveside ceremony and personalized memorial.

Miranda had her own car, as usual, and when it was all finally over and just before we parted, I said, "We gotta talk. Tonight."

She said, "Come by my house after work."

I moved in close to hug her, watching her eyes, looking for any clue to what she'd done. I got no reading, only her looking back at me, as if she were wondering the same thing about me.

On the way to my car, I saw Charlie Becker, the homicide detective and part-time regional investigator, coming out of the cemetery's main building, cell phone pushed in his ear, frowning, jabbering. He had a tie and a sport coat on for the occasion.

As I imagined it, a career in law enforcement had brought him up close and personal with hundreds of sudden, tragic deaths, where his duty was to be a peace officer, a decent human being, and a collector of quality information if it was a death unknown.

Only trouble was, he was late. He looked as if he'd stopped in the cemetery office to pick up a plot map, only to be informed that the services for Lenny were already over.

He didn't greet me, he just walked up, put his phone away, and started talking to me.

"I've been reading a lot about life insurance," he said. "And these whattaya-call-'ems? Viagra-tals?" he added with a sly grin. "I hate to read. Then I remembered: hey, I know a guy who knows all about this stuff. Why don't I find Carver Hartnett and have him explain life insurance and veggie-tales to me."

I looked at the mourners heading back to the cars in huddled clusters of two and three.

"Right now?" I asked.

"Tomorrow morning. Nine o'clock. Come down and see me. I'll call your boss and get you out of half a day's work."

"That's okay," I said. "I can take the morning off."

"We got a preliminary autopsy protocol on Lenny," he said. "Something is not right."

"What's wrong?"

"I didn't say something is wrong. I said it's not right. Tomorrow morning you teach me about selling life insurance policies, and I'll teach you about not-right autopsy reports."

"I'll be there," I said.

"Yep," he said, "and make sure you are there, because I got enough to charge you and your girlfriend right now, and the minute you do something that looks like flight, I'll charge you both on the spot. We got a detention facility in the basement of the station. I can hold you for forty-eight hours on next to nothing, and it's colder than a frozen pump handle down there. They don't give you blankets because you might hang yourself with them."

He wasn't angry or belligerent about it. He even fished the Old Golds out of his inside pocket and shook one out for me.

"Charge us with what?" I asked.

"She said the computer was off when you found Lenny, right?" he asked. "And when I asked you about that, you said you couldn't *remember* whether it was on or off. Does that sound right to you? Are you the kind of guy who isn't going to notice if Lenny's computer was on or off?"

"It was on," I said. "She didn't want people to know he had porno on the screen when he died."

"Then she tells me you all were on your way to that rave they busted up there at the Omaha Indian Reservation, but you didn't say anything about it, even though I asked you twice if you went anywhere between the Upstream and the casino."

"Because we didn't go anywhere," I said. "We were going to go, but we decided not to."

"And then, after I tell you twice not to hide drugs from me, we find a little envelope in Lenny's pants with three tabs of Ecstasy in it, and Ecstasy is what kids take at raves, right?"

Instead of lying and saying I didn't know about the E, I had to think about what would happen if Becker had gotten lucky and found the guy who sold it to me. I tried to nod without making it look like I agreed with him.

"Something's not right," he said, "and every time I try to find out why, people hide things from me, or their stories don't match."

"I feel the same way," I said. "Tonight I'm going through

some of his computer files—files from work, so I can try to figure out just what he did."

"Well, good for you," said Becker, "if you think the computer will tell you what happened, but be at my place by nine. I'm not saying something is wrong. I'm saying something is not right. Do you understand the difference? But if you're suddenly missing, I'm going to know something is wrong, and I'll come find you."

"Yes, sir," I said.

"Meanwhile," he said, mashing his cigarette butt out with the toe of his shoe, "I'm going to go stop them putting that body in the ground, so we can have another look at it."

18

DOUBLE INDEMNITY

I WAS BACK IN my cube by midafternoon, and the Dag had thoughtfully stuffed my real inbox with wads of papers and "to do" notes. Apparently Norton's plan was to dump any and all paperwork concerned with the demise of Leonard Stillmach on Miranda and me, probably because he blamed us for not keeping Lenny in line and alive long enough to prevent his inevitable self-destruction from upsetting the office.

So, not only did I have to determine the extent of Lenny's life insurance pillaging and plundering, I also had to review and respond to the all the e-mail traffic coming out of Human Resources about the claims of alleged national-origin discrimination against the twenty dead Mohammed Bilkos.

The EEOC had indeed launched the dreaded form torrent: twenty different notifications of charges, one for each of the dead Mohammed Bilkos we had discriminated against; twenty different requests for information, twenty different incident reports, and so on.

Brent Slipper, the in-house Human Resources lawyer, had clogged my virtual inbox with e-mails pertaining to the charges. He was ecstatic at the prospect of a real investigation, which would be his chance to justify the VP designation on his letterhead and all of those zeroes after his name on the company payroll. With any luck the Mohammed Bilko affair would spawn a federal complaint with interrogatories and requests for documents, which meant that the legality of those requests as well as the privileged nature of communications had to be researched, drafted up in memos, asserted in replies to the agency and to the courts. All of which would help Slipper refute his detractors upstairs who argued long ago that we should get rid of the in-house HR lawyering and send all of this discrimination and harassment nonsense to boutique employment law firms—specialists who do nothing all day every day but make government drones at the EEOC work lots harder than they want to, until they go away.

The government's testers had Lenny cold on tape saying, "We don't pay on Nigerian death claims." Not to mention a double-whammy national-origin-cum-racial slur: "You sabby, Mr. Wunga Bunga?" They would love to play that one back for the jury and watch the eyes of twelve righteous citizens catch fire with that send-a-message fervor.

Reliable had defenses aplenty. Most corporations try to show good faith by firing anybody accused of discrimination or harassment, even if the "harassment" was just an off-color joke or a moment of weakness in which an otherwise impeccable special investigator might suggest that an insurance claim coming out of

Nigeria or Russia should be examined with an extra modicum of care. In Lenny's case, Reliable had not only fired the detestable discriminator, he was dead, too. Our message to the EEOC would be: Dig him up and pound wooden stakes into his vile and prejudiced heart if it makes you feel better, but the source of the alleged national-origin discrimination at Reliable Allied Trust was gone forever.

Next, even if in the government's ossified bureaucratic imagination Lenny's thought crimes had somehow survived him and polluted all of us people-of-no-prejudices-whatsoever he left behind at Reliable, there was this: Lenny was mentally ill, certifiably manic-depressive. We'd call his doctors to the stand if the government wanted proof positive. Reliable Allied Trust was required by law (the Americans with Disabilities Act) to accommodate Lenny's disability (bipolar personality disorder) and its symptoms, which included behaviors such as calling a Nigerian lawyer "Mr. Wunga Bunga." Attached to yet another memo from Slipper, J.D., were several sexual harassment cases balancing the rights of women who didn't want to hear vulgar language against the rights of men afflicted with Tourette's syndrome, who couldn't stop themselves from muttering: "Cunt sucker! Dick licker! Go fuck your mother in bed, ya little prick." Stuff like that, and according to the photocopied case summaries Brent had found, the potty-mouthed guys who grew up riding in the short buses won every time.

Looking over all of the paperwork, I had a sudden fond hope that maybe Norton had been talking about the dead Nigerians when he'd said at the funeral that we needed to meet as soon as possible. That would be a stroll around the duck pond at the mall compared with meeting about Lenny and Heartland Viatical.

I sent GothicRage86 an e-mail from my work machine and told him outright that Lenny was dead. I explained that if someone had been there at Lenny's place Friday night, they could possibly help us figure out what had happened to him. I asked him to send the image file from the Attila-at-Home cam of whoever was there that night with Lenny. I told him to send it to my home machine, CarvedMeat@home.com.

Before I could get through more clamped bundles of paper, my phone rang and the Dag summoned me to Norton's place.

Norton was still dressed up in his funeral-go-to-meeting clothes, but now he looked grim and weary. He showed me to a chair under my own cone of light, but then instead of going around to the throne behind his desk, he pulled up another visitor's chair and sat next to me, right out there in the open. I was touched, thinking it was his way of telling me that he wouldn't be interrogating me with his Truster software or his thermo-dermo technologies—not that he couldn't still have them running in the background.

He arranged his chair just so, at an angle to mine, like he was the host and I was a guest on a talk show. On his left hand where his wedding band used to be was a gold ring with a purple stone inset with Knights of Aksarben insignias. He glanced at the crowded console alongside his desk, and for a second I thought he was probably checking our position relative to a minicam running somewhere, so he could record our conversation in digital video.

"When I was a kid, my dad took me to the movies on Saturday afternoons," said Norton. "I remember sitting in the old Admiral Theater eating popcorn, right next to my dad, the best insurance investigator in town, while both of us watched Edward

G. Robinson playing Keyes, the insurance investigator in *Double Indemnity*. Remember that one?"

"I've seen it," I said, "on video."

"Instead of dying like a dirty rat," said Norton, "Edward G. was a good guy in that one. An honest insurance investigator who went to bed every night with balled up fists and clenched teeth, dreaming about the crooked swindlers and con men he was going to catch the next day."

"It's a classic," I said, "especially in our line of work."

"And remember Keyes had that little man in the pit of his stomach who told him when he had a rotten claim on his desk?"

I nodded, and Norton's eyes glazed with moisture and sentiment.

"And remember when Keyes said"—and Norton barked just like old Edward G.—"'Every time one of those phony claims comes along it ties knots in my stomach!'"

"I remember," I said, and I took a closer look at Norton, trying to figure where he was going with this, until I noticed with horror that Norton looked on the verge of crying. He was tearing up, by God, and it collided with everything I thought I knew about him.

The rage and bitterness at the diminished stature of the Special Investigations Unit was nothing new, but the intensity had reached a new pitch.

"That was back when being a crackerjack insurance investigator meant something to the company," said Norton. "Back in those days, we were the ones who made sure that the company didn't throw more money out the window than it took in the door."

It couldn't hurt to commiserate with the poor old guy. I felt some of the same resentment, even though, compared with him, I was practically an infant in the business.

"Now they don't care about throwing money out the window," I said.

"That's right," he said eagerly, as if I were the only other person left on earth who understood how it worked. "They don't care because they just charge the customers more who come in the door. These days it's the product-development people, the marketing people, the sales teams. They're the stars. Why? Because they figure out new ways to make honest people pay the insurance fraud bills."

"It's upside down," I said.

"Don't tell those customers that twenty or thirty percent of their premium is money we throw out the window paying on bogus claims filed by fraudsters."

I shook my head like, *What can you do?* And that was just how I felt. Norton was right, but so what? What was he getting at?

"Look at us," he said and threw open his hands to nothing. "Fraudsters are easy to understand," said Norton. "They do it for the money. Why do we do what we do?"

I decided it was rhetorical, so I wouldn't have to answer. Not for the money, that was for sure.

"Because we're just good, honest people?" he asked.

We both knew that was ridiculous.

"No," said Norton. "We do it because we hate fraudsters. That charlatan who fed you forged documents, lied to you about his kids having cancer, cried on the phone about his liposuction and massage bills? You hate him, and you don't want to see him walk away with other people's money ever again."

He was right, and normal people in other walks of life don't feel the same loathing for scammers we do—that is, unless the normal people personally got screwed top to bottom, front and back by a fraudster. Only then do they understand the passions of our daily crusade, but usually not before.

"When my old man caught a grifter trying to run one past him, he had a budget! He could hire ex-FBI men and do something about it. He could enlist Hoover's G-men if he had to and go after the cons with all the rage of a fool-killing gale."

Norton was misty again. "I used to feel the same way he did about fraudsters," he said, "until—" and he paused.

Whoa. Was Norton insinuating that he didn't hate fraudsters anymore? Heresy in this department. He was right about one thing: None of us were here for the money. We could make more elsewhere as noninvestigators, and a lot more if we went crooked and decided to fleece the deep pockets that paid our mercenary wages.

"I had a long talk with Addie Frenzer over at Omaha Beneficial," said Norton.

I nodded and noticed the Dead Man Norton newsreels and testimonials still playing on his wall flat panel. And behind Norton, the Council Bluffs casinos glittering in the middle distance. The view had caused me to consider more than once that insurance is just a white-collar, more loosely regulated species of gaming, somewhere between dice and the stock market.

I felt something resembling pity for Old Man Norton.

"Remember when you went upstairs with the PowerPoint presentations and told them about these viatical outfits buying and selling life policies?"

"Lenny and I," I said.

"Since then, we've paid Heartland on a lot of viaticated

claims. We paid on a lot of medical claims to Crogan's brother-in-law, Dr. Guttman, and the Heartland Clinics. That's why I had two investigators check them out. And I had no reason to suspect that they were giving me anything but the truth. Did I?"

"They being—?"

"Lenny and Miranda," he said shortly. "And now it seems that Lenny was working a side game with them, doing just what we're not sure, or so the sales of these policies of his would suggest."

"How many policies are we talking about?" I asked, partly because I hadn't made up my mind how many to tell him I knew about.

"Well, we don't know that yet, do we?" he said.

The twinkle in his eye meant he was probably deciding how many to tell me about, also.

"I found two," I offered, vowing that I'd tell him about Miranda's after I gave her a chance to explain it, or find the policy and destroy it. Pretend it never happened. "Both beneficiaries affiliated with Heartland Viatical in some capacity."

I waited for him to volunteer any others he knew about.

"We are being canvassed on the Fraud Defense Network," said Norton. "It's like we're decorated, veteran vice detectives being charged with pandering and solicitation."

As far as Norton was concerned, he and I were peering into the dark abyss, the perverted state of modern-day industry affairs, where instead of having thirty ex-detectives for investigators, he'd been forced to hire a manic-depressive hacker like Lenny Stillmach. I should have known what was coming; it was Nub City time.

"When I was your age," he said, "I remember going down to

a hellhole hamlet in southern Mississippi, where I found a whole
town full of people who were almost all missing at least one finger—some were missing two or three fingers."

"Nub City," I said.

Norton gasped. "I told you about Nub City?"

If it was alcohol that made him forget how many times he'd
told us about Nub City, then I'd have to quit drinking before the
same happened to me. Pretty soon, he would ask me if I'd found
myself a gal yet.

Norton would go on telling us about Nub City until he died
or retired. Nub City was not the real name of the town, only its
industry nickname because half the population had mutilated
themselves and filed accident and disability claims in one of the
largest fraud rings Old Man Norton had ever busted, before his
budget was cut.

"I told you the Nub City story?"

I could see just a glimmer of panic, as if he were afraid I'd
come right out and say, *Yes, you told me the Nub City story several
times.*

The point of the story was to make us realize the forces of
human depravity at work in this business. A whole town where
people mangled themselves and their kin just for the insurance
money, and lawyers, doctors, EMTs—everybody was in on it. In
Norton's view, it was a tale from the crypt about despicable,
venal, money-grubbing, subhuman fraudsters who would do
anything for a buck. He didn't realize that modern, newbie, info-
tech investigators were more inclined to pity anybody who would
cut off their own fingers for money, even if they were fakers and
charlatans. I mean, think about working your keyboard minus a
few fingers.

"The honor, the prestige, the integrity," said Norton. "All gone. We were honest investigators. No! We were *insurance detectives* protecting honest people from con artists, who were out to steal any way they could. Now, who is honest? Who cares if the fraudsters take our customers' money? That's why somebody like Lenny goes bad. He sees the industry doesn't care about fraud anymore. So he says, 'Fine, I'll help myself.'"

"What do you think he was doing?" I asked.

Norton shook his head and grinned, as if to say, *How simple and wonderful that would be: a fraud veteran like me just telling you what I think.*

If anybody really knew, it was probably Norton. For forty years he'd lifted rocks on the claims landscape and watched every fraud mutation known to man crawl out from underneath. He'd interviewed firebugs who'd burned buildings with people in them for the insurance money, trailer-court trash who'd maimed their own children for the disability claims, and, Miranda's favorite, married couples who turned on each other and staged the "accidental" death of their spouses for term life insurance payouts.

"The insurance business has contended with people willing to kill themselves or someone else for money since the dawn of the industry," said Norton.

One of his favorite riffs. The latest scam always appears to be ingenious, but look closer and it's usually just a variation on some ancient treachery—older than the cat in the bag, the pig in the poke, the nectar in Venus's-flytrap, the Greek assassins inside the Trojan horse. Look up *fraud* in a good dictionary, the roots go to all the old languages: Latin, Sanskrit, Old Norse. The primatologists say that even monkeys practice deception to conceal newly discovered food from the rest of the troop, or to sneak a little forbidden sex on the side with the alpha male's favorite female. Fraud variations appear now and then, but the central engine never changes: Tell clever lies to gullible people until they give you their money for nothing. Telemarketers, boiler-room stockbrokers, herbal-supplement salesmen—gifted storytellers one and all. And what was Lenny's story?

"It could be as simple as that," Norton continued. "Our friend Lenny probably sensed that he wasn't long for this world because of his chosen lifestyle, so he loaded up on life insurance policies for fun and profit. He sold some for profit, and maybe for fun he decided to go out big and leave money behind for family—and friends?"

Was Norton suggesting that he knew about Miranda's policy? Maybe. If so, his theory was fine, except for some timing issues. If Lenny wanted to kill himself and leave three hundred thousand to Miranda, he knew enough to wait until the policy with her name on it was outside the contestability period. Then her policy would be just like the ones he'd sold to Heartland—incontestable. A near cash equivalent, only question being: Who gets the money?

"I can see him doing something shady," I said, "but I can't see him killing himself for money. Something else happened."

"That's the second time you've insisted that it's not a suicide," said Norton, "which makes me wonder why you're so quick to rule it out?"

He kept giving me a special look, as if all of this had double or triple meanings I wasn't getting.

"I can't prove it," I said. "Maybe he accidentally overdosed. But not on purpose."

Norton shrugged. "A distinction without a difference. Lenny slowly and intentionally poisoned himself with drugs, or he speeded things up and took them all at once one night. Does it matter which?" After a staged pause, he added, "Unless he had another, newer life insurance policy that was still contestable? Then whether it was a suicide would be important."

The Old Man could just send me a letter and tell me that he knew about Miranda's policy. Instead he wanted all of this unpleasantness confined to unspoken understandings—things we would take for granted but never discuss, like denying Nigerian life insurance claims.

Norton was not often wrong in this business, but this time unspoken wasn't good enough for me; I wanted to hear him say it, so I came out and asked him.

"Do you really believe that Lenny would buy life insurance policies on himself, sell them, gamble away the proceeds, and then kill himself, knowing that outfits like Heartland Viatical are making forty cents on his dollar?"

Norton liberated himself from his chair and paced around in deep-think mode. He began one of his customary lectures, and in his dark formal clothes he looked like a learned docent, giving me a historical minilecture and guided tour at the museum of fraud.

"In ancient Rome, people offered themselves for execution to amuse the public for five *minae*—about a hundred bucks in our money—the sum to be paid to their heirs. Historians say that the market was so competitive, candidates would offer to be beaten to death rather than beheaded, because slow, painful death provided more of a spectacle for the Colosseum crowds. That's why it used to be that we didn't pay on suicide claims. Period. Because people *will* kill themselves for money, even if it gets paid out only after they're dead, and even if they can't spend it themselves. Now of course there's that blasted two-year rule."

He crumpled up a *Wall Street Journal* and threw it in the wastebasket, as if that's what he'd do with the two-year rule if he had anything to say about it.

The insurance experts, the lawmakers, and the courts had formulated the two-year contestability period as a sensible modern compromise in the holy war against life insurance fraud and suicide for profit. The experts must have reasoned as follows: Sure, there are lots of desperate guys with big money problems and mouths to feed who would buy a policy and do themselves to leave three hundred thousand, tax-free, for the wife and kids. But desperation and patience seldom coincide in the same forebrain, so the industry put in a provision that makes suicidal desperadoes wait two years and pay two years' worth of premiums before the company will pay on death by suicide. Plus underwriting keeps a tight rein on the amounts and won't write a policy for more than five times your annual salary. Then they do a thorough job of screening out anybody mental enough to kill themselves for five years' salary paid to their kin.

"We did a lot of legitimate business with Heartland Viatical," said Norton, "including paying on legitimate viaticated policies. We've also paid on medical claims to the Heartland Clinics. It's important for us that this company's legitimate business dealings with Heartland aren't contaminated by whatever lunatic Lenny had going with them on the side. These policies showing up accelerates things. We have to go into full damage-control mode. Now."

I nodded and waited.

"Did Lenny scam Heartland?" I asked. "Or did Heartland and Lenny scam the insurance companies?"

"It's painful," said Norton, "and hard for you to accept, but this looks to be all Lenny. My dad liked to quote Mr. Alexander Colin Campbell, who wrote the definitive study on insurance crime back in 1902: 'The lure of life insurance money stands as a constant bribe to inhumanity.' That's what's happened here."

Again, I reimagined Lenny as a conniving fraudster, heisting life insurance money, scamming Heartland, scamming their investors.

"He wasn't working with anyone else here in Special Investigations," said Norton. "We hope."

I was supposed to pour this into my brain and stir it around.

"Or," he added, "if someone else is involved, we need to know now, so we can cut the cord and set them adrift, as well. Is someone else in Special Investigations involved?"

TARLON ASHWATER

It was after six and already winter dark by the time I got away from Norton and in-house counsel Brent Slipper. I was in a hurry to get over to Miranda's and extract some truth, even if I had to tie her in a chair and burn bamboo shoots under her fingernails.

Rush hour is more like rush half hour in Omaha, but traffic was still clogging the lanes and trapping cars in their metered places. I barely noticed an ancient, bruise-colored pickup with sideboards held in place by baling wire, idling in the parking lane and halfway into the crosswalk.

An old guy, seventy at least but burly as a dwarf oak, crawled out of the truck in a Western-cut wool jacket and mud-spattered boots. The license plate was a high-numbered one from outstate. He looked like he'd walked off the set of *Gunsmoke,* wearing a bolo tie and a black hat with deep curves in it, the baked leather skin around his blue eyes scored by sun and wind.

"Sir, are you Mr. Carver Hartnett?"

He had papers in hand, and a glossy magazine of some kind that turned out to be the annual report I'd seen in Norton's office last week. He looked back at Reliable's building, as if he'd just watched me walk out of there, and then pointed at my photo and the article about me and Lenny.

He didn't wait for me to answer.

"Sir, my name is Tarlon Ashwater," he said, "I don't mean to catch you in a hurry, sir. I just want a few minutes of your time, because I've tried all day to see somebody, anybody at your company."

I'd remember a name like that, and I didn't. He probably had a claim that had been denied. Probably wasn't even special enough to make it to Special Claims. Security was done letting him through the locked-glass doors, because Customer Service had already told him no three times, and now here he was.

"I can't help you process a claim," I said. "I'm an investigator. My boss assigns me claims; I don't take complaints from customers. You have to make an appointment to see one of our agents."

"I'm done making appointments," he said, and his eyes flashed like the blue tips of acetylene torches. "There's no time left for that."

He looked like he'd smile for me if I wanted him to, but he wasn't kidding.

I was just about to lope off and leave him where he was, because I could hear a growl creeping in the back of his throat, and I didn't want to deal with some cranky codger's disability claim. He even had two fingers missing on one hand, so he could have driven in from Nub City for all I knew.

Then he waved the papers at me and said, "Mr. Hartnett, sir, I'm the owner of an insurance policy for one hundred thousand dollars on the life of a Mr. Leonard Stillmach issued by your company, Reliable Allied Trust, and I want to talk to somebody about getting paid."

He pronounced it IN-surance. I walked over close enough for a look at the paper, and he handed it to me. The letterhead was from Heartland Viatical. It was addressed to Mr. Tarlon T. Ashwater at a rural route address in Mullen, Nebraska, out past nowhere in the middle of the Nebraska Sandhills.

It was a letter from Heartland to its investors describing the life insurance policies owned by the company and held in escrow. It even listed the policy numbers and the insurance companies that had issued them. I'd heard it was common practice for viatical investors to call in to the life insurance companies once a week like crows and cormorants circling over drought-stricken livestock, asking, "Has policy number 765364 matured yet?" But it was supposed to be anonymous and by policy number only. Maybe Ashwater had simply watched the *World-Herald* and found the reference to Reliable in Lenny's obit? Then found both of us in the annual report?

The list of policies included several from Reliable Allied Trust, and next to one of them Ashwater, or somebody else, had written, "Leonard Stillmach, deceased, 12/15/2001." Two other names had also been written above and below Lenny's, presumably next to policies issued by other companies. But they'd been crossed out.

"You need to take this to Heartland Viatical," I said. "They own the policies, or you do, I guess, I don't know how it works.

You invested in their company, and I think they own the policies for you, or maybe you even bought them outright, but they hold them for you in escrow?"

"Sir, I've been to Heartland Viatical," he said. "I'll go back there if I have to, but I hoped to find a way to solve this through the IN-surance company."

Ashwater looked over my shoulder.

"Look," he said, "I don't mean to make you stand out here in the street discussing business. I see a Budweiser sign over there on the side of that brick building, and I'm dry. How about I buy you a beer and tell you what I know about how this Heartland outfit works?"

It was a hole-in-the-wall bar with O'CONNELL'S PUB painted in faded letters on the brick façade. I didn't see the harm in explaining to him once and for all over a beer that Reliable couldn't help him. And maybe he had some useful dirt on Heartland.

"You wanna ride, then?" he asked. "Or you wanna walk and I'll meet ya?"

I looked in the truck at the torn upholstery and wooden boxes of tools. He even had a rifle in the gun rack, and noticed me looking at it.

"Varmint rifle," he said. "Two-fifty Winchester. Killed its share of prairie dogs, rock chuck, and coyotes."

"I think I'll stretch my legs and meet you over there," I said.

Ashwater tipped his hat. "Thank you, sir. And God bless your kindness."

THERE WAS SOMETHING about having a seventy-year-old Sandhills rancher call me "sir" like he meant it; that's why I went with him. And he had enough hard-luck stories to turn my hair white.

Three years ago, when he was flush, he'd invested one hundred thousand dollars with Heartland Viatical because he'd seen an ad in the paper promising quick 25 percent returns on "insurance-grade" investments. He'd grown up on his father's commercial ranch, twenty thousand acres south of Mullen on the Dismal River up in Hooker County. When he was barely twenty, he was out fencing and digging out a cattle gate with his old man, who stood up, clutched his chest, and died. Ashwater and his wife took over the land and ran a cow-calf operation for more than fifty years. Then interest rates went up and the drought came, worse than he'd ever seen it. The bank took the cattle first, then they took the land. His wife got leukemia. It went away once; now it was back, and he couldn't pay the medicine and hospital bills, because he was nothing but a hired man at the purebred ranch up the river.

"All I need is my money back," he said.

I tried to tell him that if anybody was going to pay him, it was the people he'd given his money to in the first place—Heartland—not the insurance companies that had issued the policies.

We finished the first beer, and he ordered another with a shot of Jim Beam, so I took a shot of Macallan with mine.

"I'm done talking to Heartland," he said. "I might do something else to them, but it won't involve words."

"Why?" I asked. "What happened?"

"I get told I own policies," he said, "but I never see any money. This is the third policy that's due to pay, and it's the third time they say I ain't getting paid out of this one. I don't even want the twenty-five percent. Just my money back."

"Have you tried calling the Nebraska attorney general's office?"

"Time is all gone, sir," he said. "Lawyers and such won't do me or my wife any good. If I have to, I'll kill as many as I can with the varmint rifle, and then I'll go before her when the government snipers take me out."

He dropped the shot of Jim down the hatch, sucked his teeth once hard, and said, "Sweet spirits of fire," while I wondered if he meant it about using the rifle, and if so whether I'd qualify as varmint.

"It's like my grandpa used to say when he started missing chickens," he said. "Lose one chicken and it's dumb bad luck. Lose two and it's probably coincidence. But when the third chicken goes missing, you can be dead sure that the coyotes are eating the chickens, drinking your beer, and playing pinochle rummy in the chicken house while you and the missus are counting sheep. And this, sir, is the third policy gone missing."

I tried to take the sting out of it for him. If Heartland was bilking investors, I explained, then maybe there'd be an investigation and they'd get busted. I could see by the set of his jaw and the cold fire in his eyes that none of it mattered if Ashwater didn't get his money back by Sunday.

"Out where I come from, if lightning kills your prize bull, the IN-surance company sends a vet out to look at the dead animal, and they pay the claim. We don't begrudge paying premiums to the IN-surance men in the Sandhills, because when you file a claim, they generally pay. Here's an IN-sured life, and it's gone, so all I'm saying, sir, is let's get around the cheaters. Pay me, instead of them."

I took a good fifteen minutes and another beer and shot of scotch to lay it all out for him. I tried to tell him he had a court case, not an insurance claim, but he wouldn't listen.

By then it was almost seven, and I just wanted to get away and go see Miranda. I was crashing again on alcohol and no sleep. Finally I made shift with a ploy and told him that I'd put his proposition before Old Man Norton, just to see if there was some way around Heartland.

I knew it was a mistake as soon as it came out of my mouth, because he seized on it like it was the Shield of Faith and Hope itself, even though I told him the chances were 99 to 1 against him.

I said I had to go, but out where he came from saying you "had to go" probably meant you'd mosey on back home before the ten-o'clock cattle-and-hog report, because he kept right on talking.

"Well, sir," he said, "I been to thirty-some county fairs and several goat-fuckings, but I ain't never seen the like of this."

I shook my head and looked at my watch, while he went off on a tear about how if outfits like Heartland could just take his money, then they were nothing but human coyotes.

I agreed, I said, but I had to go now. Well, he said, if I agreed, then I had to stay for a good coyote story.

I decided to wind things up by signaling for the bill.

"When you live in a big city like Omaha, instead of on the land, you get distorted views," he said. "One time the U.S. government sent a Fish and Wildlife female officer to Mullen, and we had a big meeting at the schoolhouse, where she got up wearing a uniform and told all the ranchers to stop shooting the coyotes. She said there were other more humane ways to control the coyote population, and that the federal government was going to fix the coyote problem by neutering the male coyotes.

"We all looked at each other like she was a Martian, of

course, and then we had to set her straight. 'Ma'am,' we said, 'the coyotes ain't having sexual relations with the livestock, they're killing them and eating them.'"

He showed me his teeth and waited for me to laugh, so I did. He called me sir several more times and thanked me. Then I paid the bill over his protests and left for Miranda's.

All the way to her place, Ashwater's stories echoed in my head, where they got all mixed up with everything else I knew and didn't know. Vulpine Lenny had slaughtered and gorged in the industry henhouse, that was clear, because there were three policies out there, at least. Maybe Miranda was just another chicken he'd had, or else she was Cher Fox standing guard outside, while Master Reynard rampaged within and drank his fill of hot blood?

I was on my way to find out.

SLOW MOTION

She met me at the door in a long Italian suede skirt, boots, and a dip-dyed shell with clingy spandex ribbing. "Merino wool," she said. "Touch it." And we did.

She had the big-bowled crystal cabernet glasses out, and bottles with fancy labels all around: reserve this, estate bottled that, signature this, barrel select that.

She had a Bible open on the table and Great-Grandma Zoe's rosary was out of its missile silo and within easy reach, She put it away, closed the Bible, and opened a *Wine Spectator* to show me an article on recent fluctuations in the Vintage Port Index.

"Do they have any articles in there about really posh detox units and Betty Ford–type clinics?" I asked.

"Of course not," she crooned in a French accent. "Wine enthusiasts aren't alcoholics, they are passionate connoisseurs and collectors of the winemakers' art."

"I don't know," I said, "I see them get just as drunk as the next fiddler's bitch."

"I think it was Alexandre Dumas," she continued, "who said that wine is the intellectual part of the meal, meats are merely the material part."

"Yeah, and I hear they had to bury old Al's prodigious intellectual liver separately."

"It's heart medication," she said. "It prevents coronary disease by cleansing the arteries of fatty cholesterol. It contains flavinoids, resveratrol, and antioxidants, and those all prevent cancer."

"I know," I said. "All I'm saying is that a bottle or two will turn you into a knee-walking, fogmatic calamity."

"It's health food, and you need to drink as much as possible."

She was only half ironic, filling my glass as she pattered along with more wine health factoids. True, she never got totally swozzled, but once a week or so she'd start mixing up her vowels and consonants before she called it a night. True, she jogged it off every morning and kept her 10K times under forty minutes and had the shape to prove it. But if she was enthusiastic about wine every night for twenty years or so, the way Norton had been enthusiastic about single-cask Islay scotches, then she'd probably start exhibiting some of the same characteristic emotional deficits and premature memory loss that he did, and if I married her, I'd have to put up with it.

She had her legs crossed, knee-on-slender-knee, with the slit in the skirt falling away on the rondure of her calf in textured black tights.

"If you ever have a kid, are you gonna go nine months without a glass of Pouilly-Fuissé?"

She was nothing but Sub-Zero, like her kitchen appliances,

even though Pouilly-Fuissé was charged with intimate sentiment, not because we ever drank it. Lenny used to call it pussy-Fuissé and went out of his way to order it just that way, whenever he was with Miranda and me.

I thought it was funny.

"I don't know," she said. "I'll discuss that with my husband."

She was pushing me like a sore tooth, which was fine with me. The more tone I got out of her the better, because it would help convince me, again, that she'd be no good for me. What did I want with a melancholic, alcoholic, Catho-holic wife? I should go find somebody normal and sober. An occasional Lite beer drinker, maternal, honest, and agnostic; one who didn't believe in hell would be better for me, and I had to be ready to go find one, if things didn't work out here, and soon.

First, I meant to find out if she was dealing off the bottom. If she was just another swindle sister, I had to be ready to walk out the door and not come back. All the way back to my place I'd be wanting to turn the car around, but I wouldn't, because she was an alcoholic-in-training. Yes! A hired liar, Mistress Sham, a con artist, a Bible-beating, obsessive-compulsive, geno-eroto-hetero-sex-o-phobic, disordered personality.

She was all dressed up, as usual, but not even Calvin Klein covered up nervous exhaustion. Feeling sorry for her was not on the schedule. The longer I studied her symptoms the less they had to do with Lenny and the more to do with herself. Maybe she was apprehensive about Becker or Norton finding out about that three-hundred-thousand-dollar life policy with her name on it, especially now that e-canvassing was in progress on the Fraud Defense Network. Pete Westfall at Guaranteed might not respond to Reliable, figuring he'd already sent me the info, but anybody seeing Addie's query would send policy info on Leonard Stillmach to her, and she'd in turn send it to Norton, or any other member who asked for it.

"You still worried I'm gonna turn on you?" I asked.

She wasn't afraid to look me in the eye. She even challenged me by holding it and not saying a word.

I poured a glass of red, and took a gulp.

"Let's get drunk and not have sex," I said. "Let's talk about sin instead."

I'd lost track of how many scotches I'd had at O'Connell's during the course of my Christian duties as a Good Samaritan for poor old Ashwater, but if she had a Breathalyzer handy, I could probably prove that I was way ahead of her.

"You said it, didn't you, Miranda? Yesterday, right? If Lenny was a scam king, then he'd be down in the tar pits with all of the other liars for hire. Forever, right? Now, what about you? If you were a scam queen, where would you end up?"

I got up and staggered over to the cedar box on the mantel and drew out the guided missile from its silo: Great-Grandma Zoe's rosary. I took it back to her on the couch and poured it into her open hands.

"Think eternity," I said. "Big mortal sins. Maybe Lenny did one on us. It looks that way, but what about you? You said you knew that Lenny was thinking about selling his Reliable policy, but you didn't know about the Omaha Beneficial policy that he'd sold to Heartland. Maybe not, but you knew he was selling more than one policy. Now tell me every other goddamn thing you know. And I want you swearing on that rosary, the Blessed Virgin Mary, and every one of your dead grandmas. I want to know everything."

She held the beads like water in her cupped palms and looked up at me.

"And before you start," I said, "I know a lot. I can prove a lot. You tell me the truth. If I hear you color it one shade of gray off a white lie, Miranda, I will walk out of here. And from here, I go straight to Norton or Becker."

I took a slug off my red, then filled up all the wineglasses, and along the way I may have accidentally on purpose filled them well over the proper halfway point, or dumped some white in some red, or committed some other passive-aggressive act of oenophilic heresy.

"You wanna make sure I don't turn on you, Miranda? You better start telling me the whole truth. Right now. Take your time and drink all the wine you need to get it out."

The disbelief on her face looked real.

"I get it," she said. "I guess you just put yourself in charge? You think I killed him to get a payout on a three-hundred-thousand-dollar life policy from Guaranteed Investment? I don't mind you calling me a murderer, but don't call me an idiot."

She walked over to put the rosary away.

"You're saying that I knew Lenny had put me down as the beneficiary for three hundred grand on a life insurance policy that was due to become incontestable in two weeks? So instead of waiting two weeks to kill him, I killed him while the policy was still in the contestability period? Why? So I could be sure that Guaranteed would be able to contest payment on any number of possible grounds: suicide, material misrepresentations on the application, fraud?"

Okay, she was right. If she was after the money, killing him last week made no sense, but if she didn't kill him, what was she hiding, and why was she being so goddamn shifty about everything?

"Turn on me all you want, Carver." She walked over to her computer desk and tore a sheet out of the printer tray. "I'll turn right back."

She handed me a printout of a scanned document sent in reply to a query posted on the Fraud Defense Network. The subject line said: "Leonard Stillmach Query." The body of the message read:

Pacific Altruistic Life & Trust
Policy #50909064
Face Amount: $200,000
Issue date: 01/06/2000
Owner: Leonard Stillmach
Insured: Leonard Stillmach
Beneficiary: Carver Hartnett

Attached was a photocopy of the policy itself. Current. Active. Two hundred grand, with me the beneficiary.

I gasped and felt hot blood burn the insides of my face.

I looked at both sides of the paper.

"It's not real," I said. "Show me originals. Somebody made this with a graphics program. I'll believe it when I see Lenny's original signature on a real document."

It was a scanned image of an original. A life policy on Leonard Stillmach. Pacific Altruistic. Term. Two-hundred-thousand-dollar death benefit. And in the beneficiary box, my name, not hers.

"It's real," she said. "All I need is a real explanation."

"Miranda, I didn't know shit about this."

"Did you know shit about giving a medicated mental patient Ecstasy the night he died?" she asked. "Was that part of what you told Becker? You told me how I needed to be honest about the drugs and so on, with Becker? Remember? Did you tell them about the Ecstasy?"

"That wasn't . . . I . . . It was a favor," I said. "Lenny asked me to get them for him—"

"Them?" she asked. "How many did you give him?"

I threw the papers at her.

"What was Lenny doing?" I yelled.

"Buying and selling life insurance policies, it seems," she said.

"And then killing himself?" I asked.

I looked at the issue date on the policy. 01/06/2000. Here, the week before Christmas 2001, the policy was still fifteen days short of two years and incontestability. In other words, if I tried to file a claim on it to collect two hundred thousand dollars, Pacific Altruistic had the right to do a thorough investigation and contest the policy if they found any evidence of fraud on the application. They could refuse to pay if the death was caused by a preexisting medical condition that Lenny materially misrepresented on his application, or suicide. . . .

Lights came on upstairs. The look Norton had served up to me that afternoon, when he'd said, *"That's the second time you've insisted that it's not a suicide, which makes me wonder why you're so quick to rule it out?"*

The dirty-bird bastard! He'd known about this policy with my name on it, and he'd been insinuating that I didn't want to call Lenny's death a suicide, because it would mean I'd lose my 200K death benefit!

"Maybe for fun he decided to go out big and leave money behind for family—and friends?"

Never mind that I would have attributed the same motive to him or Miranda or anybody else. But I didn't even *know* about the policy, and Miranda apparently hadn't known about hers, either, at first.

She got up and walked over to her machine, talking on the way, "In our line of work you don't really *meet* people the way normal civilians do, right? Remember what just *meeting* people used to feel like? You'd shake their hand, talk to them, ask them about themselves. See if they're shy, or a sloppy dresser, or moody, or pushy, or whatever. And that was all you had to go on: the impressions they left on your mother-naked senses. You weren't going to know anything else about them, except what you'd get from looking into their eyes, watching their hands for signs of nerves, seeing how they treat the waiter or anybody else who can't do much for them. If they were clever, and hiding something, you might never know it, or you might not find out for years that they filed bankruptcy ten years ago, that they've been married three times and the first two wives died under suspicious circumstances."

Her point was that information technologies supposedly had changed all of that, but I didn't agree. Even with Lenny's .pst file loaded on my home machine, he was still a bottomless pit of mysteries. And her? I might as well drop pebbles into her and listen for a splash or a clatter.

She went over and sat down in front of her machine.

"But we're different, aren't we," she said. "We're special investigators."

"What was Lenny doing?" I asked. "Something crazy? Did he buy a bunch of policies, then get AIDS, so he could sell them, and top it all off by killing himself for a big cosmic gag?"

She started clacking on her keyboard and said, "I'm not saying it means anything when *your* name shows up in the beneficiary column on a two-hundred-thousand-dollar life insurance policy on your buddy. But if I was a cop, let's say, or an insurance investigator, it might be different. Would it look funny if you had three credit cards with balances bumping their heads on their limits? Or what if you had a lien on your car? A student loan in default? People could easily get the impression that you needed money."

"Miranda, put a sock in it! I assume you found the one he had out there listing *you* as the beneficiary?"

She barely nodded, and kept going on her keyboard.

"And how about your sister?" I asked. "You didn't help her sell a policy to Heartland, did you?"

"I did," she said. "Annette had a policy she wanted to sell, and Heartland wanted to buy it. Something wrong with that? That's legal, remember? I told you about her skin condition. You know, part of the problem with our job, Carver, is that we don't see all of the hundred or so *legitimate* claims that come through here every day, we only see the bogus ones. Has it occurred to you that somewhere in the world there are legitimate viatical companies trying to help people like my sister pay for expensive medical treatments? She needed money, she sold her policy, and guess what? She didn't suddenly up and die, like Lenny."

"Not yet anyway," I said.

That wasn't fair, and I saw her flinch at it.

"I'm not accusing you of anything," she said. "Not yet. Meantime, don't stagger around drunk pointing your finger in my face and demanding explanations. If you run searches on both of us, you're the guy who looks like you need money, not me."

Norton was *still* two steps ahead! I saw the beauty of his technique: Why not assign us to investigate each other? What a way to get to the heart of the matter in double time.

"Were you in on something with Lenny selling policies to Heartland Viatical?" I asked.

"In on something?"

"Don't turn everything around into questions," I said, "I know how to do that."

"I was not *in on* something with Lenny selling policies to Heartland Viatical."

"Did you sell them any policies on yourself? The way he did? The way your sister did?"

"I did not sell any life insurance policies on myself to Heartland Viatical."

"Okay, then," I said. "Tell me about the web cam."

She gave me another cold look, like it was none of my business.

"The truth," I said. "When you called me and said you were worried about Lenny, you said you were instant-messaging him. Were you instant-messaging?"

She hesitated. "Yes."

"And using the web cams?"

"Yes," she said. "I went on-line with him right when I got back to my place. I told you I was gonna check on him. I got on

Attila-at-Home, just like everybody else does. And then we went private, peer-to-peer, through a Groove Networks subdivision. He was testing the streaming audio and video."

"Then why'd you lie about it?"

"I didn't lie," she said. "We started out instant-messaging, and then we went audiovisual, peer-to-peer. We were playing with his new web cam toys. I told you he put one on my machine. I figured you'd have a problem with it, which is why I didn't break my neck telling you about it."

"Okay," I said, "you were *playing* together on-line, then what?"

"Then he started acting . . . weird, like he was drunk or stoned or whatever," she said, "which he was, thanks to you."

"Was anyone else there with him?"

She shook her head, then made a face, as if that was totally out of the question. "No way. He was slurring a little bit, and said he was going to bed. And right after we got signed off, I thought I should call him and make sure he was okay." She covered her mouth. "But I didn't."

"What time was it when he said he was going to bed?"

"Eleven-thirty? Maybe before? Then I went to bed, and at three something, I woke up, wide awake, and sat up in bed. It was like standing next to one of those static-electricity machines. Gooseflesh all over me. I knew something was wrong with him. I called him and got his machine, then I logged on to Attila-at-Home, and there he was, passed out across the keyboard. And that's when I called you."

She had the steady look of a truth teller, her eyes naked and unafraid.

"He told me once that he had dreams about dying young," she said, and a tear tumbled down her cheek and onto the keyboard.

"Did he have AIDS when he applied for the policies?" I asked. "Did he use a stand-in for the medical tests? He's got a Reliable policy he sold to Rosa Prescott and Heartland. He's got an Omaha Beneficial policy that went from Raymond Guttman to Heartland last week. He's got a Guaranteed Investment policy with you the beneficiary. He's supposedly got a Pacific Altruistic one with me the beneficiary. How many does he have?"

She looked down at her screen. "Five, so far. The four you just mentioned, and there's another at Iowa Life & Casualty that went from Rosa Prescott to Heartland for four hundred thousand."

"He buys five life insurance policies worth a million and a half or so, then just happens to get AIDS? After that, he sells three of them to Heartland, which leaves the two with us as beneficiaries?"

"Yep," she said. "And when you sort by date, ours are the only two still inside the contestability period. Near as I can tell, he signed up for all of them at once, but as you know, the policies don't become effective until the first premium is paid and the policy is issued. The spread between the effective dates of the policies was probably caused by paperwork going back and forth to other cities. The Omaha policies issued first."

"He knew just how to get all five of them," I said, "and he lied when they asked him if he had others or was applying for others."

"He knew that if he applied for them one at a time, they'd spot him for a speculator," she said, "because when Underwriting went to MIB they'd see inquiries from other companies."

"But if he did them all at once," I said, "they wouldn't see shit until all five of them posted, days, maybe weeks later."

"Same with ChoicePoint," she said. "If companies checked it, there wouldn't be anything there until all five of them posted."

"*After* they were issued," I said. "You'd have to go to Fraud Eighty-six and the Wild Wild West for anonymous tips and hope you caught him."

"Did he know he had AIDS and somehow got the policies issued on him anyway?" she asked.

"Remember when he lost all of that weight?" I asked.

"Yeah," she said, "but that was six months ago, not two years ago. Two years ago when he *bought* the policies, he was fine. He was as close to normal as Lenny ever got."

"And six months ago, when he lost the weight—"

"That's when he was probably *selling* the policies."

Lenny had made her and me the beneficiaries of life policies and not told either one of us. No law said he had to, and the insurance companies don't mail out notices informing beneficiaries that they've been named on policies taken out by thus and so. Wealthy old men sometimes use life insurance to provide for their mistresses for the same reason: secrecy. If the old guy transfers ownership of the policy to the young lady and pays the premiums for her, the money passes outside of his estate at death. And nobody knows a thing about it. But why had Lenny done it? Was he just using us as straw names in the beneficiary blank? Place holders? While the policies ran through the two-year contestability period, until he was ready to sell them to Heartland?

I heard her leave off typing and shut down her machine.

It was too complicated to work out sleepless and with too

much drink on board, and suddenly I didn't give a damn what Lenny had done with his insurance policies, how he'd gotten AIDS, or how he'd got himself killed, I just wanted to know what he and Miranda were doing on-line together. Was it anything like what Lenny did with his old software partner, Tanya, who was married to the quad in California? But why have sex on-line if you live in the same city? I took a long swallow off a glass of half white and half red, a Neapolitan blend I'd come up with, and resolved to turn the matter over carefully in my fuddled forebrain: *Let's see, why would an HIV-positive person be interested in on-line sex?*

Okay, maybe she hadn't outright lied to me, but she was hiding important facts from me whenever it suited her.

She sat next to me on the couch. She took my right hand in both of hers and looked me in the eyes, the lines of her lovely face tendering only affection.

"You can be a good, honest person your whole life," she said. "Then fate serves you just the right mix of desperate circumstances to match your weaknesses. For one day or even just for one hour, or one minute, you're not yourself. You succumb. You do something rash, selfish, and deceitful."

"Right," I drawled with the sullen skepticism of a working Special Claims investigator, "you do something rash, selfish, and deceitful like help your buddy Lenny scam insurance companies?"

"No," she said. She kissed my hand and brought it to her cheek. "You do something like put a program on my computer so you can spy on me."

21

BURIED ALIVE

It was as if I'd walked into Miranda's place loaded for bear, and she'd grabbed the gun. In her view, I was the shifty one. All she'd done was help her sister, Annette, hook up with Lenny and sell a life insurance policy to Heartland through a viatical-settlement broker named, whaddaya know, Rosa Prescott. And so what? Nothing wrong with viaticals, per se. As for the rest of the ambiguities and half-truths about the web cam or about how many policies she knew Lenny was selling and when, she had a Clintonian facility for suggesting that if I asked a question that was none of my business, she was entitled to teach me a lesson by lying. According to her, she'd told me the truth whenever my questions didn't violate her privacy.

When I tried to find out exactly what she was doing with Lenny on-line, she dodged me, twice, like that was between her and Lenny, and what would I have wanted her to say if Lenny had asked me about her relationship with me?

I laughed at that and told her she could have told him any damn thing she wanted including the truth, which was that I usually sat around getting sick to my stomach on lust, watching her drink, then she went to bed, and next day we started over. It was the same thing Lenny and every other red-blooded male hetero did around her. That didn't tell me what she and Lenny were doing on-line; maybe they met in a Groove Networks space to discuss the latest Napa Valley wine auction?

After a while we settled into a drunken truce and grief's gravity drew us closer together. Maybe I tried to paw her once or twice, even though I was tired, drunk, and not thinking about what I was usually thinking about. Okay, I probably did it just to make her mad, because of the way she'd set me up and ambushed me with how she knew about the back door I'd installed on her machine.

Around midnight she finished up the wine and said she was ready for bed. As usual, I felt like a used truck-stop towel she was done with for the night. I was also a blue-toothed drunk with more wine than hemoglobin in my veins, so I lost my temper and said that I was going back to my place to sleep.

She told me I shouldn't drive drunk, said that she wanted me to stay, said *we* shouldn't be alone the night after Lenny's funeral. I calmly, carefully, and deliberately smashed one of her crystal Riedel wineglasses in her remote-controlled natural-gas fireplace. I calmly, carefully, and deliberately explained that I was done sleeping on her leather sofa like a goddamn shih tzu puppy, and I was perfectly fine to drive anywhere on this third-rate planet of a third-rate sun, thank you very much.

On the way home, I bought cigarettes, Old Golds! And kept sorting stories, editing and arranging scenes and lines, just the way Dead Man Norton would have done—putting the whole package together to see if it passed the smell test. Okay, so it probably wasn't Miranda at Lenny's place Friday night, but somebody had been there. I wanted to get home and see if I had an e-mail image from GothicRage86.

I was meeting Charlie Becker tomorrow, and before that I had to figure out just what I'd be telling him. If I had an image, I could just hand it to him and say, "Somebody was at Lenny's the night he died, and there she is." If I had to, I'd make up a story about how I came by it. Maybe I could get GothicRage to identify himself. Did I even know GothicRage was a him? Becker would find out about the policies sooner or later, sooner if Addie and Norton got together and started hatching industry defenses and ways to deny paying on stinky claims.

If it wasn't Miranda at Lenny's the night he died, who was it? A new girlfriend? Addie's friend and counterpart when we double-dated, Natalie Fleming? Natalie was well above average, but not quite a "Señorita Silk Fox." And GothicRage had written "brunette, lipstick, big ones, dressed for it" on instant messaging. Natalie was more like dishwater blond, ChapStick, well formed and well wrought by our Father in heaven by whom all breasts were made, but nothing near "big ones," and usually wearing a T-shirt and jeans, instead of being "dressed for it."

The AIDS thing again. If he was HIV-positive, would he have babes in his place at midnight? I guess so—Miranda had been there before. But Miranda was different. She didn't have sex. At least, not in person. She'd apparently experimented and done *something* on-line at Lenny's behest, and maybe that was the real reason I wanted to get back home, maybe see if Lenny had any . . . images of Miranda in his "My Pictures" folder.

When I got home, it was almost midnight. I still hadn't slept from the night before last and had gone through the funeral, Becker, Norton, Tarlon Ashwater, and Miranda. My head was puffed up with oozing muddy terrors and half-formed hunches.

I barely had enough life left in me to fire up Outlook and check for a message from GothicRage. His e-mail came in along with a teeming horde of spam promising me ways to be my own boss, lose weight and make money while I slept, get discounts on natural herbal Viagra, add REAL inches to my penis, and, my favorite: "FIND OUT ANYTHING ABOUT ANYONE."

No paper clip appeared in the attachment column of Gothic-Rage's e-mail, so no image.

From: GothicRage86@aol.com

To: CarvedMeat@home.com

Re: Attila-at-Home Cam

Carved Meat,

Thanks for info on poor Lenny.

Maybe I can help with sending the image, if you'll help us, first.

We'll be in touch.

Soon.

GothicRage86

I didn't take off my clothes, or drink a quart of water and take three aspirins. I just fell across the bed and zonked out.

I dreamed I was with Miranda's body in a room, and she was

propped up for viewing, like Lenny had been. And everybody was saying what a shame that she had died of a terrible venereal disease. That made me laugh right out loud. Miranda? Then just as the last of us were filing by her body, she moved her head and spoke to me. I tried to show the other mourners that she wasn't really dead, but they couldn't see that she was still alive. Only I could.

She had a wet cross of fresh black ashes on her forehead, as if she'd settled back on a chaise longue for a nap after an Ash Wednesday service.

"Do not persist in your unbelief, Thomas," she said. "Put your hand into my wound and believe!" She took my hand and guided it under her silk cerements and couture graveclothes and Ralph Lauren panne satin casket liner, steering it up between her legs. "But happy are those who have not seen and still believe."

When I left the room, Ashwater was outside waiting for me. He had a new list with Miranda's name on it and a life policy he supposedly owned. He roped me like a calf, threw a dusty gunnysack over my head, and herded me over to his battered truck, where he tied me up and tossed me in the cab. I was suffocating inside my hood, where it smelled like oil and alfalfa and Roundup herbicide.

We drove for a while, and en route, Ashwater was asking me if I was a coyote that needed to get shot with a varmint rifle. Finally the truck stopped. I heard him take the rifle out of the gun rack, then he dragged me out, leaned me against the truck, and pulled off the gunnysack.

It was midnight, and we were parked in the loop drive at Calvary Cemetery, where Lenny had been buried. Ashwater put night-vision goggles on me. He pulled a ditch spade out of the truck bed and prodded me using the handle of it on the back of my neck.

"You can die down here, or die up the hill," he said. "It don't make me no never mind."

He poked and goaded me along with the shovel handle up the hill to Lenny's grave, while I listened to him tell me more hard-luck stories: how he'd lost two fingers at a branding roping calves, how he and his wife ate plain-label macaroni and cheese from the coop, and he'd traded beer for Indian rations for weeks, how sometimes you just have to drive to town, grab your varmint rifle out the truck, and go explain to the IN-surance men and the bankers that selling cattle is nothing but selling grass, and grass don't grow when the ground is nothing but dust.

I could see the headstone glowing like kryptonite in the greenish visual field of the night goggles.

Ashwater handed me the ditch spade. "Dig," he said. "You dig the carcass up, and I'll drag it down to the company, just like I'd show my IN-surance man a head of cattle. I'll haul him down there in the truck and get Reliable Allied Trust on *Live at Five* before the Agribusiness report."

It was sweaty, desperate work, and took me a forever's worth of Sundays to get the dirt out of the grave. I was only half done when Ashwater must have pushed me in and started filling the hole with mud from a manure spreader. The mud was warm and so thick I couldn't move. I kept my eyes closed, watching meteors and shooting stars streak across the backs of my eyelids, wondering when I'd run out of air, waiting for my whole life to flash on the screen the way they say it does.

Then my eyes cracked open like unhealing sores. I was at the bottom looking up out of a poisoned well or a mine shaft with furry walls, where a hangover had settled over me like a mudslide during the night. I needed air, water, aspirin, something sweet and salty, like those athletic drinks with electrolytes.

An annoying buzz ruptured the membranes of my inner ear. Ashwater must have buried me in my underworld of mud with a huge infernal wasp, and it was hovering at the portal of my left ear, preparing to plant a saw-toothed stinger the size of a pikestaff in one ear and out the other.

It was like a question on a college entrance exam. *Sleep* is to *death* as *hangover* is to: (a) hell; (b) self-annihilation; (c) eternal despair; (d) temporary suicide; (e) all of the above. And like hell, I kept coming back to hangovers no matter how many times I swore them off. Probably because I'd been hanging around with Miranda too much. That's it—it was all her fault, proof certain and positive that she was no good for me.

If it were deadly pancreatic cancer, end-stage renal failure, or chronic lung disease, I could feel sorry for myself, but it wasn't, and I couldn't. I'd poisoned myself with too much engine additive, that's all.

The huge wasp buzzed at the porch of my ear again, and then I recognized the sound: It was my door buzzer. I sat up suddenly and gagged. Leftover wine backwashed up into my throat ahead of a tannic belch, and I almost heaved.

The digital clock said 4:07, and the windows were dark. Miranda? No way, she'd have called, maybe, but she wouldn't actually come over. Unless. Maybe she didn't want me dying on her the way Lenny had?

I staggered over to the door and had to make do with listening, since I didn't have a peephole.

"Who is it?" I asked.

"Federal agents. We have a search warrant for this address."

I recognized my old buddy McKnight's voice through the door. Maybe the rest of my life would be like a French Surrealist movie or a Kafka video loop. Every night I would hide in a different room, and every night the authorities would roust me out with search warrants, then turn me loose to find another hovel to hole up in, so that they could track me down again and serve the next night's search warrant.

I didn't want to throw up in front of them, so I went in the can and fought it all back down.

When I came out I went to the middle of the room, turned around, lifted up my arms for my old buddy Todd McNight. I even sat myself on the floor without being told.

"Get up," said the one named Mutton. "You're coming with us."

22

TROUBLE BIG

I HAVE THE RIGHT to remain silent, and mostly I have exercised that right. Anything I say can and will be used against me in a court of law. That's why I've been careful to say only things that I wouldn't mind repeating in a court of law. I have the right to an attorney, and if I can't afford it, one will be appointed by the court. So, every time they ask me a question, no matter how innocuous it seems, I pause first, and I ask myself, *Could this get me in trouble, and do I need an attorney to answer it?* If not, I answer. But mainly, as I've been trained to do, I ask *them* questions, and so far they've been forthcoming with at least some answers. For instance, I've been given to understand that the main reason I've been brought in is to assist the FBI in their ongoing investigation of Heartland Viatical. And even though they have read me my rights, if I demand a lawyer right now, it will disrupt and delay the FBI's investigation for reasons that will be explained to me when I talk to federal agents with the Viatical Fraud Task Force in Washington, D.C.

The agents here in Omaha, the Jehovah's Witnesses, Mutton and McKnight, are not investigating Heartland Viatical. That's being done from Washington, so these local guys don't know shit about the insurance business or what a viatical is, or what Lenny was doing. Or they're pretending not to know.

Instead of demanding a lawyer and making myself look guilty, I let things go forward, just a little at a time, until I could find out just what was on their minds. My plan was to cooperate with them long enough to show them that I wasn't scamming insurance companies with Lenny, I was just trying to find out what happened.

They took me to a swank new complex out west in Old Mill, northwest of where 680 crosses West Dodge Road. No handcuffs, no pushing and shoving, but the boys weren't friendly either, just blunt and businesslike far beyond their tender years.

Unlike the night at Lenny's place, where McKnight had done most of the talking, tonight it was the tall thin guy, Michael Mutton, telling me what to do. The more he talked, the more I saw that his fresh-faced youthfulness had a callow mean streak down the back of it. He kept suggesting that I was Lenny's "partner," or that we were "working together" to scam the insurance companies, which was ridiculous, but Mutton didn't know enough about Lenny or the insurance business or Heartland to understand me when I refuted his insinuations, point by point.

The two-story building had an outsized rendition of the Stars and Stripes flapping in the glare of a spotlight. Next to it was a glowing, freestanding sign, sea blue with white letters that said: DEPARTMENT OF JUSTICE, FEDERAL BUREAU OF INVESTIGATION.

Inside, it was bright and tastefully appointed commercial office space, a facility that made Becker's place look like a 1950s post office.

I spent about an hour in guarded conversation with Mutton in a small room. I was accustomed to dealing with the likes of Norton, so early on I asked, "Is this being taped? Or are we just talking?"

Mutton laughed and told me that his office didn't tape interviews. "It's against regulations," he said. "Why would we need to tape our conversations with you?"

True, I thought. And why keep secrets? They now had my computer and Lenny's, and, if they had a mind to find out, they'd soon know as much or more than me about Lenny's dealings with Heartland. And if the federal IT geeks started going through those Zip disks, or my own hard drive where I'd copied Miranda's and Lenny's .pst files, they might be asking me how other people's files got on my machine.

I told Mutton the truth, mainly, including what it looked like Lenny had done to Heartland Viatical, but he didn't seem to get it. I don't think he understood so much as how a simple viatical works, even though I'd told him twice. He just slavishly wrote everything down and occasionally said, "I'll report that to the Viatical Fraud Task Force."

I explained how I happened to be in Lenny's place when they stopped by with a search warrant for his computers. Maybe I stretched a little when I said I'd gone to his home machine to find out about Heartland, because I'd been assigned by my boss to investigate Heartland and Lenny, and I was just retrieving work-related files from his computer, because we needed them to protect ourselves from whatever Lenny had done to us and the other insurance companies.

That's when Mutton asked me a question that made me think I needed a lawyer.

"The early-morning hours of December eighteenth, when you were in Mr. Stillmach's condominium, did you use his computer to access the Internet?"

It was the same question the deaf computer guy had told McKnight to ask me, which meant that they probably knew I had used the damn thing, so why had I lied?

So I said, "Before I answer any more questions, maybe I'd like to talk to a lawyer. I don't have one, but maybe I'd like to have one appointed by the court just so I can ask him a few questions about my rights."

"That's fine," said Mutton. "I'll have the charges drawn up and all the paperwork done before your lawyer gets here."

"Wait a minute," I said. "What charges?"

"All the ones we were going to charge your coconspirator, Lenny, with," he said. "And then some extra charges that only pertain to you. See, my instructions are to take a basic statement from you if you are willing to cooperate and you have nothing to hide. If you demand a lawyer before you talk to the Viatical Fraud Task Force in Washington, D.C., then I have to charge you with everything we were going to charge Mr. Stillmach with, and name you as a coconspirator."

"But I wasn't a coconspirator," I said.

Mutton shrugged. "Then why do you need a lawyer?"

"Okay," I said, "never mind the lawyer for a minute. What charges were you talking about?"

Mutton scowled. "Well, first answer the question: Early A.M., December eighteenth, when you were in Leonard Stillmach's condominium impersonating a dead suspect, did you use his computer to access the Internet?"

"Look," I said, "what I did that night was turn on Lenny's computer and look for the work-related files on his machine. After that I turned the machine off. And if I'm not mistaken, the question you guys asked me that night had to do with was I on the computer when you guys showed up or just before you guys showed up, and the answer was no, because it had been a little while since I had turned it off."

Mutton took more notes.

"What charges were you referring to?"

Mutton frowned and acted snuffy and annoyed, as if I had asked him to do something obvious and tedious like count backward from one hundred, or name all fifty states and their capitals. He opened his folder, took out a fax, and began reading.

"Eighteen United States Code chapter seventy-three, Obstruction of Justice, criminalizes tampering with property which is the subject of a search and seizure; penalty, up to five years imprisonment. At the state level, tampering with physical evidence is a Class IV felony; punishable by up to five years imprisonment. Dual sovereignty applies so the sentences are separate and cumulative and don't run concurrently. Obstructing government operations is a Class I misdemeanor, punishable by up to one year in prison. Criminal trespass, punishable by ninety days to a year in prison. Hindering a police officer, one hundred eighty days to one year depending on whether it is charged as a city-ordinance violation or under the state statute."

Mutton turned a page on the fax.

"That's bullshit," I said. "I didn't obstruct justice, tamper with evidence, or trespass, or hinder any police officers. My friend gave me a key to his place. I got some work files off his machine. I didn't tamper with anything!"

Mutton looked surprised. "I didn't say you did. I'm saying that these are the charges we would be bringing against you unless you cooperate with us and with the agents of the Viatical Fraud Task Force in Washington, D.C. They said you were an insurance investigator and you'd cooperate. They said I shouldn't be expecting any trouble from you."

Mutton looked at his watch. "It's an hour later out there, and they should be calling soon."

He studied his fax sheet again. "That's just the little stuff. This page has all the federal computer-crime charges." He whistled and reared back. "Title Eighteen United States Code, section ten-thirty, fraud and related activity in connection with computers, makes it a crime to intentionally access a protected computer without authorization, punishable by fine and five years in a federal facility. Whew," said Mutton. "A guy could do twenty years on these alone, and that's without any of the conspiracy charges added on top. Let's see, we're in the Bureau of Prison's North Central Region out of Kansas City; you'd probably wind up in Leavenworth, Kansas, or Marion, Illinois, but they've both been full lately. So they'd probably send you to the Mid-Atlantic Region and Terre Haute, McVeigh's Hideaway. It's the noisiest place I've ever been. People get seriously hurt there. Last guy I escorted out of Terre Haute I had to take to an infectious-disease center in Indianapolis after he got AIDS from being gang-raped."

"What do you guys want?" I asked.

Mutton shrugged. "It's usually one of two things: assets or information."

"Assets?" I asked.

Mutton nodded. "Proceeds of a criminal enterprise. Do you have any, Mr. Hartnett? Or maybe you have information that will help us catch some bad guys who do have some proceeds of a criminal enterprise?"

"Hector Crogan?"

Mutton smiled. "See? Did I say Hector Crogan? No. You said Hector Crogan. Do you work for Mr. Crogan?"

Mutton opened a folder, took out a sheet of paper, and handed it to me.

"This is the biggie. Make a new fish out of you quick," he said. "Five years easy."

The printout looked like connection reports and sniffer logs showing IP origin, destination, and packet type, tracing a computer's path through server farms and ISPs.

"These are from Mr. Stillmach's Internet service provider. It shows Lenny's computer logging on night before last at one-thirty-seven A.M., at which time somebody used Lenny's machine to gain unlawful entry to a protected computer at the specified IP address. We ran right over and found you."

"She's my girlfriend," I said. "She gave me permission."

"We'll ask her about that."

The phone on the table rang, and just in time, because Mutton no longer looked like a Jehovah's Witness to me; he was "boyish" like Malcolm McDowell playing Alex in *A Clockwork Orange.*

"It's for you," he said, handing me the receiver.

The voice on the other end introduced himself as Agent Jeffrey Rhuteen with the Department of Justice's new Viatical Fraud Task Force in Washington, D.C. What a relief! I'd even sent the task-force affidavits and spreadsheets on policies before, and that's just the way Rhuteen treated me on the phone: I was a fellow investigator, not a suspect. Finally, someone who knew the real story!

He apologized for the local misunderstanding and told me how the agents who'd brought me in, McKnight and the odious Mutton, were what the FBI calls "brick agents," because they make their living walking around hitting the bricks and doing knock-and-talks, executing search warrants, and so on. Rhuteen said they went too far in grabbing my computer, and that he'd personally make sure that I could come pick it up that very morning and take it back home with me.

He explained almost everything. Heartland Viatical was being investigated for fraud, stemming from activities associated mostly with the old company Hector Crogan and his brother-in-law, Dr. Raymond Guttman, had left behind out in California. In the process of investigating Heartland, the undercover, on-line task force agents came across good old Lenny.

"You probably figured most of this out yourself by now," said Rhuteen, "but Lenny had a grand plan to scam the scammers and swindle the fraudster viatical companies he'd been busting for four years. He bought five or six life insurance policies and held them for two years. Once he started getting close to the outer limit of the contestability period, he went on a starvation diet, then he dummied up some fake medical records, and we both know he knew just how to do that."

The snippets from his e-mail messages back and forth to Miranda kept popping into my head. *"I didn't do anything illegal— well, maybe a little, but not really—all I did was sell them policies."*

"Then Lenny paid a visit to Heartland Viatical and started selling them policies," said Rhuteen, "showing them lab work and medical records indicating that his T-cell counts were falling below two-fifty, that he had thrush and was HIV-positive. Heartland bought the policies from him and had employees pay the premiums with checks from their personal checking accounts during the contestability period, so the insurance companies wouldn't know that the policies had been viaticated."

"So he didn't have AIDS," I said, remembering his e-mail again: *"I got the policies legit."*

"Well, we can't prove that," Rhuteen said, "but it doesn't look like it. When he bought the policies he was in the pink of health and able to prove it. By the time he sold them he'd lost forty pounds and had some of the best counterfeit medical records we've ever seen."

And in Miranda's car, the last thing Lenny had said before we turned around and went to the casino. *"They may be scamming somebody, but not us insurance companies. They may try to work a side deal with you. If they do, let us know, and we'll tell you how to handle them."*

"We had Lenny pretty well figured out," said Rhuteen, "but when we brought him in, he swore up and down that he hadn't forged the medical records. He said Heartland had done that, not him. All he'd done was make himself look sick and sell them his life insurance policies.

The truth was probably somewhere in between, and more e-mail snippets came to mind. *"All I did was sell them policies. . . . I told you they need all the policies they can get because they're being investigated."*

"That's the hard part," said Rhuteen, "him implicating Heartland, claiming that it was mainly Heartland duping the insurance companies, and Heartland misleading its own investors by selling them policies of people who were nowhere close to dying. People buy shares in these viatical companies, or they buy the policies themselves thinking they're 'safe insurance investments' backed by Moody's and so on, like the ads say, but they aren't, especially if the company is crooked."

"So now your witness is dead," I said, "and the big question is: Did Heartland know that Lenny didn't really have AIDS? Did they buy his policies, and then *tell* their investors he had AIDS? Make them think he didn't have but a year or two left in him? So Heartland could unload his policies on investors and get top dollar for them?"

Guys like Tarlon Ashwater had bought policies from guys like Lenny, because Lenny was supposed to have AIDS. Then guys like Ashwater sat by the phone and called in to the companies every day to find out if any of their investments had "matured."

"Lenny said he could prove it," said Rhuteen. "Lenny was going to wear a wire into Heartland for us. He claimed he'd get Heartland on tape as being willing and able to fake medical records."

That sounded just like Lenny, and he'd jump at the chance to go in and sting a viatical company after fleecing them himself.

"Hector Crogan and his brother-in-law, Dr. Guttman,

helped run a California viatical company, where there were alle-
gations they made policies more attractive to investors by sending
prospective viators across the aisle to Dr. Guttman's clinics for a
second opinion. Or that Guttman would monkey with the lab
work, or use a sick person's blood to run the tests. I don't have to
tell a guy in your line of work what kind of damage a fraudster
can do, once he gets a doctor in his pocket."

No shit. If you can order up fake medical records at will, you
can do anything. You don't even have to be in the hospital to collect on all those hundred-dollar-a-day indemnity polices the speculators trade like Pokemon cards, you just have your dirty
medical insider make up some records for you to prove you were
in the hospital when you were really taking in some sun down at
Cabo San Lucas. You just pick up the hundred-dollar-a-day
indemnity payments next time you're back in town.

"That's where you come in," said Rhuteen. "You're investigating Heartland Viatical anyway for Reliable Insurance, right?
Let's team up, just like the old days. Since Lenny's dead and can't
wear that wire into Heartland, how about you do it for us, and
for Lenny? You wear a wire and say you're there about the policies Lenny sold them."

I was going to end up seeing somebody at Heartland anyway,
I thought. Take another look at Rosa Prescott, see if she looked
like a hundred grand worth of life insurance in broad daylight. So
why not do it this way?

"Midway through your meeting with Heartland," Rhuteen
continued, "you start asking them what kind of clients they buy
policies from, and would they buy one, say, from you, for
instance? Tell them that Lenny had once suggested that you

might be able to sell them a policy, even though you were basically healthy. Something like that?"

I could find out what really happened, I thought, and I'd have the force of federal law behind me when I did it.

"I'll do it," I said.

"Then we'll make you an official confidential informant," chuckled Rhuteen, "and if you'll trust me to slant the cooperation agreement as much in your favor as possible, I can fax those to them there in Omaha, you can sign them, and we can do this quick. This afternoon, even?"

"What about all those charges Mutton was talking about?"

"We make those go away with the cooperation agreement," said Rhuteen. "You'll see it in black and white when they set you up this afternoon to wear the bug."

I was still missing twelve hours or so of sleep. "Do we have to do it today?"

"It's the best way," said Rhuteen. "When the state and locals find out Heartland Viatical owned three life insurance policies on a twenty-nine-year-old who just up and turned into a death unknown, they'll drive over there in black-and-whites with their sirens on and spook them all into lockdown. What we want is to send you over there tomorrow afternoon. Tomorrow? Hell, tomorrow's here already. *This* afternoon. Get them definitely on tape as either accepting an invitation to do a scam just like Lenny's, or turning it down cold. If the latter, then we could close our case. Because Lenny is dead. Point is we don't want the locals spooking them first."

"Right," I said. "I wanna know if Heartland was in on it. Even more, I want to know how Lenny died. I think somebody was there with him that night."

"We can help with that, too," said Rhuteen. "GothicRage86 is a confidential informant. Undercover on-line for us. He said he's ready to finish the game you started, and he's saving your image file for you. That's why the brick agents came over to grab the machines the night you were at Lenny's. We had Lenny's machine under surveillance at the provider level, and GothicRage told us somebody had logged on as a new user. We didn't even know Lenny was dead, we just didn't want the digital evidence on his machine tainted by a new user, and lucky for us the magistrate said that was enough 'exigent circumstances' for a nighttime search, so we got the warrant and grabbed his machine."

"I'm in," I said. "I'll wear it over there."

"Right," said Rhuteen, "and as long as we've got our undercover confidential informant in place, there's no need to tell the state and locals about it. The minute you walk out of Heartland, I'll call them and tell them what you did for us. They can follow up with their homicide investigation, and we'll put in a good word for you."

BEYOND NOT RIGHT

I FINISHED WITH RHUTEEN and the brick agents, who took me to my car so I could drive back to their place and pick up my computer. By then it was pushing 8:30 A.M., which gave me half an hour to make it downtown to Becker's place.

It's a straight shot down the middle on Dodge Street, which meant I drove right by the Mutual of Omaha Indian chief in a headdress, backlit by the eastern sun in all its stark winter glory. They say that grief is a species of idleness, and it must be true. I had a long red light, and there was morning traffic, which in Omaha means you might have as many as four or five cars jammed up in front of you, and more of them stacked behind you in a line that stretches for yards. I was stranded for over three minutes. Suddenly I felt too warm inside, like my guts were melting, expanding, and erupting up my gullet to the back of my throat. My eyes started dribbling like leaky hot-water faucets. I didn't *feel* sad, it was more like I was a cat coughing up a bezoar, but suddenly I was crying out of control, which, like skiing out of control in Colorado, can be dangerous. All the tear processing that I hadn't done because of crowded ceremonies and frantic rituals and the constant game of emotional wits with Miranda and Norton—hah! Imagine getting weepy while being scanned by Old Man Norton's surveillance technologies? It'd give him the same start I had yesterday: a Special Investigations man getting misty, and wearing two big tears like telescope lenses.

I was in the car, idling, having one of those cigarettes I smoke only during certain periods of my life, suddenly alone, hungover, but by myself and basically sober for the first time since Lenny had died. The damn Indian-chief logo loomed up on the skyline, and all I could think about was bipolar Lenny ranting in the backseat of Miranda's car, while she and I laughed up front, listening to him "prove" to us with manic-phase rigor that the Mutual of Omaha Indian in a headdress was Blackbird, chief of the Omahas, psychic, arsenic practitioner.

I found parking okay and cleaned myself up in the public men's room before I went in to see Charlie Becker. I knew that once I got in with him I'd have no trouble forgetting Lenny, because I'd be thinking about jail time instead.

As usual, he was gracious in an administrative way and served me all the coffee and cigarettes I wanted.

"So far you've been right about one thing," said Becker, "and only one thing. Lenny didn't commit suicide."

Maybe Becker didn't even have an office. Maybe he just drove around in his car all night and talked on his cell phone and interviewed people in small rooms like this one.

"I never thought he committed suicide," I said.

Becker lit my cigarette and drawled, "I guess if my girlfriend and I had five hundred grand worth of life insurance that wouldn't pay if the insured committed suicide, I wouldn't believe in a suicide either."

I showed him how the policies listing Miranda and me were still contestable, so it made no sense that we'd killed him. He seemed half-convinced, because I could see he got the contestability part, but what if it was one of those planned incongruities, and we only did it to deflect suspicion? So I went ahead and nailed all four corners down for him.

"Look," I said, "if I decided to turn and go dirty, I could make more than a shitty two hundred grand easy and come nowhere near jail or a murder charge doing it. *And* Lenny would still be here to help me spend it!"

He looked skeptical, so I gave him a show-and-tell on the safest, most surefire insurance scam I had ever seen.

"Pick up any magazine and shake it hard, or just open your junk mail more often, and you'll find dozens of those little 'No Return Postage Necessary' postcard insurance offers that say, 'We Will Pay You $125 a Day if You Are Hospitalized for ANY Reason. No Matter What!'

"Even the fine print promises flat-out to pay $125 per day for every day you are in the hospital and under the care of a physician. And they all say, 'This is over and above any other insurance, Medicare, or Medicaid benefits you may receive.' They're called hospital indemnity policies, and hundreds of health and accident companies offer them. The premiums are as cheap as popcorn. I don't get *one*. I don't get *two*. I apply for a *hundred* of them, all at once. Underwriting doesn't even know I exist because the premiums and the exposure on these little-old-lady specials are so low that I'm not worth the bandwidth it would take to check me out. So, I do my mass mailing, and out of the hundred I probably get at least eighty insurers to issue $125-per-day indemnity policies on me."

"Wait a second," Becker said with a grin, "maybe I should write this down, so I know just what to do after I lock your ass up in Douglas County Jail."

"I pay the measly premiums on those eighty policies for a month or two just to be safe," I said. "After that, I come down with a sudden, self-inflicted (is there any other kind?) drinking problem. I go see my doctor and tell him I can't stay away from the Dewar's and the Cutty Sark. I tell him I'm up to a quart a day and on the verge of losing my job. Hell, make it even safer: I have an accident at work, break something expensive, and let the HR workplace-safety monitors smell my breath. There's no medical test for alcoholism except liver functions, and I gotta be going steady with Johnny Walker for twenty years with a 'Johnny Forever' tattoo before I fuck those up. Now I'm driving over the limit and begging for medical help—I take a DUI if I have to, nice touch—and it's borderline malpractice if my doctor doesn't order me into treatment and rehab for thirty days."

Becker was liking it, I could see that. I was only missing Miranda to do the delivery for me.

"That's 'hospitalization' under most indemnity polices," I said, "which means I go sit around the dayroom at the Eppley Care center and play Hearts and Monopoly for thirty days. Every other day or so, I sit with the group and listen to a few drunkalogues from my fellow users, and when they ask if I'd like to 'share,' I traipse on up to the podium, smile sheepishly, and say, 'My name is Scam King, and I am an alcoholic kleptomaniac.'"

"Now hold on a minute," said Becker, "that means no beer for thirty days?"

"No beer," I said, "but when I get discharged on day thirty-one, I can party till the cows come home and then jump over the moon with them because I've got a hundred twenty-five dollars, times thirty days, times eighty policies equals . . . that's three hundred grand, and the worst thing that can happen to me is I get blacklisted on ChoicePoint and the Fraud Defense Network. Shudder! I haven't violated so much as a postal regulation, and I get three hundred grand tax-free."

"That would really work?" he asked.

"Smooth as a showgirl's ass," I said. "I can do it only once, but I can do it big. Punishable only by the entire industry flagging me for a speculator."

Becker shook his head at the elegant simplicity of the scheme.

"I never said I was going to charge you with murder," he said. "I was going to charge you with being dumber than you look."

"If it was money I was after, I wouldn't be a Special Investigations man," I said.

"Yeah," he said, pushing the Old Golds my way, "and I wouldn't be a cop. Don't tell me about money. Thanks to good old Warren Buffett and Berkshire Hathaway, there's serious money quietly stashed all over this whole damn town. I've been in seven-million-dollar houses on three-acre lots, where man and wife are trying to kill each other on the kitchen floor with a set of barbecue tools, with the kids watching the whole deal from balcony seats. Once my boys get ahold of them on the floor, I like to stoop down four inches from the guy's face and look him right in the eyes and say, 'Sir, you got more money than the Father, Son, and Holy Ghost. What the fuck are you doing drunk on the floor with the police in your house?'

"It always shocks the rookies. They grew up in South Omaha believing that money makes you happy."

"Well, I taught you about viaticals and told you how to make three hundred grand without breaking any laws. What about the autopsy? Cause of death unknown?"

"It was," said Becker. "It looked like a simple overdose, so the county let a pathology resident do the autopsy. The basic drug screen turned up some pot, some narco painkillers he'd chopped up and snorted. His blood alcohol would have got him arrested driving a car, but nothing near what it would take to kill him. So when it's cause of death unknown, everybody starts thinking spontaneous cardiac arrhythmia, which happens, even in young people, especially druggies."

"Uh-huh," I said.

"They tell me Ecstasy will kill you, too," said Becker. "Especially if you get some of a bad batch. But as far as you know, he wasn't taking Ecstasy, right?"

He read my face like it was a banner ad.

"I just—"

"I told you twice I work in homicide, not vice," said Becker. "You fiddle-faddle around and talk mush at me, and then we find the three tabs in an envelope in Lenny's pants and residues in his gastric contents. And the funny thing about this particular envelope was it had one of those little see-through, wax-paper address windows on it. Perfect medium for fingerprints. So we probably got the killer's fingerprints, if that's who gave the Ecstasy to poor old Lenny."

"You said it *was* a death unknown." I said. "What is it now?"

Becker slowly shook his head. "I had a real medical examiner take another look at the body, and things went from not right to flat-out wrong."

He puffed an Old Gold and exhaled contentedly.

I shrugged and waited.

"I'd tell you why," said Becker, "but you really hurt my feelings. Hiding things from me the way you did. I trusted you, and you kept things from me. Now I'm supposed to trust you again? After the way you treated me?"

He shook his head. "Not unless you got something else for me?"

"I'll be back tomorrow with something else for you," I said.

CONFIDENTIAL
INFORMANT

When I called Heartland Viatical to set up my appointment, I was relayed from one woman to another until I wound up with a woman named Teresa, who identified herself as Mr. Crogan's assistant. I told her I was calling to set up an appointment to see Mr. Crogan—today, if possible—about the Reliable life insurance policy that Leonard Stillmach had transferred to Heartland Viatical. She put me on hold for a minute or two, then came back to say that Mr. Crogan would be delighted to meet with me at five that afternoon.

That meant I had two or three hours before I met Mutton and McKnight out in front of Reliable, where they were picking me up in a van for the trip over to Heartland Viatical. I looked through the Heartland file I'd gotten from Norton. Lenny had some standard research in it. He'd done searches on "Heartland Viatical, Inc." in Yahoo Business and Economy. Printouts from several consumer agencies and the Better Business Bureau showed no complaints against Heartland. The Nebraska incorporation papers were in order. A Dun & Bradstreet printout listed the corporate history. He'd found a couple of slip opinions from district courts in California, but as near as I could tell when Heartland sued a big insurance company for breach of insurance contract, Heartland won—had even won punitive damages in one instance.

Heartland also had a well-designed website, and it did a decent job of spelling out all the ins and outs of viaticals, a page for people with terminal illnesses, another for investors. And if old Ashwater had a computer and an Internet connection, he could have read about how the investors in Heartland Viatical did not "own" individual policies but instead owned an interest in a group of policies held in escrow to protect the privacy of individual viators. There it was in black and white: "Our investors don't buy life insurance policies, they buy a secured interest in financial instruments—and the instruments are secured by our life insurance policies." It was just the way I'd told him: All Ashwater owned was an interest in whatever life insurance policies Heartland owned.

I clicked on the "About Us" button and learned that Hector Crogan had been honored by a California AIDS support group and had testified before the Canadian Life and Health Insurance Association in Ontario as an "authority" on the viatical industry.

Maybe Miranda and Norton were right: In our line of work we saw only the fraud outfits. Legitimate viatical companies did legitimate businesses all over the country; we just had no reason to know about them in Special Investigations Claims. The term "viatical" was new, but the concept of speculating on just when somebody might die went back to antiquity and probably reached its zenith in eighteenth-century England, where it was perfectly legal to purchase a life insurance policy on the life of a total stranger, without his knowledge or consent. Betting on which public figure or politician would not live out the week became a national pastime, like betting on sports. The gamey speculation and the growing temptation to commit insurance murders to obtain death benefits were the source of the "insurable interest" requirement you now find in the laws of all fifty states: If you want to buy a life insurance policy on somebody, you must by law have an "insurable interest" in seeing that person—presumably a family member or business partner—stay alive.

It can be argued that viaticals are an "investment" like any other. Instead of stock market speculators trying to guess just when a company might go bankrupt, viatical investors bet on just when a person might die.

I leaned over our partition and caught Miranda between phone calls.

"Remember when Lenny said, 'I'll give you the lowdown on Heartland before you get too far into it.' Remember that? Then he said, 'Unless you want to tell him, Miranda?'"

She looked at me with a brushfire going on behind her eyes, like this was not the place.

"I told you everything," she whispered. "Why are you doing this again?"

"I'm going over to see them," I said. "You can't tell anybody."

She sighed and started having aftershocks from the night Lenny died.

"Carver, leave it alone," she said, and her voice was wobbly. "Let the police figure it out. As for the policies naming us, we just don't file claims on them. Or we see if the companies will settle for fifty cents on the dollar to Vera and his sister, and nothing for us. We don't need to know if Heartland was in on it or not. Just leave it. I'm scared of it."

"I'll leave it after today," I said. "You never dealt with them directly? You never sold them any policies?"

"I told you," she said, her eyes locked on mine with her high beams on, "I didn't sell them any policies. Lenny and his friend helped my sister sell one. That's it. Get over it."

At three o'clock, I met Mutton and McKnight and a surveillance technician named Sam Growney out in front of Reliable in a van that said BANE PEST CONTROL on the side. Langdon, the deaf guy, was in there, too, probably looking for another free steak dinner.

I took all the time I needed to read the faxed "cooperation agreement," and McKnight explained it to me word for word, while Mutton looked on. It was written in plain English and covered every charge Mutton had spelled out that morning. I could see by the glint in Mutton's eye that he'd be happier if he could do a karaoke rendition of "Singing' in the Rain" while turning me over to the rump rangers in Terre Haute.

Growney showed me a special cell phone with a digital listening device concealed inside.

"Even if they search you," he said, "they'll find a cell phone and think nothing of it. It even works, if they decide to try it, and we have your number programmed to ring it. So if they get suspicious and ask you what your cell phone number is, just tell them yours, and let them call it."

They put me on the line with Rhuteen in Washington, D.C., who gave me thorough instructions. I was comforted to learn that

Rhuteen and another agent with the Viatical Fraud Task Force in D.C. would be able to listen in. The local doofuses still seemed oblivious about Heartland's business or why I was going in there wearing a wire.

"If Crogan asks you if you have a qualifying medical condition," explained Rhuteen, "you say, 'I might have something I could see a doctor about,' something like that. Don't say yes, don't say no. Try and get *them* to tell you whether you qualify. They may send you over to see Guttman, which would be great. Or better yet, maybe Guttman will give you a physical exam to evaluate your application. That way, we'll have proof that he examined you before he issues a medical opinion to the investors that you have some obscure deadly-sounding 'terminal' disease like basal-cell carcinoma or an unspecified autoimmune disorder that 'significantly increases the likelihood of your morbidity and mortality.'

"If Mr. Crogan takes that line," said Rhuteen, "let him do it, but ask him questions along the way, like, 'Really? That would qualify me?' And let him explain it to you."

When I got off the phone with Rhuteen, McKnight took over.

"If something goes wrong in there, and you need help," said McKnight, "your escape line is: 'Do you have a rest room I could use?' Got it?"

I asked, "What do you mean, *if I need help?*"

"It's standard procedure for more dangerous stuff like undercover narcotics work," said McKnight. "These guys aren't armed or dangerous, but we have to give you a code-red line, anyway. These are white-collar types all the way. You might come out of there with a paper cut or form fatigue, but you won't have any other trouble. If you do, just say, 'Do you have a rest room I could use?' And we'll come straight in and take over."

"Okay," I said, but they didn't look like they could take over an ice cream store.

"Use the can in the lobby before you go in, so you won't actually have to pee while you're in there. And if for some unforeseen reason you *do* have to pee, then use any word but 'rest room,' say, 'Where's the bathroom?' or 'Where's the men's room?' or whatever. If the words 'rest room' come out of your mouth, then we come in wearing Kevlar with big guns out, understand? Please don't forget that, Mr. Hartnett."

"I got it," I said.

On the drive over, I had more misgivings about McKnight and Mutton. They looked as bored and blasé as ticket takers at a weekday matinee. They were college grads, with ruddy cheeks, precision haircuts, crisp white shirts, subdued ties, and degrees in criminal justice, but they still looked like Eagle Scouts out trying to earn a surveillance-technology merit badge. Only Langdon, the deaf guy, seemed enthusiastic about law enforcement. He had his little disk off again, grinning and watching me like the human lie detector he was.

I'd have felt better with Becker waiting outside, and if they'd let me tell him about the operation, I would have.

WIRED

HEARTLAND VIATICAL'S SUITE OF offices was on the third floor
of an ex-shopping mall in midtown South Omaha. It wasn't a
prestigious address, but the space was big, clean, well designed
and furnished, and it came with plenty of parking leftover from
its mall days. Down the hall was a satellite office for Earwig Tele-
marketing; one level below were the business offices of Data
Media Solutions, and right next-door was—handier than salt and
pepper in one cleverly designed shaker—Heartland Internal
Medicine Associates, with Raymond Guttman, M.D., heading
up a list of three doctors. Hector and his brother-in-law had half
of the third floor, sharing a reception area and waiting room out-
fitted in upholstered wood frames and glass tables with stacks of
People, Us, We, Them.

I checked in with a receptionist installed in a walnut booth.
She ran her candy red fingernail down the ledger and told me
that Mr. Crogan would be out in just a few minutes.

I spotted rest rooms off the main lobby and went in as instructed to protect the "escape clause" Agent McKnight had given me.

"Do you have a rest room *I could use? Got it? Pee before you go in."*

I didn't have to go, but I went anyway just to be sure, and it occurred to me that we lived in one heck of a connected world if FBI agents in Washington, D.C., could listen to my urine spurtling in a porcelain toilet in Omaha, Nebraska.

"If the words 'rest room' come out of your mouth—"

I washed up and patted the cell phone in my interior sport coat pocket. It was one of those ultrathin StarTAC units and didn't make so much as a bulge that I could see in the mirror.

Back out in the lobby, I had a good view into Guttman's clinic, and it looked semibusy. Every third or fourth chair had a patient waiting in it, from moms with little kids, to gimpy old guys, to a healthy-looking woman in a dark suit reading a *Forbes* magazine. Maybe Guttman handled Hector's viatical medical exams and chart reviews, but he or his associates also had what appeared to be a decent clinical practice, as well.

While I waited for Hector I saw a surveillance camera staring back at me. It was mounted just below the ceiling between the office suites, and I wondered if it came with the building or if Hector and Guttman had installed it.

A lock buzzed on the glass doors that said HEARTLAND VIATI-CAL, INC. in silvery lettering, and out came a guy who looked like he'd walked off the pages of a men's wear catalogue. He had my six feet beat by another four inches at least, all angles in the jaw and shoulders and sandy hair blown back in gelled waves, but with the edges trimmed close in straight lines all the way from his missing sideburns to the squared edges at the collar of his shirt. He'd gotten a tan somewhere besides a booth, because he had a vizard that was two shades lighter where his sunglasses or ski goggles had been. Here in the depths of a Midwestern winter he looked like a fair-haired George Hamilton. I'd been expecting a middle-aged businessman, but Hector looked my side of thirty, prosperous, and professional.

"Mr. Hartnett, come in, please," he said.

He had the stiff, polite carriage of an ex-military guy but was dressed out in a thousand-dollar suit and a dark tie. The only unfortunate wardrobe choice was the cowboy boots; somewhere along the line Hector had come down with the mania you see in these parts for hand-tooled saddle boots made out of alligator tail, diamondback rattlesnake, Malaysian gecko, or full-quill ostrich skins. All I knew was that they probably cost more than my car and my home computer combined.

Firm grip on the handshake, friendly blue eyes.

He opened the tinted glass door with the panache of a Park Avenue doorman and led me through a cube farm with computer monitors and phone-bound employees whose voices melted in the invisible soft hiss of noise-reduction technologies. He traded wisecracks with several of them about having an insurance investigator on the premises, his manner a perfect blend of authority and camaraderie. Maybe I'd never know if Hector was a fraudster, but one thing was clear: He was a nice guy, and his employees liked him.

At the outer perimeter of the circular floor plan every office was a corner one, and Hector had the biggest slice, with the rest of the pie carved into smaller tinted-glass offices. More young men and women dressed in office casual sat in front of workstations, staring into their flat panels.

As Hector walked ahead on into his office, I got the definitive pedigree on the boots: etched in gold lettering on the back of the left heel it said "Burmese" and the right heel read "Python."

Hector's office was done in peg-wood floors with a nine-by-twelve Karastan rug, and every stick of furniture was part of a matching set that looked like he'd ordered it out of the Levenger catalogue.

He put his hands on the back of an upholstered armchair with leather armrests and brass buttons—the middle chair in a matched set of three. I sat in it, while he went behind his desk and settled back in a chair that was the twin brother of Norton's Herman Miller.

"You don't find people from our industries sitting down together too often, now, do you?" he said with a chuckle.

Given what guys like Lenny and I had done to the viatical-fraud industry, I expected suppressed hostility to singe the edges of his joshing. Some of the bigger life companies were canceling and rescinding *all* viaticated policies and telling the viatical outfits to bring on the lawyers if they wanted to be paid. Insurance companies keep platoons of lawyers on retainer the way other companies lease equipment or hire temporary line workers. Protracted litigation put even legitimate operators in a terrible squeeze with investors like Ashwater or worse breathing down their necks, federal agents sniffing up their ass, and insurance companies telling them to bend over. But so far Hector was nothing but professionally cheerful.

"It's a truce," I said. "I thought we should meet because we got a policy at Reliable to pay on. Leonard Stillmach's policy, and according to our computers, Heartland Viatical owns it."

Hector glanced at his monitor and clicked once on his mouse, then gave me his full attention.

"Lenny was an exceptional investigator," said Hector. "Most people in your business assume that if it has *viatical* in the name it's a fraud outfit. Lenny outgrew his industry prejudices. We gave him access to everything he needed to see us for what we are—a legitimate, professional viatical-settlement company. We'll do the same for you. All you have to do is ask. The main reason insurance companies hate us has nothing to do with fraud," he added with a genuine smile. "It's because we keep policies in force that would otherwise lapse."

Some truth to that, I thought, and again it was AIDS behind it. Not many people can afford to pay all the AIDS bills *and* keep up the premium payments on the old life insurance policy. If they get too sick to work, the budget gets even smaller. So they cancel the policy or let it lapse. The insurance company gets to keep all the premiums paid over the years and doesn't have to pay a nickel in the death benefits when the inevitable happens.

"I found more policies on Lenny," I said. "Several. Most of them assigned to your company."

Hector looked stoic, almost sad, as if he were an oncologist and Lenny was a favorite patient who had succumbed to the big C.

"We work hard here," said Hector. "We built our own business in a new, formerly unregulated field trying to help sick, desperate people sell their life insurance policies to qualified investors. It has its own rewards, but I can't tell you what it meant to us here at Heartland to have a crackerjack Special Claims investigator of Lenny's caliber, a guy who started out investigating us and ended up turning to us in his hour of need."

I'd dealt with enough lawyers to know that Hector was of the courtroom variety, or had been for long enough to learn just how to talk to juries and anybody else who needed talking to, but his charm seemed more a gift he was sharing with me than a mere tool in the cynical service of self.

"When you say, 'his hour of need,'" I said, "was Lenny in more than the usual trouble? Medical trouble?"

Hector shook his head and smiled a big, friendly one. "You know the industry's privacy policies better than I do, especially when it comes to medical records. We can't discuss Lenny's medical records or his transactions with this company. You understand, of course?"

"I'm just curious," I said. "Lenny didn't look that sick to me, but you bought a lot of big life insurance policies from him. Was Lenny typical of your clients?"

"Ah!" he said, as if he knew just what I was asking. He pushed a button on his receptionist phone and did a one-minute wave of his finger while the open line trilled.

"I think I can answer your question," he said.

"This is Teresa," and I recognized the perky voice of Hector's assistant coming out of the speaker.

"Teresa, is Don with anyone?"

"No," she said, "but he's on his line. I don't think he's going to be long, if you want me to send him over after?"

"That would be great," said Hector, and clicked off.

He swiveled back toward me and patted a Waterman pen lying askew on a blank legal pad.

"Don sought us out first as a client, but then he came to believe so strongly in our services that we hired him to help us target market segments and articulate our mission to the people most in need of our services. The viatical-fraud outfits have made for some hideous publicity. It forces legitimate businesses like us to do a lot of aggressive remedial marketing and advertising, so we try to be flexible when clients come to us with insurance polices they wish to sell."

"Even if they aren't sick?"

"Well, in the case of, say, the new senior life insurance settlements, there's no requirement that the viator or settlor have a terminal illness, or any illness for that matter," Hector explained. "Most of our senior clients owned relatively large policies with increasing premiums that had become a burden with age. When we buy the policies from them we assume the premium obligations, of course, and we are able to provide them with a settlement they can spend to increase the quality of life in retirement. When the policy matures, meaning the viator passes, then our investors enjoy a reasonable profit."

"Lenny had big policies, too," I said, "but he wasn't old."

Hector nodded good-naturedly. "I was just explaining our willingness to be flexible when prospective clients approach us with insurance products they wish to sell to our investors. Most of our clients aren't seniors, most of them are—"

Somebody knocked twice lightly on Hector's open door, and I looked over to see that it was the Angel of Death himself standing there dressed in black everything—black jacket, black knit T-shirt, black baggies, even black shoes and socks—all of which highlighted the sallow pallor of his gaunt neck and hairless head. He looked like an emaciated Johnny Cash in a burning ring of dire.

"Don, come on in," said Hector.

Don weighed all of ninety or a hundred pounds. He had a purplish blotch on one side of his neck, and wet sores around his mouth. You didn't need to read the lettering over his shirt pocket that said: PROUD TO BE POSITIVE to guess his condition. Even the portable oxygen tank he had slung over one shoulder was in a black sheath, with clear tubing running from the O_2 nozzle to a nasal cannula that looped around bloodless ears with all the color of paraffin wax.

I got on my feet quick, the way people do when somebody famous walks in the room. Hector introduced me as a Special Claims investigator from Reliable Allied Trust with questions about what kind of clients Heartland Viatical served.

"Nobody articulates our mission statement better than Don," said Hector. "He's my all-American lineman. I'm just a rookie running back."

Don drifted like a spirit over to me, weightless on his black crepe shoes, and I kowtowed with the excessive politeness that often accompanies terror.

He smiled serenely and extended his hand. He had wire-rim glasses with huge black pupils behind them that seemed to be seeing more of everything than everybody else. He seemed to be living Eternity right now, not the infinite temporal duration of heaven or hell, but the true timelessness of *being* completely in the moment.

I gave him a hearty Midwestern handshake, just the way I'd shake the hand of any regular guy, just like I wasn't thinking about getting AIDS from that tiny open sore on the back of his right-hand ring finger.

Don settled himself like a leaf on the captain's chair to the left of mine.

"Mr. Hartnett," he said, "when death approaches, people speak the truth. There's no time left to gain anything by lying. Even the law says a dying declaration is more than hearsay. This man," he said, with a moist glance at Hector, "and this company gave me back my dignity. In my good years, my prescription-drug bills were twenty-eight hundred dollars a month. Now I'm in and out of the ICU, so it's up over ten grand, easy. In between, I had enough food, but I was too sick to prepare it."

He coughed, and I could see a blue vein squiggle under the translucent skin of his forehead.

"I had a five-hundred-thousand-dollar life insurance policy. I have no children. My parents are both dead. I have one sister who thinks I killed my parents by telling them I was gay. I was too sick to work. What would you do, Mr. Hartnett? First I went to the insurance company and said, 'I'm going to die soon, and my partner is going to collect on my insurance policy for five hundred thousand tax-free. How much would you give me for my policy right now?' The answer was nothing, probably because they were hoping I'd go completely bust so I couldn't keep up the premium payments, and the policy would lapse."

From the sounds of it, Don had a legitimate policy, too, just like Lenny's. The 500K would trigger a medical exam, and Don must have passed it, way back when. From the looks of him now, if he'd sold it recently, he'd gotten top dollar, probably seventy or eighty cents on the dollar, because he was definitely on his way up the ladder and out of the pool.

"So," he continued, "what kind of clients do we serve at Heartland Viatical? Mainly people just like me."

Hector looked smitten with tenderness, on the verge of touching himself, and I paused to consider how all of this was sounding to the boys in the van. I began to wonder if Rhuteen and the guys in D.C. had anything more to go on than hunches that these guys had a viatical fraud mill going here. I had the distinct impression that if I proposed anything illegal, Hector and Don would take offense at the stereotype, but I figured that it was my job as a confidential informant for the U.S. government, so I plowed ahead.

"I understand," I said to Don. "When Lenny and I saw the viatical policies start rolling in, we told the people upstairs in Product Development that Reliable needed to come up with an accelerated benefits option, so that we could in effect buy policies back from our own customers, instead of forcing them into the sometimes, uh, treacherous secondary market."

Then I looked Hector's way. "But Lenny once said something about how even somebody like me could sell my policy to a company like Heartland, especially if Heartland found itself needing more policies for one reason or another. I mean, I have a policy now, and I could get others, if I thought I could sell them."

"Do you have a qualifying medical condition?" Hector asked. He glanced at Don, then back at me. "No need to say *what* condition, of course, but do you—"

"I might have something I could see a doctor about," I said, using the very words Rhuteen had recommended, and the cell phone banged against my pattering heart, as if I could feel them right there listening.

"Interesting," said Hector with a smile and elaborate nod. "I can print you an application form right now. I'll go over it with you, and then you can either fill it out here or take it with you."

Hector looked to be calling up a file on his screen, but his monitor was angled away from me.

He typed on his keyboard, and said, "That's H-a-r-t-n-e-t-t, right?" asked Hector.

"Right," I said. "Here's a card."

Hector took it from me, slid it alongside his keyboard, and went back to typing.

"Don," said Hector, "see if Dr. Ray's with a patient. If not, ask him to come over and meet Mr. Hartnett."

"Sure, Hec," said Don, and took a couple of deep breaths to prepare himself for the journey, exhaling through pursed purple lips.

"Tell him to bring the lab tote with him," said Hector, "in case Mr. Hartnett wants to get the application blood work and urinalysis out of the way. Then he won't have to come back for another unnecessary appointment."

"I will," said Don, and he vanished without a sound.

Hector chattered while he typed. "Sometimes we're able to help clients who have medical conditions not commonly thought of as terminal," Hector explained. "Suppose, for instance, the prospective viator has a large life insurance policy and was recently diagnosed with severe coronary artery disease, or a stage-two or better melanoma or an autoimmune disorder. Terminal? Hardly, but the policy owner now has ratable risk factors and the insured has a greater likelihood of morbidity and mortality, a risk we or our investors may bet on if the price is right. It's not rocket science. It's no different than buying corn futures in a drought."

"I see," I said. "But what if I don't have anything too serious—"

Hector stopped me with a traffic cop's open hand. "That's Dr. Ray's end of the business," he said with mock solemnity. "Once we have an application and medical records, he'll spell out your options."

Don's sickly double knock sounded again on the open door, and he had the good doctor Guttman in tow.

"Ray, close that door for us," said Hector.

Guttman was not much older than Hector but was pudgy and puffy, with prematurely thinning hair and bags under his eyes. I remembered how Lenny had told me that if I ever had the chance to party with Ray, I should ask him to bring his black bag of goodies. His white lab coat had HEARTLAND INTERNAL MEDICINE ASSOCIATES stitched in royal blue over a pocket protector bristling with penlights, tongue depressors, and rubber reflex hammers. And instead of a black bag, he had a rubber tote with slotted compartments, stoppered vials, sterile-packaged needles and syringes, and sealed specimen cups.

Don drifted to my left, where he leaned against a file cabinet veneered in oak. I saw him adjust something in his black sport coat pocket. A Palm Pilot? Cell phone? Then he took off the sport coat, folded it, and set it on the file cabinet. His arms looked like bleached bones and black veins shrink-wrapped in wax paper, but he was still beaming eternity at me. I thought, *God bless you, Don.*

"I'm Dr. Guttman," said Ray with a handshake that squeezed once, then melted and withdrew. "Any friend of Lenny Stillmach gets the red carpet here," he chuckled, "even if you're still working for an evil corporate insurance behemoth."

His tone was sardonic and playful and suggested that he didn't take anything, including medicine, too seriously. I could see how he and Lenny might wind up on the same antic and agreeably deranged page together, both devotees of the work-hard-play-hard school of thought.

He pulled up another captain's chair and set his lab tote on it. The syringes were all sealed in paper and plastic, the needles each in its own sterile bubble on a perforated sheet. It all looked autoclaved and safe, and if I had to let Dr. Ray draw routine blood work on me to further an FBI investigation, I guessed I would.

"You probably should lose the sport coat," said Guttman.

"Nah," I said, pulling up the right sleeve well above my elbow. "See? It's a baggy coat over a short-sleeve shirt."

He shrugged for me to suit myself and sorted sterile packets in the tote, gathering his paraphernalia.

I smiled at Ray and turned my right arm supine, the crook of my elbow naked below the coat sleeve and shirt.

Mainly I was thinking that no matter what happened here, I had discharged my obligations to Agent Jeffrey Rhuteen and his Viatical Fraud Task Force. GothicRage86 would send me the image of whoever was at Lenny's, and I could hand it to Becker tomorrow. I could clear Lenny of a suicide and maybe even prove that it was Heartland, not Lenny, that had done the lion's share of the scamming when it came to selling his insurance to viatical investors like Ashwater.

Hector grabbed some sheets as they came off the printer. I could see that the top page was written in all capital letters. A disclaimer or a legal waiver of some kind?

"I know it's tedious," Hector said, and smiled with teeth so perfect they had to have been whitened by the new argon lasers, "but I always sit right here and wait while a prospective client like yourself reads our application. Most misunderstandings can be avoided if applicants just take the time to read the paperwork very carefully. I'll answer any questions you may have."

Hector slid off the top sheet only, the one with the capital letters, and he didn't really give it to me, he turned it around and held it up in front of my face so I could read it. The top two lines said:

(1) WEARING A DIGITAL LISTENING DEVICE! HOW AWK-WARD!

(2) READ THIS VERY CAREFULLY **OR YOU *WILL BE DEAD.***

Right about the time I read the word *dead,* I heard a cough and a muffled click to my left, where Don's right hand had been inside his folded black jacket. Then he was standing in the periphery like the proverbial Footman, only he wasn't holding my coat and snickering, just pressing cold metal against my left temple.

Hector's face was still a beacon of professional good cheer, and he held up what looked like a small, black walkie-talkie with a stubby black antenna that was as thick as a cigar. The LCDs on the face of the device were silently streaming numbers and lights, and the white lettering above the readout said, "Digital Range Finder."

On Ray's side I felt something soft and plastic brush the top of my wrist, like those hollow rubber tourniquets they use to tie off your arm for a blood sample.

"Do keep reading," Hector said.

(3) PRISON TERMS AND DEATH SENTENCES HOLD NO
TERRORS FOR MY GOOD FRIEND DON. AND WHO WILL
BLAME HIM IF HE LOSES IT AND COMMITS JUSTIFIABLE
HOMICIDE AGAINST AN INSURANCE NAZI WHO DENIES
MEDICAL CLAIMS FOR A LIVING?

(4) SAY ONE WORD. ANY WORD! ONE WORD COMES
OUT OF YOUR MOUTH AND YOUR BRAINS WILL EXIT YOUR
SKULL STAGE RIGHT.

(5) DO NOT MOVE.

(6) DO NOT SAY ONE WORD.

(7) JUST LISTEN.

(8) DO THAT AND YOU'LL LEAVE ALIVE, MAYBE EVEN
UNHARMED.

I started shaking hard and taking breaths wherever I could fit
them in. Guttman reached across my lap, and I felt another delicate brush of tubing or string on my left wrist. Then two light
clicks, and when I looked down my wrists were strapped to the
chair arms with thick plastic zip ties, the kind electricians use to
bundle cables, the kind you don't get off without wire cutters, or
maybe that's why Guttman had that huge pair of surgical scissors
in his tote? Only question, I guess, was whether I'd be alive or
dead when he cut them off.

Hector shrugged as if he truly regretted the poor choices I'd
made in life but was helpless to do anything about them at this
late hour.

Don coughed, and the muzzle nudged my temple.

My adrenals were sparking like 220 volts ungrounded, firing

currents all the way out to my fingertips. My internal organs swelled up with fight-or-flight juices. I discovered that terror dramatically affects vision, because suddenly I could see everything—the minute textures of every surface in my field of vision, as if I were a bird of prey scanning the forested terrain of the desktop, the floor, the tote, the file cabinet, searching not for prey but for a tool, a clue, any new detail—the letter opener in Hector's pencil cup, the syringes and scissors in Dr. Ray's lab tote, the distance between my restrained left wrist and the gun Don held to the side of my head—any speck of hope I could fall upon and embrace, any byte of information that might help me convince these men to let me leave that room alive. But I had to do it *without saying one word. Without moving?*

Hector shook the same paper in front of me. His voice was still ringing like a bell. Perfectly natural. He could win friends, influence people.

"And for their own protection, we always insist that our prospective clients read the application twice, so please take another careful look, Mr. Hartnett. It's standard procedure, and it's to protect you and every single one of our valued clients."

My eyes were twitching in their sockets now, but I could see he was waiting for me to read it again, and I felt Don give me a patient nudge with the barrel. Along with my new OmniVision technology, I felt the scales of religious skepticism fall from my eyes. I suddenly believed every single word of the Apostles' Creed with a new fervor that would have taught Job a thing or two.

I believe in God, the Father Almighty, Creator of Heaven and Earth,

and in Jesus Christ, His only Son . . .

"Pay particular attention to lines four, five, and six," said

Hector, "where it lays out the necessary preconditions for a successful application."

They were easy to find because Hector had thoughtfully bolded them for me.

(4) SAY ONE WORD. ANY WORD. ONE WORD OUT OF YOUR MOUTH AND YOUR BRAINS WILL EXIT YOUR SKULL STAGE RIGHT.

(5) DO NOT MOVE.

(6) DO NOT SAY ONE WORD.

Dr. Guttman tore open a syringe packet with a practiced snap of his wrists and popped one of the bubbles for a needle. I smelled alcohol when he tore the seal on a prepackaged wipe.

The cell phone was banging hard against my thrumming heart muscle, and I knew just what they were hearing outside: "Pay particular attention to . . . Review the application carefully . . ." I'd be dead five times over before the FBI knew what was going down, especially since one of them was deaf!

Deep inside my limbic system—somewhere in my squirming brain—a little homunculus sat at his console screaming the escape clause that McKnight had given me: *Do you have a rest room I could use? If not, I'm about to have an accident and flood command central with pure adrenaline.*

Hector propped his paper up on the front of his desk so I could still read it. Guttman donned double surgical gloves and finished preparing the syringe.

Hector pattered along in the mundane singsong voice he would use to convince any skeptical applicant of the worth of his services.

"Now it's true you probably wouldn't be a typical Heartland Viatical client," he said. "God knows, Lenny was anything but typical."

"Too true," Guttman chimed in. "Nothing typical about dear Lenny."

Hector opened a file and took out a big glossy photo and handed it to Don.

"You see, Mr. Hartnett," said Hector, "you are accustomed to seeing us and our mission to serve our clients from *inside* the Special Investigations Unit at Reliable Allied Trust. Our goal is to help you see Heartland Viatical the way our patients and clients see us. Imagine that you or perhaps a loved one had a terminal illness."

Don held a grainy eight-by-ten digital photo of Miranda up in front of me, where the afterimages of Hector's printed death threats were still swimming in the air. It was a head shot of her coming out the revolving door of Reliable's offices, unaware of the camera: right between her eyes was a big bullet hole in the photo, with real powder burns around it, from the looks of it.

"When you or a loved one has a terminal illness, life becomes a desperate struggle to survive at any cost," said Hector in the soothing voice of a financial consultant or a bereavement counselor.

Guttman had slipped out of his chair on my right and had come around to my left where Don was holding the photo. The doctor wasn't looking at me, and I was damn glad because I'd decided ixnay on the blood work. Maybe next time.

Guttman took the photo and handed it back to Hector. Don extended his left arm, so Guttman could palpate a vein.

"Unlike you, most of our clients are desperate when they

come to us," Hector continued in the same maddening, routine tone of voice, pausing briefly now and again to shuffle papers.

"You should take a moment and imagine yourself like poor Lenny," offered Hector. "Because before I accept your application, and before we enter into our agreement, I need for you to *believe* in us and our services, *believe* in Heartland Viatical, and know with all of your heart that we are a legitimate, professional viatical-settlement association."

I opened my mouth to say something like, *"By the bleeding wounds of Sweet Jesus Christ my Savior, I believe!"* But then everybody froze in horror and looked like there was going to be an awful mess to clean up if I did.

I believe in God, the Father Almighty, Creator of Heaven and Earth, and in Jesus Christ, His only Son, and that Heartland Viatical is a legitimate, professional viatical-settlement association . . .

Without moving my head, I tried to strain to the left for a look at Don. He must have felt my eyeballs roll against the gun barrel, because he leaned forward a little, as if to reassure me that he was still there, placid countenance and all, manifesting not a trace of malice or ill will; nothing but angelic tranquility and inner peace, except now he happened to be poking a gun barrel against my head.

Guttman had finished drawing Don's blood and pushed a cotton ball over the hole he'd made. Don folded his arm over it and mashed it in place between his bony forearm and biceps.

"Lenny had insurance policies to sell," said Hector brightly. "And he supplied us with medical records that would indicate he had a qualifying medical condition."

Guttman's eyebrows flew up and he made an exaggerated face that wordlessly said, *"Yeah-right!"*

Guttman walked back around to his lab tote, but he still had the needle uncovered, and he went right past the tote and sat down in the captain's chair next to me. He held the needle about six inches from the crook of my elbow and frowned, as if he was thinking about what to do with it.

My eyes stayed on the needle, where a black tear of Don's blood quivered and hung from the tip. It was like a tiny dark convex mirror, and if I kept zooming in on it with my new panoptic, high-resolution eyesight I could see the whole room, I could see to infinity and beyond reflected in it.

Show unto us the blessed fruit of thy womb, Jesus! O clement, O loving, O sweet Virgin Mary!

"But you must understand that Lenny's transactions with Heartland Viatical, and indeed *your* transactions with us here today, are *strictly* confidential," said Hector.

Guttman held my right arm down even though he didn't need to, if I struggled, the zip ties would tear into my flesh like razor wire and weasel teeth.

Guttman wasn't smiling really, just lowering the needle an inch or two at a time toward the bulging vein at the inner aspect of my right elbow, with his thumb on the plunger of the syringe.

My pores flushed sweat, and I kept wondering what the juvenile government morons in the van were thinking about my gasps for air.

Hey, Growney. Does that guy you wired have asthma?

Would Don and Hector and Guttman consider it an innocent mistake and excusable error if I suddenly said, *"Do you have a rest room I could use?"* Under the circumstances, they had to know I needed a rest room.

*Do not say one word? Fellas, I took it to mean unless I was about
to have an accident and needed to go to the rest room?*

That gun had to be getting heavy for poor Don, I thought,
and our telepathic link must have transmitted the data in real
time, because he went for the two-handed grip and kept the gun
in place. He leaned forward again and gave me another face full
of beatific serenity, as he silently mouthed words to me: "ONE
WORD. SAY ONE WORD."

I realized that unlike Hector or Ray, I, too, had stepped right
out of Time onto Don's side of the relativity equation, and we were
both looking at each other and sharing the black magic of the
moment standing still forever. It was just like old Einstein had said:
God invented Time so that everything doesn't happen at once. It
didn't last longer than any other single moment in my life, and
under other circumstances I'd probably have filled it with a lazy
half notion about what to drink that night or what new stratagem I
could employ to get Miranda into bed. Instead I was deep in *now-
ness* with Don, capable of satellite imaging and of thinking several
hundred thoughts all at once, not all of them rational. For instance,
I was wondering if I could look down at the growing damp spot
between my legs and say by way of explanation, *"Rest room?"*

Now that Ray was back on my right, would Don really splatter him with—?

Hector courteously held the paper back up, with his fingertip
helpfully bookmarking line 6:

(6) DO NOT SAY ONE WORD.

Deserts, mountain peaks, and vast oceans of eternity all
around, but still not a drop or glimmer of hope. Ray was lower-

ing his needle little by little, or I was imagining it, or terror was inflating my muscles, bulging my ripe blue vein out toward the needle. I made up my mind that if Ray stuck it in, I was going to say, "Rest room," before he could push the plunger down. If he did that, then I wanted Don to finish things for me right here, so I wouldn't have to count on myself to do it later. But wait, didn't that mean I should wait and see if he gave me the plunger?

To thee do we cry, poor banished children of Eve! To thee do we send up our sighs, mourning and weeping in this vale of tears!

"Without mentioning names," Hector continued, "or disclosing privileged medical information, we can give you demographic and statistical information on some of our clients whose needs and circumstances may resemble your own."

Hector fetched another sheet of paper and politely held it up for me.

"Here's a young woman just about your age who came to us with a term life insurance policy she wanted to sell."

It was a life insurance policy, or a copy of one, for three hundred thousand dollars from Omaha Beneficial.

> **Owner: Miranda Pryor.**
> **Insured: Miranda Pryor.**
> **Beneficiary: Annette Pryor.**

That didn't make sense, because Miranda's sister was the beneficiary, not the owner or the insured. It was Miranda's own life insurance policy.

Hector took that paper away and held up another one.

"And after we purchased the policy and added it to our portfolio of life insurance policies, it looks like this," he said.

Same policy, only now it had obviously been sold.

> Owner: Heartland Viatical
> Insured: Miranda Pryor
> Beneficiary: Heartland Viatical

Sins don't come any blacker than the lie she'd told me. *Good eye contact, too, Miranda! No blinking! That must take a lot of practice!* I saw the whole thing now. It was Lenny and her. She knew what kind of outfit this was, and she'd let me walk in here to find out the truth and get my head blown off or my blood infected.

"I didn't sell them any policies. Lenny and his friend helped my sister sell one. That's it. Get over it."

But Miranda had sold them at least one policy. It was right there in black and white with her signature on it. She and Lenny had both made good money, only difference was Miranda must have invested hers, while Lenny donated his to Harveys and Harrah's. She matched lies the way she matched scarves and gloves, textured tights and wool sheaths, sofa pillows and chenille throws. Maybe the Catholic bit was a tapestry of fine lies, too. Maybe the strict chastity rules only applied to me, because I might be useful, and it allowed her to keep me around without me despoiling the merchandise.

If I was really on the final jetway to Air Eternity, I'd be taking the last trip knowing she was all sham and scam. I was a fool in the court of her intrigue. I dressed myself in bells and motley, making merry whenever she pushed my remote. "Yes, Your Most Excellent Fraudulency," I'd sing before curling up on her leather sofa with a bone between my legs.

"So, to answer your question," said Hector, "yes, we have expanded our services to accommodate the needs of our clients, but we're careful to disclose the particulars of any diagnosis to our investors, so they have the benefit of our thorough medical testing before they make their decision to invest."

She could weasel and equivocate about every other bogus story she'd told me, but I had flat-out demanded the truth about whether *she* had sold any policies to Heartland, instead of just arranging a sale for her sister.

"I did not sell any life insurance policies on myself to Heartland Viatical."

There it was, and here I was. My only regret was that I couldn't stop by Miranda's place on my way to the airport for my last flight out on Infinity Airlines. I'd smash all of her crystal stemware, then tie her up and make her watch while I poured her treasured '97 Whitehall Lane reserve cabernets one by one into the toilet.

"If he was a scam king who conned Omaha Beneficial out of half a million, then yes, he'd be down there with all of the other liars for hire."

Liars for hire?

"I did not sell any life insurance policies on myself to Heartland Viatical."

And all the while my mind deep inside my matter was screaming: *Do you have a rest room I could use?*

Glory be to the Father, to the Son, and to the Holy Spirit. As it was in the beginning, is now and ever shall be, world without end. Amen.

If I could leave here without any bullet holes or needle holes in me, O clement, O loving, O sweet Virgin Mary, I'll say the rosary every morning for the rest of my goddamned life! And I'll be praying that somebody with divine authority will please send Miranda's soul to Rung Nine with the violent and the bestial, where fraud kings and queens gnaw on each other's scalps for all Eternity.

My heart beat like thunder, coming in waves every decade or so. I was expecting that Bird of Eternity to come along any century now and sharpen its beak on the barrel of Don's gun. I kept trying to snag sweet Hector's eyes with mine, so I could silently plead with him, using only my face and my eyes.

"If you come away from this meeting with only one thought," said Hector, "please let it be our policy of absolute confidentiality."

Hector handed two more glossies to Don, who fanned them in front of my face. The photo of Miranda with a bullet hole between her eyes, and right next to it a glossy of yours truly with three bullet holes, one in each eye and another in the center of my forehead.

"If we discover that you've breached our confidentiality policies," said Hector, "we would have no choice but to cancel everything. Including you . . . as a client, I mean, of course."

The universe came to a complete stop when Hector gave Dr. Ray a curt nod. It meant Eternity was ending and something was going to happen. But what?

26

ETERNAL LIFE GRANT UNTO HIM, O LORD

THE DOOR OF THE black van slid open, and the boys were inside eating Burger King Whoppers and frowning at me. I fell into the jump seat and panted for air, rubbed my arms, savored the horrible metallic taste in my mouth. I revelled in every last bit of my unmolested flesh. Maybe somebody would kill me tomorrow, and maybe tomorrow I'd be worried about it. But right here, right now, I had one roomy second after another—thousands of them if I stayed up again all night and examined each one—thousands of seconds to squander just sitting here feeling wet and cold, smelling my own urine and sweat and hideous breath. Air was a rare delicacy. Like Hamlet, I could be bounded in a nutshell or a pest-control van and count myself a king of infinite space.

McKnight wiped mayonnaise off his lips with a napkin.

"What happened? Why'd you stop talking?"

Like so many extreme states of consciousness, its effect was paradoxical. I had lived the terrors beyond the grave and now had come back fearless and reckless as Lazarus about the tiny threats of this one.

I was cold and shaking, my damp clothes clinging to me. I touched my face, my fingertips delighting in the tactile pleasures of my intact skull.

Hector had given the nod, and the good doctor Ray—God bless him! He was probably a good person who meant well!—had cut the zip ties. All I had to do was sign my application, while Hector pattered along in his unctuous, we're-here-to-serve ministerese: "Any breach of confidentiality has dire consequences, as you know."

Don had nudged me with the muzzle of his gun, and Ray had put the cap on his needle.

"We'll save this sample for you," he said. "So you won't have to come back. We hope."

Agent Langdon, the handsome, deaf one, was watching me. His little beige disk was off the side of his head and dangling against the lapel of his tweed jacket, meaning, I guess, that he just wanted to watch me again, without being distracted by sounds or words or explanations. See if I was telling the truth.

When he finished looking me over, he laughed and signed something to McKnight, who smiled.

"What?" I asked, and handed McKnight the cell phone that had almost gotten me killed.

"He says, 'Maybe Hector Crogan is not a nice man?'"

27

ESAU AND JACOB

S OME SAY THAT THE gods have two ways of dealing harshly with us: The first is to deny us our dreams, and the second is to grant them. For the moment, my dreams were stamped "granted," and I had plenty of infinite seconds left on earth to plan my next move, which would not entail working as a confidential informant for the Federal Bureau of Investigation.

Fuck the junior G-men and the Jehovah's Witnesses and the Eagle Scouts and the Viatical Fraud Task Force in Washington, D.C. Bend them over in the Terre Haute showers and zip-tie their hands to their ankles. I was picking up my chips and leaving the federal table. Tomorrow morning I'd stack them up in front of Charlie Becker in his interrogation room.

When Mutton asked me what had happened, I told him. He got a quizzical expression on his face and consulted with Mc-Knight. Whenever their whispers and murmurs surfaced above the traffic noise, I was able to gather the following: I seemed to be traumatized and emoting about a personal misfortune that was tragic and compelling, but had nothing to do with federal jurisdiction. Even if they decided to believe me, I was describing a simple assault, a local matter. They had nothing in their digital recordings to suggest that I'd been threatened. Mutton and McKnight's reasoning went this way: *This is the same guy who's lied to us how many times? Maybe we should check with the Viatical Fraud Task Force before we go barging in and spoil their investigation. What if we screw up their investigation, all because some lying insurance adjuster complained that somebody made him read a threatening note?*

No, they said. I should tell Becker about the assault, because then it would become part of his homicide investigation. They didn't even thank me for wearing a digital listening device into Heartland Viatical—because the recordings were useless, I guess, and so was I.

The only numbered clause I cared about in my cooperation agreement was the one I'd handwritten in and faxed back to Rhuteen for initials before I went into Hector's place: the clause that promised me the image file of whoever had been in Lenny's place the night he died. And according to my specific instructions and the terms of our agreement it should be on my home machine attached to an e-mail from GothicRage86, right about now.

Before I went home to get it, I had to stop by and see Eve, Lilith, Lorelei. Tie myself to the mast and sail by Siren Miranda's place. I wanted to sit with her in one of those eternal moments I'd shared with Don, make her see Eternity from this side of the grave the way I had.

She opened the door, took a look at me, and knew that bad things had happened to me, and that I was thinking about doing worse.

"What happened?" she asked, her voice quavering.

"I been through hell, Miranda, and I brought something back for you."

I'd learned a few things from regional investigator Becker in the short sessions I'd spent under his tutelage. Don't say a word, just let her talk. If she asks a question, don't answer, ask one back. If she tries to tell me a story . . . ?

I didn't want to hit her, I wanted to kill her. But even on rampage autopilot I knew that if I did that, I could wake up in Terre Haute, BOP Mid-Atlantic region, or in that nightmare penitentiary I'd dreamed about the night Lenny had died. I could kill her and then kill myself, which seemed to be the modern solution to these intractable crime-and-punishment dilemmas. Strangling her would be the easy part. After that, I was afraid I'd find myself in that Deep Valley of No Time I'd shared back at Heartland Viatical with my old buddy, Don Juan Gandhi—the moment standing still. I'd have a century or two to think about whether to turn a gun or knife on myself. A loss of nerve would land me in lockdown at Leavenworth with my new boyfriend, Butch the Dungeon Master.

She was afraid of me, and that was a thrill. I was a lot bigger and stronger than her and ready to enjoy every minute of it. She had her Christless Bible open on the table and that sent rage like a lightning fork to my brain stem. I tore out a fistful of onionskin sheets and threw them at her.

"Three hundred thousand," I said. I kept it businesslike, easy to understand. Why get emotional? "Omaha Beneficial. Owner, Miranda Pryor. Insured, Miranda Pryor. Beneficiary, Annette Pryor."

She looked like she was sorry she'd opened the door. Too late

to change that. Time goes forward, and treachery has consequences, my darling.

"Okay," she said. "I lied to them. I told them I had a qualifying medical condition."

I looked her up and down like the infected carcass of lies she
was, and I said, "Right, Miranda. What's your qualifying medical? Your bad back? Your mental illness? Pathological lying?
Mythomania? I can vouch for it being a ratable risk factor,
because it makes me want to rip your pretty head off. Like right
now."

"I didn't have a choice," she said. "I had to—"

"No, Miranda," I yelled. "No more stories from you. It's my
turn, and have I got a story for you! It's a really dark one, just the
way you like them, but I didn't get it from the Fraud Defense
Network or the *John Cooke Fraud Report*."

I ripped another wad of Bible pages and shredded them.

"No, I know how much you like religion and the Bible, so I
went to Bible-Dot-Com and made sure it's a fucking bona fide
Bible fraud story."

If she was breathing, I couldn't tell. She leaned over the coffee table and picked up her wineglass, but she was shaking too
much to get it to her mouth. Then she looked as if she was thinking about throwing it at me instead.

"I hate all that namby-pamby, New Testament, sign-of-
peace, love-your-neighbor crap, Miranda. I'm an Old Testament
guy. I wanna trade eyes and teeth."

She looked at the phone and knew she wasn't going to get to
it in time to dial 911 if it came to that. Then she looked at me.
Maybe I should let her *think* she was gonna make it to the phone,
even though she wouldn't.

"My name's Isaac," I said. "Remember? Abraham and Isaac? I'm Abraham's son, Isaac? My old man came within a gnat's ass of throwing my twelve-year-old flesh on a bonfire because he thought God was talking to him and asking him to sacrifice me so He could have some filet of firstborn son."

She took a shaky sip and tried to pretend we were just talking.

"An angel saved my bacon on that go-round. He probably gave old Abraham six hundred milligrams of Thorazine in the butt muscle and threatened him with commitment proceedings if he ever tried to serve me for lunch again. After that, Abraham, my crazy old man, lived to be a hundred seventy-five years old and left everything to me. We buried him next to my ma in a cave, and I took over as chief of operations."

"You're drunk," she said.

I picked up the nearest half-full wine bottle and sucked it dry.

"I'm tasting currants, anise, black cherry, coffee, herb, sage, chocolate, toffee, licorice, and spice with a long integrated finish," I said. "The nose on this is so perfect it makes me wanna break it black and blue with a sucker punch. Do you have any Pussy Fouissé?"

She tried to get up, and I pushed her back down on the leather sofa, right in front of old Gustav's *The Kiss*.

"I've listened to all of your play-acting fraud stories, Miranda. Now you're gonna listen to mine. My name's Isaac, Miranda. Read all about me in Genesis, Miranda. I married a woman named Rebekah, and we had two sons, twins actually: Esau and Jacob."

I could see it come home to her now, which was fine. I wanted her to know where I was going so I could force-feed her ears with every word of it. I let her think about it while I sucked on another bottle.

"That's where you come in, Miranda. Your name is Jacob. Your twin brother's name is Esau. Esau came out first all covered with hair, so guess what? He's my firstborn son. You came out second, just your basic naked newborn babe riding dead last in terms of inheritance.

She brushed shredded Bible pages off her lap and thought about trying to get up again.

"Both of you grow up and Esau becomes a skillful hunter, a rugged outdoorsy-type guy, with hair all over him. Esau is my personal favorite, because I like meat, and he brings me lots of it. You? You're a simple, smooth-skinned guy with soft hands, who likes to sit in his tent alone and think up news ways to fuck people out of what's rightfully theirs. Your mother's slippery herself, so she takes more of a shine to you than to honest Esau.

I poured another three fingers of wine into the nearest glass, drank it, and tossed it into the fireplace, just like they do in the movies.

"This wine is really good, Jacob. I'm tasting pear, lemon, fig . . . Where was I? That's right, I'm Isaac. Before long I get old, too, just like Abraham, my dad, did, and soon I'm older than the dirt in King Tut's tomb. I'm blind, I'm sick, I'm dying in bed. I can feel myself taking the far turn and headed for my last meal, so I call in my firstborn son. Not you, Jacob. Esau.

" 'Esau,' " I say, " 'take your bow and arrow and scare up some game. Cook it up rare the way I like it, and bring it in here on a platter. We'll have ourselves a real last supper, and then I'll give you my special, final, irrevocable blessing.' "

Miranda slowly turned and lowered her head into her arms, burying herself in the sumptuous leather interiors of her sofa, like maybe she couldn't hear me there. She was at least pretending to sob.

"As it happens, Miranda, I mean, Jacob, you had already fucked Esau over once before when he was starving, and you made him surrender his birthright to you before you'd give him a bowl of soup. It's right there in Genesis, Miranda. You're such a greasy greedhead, Jacob Miranda, that even a guy's birthright ain't enough for you. Now you want the blessing that I, Isaac, plan to give Esau, too, because my blessing will say who's who and what's what until Christ rides the pony into Jerusalem. And once it's done, it's done. In the Old Testament there were no take-backs on blessings, and what was done was done."

She got up off the couch and started up the loft stairs to the bedroom, and I followed her, chewing her shapely ass the whole way.

"So, what do you do, Miranda? While I'm out hunting, you and your mother, Rebekah the Rat, cook up two choice kids from the goat flock, and the old lady fixes them just the way I like them. She dresses you up in Esau's clothes, and she covers the back of your hands and the skin of your neck with goat hair and sends you on in with the food to see me.

She was crying hard, and what of it?

"So you come on in dressed up like your twin brother with our feast in hand, and you say, 'Father!'"

I was right behind her head, making my voice high when I was doing her and Jacob's part, following her through the bedroom so closely that if she stopped I'd probably break a tooth on her ivory hair comb.

"I'm fucking blind, feeble, and decrepit on my deathbed, Miranda, so I say, 'Yes, which of my sons are you?'"

She opened the bathroom door and turned to look at me, her cheeks tinseled in wet streaks, and her lower lip twitching, all the shit I'd seen before whenever she thought it would help grease the chute for another run of lies.

"So you *lie*, Miranda, like the siding salesman you are, and you say, 'It's me, Dad, Esau, your firstborn,' you say. 'I fetched some meat just like you told me, Dad. Sit up and eat it, and then hurry up with the special blessing.'"

She slammed the door, but I had my foot in it, and I could still see her in the mirror over the washstand.

"I'm blind, Miranda, and I'm dying in bed, but I still got half my wits about me, so I ask, 'How in the name of Methuselah's mother did you find meat so fast, Esau?'"

She glared at my reflection in the mirror, like she was one of those legendary, ancient reptiles that could kill you with a glance.

"What do you say, Miranda? I mean, Jacob? What do you say, Jacob Miranda? Maybe you're both. Maybe you're a fucking hermaphrodite, Jake, and that's why you don't like sex? What do you say, Miranda?"

The door was pinching my foot, and she was shoving hard on it and sobbing. I tried to reposition it, but the second I moved it she got the door shut and locked. I put my mouth right up where the door meets the jamb so I could keep on her.

"You say, 'I dunno, Dad! The Lord, your God, must have planned it that way.' And that's just the kind of shit you would say, wouldn't you, Miranda? It's God's will that you're a chiseling insurance cheat, isn't it?"

I stood there staring at the door, thinking about whether I ought to just break the fucker down. I wouldn't hit her. Probably wouldn't kill her either. Just break something big, like a door, and if the cops came, she could sue me for damages but that's about it.

"My mother, Sarah, didn't raise any fools, Miranda, so I say, 'Come on over here so I can feel you and see if it's really my son Esau or not."

"You walk right on over, barefaced as brazen brass, and come stand right next to me, and let me feel the goat hair on the back of your hands. And I say, 'Fuck me silly and turn out the lights. It's Jacob's voice, but the hands are Esau's. How in the fuck can that be?'

"So, I say it again, Miranda. I ask you point-blank, 'Are you really my son Esau?' "

I hammered on the door and yelled in to her.

" 'Are you really my son Esau, Miranda?' And what do you say, Miranda? What do you say?"

I had my leaky hot-water faucets going all of a sudden. Not sad, really, just purging fluids.

I hammered on the door, big loud ones, one for each syllable. "You lie and say, 'Fuck yes, it's me, Dad. It's Esau! Who in the fuck did you think it was? You didn't think it was that scam artist, Jacob the snake, did you?'

"I fall for it, Miranda. I fall like Cain falling into hell with the wicked. I fall hard. You and I eat food, we drink wine. We party righteous, Miranda. Then, I say, 'Come closer, son, and kiss me.'

"Not a problem for you, is it, Miranda? You kiss me, and you're so close I can smell you, smell your clothes—smell Esau's clothes, not yours. You kiss me, just like Judas kissed Christ, you bitch!"

Wham! I hit the door a good one.

"Then I let loose with your blessing, Jake. Jake the snake!"

I whacked it again, and the hurt in my hand bones felt good, just like everything else I'd been feeling since I got my new lease on life at Heartland Viatical.

"I love the smell of you, Esau, and I say, 'Ah, the fragrance of my son is like the fragrance of a field that the Lord has blessed! May God give to you of the dew of the heavens and the fertility of the earth, abundance of grain and wine. Let peoples serve you, and nations pay you homage. Be master of your brothers, and may your mother's sons bow down to you. Cursed be those who curse you, and blessed be those who bless you.' "

I pushed on the door, and it opened with no resistance, which left me suddenly with nothing to bang on. She'd turned out the lights over the washstand, but there was a walk-in closet behind her, where I saw the clothes she'd been wearing scattered on the floor.

She wore a kimono-style pink satin wrap with the sash tied, her breasts roaming around free underneath as she walked toward me. Her face was twitching with hate, and her eyes were on mine like missile-lock.

"You wanna feel my skin and find out if it's really me, Isaac?" she said.

I hadn't planned on getting in without breaking down the door, and now I was suddenly in here, with nothing to do, except maybe the second-oldest crime known to man and woman.

I just stood there, breathing heavy, sweating, watching her, like you'd watch a new species in a lab, continually amazed by her surprising behaviors. It was a maneuver of some kind. She was making me think she was going to give it up. She'd move us out near a phone or a weapon, or maybe she'd make a run for the neighbor's place, call Becker and tell him that Carver Hartnett had assaulted her in her boudoir.

"Close your eyes, Isaac," she said, her face still on low boil. "You're blind, remember? Close your eyes, and I'll put you back in bed, and let you feel the back of my hands and my neck. See if it's really Esau, or not."

She moved closer to me and reached for my hands. I jumped at first, like I was expecting she'd palmed one of good doctor Ray's uncapped syringes. Maybe she'd done the same thing to Lenny the night he died? Maybe she'd killed Lenny just this way. Maybe she was a double agent or an operative in one of those James Bond video games, and she'd walk me over to the bed, and just when I thought I was going to get some, she'd finish me off with a lipstick gun, lethal acid perfume, or a diamond-chip and titanium-strand garrote spooled inside her fake-gold watch.

The fire went out of her eyes. I let her take my hands, and I could feel her shaking. She was afraid, too, and not just mad.

"Close your eyes," she said.

I did, but I still had plenty of hate in me making my eyelids jitter like I was watching ancient, overexposed film race through the sprockets of my internal projector: blood reds and midnight shadows, skipped frames, flashes of light from sharp instruments and blunt weapons she'd use to hunt me in the darkness to which I'd acquiesced. Because I trusted her? No fucking way. I had to know what she'd done with Lenny on-line and otherwise, had to know if she went all the way and murdered the poor fucker, or helped a hale fellow well-met like Hector or Guttman do the job. If she told me that the only way I could know the truth about Lenny was to let her show me, I was going to let her. I'd drink the coffee with the sleeping pill, and maybe I'd wake up alone in a coffin, hearing her dump shovelfuls of dirt on the coffin lid. *Thrump. Thrump. Thrump,* and me alone in the box, with nothing but a butane lighter to watch the last of my oxygen burn. No, that wasn't like her; she'd run a pipe down there so I could breathe and have an extra week to think it all over.

She backed me up out of the washroom. She was gentle about it, but maybe she was just putting me off guard.

"That's it, Isaac."

I opened my eyes and watched her, holding my hands, walking me backwards, guiding me over to her bed. She looked bitter and resolved, her face somber and agloom, as if she were leading me outside to a skyless gray dawn on the morning of my execution.

She turned out the lights when we went by the switch, and it was suddenly as dark as the tombs under the Sphinx.

She sat me on the bed, and I figured once she got me off my feet, she'd bolt, or smash my face in and run for it, but she didn't.

She let go of my hands and said, "Wait."

She struck a match and lit a blue candle on her nightstand.

I swallowed hard and watched her bending over the candle, her dark hair spilling onto the pink satin. Her runner's legs looked basted in oil and ready to eat.

She caught me watching and said, "Close your eyes, Isaac. You're blind, remember?"

Her voice was farther away from seduction than heaven is from earth; instead it was clotted with sadness and hope forlorn.

"Lie down, Isaac," she said. "You're old and sick. I'll give you what you want, and then you'll give me your blessing."

I obliged and lowered myself back on her fat pillows, but I cheated and peeked, so I could watch her walk around the bed to the other side, where she climbed in with me, and with no weapons, as near as I could tell.

I needed some spit bad, because my mouth was open and moving a lot of air.

She crawled over close to me and rolled onto her side, still looking nothing like romantic. She kissed me a good one, tongue and all, then she drew back and stared.

"Miranda?"

"Wait, Isaac," she said.

She found the satin sash and untied it.

That was enough for me. I went in for another deep kiss, and she kissed me back.

I took a breath and watched her move under the robe, the candle glow flickering like flames on her silk-draped curves. I felt my damp pants rising like a pup tent on a pole.

We could hear each other breathing.

I touched her breast, and she pushed it into my hand, her eyes watching me. Touching her.

She had to know how hungry for it I was, and if this was another scam of hers, it wasn't going to end with me going out to the couch with a hangover hard-on and blue balls. Long ago, I'd decided that if her sex phobias were Catholic, then I'd have to marry her after I did it, or she'd have a nervous breakdown or a psychotic break. It made me pause on the brink, but then I slid my hand under the silk robe.

My throat parched and hurt when I didn't have enough moisture for a swallow.

"Close your eyes, Isaac," she said, with that same haunted tone.

I obeyed, even though it occurred to me that she might have an ice pick at the ready. Instead, her left hand took my right and steered it under the gown, just like she had done in my dream.

"Come closer, Isaac," she whispered.

I moved up from her hip to the curve at her waist, where I felt something rough, and my first thought was that she had a huge gauze bandage on under her silk kimono, which didn't make a lick of sense.

I opened my eyes, and she pulled the flap of the gown away, showed me those glorious breasts I'd wanted my hands on from day one. But where my hand was, at her waist, was Annette's giant nevus, as big as a catcher's mitt. The skin was black and bumpy, just like the photos I'd seen attached to her e-mail to Lenny.

My hand went limp, but I had enough sense not to jerk it away. I just left it there, trying to shut down tactile sensations from my fingertips. It felt like busted Styrofoam or dried leather.

Her eyes were afraid, like the family dog on her way to the pound to be put to sleep. She was just a big organism, like me, but she'd lost the power of speech and had only her eyes—complex, light-sensitive organs, open and laid bare, like gutted shellfish, with all the soul removed.

I didn't know how many other guys had made it this far, but I wasn't going to do whatever they had done. I looked right at her, straight into her naked eyes. I touched it, too, just like I wasn't a bit afraid of it. I imagined the other guys, excusing themselves to go dry-heave in the can and then come back for a long discussion about her affliction. Probably not one of them had just gone ahead and done their duty.

"Miranda," I said, "I don't care about that. We can just cover that up any time we want."

My intention was to believe those words, and soon. My plan was to wake up tomorrow and say aloud to her and myself for the rest of our lives, "Miranda, I don't care about that." It would be like Faith, something I had to say over and over and work on every day to make sure I didn't take it for granted, and then maybe one day I'd wake up really believing it. But I was also afraid that I couldn't do it, afraid that I *would* care about it. I wanted to take a day or two and think about whether I cared about a big black mole on my wife's hip. It wasn't going away soon, I could see that. And I could see the flatter, scarred places where they'd tried to fix it, and I had a good idea of how it would look even with the rest of the black mole removed.

Somehow she believed in God, even after being born with that on her, or maybe that was why she believed, because God was all she had.

"Now you know why I spend on clothes," she said.

Then she reached down and touched me, right through my damp pants.

Right then I knew what had happened with every other guy who'd been here before me. They hadn't had anything down there for her to grab on to. They'd lost it, because they were squeamish, half-assed amateurs.

Not me.

PISS FOR COLD BEER

I CHANGED MY MIND," said Becker. "I'm not going to charge you with being dumber than you look."

I knew it! Agent Rhuteen of the Viatical Task Force obviously had kept his promise and had called Becker to report my services above and beyond the call of duty.

He poured more coffee for me and spilled some Old Golds my way.

We were back in our little interrogation room, which I was starting to think of as our office, where we would be working together to solve crimes, arrest Hector and his minions, find out which weasel killed Lenny. Soon Becker would be proud of me indeed. I had the image file from GothicRage right there in front of me.

"You're not going to charge me?" I said, trying not to sound too proud of myself.

"Not with being dumber than you look," said Becker.

"Instead I'm going to charge you with being a water-headed, Mongolian clusterfuck."

Becker was expressionless, as usual, but not without emotion. He ran the gamut from scathing sarcasm to flashes of tenderness whenever he mentioned "poor Lenny" or "the victim's family," all without moving a facial muscle.

"Somebody was at Lenny's place the night he died, and I've got a time-stamped JPG image of her right in here," I said, tapping the folder.

"And JPG," he said, "that must be Mongolian for something I could use to swat you upside the head? You and computers." He shook his head. "That's why you ran off to pretend you were a secret agent for a day, right? Those FBI guys are all computer techies now. They don't even talk to people anymore. They leave that to us menials who work on unimportant local matters, like homicides."

I pulled out the digital image GothicRage had sent me and passed it across the table to him.

"I've seen that," said Becker. "The *federales* sent it to me yesterday after you came out of Heartland Viatical without any holes in your head. They couldn't even ID her. Not a clue. They're asking *me* if I know who she is. I said, 'Sure, I know who that is. It's Miss Scarlet and she did it in the billiard room with a candlestick.' Earwax for brains!"

His ingratitude was shocking. I'd risked my life to get that image.

"The task-force agents told me that if I wore the wire, they'd call you and tell you what I did for them, and then they'd help you with your investigation."

Becker laughed through his teeth and grunted. "You're funny. You could do comedy at the fund-raisers we hold down at the union hall. You should see about getting in the Omaha Press Club Show. You're good."

"They said—"

"Let me tell you about the FBI," said Becker. "The FBI will trade you piss for beer, as long as your beer is cold. You gave 'em their cold beer by wearing a wire for them, and then they let you sit in there and piss yourself, while they ate Taco Johns out in the van. Do they even carry guns anymore? No, probably just those little pocket computers. Go on, and get out." He waved his arm at the door. "Go on out West Dodge Road and let the FBI take care of you."

I picked up the image and turned it around for him.

"This woman's name is Rosa Prescott," I said. "She was at Lenny's place the night he died. She works with Heartland Viatical."

"Her real name is Juanita Sanchez, and she's downstairs in a holding cell," said Becker. "She made a run for it the minute she heard about your viagra-tal adventures. We put out the all-points, and the State Patrol pulled her over on I-80 out by North Platte. You see how it works with us simpleminded local cops? We don't have time to play on computers. While you and the FBI type love notes to each other in chat rooms on the Internet trying to trick each other with your computers and digital listening devices, somebody back here in the real world has to actually drive around in a car, find the bad people, and arrest them."

"She's downstairs?"

"She had her name on two life insurance policies worth four hundred grand," said Becker. "And she works with Heartland. I got every insurance company in North America calling me and telling me about life insurance and viagra-tals. You know how easy insurance murders are—when the policies start popping up, all you gotta do is see who's getting all the money when Lenny dies. Look at Heartland. He sold them a million dollars' worth of life insurance policies on himself."

"Because he knew they needed policies," I said. "Any policies, to answer the federal subpoenas and prove they were legitimate."

"And if Lenny dies," said Becker, "they get their policies, and make a million clear."

"Cash," I said. "Cash to pay investors. Cash to buy more policies. Cash to help them prove they're legit when the FBI comes around. They needed policies and they needed money, and with Lenny they got both."

Becker lit a cigarette.

"Even before we got a second look at the body," he said, "we knew it wasn't the Ecstasy and the pot and the painkillers and booze that killed him, it was *somebody*, probably one of those beneficiaries on his policies, or maybe it was all of them, or it was a freak heart attack."

"You just have to figure out who all is in on it," I said.

"Right," said Becker. "You? Your girlfriend?" He pointed his finger at me, like he was Norton warning me about finding a gal. "You keep hiding things from people, and you're gonna wind up in a cage with nothing but a toilet and no lid, my friend. I was ready to lock all of you up and hold you for forty-eight hours while I sorted it out."

"But then they took another look at the body," I said, "and something was not right? No, you said it went from not right to flat-out wrong."

"This is just like a death unknown I had ten years or so ago," said Becker. "Found a young guy drunk and dead, slumped over the steering wheel, with the front end of his Mazda smashed in by a light pole out on Military Avenue. Looked like a basic one-car accident all the way. Nothing suspicious, so the medical examiner lets the pathology resident handle the autopsy. Blood drawn at the scene showed a BAL of point-two-five, plenty drunk enough to smash up a car. Autopsy didn't show squat, except maybe trauma to the heart from being smashed against some ragged broken ribs and the steering wheel. They went ahead with the funeral and buried the guy. Two big life insurance policies turn up, recently purchased by his wife and held just long enough to make them incontestable.

"I never hesitate to exhume a body," said Becker, "or to stop one from going in the ground in the first place. The body is all the victim has left to tell you who killed him. Wounds don't heal once you're dead, and for a few weeks or months you got a nice skin map and legend of trauma, anything from faint scratches to a puncture wounds.

"When we dug that one up, we found a hole in the guy's left armpit, just about the size of the ice pick the wife's boyfriend ran into his heart before propping him over the wheel."

I knew where he was coming from; bodies to him were like original documents to us in Special Investigations.

"You found an ice-pick hole in Lenny?"

"Syringe hole," said Becker. "Left foot, right between the little piggy that had none and the one that ran wee, wee, wee, all the way home, but we couldn't find lethal amounts of any of the usual suspects in his blood. So the examiner was thinking it's a Claus Von Bulow insulin special. No. We sampled the tissue at the wound site and found our substance: potassium chloride. Same thing old Dr. Kevorkian and the mercy killers use. A massive dose delivered quickly brings on sudden cardiac arrest, and after that, it gets absorbed by the body. But the killer missed the vein at first and injected a sample into the surrounding tissue before she pulled back again and found the vein."

I remembered Lenny in the back of Miranda's car again. He'd practically predicted his own death. *"Guttman has a history of being disciplined by the medical board in California because he helped a terminal cancer patient do the Kevorkian with a big injection of potassium chloride in a California mercy-killing case."*

I flashed on Rosa back at Harrah's the night Lenny had lost five grand to Charlize, Blackjack Princess of the Night. Rosa had known where to find Lenny: at the tables. Then Miranda said we had to leave, and Rosa had whispered in Lenny's ear. Were they arranging to meet later? Was she telling him she'd be by later?

"It's easy to murder a druggie and get away with it," said Becker. "All you gotta do is party hard with him until he gets fucked up as per usual, then stick around and convince him it's a special occasion and it's time to get way fucked up. Keep him going until he passes out, then you can do anything you want with him. Mix pills in water and pour them down his throat, or give him a hot shot of something two or three times the purity he usually gets. Even a guy like Lenny who doesn't do needles, you just help him get beyond fucked up until he passes out, then roll him over on his back, prop him up on some cushions, and keep dribbling liquor down his throat. He'll do some gagging and coughing and spitting, just like any other random drunk, but eventually he'll stop breathing, or aspirate booze or vomit, and die. If you're worried about evidence, light a cigarette for him, drop a match in a puddle of tequila, and excuse yourself. Either way, it don't look nothing like murder. He looks like just another drunk fuckup who poisoned himself."

"She was with him at the casino when he lost the hand," I said. "She must have stopped by after we dropped him off."

"And thanks to you he was already normal fucked up," said Becker. "All Juanita's gotta do is help him take it to the next level of totally fucked up. After he goes out, she slips him a needle between the toes. He maybe murmurs wha-the-fuck-ya-doin'-down-there-Rosa and drops under the cold waves in the Dead Sea.

"Then she props him up at the keyboard, turns his web cam on, and it looks like he passed out at the controls."

"Then you were thinking it's somebody with some medical background, because they'd know about potassium chloride, and how to deliver it, right?"

Becker nodded, as if he'd always expected more of me, and was glad to see me coming along after all.

"And one of those policies had Dr. Guttman's name on it," I said, "before he transferred it to Heartland. Guttman's a doctor. And my friend Addie said Rosa, or Juanita, I guess; Addie said she was an ex–hospice nurse turned viatical broker."

"Yeah," said Becker, "she was a good nurse, and when you get another look at her you'll see why Lenny was anxious to try some viagra-tickles and veggie-tales out on her. But so what? You see the problem? Just because I know *how* Lenny died doesn't mean shit. We got nothing but a hole in a foot and some potassium chloride. Even if you got a picture of Rosa Juanita on the Internet camera. She's gonna say she stopped by Lenny's neck of the woods on a snowy evening for a drink on the way home and then left. So what?"

"Fingerprints?" I asked.

"Only a total amateur," he said. "Anybody medical is going to be wearing latex gloves at the scene."

"So you gotta find the syringe?"

"Literally a needle-in-a-haystack deal," said Becker. "We got a search warrant for the medical waste at the Heartland Clinic. We gotta hope she takes it back to the clinic and properly disposes of it in one of those red needle chop boxes that has 'biohazard' written all over it."

"If she pulled back on the syringe," I said, "then it's got potassium chloride *and* Lenny's blood."

"Even if she don't pull back, it's *in* and *on* the needle barrel. Blood, Lenny's DNA, and potassium chloride."

"She can't be dumb enough to keep it."

"She's not dumb," said Becker. "She's smart, so smart she knows not to trust Hector and his brother-in-law. Juanita goes way back with Hector and Dr. Ray. She was with them at the old veggie-tale company out in L.A. She saw them turn on the other half of the outfit once before. Those California guys all went to jail, and Hector and Ray got off with wrist slaps from the licensing boards. Murder's too fast for her, but they find her price and talk her into it. They keep telling her that the chances are we're not even going to find the hole, and even if we do, our first thought is going to be that crazy Lenny had moved on to needle drugs and was trying to hide his tracks.

"Still, she's smart enough to realize that if we *do* figure it out, Hector would toss her overboard at the first sign of trouble. So she's got to protect herself. Guttman prepares the big syringe for her, loads it with potassium chloride so it's all ready to go. Caps the needle. Gives her a couple pairs of latex gloves and cotton balls. Puts it all in a Ziploc bag for her. All she's gotta do is make sure that the bleeding stops after the injection, and take the syringe with her when she leaves. She might be dumb enough to throw the stuff in the closest Dumpster, but that's the first place we look when we walk out of a crime scene. No luck. All she had to do was throw that needle away in any trash can on any street corner in town."

"But she not only took it, she kept it?"

"It's got Guttman's prints on it," said Becker, "not hers. He's got no reason to wear gloves drawing up a syringe full of potassium chloride. No. *She* wears gloves while she's working on poor Lenny, and you know she's gonna take the syringe and the needle with her when she goes. But instead of throwing it away, she keeps it, because if Hector or Guttman turn on her, she's gonna say, 'I didn't do it. Dr. Ray did, and I can prove it. I got the syringe with his prints on it.'"

"You grabbed her," I said, "and threatened her downstairs?"

Becker raised a single eyebrow. "I talked to her in a special way. I didn't threaten her. If criminals trusted each other," he said, "we'd never catch them. But there's no honor among snakes, and no law that wasn't made to be broken, even the one that says Never turn on your own. When the cops hand you a few affidavits from cooperating witnesses and confidential informants who all say things only your best crooked buddies know about—"

"She turned on them," I said.

He nodded. "I got 'em all downstairs," Becker said. "Guttman says she did it. She says Guttman did it, and they both blame it all on Hector."

"And Hector?" I asked.

"Hector won't say shit until it hits the fan. He's a lawyer. Those guys are always careful, but in the end they do whatever it takes to stay off of Old Sparky."

"But you wouldn't have Rosa without the image file," I said.

Becker shrugged. "True. You got her picture. I owe you there."

TURN OUT THE LIGHTS

AFTER A WEEK OR SO of big news stories on Lenny's murder and coverage on the ensuing pretrial skirmishes, the paper was saying that the government was going to get guilty pleas and big prison terms on most if not all of the Heartland defendants, and any holdouts would be tried for capital murder. The corporate officers of Heartland Viatical, including Rosa/Juanita and my spiritual mentor, Don Gandhi, had all been moved from Becker's basement to the Douglas County Jail, where they were awaiting trial and turning on each other by the day. I only wished I'd been able to set up Attila-at-Home web cams on the walls of Becker's holding tanks, so I could watch playbacks of his technique. I could eat popcorn as he serially interrogated them, constantly reminded them of their inhumanity and duplicity, administered one deniable insinuation after another, confronted them with mismatched stories.

Meanwhile, I had the good fortune to work on another case

with Becker. He had a house fire and a charred corpse, which always makes the cops suspicious, because murderers love to clean up a crime scene by starting a body-of-evidence bonfire on their way out the door. This one was a gas fire in the garage of Sally and Howard Turnbull, a childless, thirty-something couple living in deep South Omaha. Howie had his tool bench in the attached garage, with shelves above it for paint cans, paint remover, motor oil, propane tanks for the grill, and, yes, a gas can for the mower. He'd taken his wife, Sally, out to dinner, because she was leaving town for the weekend and going to her Class of '81 Wyandotte High School reunion down in Kansas City.

Howie dropped Sally at the airport and came home to a raging house fire. The garage had burned to the ground and most of the house, too. Inside the garage, the arson boys found the charred remains of a body.

For weeks, Becker and his men operated under the assumption that it was breaking and entering gone tragically awry when the burglar must have set off a spark while stealing Howie's tools. That was too far-fetched for Becker, who thought that maybe Howie had hired somebody to torch the house for him so he could collect on the insurance money, and maybe whatever his buddy had used to start the fire got out of hand too soon.

That's when Becker called me.

I checked the property-insurance angles for him, and when I did I also found some recent life insurance activity on the Turnbulls, namely, three different policies at three different companies for a grand total of almost a million on Howard Turnbull, with Sally Turnbull the beneficiary on all three. When Becker asked the Turnbulls about those, husband and wife said that they were trying to get pregnant and Sally had been having nightmares about having a child and no husband if something went wrong down at the salvage yard where Howie ran a backhoe for a living.

Meanwhile, Becker put a missing person's report together with the charred body and found out the dead guy's name was Sonny Lisko, the line supervisor out at the packing plant where Howie's wife, Sally, worked. What was Sonny doing at the Turnbulls' house? Sally said she didn't know, and Howie said he'd heard his wife mention Lisko's name once or twice in connection with work but had never met the guy.

When I told Becker about the life insurance policies, he went out to the packing plant to ask around about Lisko and found out that he was a supervisor who had been counseled about having a workplace relationship with Sally Turnbull: sex in the parking lot, drinking after work together, carrying on in public.

Uh-oh. I almost told Becker to stay on the line while I patched Miranda in.

Becker and his men took another look at the evidence gathered at the scene, and I recommended an arson investigator I'd met through Old Man Norton. On the second pass, they found a single fragment of a lightbulb out in the driveway with a frayed shred of duct tape stuck to it and some residues that later proved to be paraffin, epoxy, and gasoline.

I was sitting at my desk when Becker called and told me about the lightbulb fragment and the residues. He thanked me for finding out about the life policies, then he asked me what I thought had happened.

"I don't know," I said, "let me mull it over."

"Well, I do," he said, "because the fire boys told me. And I'll buy you drinks at the Holiday and dinner at Jams if you get it right. I think you pretty much have to be an arson man to figure this one."

I had my machine up and running with the Google search engine sitting right there blank, so I typed in *"paraffin lightbulb gasoline epoxy duct tape"* and clicked on the Google Search button.

There it was, on top and first in line: "How to make a lightbulb bomb." First you heat the metal base of a lightbulb with a butane torch until the bulb separates. Then, after it cools, you fill the bulb with gasoline, glue it back onto the base with epoxy, seal it with paraffin, and wrap some duct tape around it for good measure, and then screw it back in the socket. The lights go *out*, not on, for the next person who flips the switch, especially if you got a can of gasoline and two propane tanks on the shelf underneath the bulb.

"It sounds like a lightbulb bomb to me," I said in a bored tone of voice, like I'd already seen ten or twenty lightbulb bombs in my day, and what else did he have for me.

"You circus-freak fuck!" cried Becker. "How'd you do that?"

I could hear him pounding the table and stamping his foot on the other end, like he was Rumplestiltskin and I'd just guessed his name.

Lisko must have made his lightbulb bomb, and then won himself a Darwin Award by forgetting to make sure the switch was off before he screwed in the bulb. Becker liked that part, too, because I told him just how it could have happened. What if when Lisko arrived at the Turnbull house the light switch was on, but the bulb was burned out? Lisko would think the switch was off, would then remove the dead bulb and screw the lightbulb bomb into a live socket. *Kabloom!*

Later, over dinner and drinks on Becker's nickel, I put him

out of his misery and told him how I'd done it. He was intrigued, maybe for the first time, about what could be done with a computer. He was also going to retire soon with a nice pension and was thinking about going private and starting his own investigation business.

If he did, would I like to join him, and run a computer for him?

DAGMAR SLEPT
WITH HITLER

I WAS USED TO it now. Every time I managed to escape the malign and deadly forces of the universe and struggle back to my cube to do a little work, I'd find a note from Comrade Dagmar on my keyboard advising me to "See Mr. Norton. Urgent." She didn't trust the electronic versions of pink slips checked URGENT, she had to take the precaution of adding a real pink slip when it was *really* important.

Maybe Becker and I had the real world under control, but the Special Investigations Unit was a bleeding beast, mortally wounded by the antics of Leonard Stillmach. I had e-mail and phone calls looking for dirt on Lenny the viatical scammer, and more e-mails and phone calls from HR looking for evidence against Lenny the national-origin discriminator, along with some sidling, personal e-mail inquiries saying, in effect, "Such a tragedy, he was so young, you must be devastated . . . but what the fuck happened?"

All of which landed me back in Norton's environment, this time in our customary positions: He was behind the desk tapping on his "book rest"; I was out front under my own cone of light.

"Nobody knows paper the way we do," said Norton. "That's why taking good care of files is so important."

"True," I said.

I figured he was headed off on another rant against management. How they hated the expense and space required to store paper, even if having real paper files helped us deny bogus claims, claims that would otherwise cost the company millions. How brave, old-schooler Norton was going to have to fight them again and make sure that the company kept saving paper files and original documents and kept one or two real investigators around who knew how to review a Special Claims file.

I started feeling sorry for him again and knew I'd have to pick a time soon to tell him that Miranda and I were going to work for Charlie Becker when he retired in March.

"On the other hand," said Norton, "if you have a problem file, one with a stinky claim in it that got paid anyway, or paid to the wrong person . . ."

He wasn't saying what was on his mind, which had me worried.

"If the file winds up missing," said Norton, "myriad sins just vanish."

I knew what he was talking about. It was practically a cliché in the business. A Special Claims investigator enters an order to pay a claim in the main system, and it gets paid. Later, a question arises about the claim, usually because of an inquiry from some external entity—the Nebraska Insurance Commission, the state attorney general, the postal authorities, litigants in some ancillary civil litigation. When a request for information on the claim comes in, somebody at Reliable goes looking for the file. And guess what? *Poof!* No file. No supporting documents to explain how or why the claim got paid; it just did. The only record is a draft or a check issued, along with the auditor number of the person who ordered payment. Nobody expects an investigator to remember why he paid claim number 7684763-01 without the supporting documents. Everything must have been in order, or he wouldn't have entered an order to pay on the claim.

"It's curious that the file on Lenny should suddenly be missing," he said. "More than curious, since the fraud investigation is now a murder investigation."

If Lenny's file was missing, who would bury it? Miranda? What for? I knew just about all there was to know about her, including the exact size of her left ring finger. The policy had been viaticated to Heartland. What possible reason could she or any other investigator have for making it disappear? Why would anybody bury it? It was going to get paid, if it hadn't been paid already.

"We don't have a file on Lenny's policy anymore," said Norton. "Troubling enough, but even more troubling is what we do have."

"Was it paid?"

"It was paid," Norton said.

Maybe the file was missing, but if the claim got paid, they shouldn't have any trouble figuring out who ordered payment. You can't get a check or a draft issued without putting in your auditor number.

"Whose auditor number?" I asked.

"The death benefit was for one hundred thousand," said

Norton, "so the file was supposed to come back to Dagmar Helveg for quality control," said Norton. "Dagmar didn't get a file, all she got was a record of the request for payment and a copy of the check from processing. The file is nowhere to be found. You had it last, right? I gave it to you."

"So somebody paid Heartland on Lenny's life claim," I said. "So what? It was incontestable. It was going to get paid no matter what."

"True," said Norton. "I paid Heartland *three* days ago. But that's what's puzzling, because *two* days ago, a second check was issued on the same claim. Are you related to a Tarlon Ashwater by blood or marriage? Is he a friend of yours?"

Hot flash, and of course he had the thermal cameras going and the Truster software.

"Ashwater got a check?" I asked. "Who met with him? You? Dagmar? Who paid him?"

Norton didn't answer, just watched his book rest.

"I talked to him out front one night," I said, "and told him to go see Heartland, or go find a lawyer. Who'd he get to pay him on Lenny's policy when he's not the beneficiary? Heartland was the beneficiary."

"Well, Heartland has been paid," said Norton, "and so has Mr. Ashwater. Just who is he?"

Norton's tone of voice suggested that Tarlon Ashwater was about as real as a wood nymph or a leprechaun.

"He's a destitute rancher who was dumb enough to invest a hundred grand in life insurance policies held by Heartland Viatical. That's all I know about him. Who paid him?"

Norton just kept looking at me, waiting for me to figure things out for myself. He shook his head.

"Unlike Lenny, you are an excellent actor," said Norton. "Where's the file?"

"I didn't bury the file," I said. "What possible reason—"

Norton's eyes flashed like sharp knives in the sun.

"It's your auditor number on the order to pay the claim," he said. "And then conveniently the file winds up missing. I'm just not understanding why. Why issue a one-hundred-thousand-dollar check to a Sandhills rancher you supposedly don't know? Is he a dummy ID? Do you have a bank with an account in the name of Tarlon Ashwater and a phony driver's license to go with it? Some obscure little Sandhills bank where you could cash that check? Tell me how it works, Carver."

The son of a bitch was filthy dirty. I'd ravaged my heart and almost got myself killed suspecting the woman I loved. Now it was as if Norton had passed me a note in the back of the classroom.

In the Reliable Special Claims Unit, two people have the list of auditor numbers: Norton himself and Dagmar. One or both of them had entered my auditor number on an order to pay a claim on Lenny's life insurance policy for one hundred thousand dollars to Tarlon Ashwater. Hell, they'd probably even done it from my computer, because they had the passwords, too.

Just in time, Cecil Norton, Dead Man Norton himself, popped up on the multimedia screen saver. And the newspaper headline spun onto the screen: RELIABLE ALLIED WINS INSURANCE FRAUD VERDICT.

I recalled how life used to be back when it matched my expectations. Lenny would always be crazy and high and transported in wacky flights of fun in the backseat, but he would always stay just this side of going too far. Then he would wake up the next morning ready to rule another day. Norton would always be a paragon of fraud-loathing virtue, no matter how much he despised the cynical machinations of management and the product-development hot shots who cut his staff and his budget semiannually. Miranda would always be an unattainable goddess.

Now, Lenny was dead. Old Man Norton, the head of Special Investigations, the son of Dead Man Norton—whose hatred for fraudsters gave him chest pains—now, the scion of Dead Man Norton was filthy fucking dirty. Miranda was still a goddess, but now she was signing on with me.

Why would Norton pay off Tarlon Ashwather? I needed more time to think. I didn't have the particulars sorted out; all I knew was that Dagmar and Norton had both warped all the way to crooked. Dagmar? Do something like that on her own? It would be like Eva Braun calling off Hitler's invasion of Poland.

"A check for a hundred thousand dollars," said Norton. "Not a draft. A draft we could stop payment on. A check we can't stop because it was cashed the day this mythical being named Mr. Ashwater picked it up downstairs."

Norton's phone rang and he answered it, turned up his white noise so I couldn't hear him, and had himself a quiet, private conversation.

While he talked on the phone, I imagined myself contesting my impending termination. Maybe insurance money and insurance fraud would be the topic on the table upstairs in front of the big boys, but to them it would be elderly, obedient, long-suffering Dagmar Helveg versus Carver Hartnett, J. Random Slacker of the Omaha insurance world. My word against hers.

Why pay Heartland *and* Ashwater? Only one explanation

made sense: Norton was in dirty with Heartland Viatical. Ash-water was at the end of life's rope, roaming around town with a varmint rifle, ready to make serious trouble for Heartland and Reliable if he had to. Why not pay him off? And do it so it wouldn't cost Heartland a cent?

Who changed the beneficiary form from Rosa Prescott to Heartland Viatical on Lenny's Reliable policy the day before Lenny's funeral? Norton. Who kept assigning one investigator after another to investigate the fraud outfit he'd bought into? Norton. What better way to paper the files with somebody else signing the orders to pay on claims to Heartland Viatical and Guttman's Heartland Internal Medicine Associates? Plus, the Heartland file would be full of memos from his investigators showing no evidence of fraud pertaining to the operations of the new entity, Heartland Viatical, only stale maybes from its prior California incarnation.

I could see Norton explaining himself in the corner offices upstairs when the Heartland bust hit the papers.

"I had not one, not two, but three *investigators look at that out-fit, and they all told me it was legit."*

True, Norton assigned us to investigate Heartland, accompa-nied by disclaimers and easy outs, such as, *"Run Heartland's poli-cies in your spreadsheets, and you'll see there are no viatical-fraud flags."*

Of course the normal viatical flags were missing; the premi-ums on the policies were being paid by *individuals*—Ray Guttman, Rosa Prescott—not by Heartland Viatical. And who could best show them just how to do that?

"We did a lot of legitimate business with Heartland Viatical,"

Norton had said. *"It's important for us that this company's legitimate business dealings with Heartland aren't contaminated by whatever lunatic Lenny had going with them on the side."*

Lenny had said it in the backseat on the last night of his life: *"Miranda already told Norton that she thought Crogan's old company had recruited sick people to apply for fifty-K jet-issue policies,"* and Lenny had told Norton, too, *"I told Norton I thought Crogan and his partner were running swoop-and-squats out in Orange County,* and *representing the capper."*

And every time his investigators came back with something that smelled funny, Norton insinuated that it wasn't enough, not the beyond-a-reasonable-doubt stuff that would move a company like Reliable to lift a finger to accuse an outfit of criminal fraud.

Norton could show Hector just how to set it up so insurance companies, including Reliable, wouldn't catch his policies running through the system until they were incontestable. Norton would show him how to spread the policies around so you didn't get too many at one company. He could sell Hector black-market insurance information on AIDS victims with life policies. Christ, he was the head of Special Investigations! He could do anything! Including control us while we "investigated" Heartland. And what did Hector bring to the table? The dream nuclear weapon of every fraudster, a dirty doctor in his pocket.

I watched Norton speaking into his phone. I blamed him, yes, but I also knew just why he'd gone dirty. He'd said it himself!

"The honor, the prestige, the integrity. All gone. We were honest investigators protecting honest people. . . . Now, who is honest? Who cares if the fraudsters steal money? That's why somebody like Lenny goes bad. He sees the industry doesn't care about fraud anymore. So he says, 'Fine, I'll help myself.'"

Maybe Lenny knew Norton was dirty, too. Maybe he'd sensed it every time he went back into Norton's environment with more dirt on Heartland only to be gently rebuffed. Lenny probably took the lay of that landscape and had a great idea. Every fraud investigator's dream: Scam the scammers. Scam Heartland by selling them big incontestable life policies. And Heartland let him do it, because they were being investigated and subpoenaed and needed policies more than anything to prove their legitimacy.

If Norton called him on it, Lenny could turn the tables on him. When Norton found out that Lenny had cut his own deal with Heartland, the old man had probably panicked and fired him. Lenny's shenanigans could blow the whole mess wide open. And the one big miscalculation? Murder. Norton probably hadn't figured Hector would go that far. He was wrong.

"It's painful," Norton had said, *"and hard for you to accept, but this looks to be all Lenny. He scammed Heartland. He wasn't working with anyone else here in Special Investigations. We hope."*

Norton hung up the phone and turned off his white noise. He was pale and wearing a look of complete resignation, the like of which I hadn't seen since my encounter with my friend Don.

I almost thanked him for giving me the time to make sense of it, so I could take a long look at him knowing that I had a kingpin scammer in my sights. Not that I could prove it. That would never happen. Why? Because Old Man Norton is always two steps ahead.

I knew what was coming down now. It was liberation day.

"Norton," I said, without worrying about whether I'd get my next paycheck if I crossed him, "we both know that sometimes dirty just happens to people. A basically honest person agrees to pad a claim or let the doctor bill a facelift as temporal mandibu-lar joint disorder."

"Don't give me that everybody-does-it excuse," said Norton. "Paying Ashwater off is a sight worse than padding a claim."

The line was too perfect, so I didn't bother touching it. I just watched him hear his own echo. He was squirming now. He knew I knew. He also knew I couldn't do a thing to him, but it still had to be embarrassing for an investigator of his pedigree.

"I guess it's like smoking cigarettes only during certain periods of your life," I said. "It won't be permanent, just temporary. And if management keeps doing you dirty, don't they deserve the same?"

Maybe he was getting so old, he could momentarily forget I was even there, because he looked to be drifting off into mem-ory's landscapes, his hand still lingering on the phone receiver.

"We had something worth more than money," said Norton. "We had integrity, and smarts, and we worked hard. And sud-denly—"

"That was then," I said.

"This is now," said Norton.

He wasn't even looking at the book rest anymore. I could see him decide that it was time to pretend everything was normal again. Put me at my ease. Sure, we'd had our differences, but I'd been a good investigator. Honest, too.

I saw the dreamy, sentimental, paternal look come back into his eyes. I knew it was coming, so I headed him off.

"I found myself a gal," I said.

I could see that he felt ambushed, as if now he had to worry that he was becoming too transparent, maybe missing a step, so that instead of being two steps ahead, he was getting old and could only stay one ahead. Not to worry, one was enough.

"That's excellent news," he said, glancing at his watch. "I'm looking forward to hearing all about it in our next meeting. But I've got an appointment upstairs with the Product Development people. They're finally taking a look at adding an accelerated-benefits option on our life insurance products."

I stood up.

"Good-bye, Norton," I said.

I looked at the screen saver on his wall monitor and waited for Dead Man Norton to pop back up on the screen.

"It's a shame that your dad couldn't live to see how far you've come in this business."

Outside the door I didn't see any rent-a-cops, and I could tell the Dag was alarmed. She was on the phone, trying to find them. I even heard her say, "They were supposed to be here fifteen minutes ago!"

Down the hall I saw Charlie Becker rounding the corner with two plainclothesmen and a Reliable security guard. I smiled at Dagmar and waited. Maybe that was the phone call Norton had just received. Somebody had called to say that a homicide detective named Charlie Becker was coming up to see him.

Charlie shook my hand like I was already his partner.

"What are you gonna charge me with now?"

He just grinned, put his men in two chairs across the way from Dagmar's sentry booth, and pulled me aside.

"I ain't got enough to charge him, because nobody dealt with him except Hector. But I can always put him down in the basement for forty-eight hours and see what happens."

"Yeah," I said, "and I got a Sandhills rancher I can put you in touch with who got paid a hundred grand three days ago on a Heartland Viatical policy. He might be able to help, too."

Becker straightened his sport coat and winked. "We'll see what Norton's made of."

"He's no killer," I said. "He just bet on the wrong side in the game of wits."

Dagmar showed Becker into Norton's environment, then she scurried back to her desk, nervously glancing down the hallway where the security guard had gone.

All I could do was watch the face Dagmar showed to the rest of us and wonder about the other one she wore inside. Did she ever get them mixed up, or wonder which one was true? Did she sleep at night, or just stay up and dream of cunning new ways to serve master Norton? Does old age make it easier or harder to be filthy fucking dirty?

Maybe Miranda had it right. Maybe the Dag and Norton had been good, honest people their whole lives. Then fate served them just the right mix of desperate circumstances to match their weaknesses. For one day, or even just for one hour, or one minute, they weren't themselves, and succumbed. Maybe, after the initial shock, being a fraudster wasn't so intolerable, and so they let it go on a little longer. Pretty soon, the hard part was over, and they just kept on being bad, because the money was good.

"Don't worry, Dagmar," I said, "I'll go find a security guard to escort me to my cube. I know how it works. Lenny told me all about it."

Acknowledgments

Three ace insurance investigators—Ron Thorngren, Sharon Broughton, and John Plummer—generously taught me about the old-school street smarts and the new-school information technologies of Special Investigations, with tales of fraudsters, scam artists, and insurance murders tossed in along the way.

I also relied on *A Game of Wits* by John J. Healy, and the Insurance Forum's excellent collection of articles, *Viatical Transactions: The Frightening Secondary Market for Life Insurance Policies*, edited by Joseph M. Belth. And thank you, Dan Koch, for sparking my interest.

I thank Scott Charney, John Alber, Gary Hodge, John Albrecht, and Joel Hollenbeck—IT cyber wizards one and all—for reviewing the early drafts of this manuscript and suggesting ways I could pretend to have more than an amateur's grasp of computer technology.

Jason Brown showed me how cyber athletes play the game,

and my friend, Rick Barba, the king of computer game guides and a great fiction writer, also reviewed the manuscript and told me not to throw it away.

I am grateful to Julie Kirkham, LeAnne Baker, and Deirdre Faughey for their story suggestions and for their careful reading and editing of this manuscript.

Thanks also to Dana Meyer, Julie Burt, Tom Monaghan, Joe Bataillon, Jim Fogarty, and Sharon and Jerry Conneally.

Dr. Thomas Mustoe, Dr. Blaine Roffman, Dr. Kenneth Maxwell, and Dr. Chris Huerter all generously provided free medical advice to the characters in this book and great story-telling advice to their creator along the way.

Assistant United States Attorney Laurie Kelly put me in touch with the scourge of the fraudulent viatical outfits down in Florida, AUSA Ellen Cohen, who taught me how these criminal enterprises operate and how the justice department brings them down.

Omaha's greatest detective, Charlie Parker, told me all about crime scenes and how to interrogate bad guys.

As usual, Daniel Menaker first told me what the book was *really* about and then published it.

My children are grateful to Gail Hochman and Marianne Merola for feeding and clothing them.

Finally, thanks to Snoutman for the 2K-a-day technique.

—Richard Dooling